## PRAISE FOR

### *The Midnight Show Murders*

"*The Midnight Show Murders* is great fun, full of nifty twists and turns."                    —Carl Hiaasen

"The laughs are frequent and belly-deep, and the personable tone is akin to a television mystery/comedy like *The Rockford Files* or *Columbo.*"   —*BookPage*

"Fast-paced, exciting . . . Wry humor lifts this above most celebrity-written fiction." —*Publishers Weekly*

"Roker and Lochte offer a satisfying entrée to follow the appetizer they provided in *The Morning Show Murders.*"                    —*Kirkus Reviews*

"The authors succeed in entertaining readers with a crime drama flavored with some of Roker's familiar charm and humor. . . . For a murder mystery, it's great fun."                    —Fredericksburg *Free-Lance Star*

# AND

## *The Morning Show Murders*

"Al Roker's first mystery thriller is a winner. Terrific plot, fast, funny, and full of action and adventure with even a touch of steamy romance. And I love his leading man, TV personality, restaurateur and amateur sleuth Billy Blessing. Billy's not only heroic, witty, and self-effacing, he can whip up little snacks in his kitchen that taste better than Butterscotch Krimpets. I think Stephanie Plum would love him, too, even with some of the misguided things he has to say about New Jersey."          —Janet Evanovich

"Roker brings his A-game to the table when it comes to giving readers a bird's-eye view into the behind-the-scenes action on a television show."

—*Chicago Sun-Times*

"This is a funny, funny, very funny mystery that really gallops along and has several cool twists. Maybe Al Roker should quit his day job."       —James Patterson

"Great fun! Al pulls back the curtain to reveal what really goes on when the cameras go off."

—Harlan Coben

By Al Roker and Dick Lochte

*The Morning Show Murders*
*The Midnight Show Murders*

And look for

*The Talk Show Murders*

Coming soon from Delacorte Press

# The MIDNIGHT SHOW Murders

## *Murders*

### A BILLY BLESSING NOVEL

# AL ROKER
## *and* Dick Lochte

DELL | NEW YORK

2011 Dell Mass Market Edition

Copyright © 2010 by Al Roker Entertainment
Excerpt from *The Talk Show Murders* © 2011 by Al Roker Entertainment

Published in the United States by Dell, an imprint of The Random House Publishing Group, a division of Random House, Inc., New York.

Originally published in hardcover in the United States by Delacorte Press, an imprint of The Random House Publishing Group, a division of Random House, Inc., in 2010.

Excerpt from *The Talk Show Murders* © 2011 by Al Roker Entertainment. This excerpt has been set for this edition only and may not reflect the final content of the forthcoming edition.

ISBN 978-0-440-24581-0
eBook ISBN 978-0-440-33978-6

Cover design: Carlos Beltran
Cover art: Ben Perini

Printed in the United States of America

www.bantamdell.com

9 8 7 6 5 4 3 2 1

Dell mass market edition: October 2011

*This book is dedicated to my wife,*
*Deborah Roberts.*

*How I ended up with such a*
*special woman is still a mystery to me.*

*To Courtney, Leila, and*
*Nicky: I know you are surprised*
*I wrote a mystery because you*
*think I don't have a clue.*

*I love you all.*

# Chapter
## ONE

My love affair with Los Angeles began to wane twenty-three years ago, the morning a cleaning crew found Tiffany Arden's body in a dumpster behind Chez Anisette, a very popular restaurant of the day. Her head had been pulverized. If you're ghoulish enough to want a more detailed description than that, then go ahead and Google the media coverage of the murder.

There was a lot of it.

Much of it was accurate. Some was not. For example, it was widely reported that her murderer was unknown. Not true. I was pretty sure I knew who he was. And I knew that he was still at large, enjoying a rich, full life in the City of Angels.

"Just listen ta this, Billy." The gruff but lilting voice of Irish pop singer-guitarist Jimmy Fitzpatrick interrupted my morose thoughts with a statistic almost as disturbing. "There are two thousand, nine hundred an' forty-three things that can cock-up the average airplane, any one of 'em capable of plummetin' us to earth an' certain death. Would ya believe it?"

Fitz, my seatmate aboard American Airlines flight 349 to Los Angeles, was reading a cheery little non-book he'd picked up at JFK, *What Could Go Wrong?*

"Thanks for sharing," I said, and picked up *my* airport purchase, a Walter Mosley paperback, from my lap, where I'd rested it while musing about poor Tiffany.

"O' course, this is not the average airplane, since we're travelin' in the comp'ny of the future king o' late-night tele," Fitz added, making sure he was heard by the king, who was sitting across the aisle.

Off camera and semi-relaxed, the comedian Desmond O'Day was a wiry bantamweight in his forties with a V-shaped face and short, neatly coifed hair so blond it was almost silver. He had a penchant for tight, black apparel, which presently included linen trousers and a T-shirt designed to display his workout arm muscles and mini-six-pack. He paused in his perusal of a script to glare over his rimless half-glasses at his shaggy-haired, bearded music director.

"Stop botherin' Billy, ya sod," he said. "The man's doin' us a big favor, travelin' all across the country to help us kick off the show."

Fitz, wincing from having incurred the displeasure of his old pal and new boss, said, "Sorry, Billy."

He gave me an apologetic smile and leaned back in his seat, silent as the late King Tut.

"A little conversation would be fine, Fitz," I said, "as long as it's about something other than us plummeting to the ground in a screaming death plunge, then being vaporized in a fireball of death."

He kept his lips zipped, evidently convinced that a command from Des O'Day was not to be taken lightly. He was a better judge of that than I. He'd known Des since they were boys together on the Emerald Isle, while I'd just met the man.

Oh, I'm Billy Blessing, by the way. Chef Billy Blessing, to be formal about it.

For a decade and a half, I served in other chefs' kitchens before opening my own place, Blessing's Bistro, in Manhattan. It's famous for its steaks and chops, and the food we prepare and serve has earned a top rating in Gault Milleau, of which I am quite proud.

My fame, such as it is, comes only indirectly from my culinary skills. I'm a cohost on the Worldwide Broadcasting Company's morning news and entertainment show *Wake Up, America!* weekdays seven to nine a.m. If you're one of the show's four million viewers, you've probably seen me, the guy who, I've been told, looks a little like a slightly stockier, clean-shaven (head as well as face) version of Eddie Murphy.

I provide a daily *WUA!* segment on food preparation, but I have other chores, too. I do remotes, interview visitors to NYC who line up on the street each morning outside the studio, review books, chat with authors who are flogging their wares, and, whenever possible, flog my own wares, which, in addition to the Bistro, include a weekly cooking show on the Wine & Dine Cable Network, *Blessing's in the Kitchen,* a line of premium frozen dinners, and a couple of cookbooks.

At that particular moment I was flying from New York to Los Angeles to add two new credits to my list. One of them involved the Irishman across the aisle. Though you couldn't have told it by his sour scowl, Des was very funny and quick-witted, and he'd parlayed success on the stand-up circuit and a featured role as the cynical, sex-obsessed photographer in the popular sitcom *A Model Life* into an upper-strata gig as host of his own show, *O'Day at Night,* WBC's entry in the post-prime-time talk-show sweepstakes, set to debut in precisely nine days.

I'd been tapped as the new show's first weekly guest announcer. Its producer, a Falstaffian wheeler-dealer named Max Slaughter, told me I'd been Des's first choice. My agent-lawyer, Wally Wing, who, unlike most members of both of his professions, has never heard the term "candy-coating," admitted that Des had wanted someone on the order of Tom Cruise or Brad Pitt or, at the very least, the ex–governator of California, Arnold Schwarzenegger. Gretchen Di Voss, the head of the network, somehow avoided laughing in his face and offered him Howie Mandell or me. Howie had other commitments.

"Why wouldn't I have other commitments?" I'd asked Wally.

"Well, one reason—Gretchen wants you to do it. She feels it would be, in her words, 'an act of synchronicity.' You'd be the bridge between *Wake Up* and *At Night,* getting viewers of the morning show to sample the late show while at the same time giving *At Night*'s fans a taste of the morning show."

"I'd love to meet these viewers who are up from seven in the morning till after midnight," I'd replied. "But, okay, that explains why the network wants me to do the show. Why in God's name would I agree to spend two weeks in L.A., away from home, hearth, and restaurant?"

Wally had grinned and said, "The real reason's got nothing to do with the O'Day show. It's . . . wait for it . . . Sandy Selman wants to make a movie about you and the Felix thing."

The Felix thing. A typically Wally way of summing up one of the more unpleasant events of my life. A little more than a year ago, an executive at the network was murdered, and for a number of reasons, real or imagined, I was put at the top of the cops' suspect list. Then an international assassin known as Felix the Cat got involved and all hell broke loose. I was threatened, nearly roasted alive, and shot at. And I lost a woman I cared for.

The Felix thing.

"Okay," I said, "a guy I've never heard of wants to make a movie about a devastating experience I've spent the last year trying to forget. Tell me why I have to go to L.A.?"

"You've never heard of Sandy Selman?" was Wally's response.

"Okay, I've heard of him. He makes movies that are ninety percent computer graphics, eight percent sex, and two percent end credits. So why do I have to go to L.A.?"

"To write the book," Wally said in the singsong manner Big Bird uses to speak to kids.

"What book?"

"The book you're going to be writing in L.A."

"What makes you think I can write a book?"

"How hard can it be? Paris Hilton has written a book. Miley Cyrus has written a book. Hell, the goofy weatherman on the *Today* show's written five books. You may be the only person in show business who hasn't written a book."

"Well, I did the cookbooks," I said.

"My point exactly," Wally said.

"Why do I have to go to L.A. to write it? Last I checked, it was possible to write one in Manhattan."

"Not if we want Sandy Selman to produce the film version. He likes to be able to look over his writers' shoulders as they work. And don't worry about that. It's Harry Paynter's shoulders he'll be looking over."

"Ahhhhhh. Suddenly, it all becomes clear," I said. "I'm guessing Harry is one of your literary clients, and he's going to be helping me write the book."

"On the nose," Wally said, tapping his almost nonexistent schnoz in an impressive display of his expertise at charades. "He'll also be writing the screenplay."

"How altruistic of you, Wally! Oh, wait . . . in addition to your agent fees for both of us, you'll probably be getting a packager percent, too, right?"

"What's with the 'tude, bro? I assure you, this little jaunt is gonna be worth your while."

"It's not the money," I said. "I trust you to handle that. It's going to L.A."

"Spending two or three weeks on the coast is gonna kill you, Billy?"

Little did he know.

# Chapter
# TWO

"Change seats with me, mate," Des O'Day said to Fitz, who leapt to meet the request. Unfortunately, in his zeal, he'd neglected to unsnap his seat belt, and it nearly cut him in two.

"Uh, oh, Jaysus! Sorry, Des," he said, freeing himself this time and hopping into the aisle.

"Save the low comedy for the show, boyo," Des said as he eased past the bearded man and slid onto the vacated seat.

"Man's as thick as two short planks," he said, winking at me.

I said nothing, merely gave him a questioning look.

"Well, Billy, suppose you tell me what ball of shite's awatin' me in lotusland?"

"Could you be a little more specific?"

"What's the city like? I know the jokes. It's a great place to live if you're an orange. In Malibu, you can lie on the sand and stare at the stars, or vice versa. I've heard 'em all. But what's it really like?"

"Your guess would be better than mine," I said. "I haven't been out there in years."

"Twixt you and me, mate," he said, lowering his voice, "the longest I've spent in the so-called Angel

City has been forty-eight hours, and most of that was in the airport."

"But you've been there preparing for the show, right?"

"I've taken some quick runs in and out, mainly to meet with our fearless producer, Slaughter. And to check the progress on the theater conversion. It's near the WBC lot in Hollywood. For the last thirty or forty years it was a playhouse where they put on live dramas. Last time I was there, some of that 'Don't throw away our history' bullshite was goin' on, but I hear that's mellowed some.

"I didn't see the point of gettin' involved in any of that. So I've been puttin' off the big move, and the publicity, till the last bloody minute."

"Last, indeed," I said. "You go on the air in nine days."

"They don't need me to cobble the feckin' set," he said angrily. "All I'm expected to do is move kit and caboodle to a strange and, from all reports, loony land; get me fixed up in a proper house; keep my pale Irish flesh from the incessant, cancerous sun; find a whole new stable o' slappers; and, finally, hobble in front of a camera and try not to look like bloody Fecky the Ninth."

Not having an Irish slang dictionary handy, I was pleased with myself for making sense of at least a third of everything Des said. "You're a funny man," I told him. "You'll do fine."

"Don't go Father Feeney on me, Billy," he said. "I haven't got a baldy, and I know it. I tried like hell to convince Gretchen to do the show from New York. It's my bad cess she didn't see the logic of it. I mean,

Christ, look at the crowd of shows out here every night. Leno, Kimmel, George Lopez. And the bloody Scot. And now feckin' Conan's back. All hustlin' for A-list wankers an' makin' the same bloody jokes about smog, agents, and the stupid culchies.

"Meanwhile, Dave and Fallon, bein' the only players in Big Town, can afford to do hardball comedy, pick 'n' choose from the top-name caffers, and still get the ratin's. I mean, what's Gretchen thinkin'?"

At this point I should confess I had given up deciphering what Des was saying, and to a failure of character. I was romantically involved with Gretchen until she suffered a lapse in taste and dumped me. There's more to that story, of course, and if Wally has his way, you may be reading about it someday or seeing it in some exaggerated context on a movie screen. For the now, I mention it only to explain why I was secretly amused at the thought of Gretchen reacting to the carping and complaints of a sometimes-incomprehensible brash comic she was about to transform from sitcom sidekick into brand-name headliner.

I could imagine her biting her tongue, secretly cursing Des. Possibly even cursing her father, Commander Di Voss, for deciding that the network (of which he was president and chairman of the board) needed a late-night talk-show presence. Was it wrong of me to take some delight in an ex-sweetie's distress? An *unfaithful* ex-sweetie? I think not.

"The fact of it, Billy," Des was saying, "I need the edginess of a real city, like New York or Dublin, to keep the noggin noodles crisp. I'm afraid of what the feckin' sun and the smog does to your wit. Not to mention everything being all spread out like bloody cheese on a cracker. Hell, I don't even know how to steer a car. I'm gonna have to depend on a bloody chauffeur. Or Fitz."

"Life is tough in paradise," I said.

"If it was like Vegas, maybe I could work around the sun and the rest of the shite. You know, just hang in the hotel, do your work, and order up the food, drink, and scrubbers. But Gretchen says I've got to use the feckin' city in my stand-up. And to use it, you've gotta know it."

"Then it's a good thing I won't have to use it," I said.

"As much as you've bounced about, I can't believe you never spent serious time in L.A."

"Nothing worth mentioning," I said.

"Then why am I wastin' my scintillatin' personality on you?" he asked, giving me a half smile to show he was only half kidding. He removed his glasses and tossed them on the empty seat next to his script. "Might as well go check the talent on the flight."

I wasn't unhappy to see him wandering off to treat the hostesses to his dubious charm. Aside from his being pretty much the antithesis of a good traveling companion, I really didn't need anybody to quiz me about L.A.

I pressed the button that lowered my seat as far as it would go, leaned back, and closed my eyes. I was hoping for sleep. Instead, I was visited again by the memory of Tiffany's murder, the events leading up to it and the aftermath.

Especially the aftermath.

## *Chapter*
# THREE

As I said, my short-lived Angeleno life began about twenty-three years ago, not long after I decided to exchange a somewhat dubious and unlawful youth for a future fueled by ambition and a strong sense of purpose. During a brief stretch in prison, I found my true calling in the kitchen. Once I'd served my time, a jobs program landed me an apprenticeship under Chef Ambrose Provoste at La Provence in Detroit. I was one of three chosen to assist him in the kitchen of a restaurant soon to debut in the heart of Hollywood, owned and managed by an oily Frenchman named Victor Anisette.

Just weeks after its opening, Chez Anisette became the favorite watering hole of a cadre of celebrities who followed in the wake of one of its daily diners, a famous, fabulously overweight director whose reputation as a gourmet was almost as impressive as his work on film.

For nearly a year, it was a wonderful adventure. The stars, superstars, and their acolytes and fans kept the kitchen busy, and, thanks to Chef Ambrose's kindness, I was transformed quickly from apprentice to line cook.

I lived at the beach in a ritzy condo on the Venice–

Santa Monica border. It was owned by an actress friend who was in New York, appearing in one of the few nonmusical hits of that Broadway season. The deal was a good one—I paid her monthly mortgage fee, which was not excessive, and kept the fish in her aquarium as well fed as the customers at Chez Anisette. In return, along with a furnished suite that included access to a gym and swimming pool, I was also able to hop across the hot-sand beach and treat my body to a saltwater immersion while freezing my ass off in the always frigid Pacific Ocean.

It was, actually, paradise. But like any paradise, only temporary.

The working relationship between Ambrose and Victor Anisette had been edgy from the jump, a classic case of genuine genius versus the self-deluded variety. It eventually deteriorated past the point of no return.

"You know who William Goldman is, Billy?" Ambrose asked me one night at the bar at Kathy Gallagher's, a restaurant on Third that we frequented because it stayed open several hours past Chez Anisette and its bartenders made excellent full-measure gin martinis.

"Goldman?" I said. "Sure. He writes novels and screenplays. Including *Butch Cassidy*."

"There's a story going around, maybe true, maybe apocryphal. A couple years ago, he wrote this script for a TV comedian who's now a big movie star. There were disagreements, and both Goldman and the director quit. Just the other day, the comic tried to bring Goldman back on board. He was in the middle of enumerating the script changes he wanted when the writer stood up and headed for the door. The comic asked where he was going, and Goldman replied, 'I'm too old and too rich to put up with this shit.'"

Ambrose took a sip of his icy martini, swallowed it slowly, and smiled. "Earlier tonight, I said those exact words to Victor."

"What are you going to do?" I asked, though what I was really thinking was what was *I* going to do?

"I am rich, in a minor way," he said. "And a dollar goes pretty far in Louisiana real estate. Especially around my hometown of Alexandria. I've been thinking about opening a restaurant in Alex. It'd be like following in my old mentor Chef Louis's footsteps."

Chef Louis was Louis Szathmary, a Hungarian refugee who, with his wife, began a tiny place on Chicago's Near North Side called The Bakery that eventually expanded into one of the city's most treasured restaurants.

"I'll start out small," Ambrose said, "maybe fifty chairs. Then, as business demands, expand."

It struck the self-absorbed, cynical, youthful me as being something of a dream. I was familiar enough with the territory to know that unlike Chicago, Alexandria, Louisiana, was not a hotbed of gourmets. Nor was it a city where diners were open to new culinary experiences. Worse yet, it was clearly not a stepping-stone to bigger things for an ambitious young black chef, even if Ambrose was to make me an offer. Which didn't seem to be in the cards.

"What about Tiff?" I asked, just making conversation. Tiffany Arden was a very pretty twenty-six-year-old failed-starlet-turned-Chez-Anisette-maître d'ess and bookkeeper. She'd moved in with the twice-divorced fifty-four-year-old Ambrose about three months before.

"She'll come with me," Ambrose said with certainty.

"You've talked it over?"

"Not in so many words. I really just made up my mind tonight," he said. "But Tiff's a trouper. They'll love her in Alex."

Actually, they never got the chance. Trouper Tiff wasn't quite ready to give up the fast life in L.A. for a city where folks like to crack crawfish for entertainment. So Ambrose returned to his hometown single-o and brokenhearted. He started a small restaurant that he called Ambrosia and, last I heard, was a new grandfather happily retired from kitchen work and teaching a course in nutrition and food preparation at Louisiana State University at Alexandria.

As for Tiff, well, the way things turned out, her decision to stay was not a wise one.

Ambrose's replacement in the kitchen of Chez Anisette, and, not surprisingly, in Tiffany Arden's bed, was an admittedly talented, if arrogant and obnoxious, young chef named Roger Charbonnet. He was a massive six-foot-three, gym-toned, ill-tempered jerk who made Gordon Ramsay sound like a food whisperer. His yelling and screaming were so loud that Victor Anisette was forced to soundproof the kitchen.

Giving the devil his due, Roger helped me become a better chef. Mainly because he scared the hell out of me and I did not want to become one of his kitchen smash toys.

Things went smoothly and uneventfully for nearly five months. Then, one morning, the cleaning crew arrived at the restaurant to find the front door unlocked, the cash register open and empty, and Tiffany's body in one of the garbage bins out back.

The crime scene technicians (perhaps they called them CSIs in those days, though I doubt it) decided that she'd been killed in the kitchen and dragged to the bin. "Death by blunt instrument" was the official pronouncement. The specific blunt instrument, discovered in another bin, was a meat tenderizer bearing Tiffany's blood but nary a fingerprint. The time of death had been approximated as between one a.m. and five a.m. that morning.

I and the other members of the kitchen crew testified that we'd last seen the victim when we'd left the restaurant at a little after eleven the night before. She and Victor had been toting up the lunch and dinner numbers, while Roger sat at a nearby table, scribbling his critique of our kitchen performances.

The detectives assigned to the murder were on Roger like white on rice. He'd not only worked and played with the victim, he'd shouted and screamed at her, and she at him. And their frequent outbursts of mutual animosity had been observed by many. Roger had had the opportunity to murder Tiffany, the proximity, and the motive. A prosecution trifecta, if you will.

But just as the case against Roger seemed a sure thing, it ran out of the money when Victor Anisette stepped up to provide him with an airtight alibi. According to the restaurateur, after we'd left that night, Roger and Tiffany had had another of their rows, this one, like the others, involving the chef's roving eye. And other body parts.

When Tiffany furiously declared that their romance was kaput, Victor and a morose Roger had departed together, leaving her to close up the shop. The two men had traveled by separate cars to Victor's home in Brentwood, where they drank and discussed the vagaries of women until the early morning, when Roger passed out on the sofa and Victor went to bed.

That had been at approximately six a.m. Victor was certain of the time, because he had set his alarm for ten a.m. When the device did its job and he awoke, Roger was still asleep on the sofa.

Victor assured the investigators that Roger had remained in his presence during the crucial hours. Yes, both he and Roger had relieved themselves from time to time, but not for periods longer than a few minutes. It was at least a twenty-five-minute drive from Victor's home to the restaurant, even without traffic.

Faced with the restaurant owner's statement, the detectives were back at square one. They put us all through the wringer again. They even checked Ambrose Provoste's whereabouts and that of Tiffany's other significants, going back to her college years. But they were unable to build even a circumstantial case. And eventually they were shifted to warmer investigations.

Life went on. Except for Tiffany's. We of the kitchen ensemble settled back into our pre-murder routines, and a new one that Victor established to chase away our postmortem blues. Chez Anisette was dark on Mondays, so, at the close of the kitchen on

Sunday nights, he broke out the booze and hosted a little end-of-the-week celebration for the staff.

It was near the close of one of those Sunday-night soirees that I found myself last to leave, observing Victor drain the dregs of a bottle of absinthe that he'd smuggled into the country after one of his infrequent Paris visits. I've never been fond of the flavor of anise, so I'd sipped my cloudy cocktail and was reasonably sober. Victor, for reasons unknown, had tossed his down like Coca-Cola and had all but succumbed to the so-called *la fée verte,* the Green Faerie.

After much boozy palaver about this and that, just as I was racking my brain for an excuse to get out of there, Victor shifted the subject to the feeling of loyalty he had for his Chez Anisette "family."

Falsely interpreting my lack of response as disbelief, he pounded the table, causing the cloudy liquid in my glass to hop. He did care about us, he shouted. Then he added, and I still remember his exact words, "If I hadn't cared, why would I have lied to save Roger's ass?"

Even if I'd been swigging the absinthe, that would have sobered me. "Roger wasn't with you the night Tiffany died?" I asked.

"What?" He stared at me, glassy-eyed. "What the hell are you talking about?"

"You said you lied to save Roger's ass."

"I said nothing of the sort. You're drunk. We're both drunk." He stood up, weaving. "Bar's closed. Go home, Billy. Sleep it off."

I went home. But I didn't sleep it off.

He'd said it. And I'd heard him.

After my real father's death, I'd spent some of my

teenage years traveling across the country with my foster father, Paul Lamont, a surprisingly moral con man, but a con man nonetheless. Because of that and my incarceration, I was not exactly a stickler for law and order. But Paul had died at the hands of a villain who'd escaped legal punishment. And my feelings about murderers roaming free were still strong and raw.

The next morning, I contacted the homicide detectives who'd been assigned the Tiffany Arden investigation, an easygoing, old-line cop named J. G. Penny who was only months from retirement, and his much less tolerant partner, Pete Brueghel, a wiry, intense hero of the Vietnam War who'd told me more than once that he believed police work wasn't merely a job but a calling.

Victor told them I'd been drunk and must have misunderstood or perhaps even imagined he'd said any such thing. He held to his statement that he'd been with Roger at the time of the murder.

Penny had accepted that, but Brueghel, who was definitely not a member of Roger's fan club, bullied his partner into reopening their investigation. What followed was a series of rigorous interviews that, in Victor's words "formed a pattern of harassment that interfered with the operation of my restaurant and bothered my Brentwood neighbors to distraction, forcing me to secure the services of a very expensive law firm." He told me that at work shortly after hearing from his expensive firm that the detectives had found no substantive proof that Victor had lied and therefore were closing that part of their investigation. With the burden of suspicion lifted, Victor felt he was able to kick me to the curb, which he did with a smile. The fact that he hadn't fired me sooner was, to my mind, another indication of his guilt.

Though there are thousands of restaurants in the greater Los Angeles area, the list of notable eateries was not long. And Victor Anisette had been quick to put their owners on notice about my "lack of skill and disruptive kitchen presence."

Still, naïvely optimistic, I persisted. Several weeks and upward of thirty turndowns later, I departed a classic Old Hollywood establishment on the Strip to find Roger Charbonnet leaning against the front of my car.

He straightened and, nearly seething with fury, told me that he'd been in love with Tiffany Arden, that he had not killed her, and that he was not going to allow me to continue telling people that he did.

I replied that I hadn't told anyone he'd killed Tiffany, merely that Victor had lied about his alibi, which I knew to be the case. I added that I didn't need him to "allow" me to do anything.

Roger drew back his jacket, exposing a gun tucked behind his belt. He raised his right hand and hesitated, as if counting to ten before doing something he might regret. He blinked and lowered his hand. He shrugged the jacket back in place, covering the weapon. "I'll *allow* you a week to leave this city. After that, if I see you, I'll kill you."

I watched him cross Sunset and get into his new, shiny black Corvette. I got into my twelve-year-old formerly owned Mercedes sedan, which I still hadn't quite paid for, and considered my options. What good were a lovely townhouse, the Pacific at your door, great West Coast seafood, fresh vegetables and fruit, and beautiful women if you were dead broke? Or worse, just plain dead?

I went to the townhouse and phoned Ambrose. Through his auspices, I left four days later for a job in the kitchen of the Quarterdeck Club in Aspen.

Now, twenty-two years later, I was returning to the city where the murder of Tiffany Arden was still unsolved and Roger Charbonnet had become something of a food icon, the very visible partner of a reclusive Victor Anisette in several of the better restaurants.

I'd have to settle for other places to eat. Nothing spoils a dinner on the town more than wondering if there might be arsenic on the arugula.

## *Chapter* FOUR

Against my better judgment, I let Des talk me into staying with him at the Malibu beach mini-mansion he was leasing with an option to buy. "My business manager said leasin' was the way to go with the hut," he told me on the drive from LAX. "Dekko the grounds before I lay down my nicker."

We were traveling by chauffeur, of course. Two limousines, he and I in the lead, Fitzpatrick bringing up the rear with the luggage and a pretty brunette flight attendant who'd caught Des's eye on the plane.

" 'Dekko the grounds'?" I asked.

"Look the place over," he translated. "Like I said, I'm a stranger here, mate. Max's gofer sent me photos of this Eye-talian viller. They look pretty good, but I wanna see fah m'self."

"What are the criteria?"

He smiled. "Simple. It's gotta be the feckin' biggest and the dearest."

I didn't know how dear it was, but the Villa Delfina was definitely feckin' big, a stunning re-creation of an elegant, Old World Italian villa resting on a large section of a gated and secluded beachfront strip of high-ticket residences known as Malibu Sands Estates.

Two Angelenos awaited us. One, a thin, pale young man who'd been leaning against a silver Prius, hopped to attention as our limo convoy drove past the wrought-iron gate into a flagstone circular drive. The other greeter, a leather-tanned woman of a certain age, emerged from a silver Mercedes-Benz sedan and strolled to the villa's heavy wooden door, which she unlocked with a key.

When we got out of the car, the pale young man was right there, extending a hand to Des. "I'm Trey Halstead," he said. "Assistant producer of the show."

Des gave him an airy look, hesitated, then shook the hand.

"We've talked on the phone," Halstead said.

"Right. When Max was too busy. Guess he was also too busy to do the welcome thing, eh?"

"He's hoping to see you tonight. He's got quite a

few events lined . . ." Halstead stopped talking when he saw he'd lost Des's attention.

The comedian was watching Fitz emerge from the second limo with the airline hostess, who was sniffing a little and whose demeanor had taken on a vibrant quality I hadn't noticed on the flight.

Our assistant producer turned to me and frowned. "Hi, Mr. Blessing. Trey—"

"Halstead. Right." I shook his hand.

"Uh, I wasn't expecting . . . I thought you'd be heading toward your hotel."

"Des has graciously invited me to stay out here for the week."

"Oh."

This news seemed to perplex him. I got the impression young Mr. Halstead was not a fan of improvisation.

The tanned woman had been watching us with a frown that she replaced with a professional smile when she approached.

She was dressed in a too-tight midnight-blue business suit and a white silk shirt unbuttoned to show maximum cleavage. To my jaded eyes she seemed to have had work done on every section of her body, from her dyed fluffy blond hair to her tiny nose, and from her bulging breasts and tucked tummy to the sparkled silver polish on the toes of her sandaled feet.

Trey Halstead opened his mouth to say something, but the woman rolled right past him and presented Des with the door key to the villa and a leather box the size of a trade paperback book. Parting her plumped lips, she said, "Welcome to Malibu Sands and your new home, Mr. O'Day. I'm Amelia St. Laurent from Crockaby Realty."

"Of course you are," Des said.

Unblinking, Amelia St. Laurent turned to me and in lieu of a leather box proffered a hand with long silver nails. It was cool and very strong. "And I know you. You're . . . the man from the morning show, which I watch every single day of the week."

"Billy Blessing," I said, making it easy for her. "Nice meeting you, Amelia."

She turned back to Des. "In the box, Mr. O'Day, you'll find three additional sets of keys that fit the doors in the villa, and three wireless wands for the front gate. If you need anything more"—she batted her extended eyelashes—"anything, just call. My business card is in the box with the keys."

"Lovely," Des said.

"I'd be happy to give you a little tour of this marvelous property," she said.

"Tell you what, darlin'," Des said, nodding toward Fitz. "Why don't you show my associate, Mr. Fitzpatrick, the grounds?" He reached out and grabbed the arm of the seemingly befuddled stewardess. "I'll be taking my own tour of this young damsel."

With that he whisked the young damsel into the villa.

Trey Halstead introduced himself to Fitz and began edging toward the Prius. "I, ah, better get back to the production company. I'll call you about tonight, Mr. Fitzpatrick."

"Sure," Fitz said. "Whatever."

He then told Amelia St. Laurent that though he

was very much up for the tour, he had to supervise the removal of the luggage from the limos. "I'm bettin' Billy would enjoy the tour," he added with an evil Irish grin.

That's how I discovered that we were on "the sandiest section of the Sands, with a fifty-six-foot frontage." The main house, the villa, had "beautiful new hardwood floors" and "a gourmet kitchen," where I would have been happy to spend a little more time. But Amelia St. Laurent, probably thinking about all the prospective house hunters awaiting her back at Crockaby, rushed me to, and past, "the spectacular pool area," "the lovely, tranquil koi pond," and "the flowering gardens."

At "the attractive detached two-story, two-bedroom guesthouse," where one of the limo drivers had deposited my luggage, she asked, "Will you be moving to this coast, too, Mr. Blessing?"

"Doubtful," I said.

"Oh?"

"I'm a New Yorker."

She gave me a look that is usually accompanied by the words "trailer trash," then regained control of herself, flashed me her puffy-lipped, ivory-white, bonded-tooth smile, and bid me adieu.

I spent the next half-hour unpacking and puttering, after which I phoned Harry Paynter, my collaborator on the book, to say hello and settle a time when we might meet. Since I wasn't sure about the availability of the limousines, I suggested he drive out.

He clearly did not warm to that idea. "Uh . . . I guess I can. But I'll need a couple hours to clear up a few things."

I looked at my watch, subtracted the three-hour difference, and told him that I'd expect him around four-thirty his time. Now my time, too.

With Des and his flight attendant amusing themselves and Fitz off who knows where, I decided to take a stroll along the beach. I got out walking shorts and the T-shirt that read "I'd rather be watching *Wake Up, America!*" and began bare-footing across the sand past homes that, if sold collectively, would reduce the heart-sickening national debt to a few pennies.

I'd barely moved beyond Des's villa when my phone rang. It didn't actually ring. It played the opening bars of "The Frim-Fram Sauce," an old bebop tune made famous by Nat King Cole. There aren't a lot of songs appropriate for a chef-restaurateur's ringtones. Maybe "Food, Glorious Food," from the score of *Oliver!* Or "Gimme a Pig Foot and a Bottle of Beer." Or "Life Is Just a Bowl of Cherries" . . .

But I digress.

The call was from my agent, Wally Wing, finding time for me in his busy day. "Billy, I'm stuck in traffic on my way to Le Bernardin and thought I'd check in, see how the trip went."

In other words, "I have nothing else to do, so I may as well rack up some billable minutes."

"Trip went fine. Very uneventful."

"Hotel accommodation okay?"

"I canceled the hotel. I'm staying at Des's place in Malibu."

"Wrong move, my brown brother," he said. "As the great Herman Mankiewicz once said, they don't even allow brunettes in Malibu."

"Herman hasn't been out here for a while." In point of fact, the cowriter of *Citizen Kane,* whom critic Alexander Woollcott once called "the funniest man in New York," died in the mid-1950s. "Attitudes change in sixty years."

"In any case, it's not smart to bunk in with someone you're working with. Things go wrong on the job, you take the problems home with you."

Wally married one of his assistants. It didn't last.

"We're not bunking," I said. "I'm in an 'attractive detached guesthouse.'"

"Yeah, but there's all that sun at the beach. You're courting melanoma."

"The thing that elevates you above all other agents, Wally, is your positive outlook. Don't forget about the earthquakes, mud slides, and wildfires."

"It's that kind of world, Billy," he said, and began rambling on about his dinner guest at Le Bernardin. Either a new flame or an old client. I wasn't sure, because my attention had drifted to a vision limping toward me from the ocean.

She had to be six feet tall, a sun-bronzed beauty wearing a bright white bikini. Early twenties. Her short black hair was in wet ringlets around a face twisted in pain. "Could you help me?" she begged.

# Chapter
# FIVE

"Later," I said to Wally, not bothering to wait for a reply before clicking the phone shut and slipping it into my pocket.

I walked into the ankle-deep surf, offering my arm.

"Oh, God, thanks," she said, shifting some of her weight to my arm and shoulder. "I cut my foot on something out there. Could you walk me to my towel?"

"Sure," I said.

With her hopping to keep her right foot above the sand, we struggled to where she'd laid out a bright orange-and-yellow towel sheet. Beside it was a second towel sheet.

"If you could just lower me . . ." she said. "Ahh, yes. Thanks. One more favor? Tell me what you think?"

She was so physically stunning, it took me a second to realize that she was asking me to gauge the wound.

"Sure," I said.

I knelt down on one knee and lifted her foot by the heel to check the damage. "A little cut on the ball," I told her. "Maybe an inch long. Doesn't look very deep. The saltwater is adding to the pain, but it's doing a little healing, too."

"I suppose I should put something on it, just to play safe."

"How far is your house?"

"Over there," she said, pointing to a two-story traditional enough to have been dragged kicking and screaming from one of Pasadena's more exclusive zip codes.

She turned to look over my shoulder at the ocean. "But you've been kind enough. I see that help is on the way."

I followed her line of sight to where a man was riding the wind on a sailboard. Tall and tanned and fit. He was heading inward, toward us, at surprising speed.

"He'll be here in a second," she said.

As he sailed nearer, I saw that he was gray-haired and probably a little long in the tooth to be keeping company with a brunette in her twenties. But this *was* Southern California.

He rode the board past the shoreline and up onto the sand. He hopped off and began taking in the sail before looking our way. When he did, we recognized each other, and his face broke into a broad grin. "For Christ's sake!" he shouted. "Billy Blessing. Where the hell did you come from? And don't tell me you've got a camera crew hidden somewhere."

"No cameras," I said. "I'm traveling light."

His name was Stew Gentry, and he was one of a diminishing group of legendary movie actors still appearing before the cameras. I wondered if Eastwood or Garner or any of his other remaining contemporaries went in for sailboarding.

I meet hundreds of celebrities, and most stay in the professional-acquaintance category. But when I spent time with Stew last year, interviewing him on *Wake Up* and for my own show on the Wine & Dine—where he prepared an almost-edible baked Alaska—we established a friendship.

He gave me a powerful handshake, wet and gritty with ocean salt. "You lied to me," he said. "You told me you never set foot on this coast."

"That was the truth at the time," I said. "This is a very temporary work visit. But before we get to the details, your . . . friend needs a little medical attention. She cut her foot."

"Shit," he said. He dropped the sail and his smile, and ran to the brunette. "What happened, baby?"

"It's not much of a cut, but I'd like to clean it off, if you could help me up to the house."

Stew made his own appraisal of the wound. "Barely a scratch," he said. "But let's take care of it."

He bent down, cradled all six beautiful feet of her in his arms, and stood. My back almost gave out just watching him. "This lovely, if heavy, young woman isn't my friend, Billy. She's my daughter, Dani Kirkendahl. Dani, this is—"

"Chef Billy Blessing," she said. "I *do* watch TV from time to time, Daddy."

I'd been momentarily surprised by Stew's revelation, mainly because I thought he'd told me his daughter had died. Keeping that thought off my face, I said, "Pleased to meet you, Dani."

"Come on up to the house, Billy," Stew said, carrying her across the sand. "I'll brew up a batch of Manhattans to honor your arrival."

I followed them to chez Gentry, stepping gingerly along a path of tree trunk slices laid in sandy gravel. To my left was a swimming pool, as clean and blue-green as one you'd find on a David Hockney canvas; to my right, a redwood deck only slightly smaller than a basketball court housed a glass-top table with a wrought-iron frame, matching chairs, a large umbrella, a gas barbecue, and a half-dozen beach loungers resting side by side.

I paused at the open French doors to brush the sand off my feet, then entered what could have passed as a set from one of Stew's Western films—the wealthy cattle baron's comfortable living room, complete with thick dark-wood ceiling beams and heavy planked hardwood floors covered by handcrafted Indian rugs in subdued earth colors.

The room, the house, was a beehive of activity. A cleaning crew of supple young women, mainly Latina, was vacuuming, dusting, and applying some kind of liquid wax or cleanser to a chocolate leather sofa and chairs that faced a huge white stone hearth. One of the workers was using a dustpan to capture the ashes from last night's fire.

Stew was halfway up the curving stairwell, Dani still in his arms. "Be just a minute, Billy," he called down. "Don't flirt with the ladies. They've got work to do. Make yourself comfortable."

I took that as a license to snoop.

Staying clear of the ladies, I strolled around the room. The walls were filled with what I assumed were mementos from hunting forays. No buffalo or moose heads, but mounted antlers, a mounted snake at least seven feet long that was being carefully avoided by a lady with a dust rag, and the pelt of what must have been a good-sized mountain lion. There were oil paintings of Western scenes in ornate gold frames, and a tall, spotless glass case displaying an assortment of handguns and rifles.

In a corner of the room was a round, scarred wooden table covered in green felt, on which was displayed a collection of framed photos. Some were movie oriented—Stew on location, goofing with the crew, riding a horse, embracing a leading lady. Some were portraits of celebrities with inscribed messages of friendship. There were several daguerreotypes—his parents or grandparents? There were shots of Stew, in the late 1960s maybe, aboard a yacht with a handsome blonde—a former wife?—and others in what appeared to be a foreign locale with a lovely brunette and a little girl, probably Dani. There were pictures of a beautiful young bride, definitely Dani, in a wedding gown, with Stew at her side, wearing a morning suit and looking dashing if slightly in the bag.

I paused in my photo perusal, distracted by the aroma of something intriguingly spicy that had drifted into the room, when one of the staff entered through a kitchen door. I headed that way and pushed open the door to face several women in white aprons and caps preparing a Mexican feast.

One of them was creating a seafood salad, tossing peeled shrimp and hunks of crabmeat into a bowl so gigantic that Stew was either having a very large crowd for dinner or was opening his own restaurant.

It had been nearly thirteen hours since I'd had breakfast in Manhattan. I'd passed on the first-class lunch fare, maintaining my belief that if God had wanted flying creatures to eat while in the air, he would not have given the pelican that deep pouch to hold its food in for later. And he'd have definitely done something about the food prep on planes.

Thirteen hours of abstinence and the food aromas were causing my brain to short-circuit. Before I did something totally uncivilized, I backed out of the kitchen and escaped to a study just off the other side of the main room.

It had the rumpled, lived-in look of a special place. There was an Eames lounge-chair-and-ottoman combo (which I've always wanted but could never figure out why), and beside it a floor lamp and a Mission-style end table on which rested a highball glass with about a half-inch of melted ice, a folded newspaper, several scripts, and a copy of the late Senator Ted Kennedy's autobiography. If that didn't suggest that Stew was more of a reader than his rough-hewn image indicated, one wall was lined with hardcover books, mainly biographies and historical tomes.

There was also a dish containing very stale cashews that I scarfed gratefully while studying the art hanging on the walls. It was as modern as the living room art was trad. Some were by painters whose style was unfamiliar—an expressionist work that seemed to suggest water breaking against rocks, a black-and-white portrait of a bird emerging from its shell, and a jumbled streetscape. But there was also a bright, riveting de Kooning woman and one of Mark Rothko's very valuable color swatches.

I was so caught up in the de Kooning that I didn't hear Stew enter the room and jumped a foot when he announced, "Cocktail time."

He had a glass pitcher of brown liquid in one hand and two long-stemmed glasses in the other. "Sorry," he said. "Didn't mean to sneak up on you."

"Nothing a trip to the cardiologist won't cure," I said, taking one of the glasses from him. "How's Dani doing?"

"Fine. It's nothing. She'll be down in a minute. Meanwhile . . ." He filled my glass. "Let the trendsetting assholes slurp their bubblegum cocktails," he said. "I'll stick to the classics."

I took the cocktail to a soft leather couch that faced the Eames chair, where Stew sat before filling his own glass. He raised it and said, "To your arrival on the best coast."

I sipped the cocktail. It was about as good a Manhattan as one could blend in a pitcher.

"So, Billy, what kind of work brings you out here against your will?" he asked.

"The network is launching a new late-night show."

"Like Leno's?"

"Yes," I said. "There's been some publicity. Not enough, apparently."

He waved his hand dismissively. "I'm no judge. Except for sports, I don't pay any attention to what they're doing on TV. But this show must be something special to lure you out here. And living in Malibu Sands? Which place, by the way?"

"Villa Delfina."

He was silent for a beat, then said, "The villa, huh? I heard the asking price was twenty-six mil."

"Well, because of the recession, I got them to come down a few thou," I said.

When he didn't smile, I added, "I'm just a guest of the owner's, a chimney sweep in this sunny hall of kings."

"Who's payin' the freight?"

"The guy who's hosting the new show, a comedian named Desmond O'Day."

Stew cocked his head and frowned.

"You know Des?" I asked.

"Not that I recall," he said. "Comedian, huh? One of those always-on guys?"

"I don't think so," I said. "But I've only just met him. We flew in earlier today, and he very kindly offered me the comfort of his guesthouse."

"I'll have to thank him for bringing you to the neighborhood."

There was a thumping noise coming from the other room. It grew louder until Dani appeared at the door, looking beautiful and healthy in an aqua tank top, white slacks, and sandals.

Stew's smile of fatherly pride left his face when he saw that she was carrying a blackthorn walking stick. "Where the hell did you find that goddamned thing?" he growled.

"In your room," she said, surprised at his sudden anger. "I'm sorry. Shouldn't I have—"

"No, no. It's fine. Come and sit."

"Better not," she said. "There're only a few hours before the guests will be arriving. I might just take a little nap." She graced me with a smile. "It was lovely meeting you, Billy."

"The pleasure's all mine," I said, rising. I placed

my barely touched Manhattan on a table and added, "I'd better be going, too. Work beckons."

Stew walked with us into the living room. While Dani hobbled toward the stairs, he saw me out the way I'd come in. "As you may have gathered, we're having a little dinner party here tonight," he said. "Mixing business and pleasure. There'll be some folks who are investing in my next screen masterpiece, some friends, and even some enemies. But a convivial crowd in the main. Please drop by."

I hesitated, mainly because I was weak from hunger and just a little jet-lagged.

"I really would love for you to come, Billy. We'll have lots of food, lots of booze, a few lovely ladies. And you won't even have to worry about driving home."

"You didn't cook any of the food, did you? I still have nightmares I blame on the baked Alaska you whipped up on my show."

He chuckled. "That really wasn't my specialty," he said. "The publicity people thought it would make a good visual. Actually, I'm a damn fine chef, and I hope I get the chance to prove it to you while you're here. But tonight's feast is being prepared by professionals such as yourself."

"In that case, I shall return."

"Excellent. Any time after eight," he said. "Bring your Irish host. I'd like to meet him."

Walking back to the villa, I wondered how Stew knew Des was Irish if he'd never heard of him. Then I laughed at myself. What else would Desmond O'Day be? Iranian?

# Chapter
## SIX

Harry Paynter, the novelist-screenwriter with whom I was supposed to form a literary alliance, was a plump young man with a baby face and sad, weary eyes that gave him the look of a debauched choirboy. He seemed surprised, but not impressed, that a pop-music star like Fitzpatrick had unlocked the gate and escorted him to my digs. Harry would probably not have been impressed to find Prince doing my laundry.

"So Billy," he said, when we were seated in the guesthouse living room, "don't suppose you've got any Diet Mountain Dew?"

"Doubtful, but I'll check." I walked to the small kitchen, looked in the fridge, and reported back to Harry, "No to the Mountain Dew. Thanks to somebody—the realtor, I guess—there's tomato juice, carrot juice, and bottled water."

"Pass," he said.

"I'll add Mountain Dew to my list."

"Don't bother," he said. "Here's the thing, Billy. My time is fucking valuable. I've got two scripts due next week—a contemporary remake of *The Pit and the Pendulum* for Sony and a musical thriller that'll star The Peezy Weezies, we all hope. I can't afford the time it takes for me to drive out here. I spent five minutes just waiting for the security guys at the gate to find my name on their list. There's no reason we have to be in the same room to collaborate. We can use the phone, text, Skype, whatever. Right?"

"Sounds right to me," I said, though I had no working knowledge of Skype. As for The Peezy Weezies, well . . . the only Weezy I knew had the last name of Jefferson.

"Okay, that's how we'll handle it. But I'm here now, so let's get to work," he said, sliding a laptop from a leather shoulder bag. "I can give you ninety minutes. And I'll try the fucking carrot juice."

I returned to the kitchen, poured two glasses of the thick, bright-orange liquid, and returned to the living room.

Harry had the laptop open and balanced on his knees, ready for action. He took a gulp of juice, shuddered, and said, "Yuk."

"Fresh-squeezed," I said.

"That's the problem. I can't stand fresh. Tastes like medicine. Okay, let's get going on this bad boy. We need a title. How about *TV Can Be Murder*?"

"A little jaunty, don't you think? What about *The Morning Show Murders*?"

"Too on-the-nose. *Murder on Camera*? *Blood on the Camera*?"

I winced.

"*High Def Death?*"

"Too hard to pronounce," I said.

"Why don't we follow Raymond Chandler's lead?" he asked. "*Good Morning, Murder.*"

"What's that got to do with Chandler?"

"*Farewell, My Lovely. Good Morning, Murder.*"

And so it went for the next ninety minutes, at which time, as promised, my collaborator departed. Without a decision being made on the title.

Having picked up on Harry's anxiety, I strolled over to the villa, where I found Des, Fitz, and a new-comer—short, soft, with a pug nose, tiny ears, and a shock of jet-black hair—in what appeared to be a big-boy's playroom, complete with dartboards, pinball machines, and the like. Fitz was playing pinball, while the other two men were stretched out on leather chairs and ottomans in front of a giant flat TV screen, engrossed in a videogame called Brütal Legend.

"Yo, Billy," Fitz said, by way of welcome.

"That you, Billy?" Des said, not taking his eyes from the TV screen. "Say hello to Gibby Lewis, head writer on our little show."

Gibby, evidently not quite as committed to the big-screen competition, turned a peeved baby face toward me. He broke it with a brief forced smile, a nod, and then it was back to Brütal Legend.

"Des," I said, trying to talk over the noise, "a friend is throwing a dinner party a few houses down. Around eight, if you're interested."

"Can't make it," Des replied, keeping his eyes on the screen, where a buffed and bearded character re-sembling both Jack Black and Popeye's nemesis, Bluto, was using his odd-looking guitar to thwart evil. "That feckin' little twerp who was here earlier called to say Slaughter's hostin' a hooley for me with a bunch of doxies."

The twerp was our associate producer Trey Hal-stead. Slaughter was, as mentioned previously, Trey's boss, producer of the new show. A hooley was a party. The doxies were, well, doxies.

"Max didn't mention any party to me," Gibby said. His delivery was as peevish as his mug. "Not that I coulda gone. I've gotta spend the evening with my lovely sister and her adorable kids. Unless I can think up an excuse. Like a hernia. Then I'll go find my own doxy."

"Pull up a chair, Billy. This game's a gallery. That's Jack Black with the gizmo, doin' the arse-kickin'. Ozzy Osbourne's in it, too."

Regardless of those attractions, Brütal Legend seemed to be a combination of unrelenting violence and headbanger music, two of my least favorite things. "I'd better get myself in gear for tonight," I said.

"Your call," he said.

According to my watch, it was ten after seven. Ten after ten in Manhattan. I'd already searched and found nothing remotely snackable at the guesthouse. "Mind if I raid your kitchen?" I yelled over the sounds of Jack Black's arse-kickin'.

"What's that?"

I repeated the question, and he told me to help myself to whatever.

In the large, brightly tiled gourmet country kitchen capable of feeding a tribe, I discovered the perfect dinner foreplay—a wedge of Jarlsberg cheese, saltines, and green seedless grapes. And to wash it down, a brisk, melony Chimney Rock Napa Valley Elevage Blanc.

Feeling considerably refreshed, I returned to the

guesthouse and put in a call to my restaurant's manager-hostess, Cassandra Shaw.

"Oh, Billy," she said, heavy on the sarcasm. "I was beginning to wonder if you'd forgotten us, out there in lotusland."

"The time difference threw me off," I said.

"No problem," she said. "We had an excellent night. Near capacity. Service was smooth. Morale high. Don't worry about us, Billy. We always seem to prosper when you're not around."

Cassandra is a tall, relentlessly beautiful blonde and, more crucial to the success of Blessing's Bistro, an extremely self-reliant, smart, and dedicated second-in-command. But as long as I've known her, nearly seven years, she has carried a chip on her shoulder the size of the Manhattan phone book. Our customers not only accept her snarky attitude, they seem to be amused and even enchanted by it. I have to admit, there are times I'm amused by it myself. This wasn't one of them.

"Well," I said, "if, by some miracle, you do need me, you know how to reach me."

"I seem to have misplaced the phone number of your beach cabana."

"I'm working here, Cassandra. No beach cabana."

"How sad for you," she said. "Billy, to be serious for a moment, the women out there are as self-obsessed and predatory as they are beautiful. Please try not to disgrace yourself or the Bistro. Keep it zipped."

I told her I'd do my best. I didn't tell her I was wearing breakaway pants.

In any case, her advice, sincere or not, went in one ear and out the other.

Only an hour later, at Stew's dinner party, over-dressed in a sport coat in L.A., I found myself sharing personal space with one of the most attractive females present, pretending to be enthralled by her explanation of why she'd had to take Balthazar, her Pomeranian, to "doggie rehab."

I'd spied her the moment I stepped through the door. Stew had welcomed me, expressed regret that Des had been unable to make it, and was about to lead me to a group of pleasant-looking, affluent, middle-aged couples when I asked if he'd mind introducing me instead to the beautiful lady who, like myself, disproved Herman Mankiewicz's quip about Malibu racial intolerance.

Now she and I were standing poolside with a couple dozen other guests, enjoying a mariachi band and margaritas and appreciating the way the patio heaters kept the night balmy in spite of a chilly breeze off the ocean. So fascinated was I by the way her no doubt enhanced sea-green eyes contrasted with her dark brown skin, I was able to keep a straight face while she told me about "poor Balthy" nibbling on a marijuana plant in the garden behind her house. I assumed Balthy was one of those accessory quasi-dogs so popular in L.A., and, in fairness, NYC.

"It got so I just couldn't keep him away from it," she said. "I decided I had to . . . Why is that fool gawking at us?"

It took me a second to realize she'd not only changed the subject, she'd asked me a question.

Reluctantly, I turned from her to observe the fool.

He was a big, arrogantly handsome guy in his early fifties. Salt-and-pepper hair cut close to his balding scalp. Black leather jacket. Several days' growth of beard on his chiseled chin. He was standing with Stew's daughter, Dani.

"Do you know him, Billy?"

Oh, yeah. I knew him.

The last time I'd seen Roger Charbonnet, he'd threatened to kill me. Twenty-two years may have passed, but, judging by the expression on his face, he still remembered me, and it was not a fond memory.

## Chapter
## SEVEN

"Isn't he the chef with all the hot restaurants?" the lady with the green eyes was saying. "I think he just opened a place over on Kanan Dume Road."

I couldn't respond. I couldn't even remember her name. And I'm usually very good with names. My problem was that I'd just lost twenty-two years. I was no longer a moderately self-assured adult attending a dinner party. I was a hesitant, self-conscious, out-of-work kid being faced down by a seething lunatic with a gun tucked under his belt.

Roger Charbonnet smiled suddenly. Not a pleasant sight. He raised his hand, made a gun with thumb and forefinger, and pointed it at me. Then, continuing to face me, he bent down and whispered something in Dani's ear, draped his arm around her shoulders in a possessive gesture, and escorted her back into the house.

I'm not sure how long I continued to stare at the now vacant section of the patio. What brought me back to the party were the mariachis hitting a high harmonic note on "Guadalajara" and the slightly distant sound of the sister with the green eyes talking about a "wonderful dog whisperer who saved little Balthy from his addiction."

She'd abandoned me for a younger, tanned and toned guy in a flashy Hawaiian shirt and white slacks who was so attentive to her shaggy stoned-dog story that if he stood any closer to her, he'd lose the pleats in his pants.

It probably would have been more prudent for me to head back to the Villa Delfina at that point. I could raid Des's fridge again and then waddle off to sleep away the jet lag and other excesses of the day. But it was still early, on this coast, at least, a dinner including fresh seafood salad and grilled top shoulder of lamb was imminent, and, most important, having regained my senses, I was not about to let an asshole like Roger Charbonnet think that he'd chased me off a second time.

I found him inside the house, treating Dani and a small group of partygoers to a play-by-play of a recent trip to an estate in Sardinia as the guest of an Italian American film director. Hearing a slur in his voice, I realized he'd been sipping more than his share of tequila.

Sloshing through a vignette centering on "the auteur's fucking amazing Ferrari Enzo," he noticed me standing just outside his conversation circle, observing him with the same unreadable smile I'd perfected as part of my on-camera interviewing technique.

My presence was apparently distracting enough to cause a momentary gap in his monologue. Dani followed his glance and saw me, smiling pleasantly. She waved, and I returned her wave.

Roger's neck turned pink, and as the flush spread to his face, I sensed he was about to blow. An ugly confrontation would definitely detract from the party mood. Before that happened, I broke eye contact and moved on.

There were signs that the dinner bell was about to be rung. Smiling Latinas in beaded blouses and colorful full satin skirts, and their male counterparts in embroidered guayabera shirts and black trousers, were transporting the fragrant dishes on silver salvers from the kitchen to the dining room, where three long groaning boards had been pushed together to form a U. Lured by the heady aroma of the spicy foods, the guests were gathering.

"You look like you could use this."

Stew had made another of his silent approaches, but this time I took it in stride. I'd already had my startle reaction of the evening. He was holding out a salt-rimmed glass containing a fresh margarita in crushed ice, a duplicate of the cocktail in his other hand.

"You walk quieter than a ninja," I said, taking the drink.

"My Indian blood," he said. "It makes me aware

of things, too. Like the friction between you and Charbonnet. What's the deal?"

Maybe I should have told him that I suspected the guy fondling his daughter had murdered his girlfriend twenty-three years ago. But that kind of accusation can at worst get you sued and at best get you hopelessly ensnared in an ugly family scene. I took a sip of the margarita. "We chefs are a competitive crew," I said.

"As opposed to actors?" He sampled his margarita. "Well, don't let your competitive sense interfere with your enjoyment of tonight's feast."

"Don't tell me Roger's responsible for the food?"

"No way. The chef is Zapopa Estevez. From Camino Real in Brentwood, for my money, the best true-to-Mexico *restaurante* on the West Coast. And believe me, I've tried 'em all."

"You've sold me," I said, heading in the direction of the gathering crowd.

Stew put a halting hand on my shoulder. "It'll take a while for the line to go down. Let's us get some air and have a little chat."

He led me out to the patio. It was suffering from dinnertime loneliness, except for the mariachis, who were taking five. When one of them noticed us, he tossed away his cigarette and picked up his guitar.

"Relax, *amigo*," Stew called over to him. "Take your break. You guys earned it."

I followed him to the far edge of the deck, where he stood looking out at the ocean. The dark water was touched by shimmering streaks of reflected moonlight. "Goddamn it! There. See that?" Stew asked.

I saw nothing at first. Then I caught a few shadows disturbing the natural pattern of the ocean. "That a boat out there?" I asked. "What are they doing?"

"Hell if I know. Maybe some kind of new-age fishermen. More likely they're there because they can be. According to coastal-access laws, the other side of the high-tide line is open to the public. But even though they're not breaking any laws, they don't belong out there."

He shook his head. "I guess I sound like an uptight asshole. But the fact is, there are twenty-one miles of beach in Malibu. And no matter what you want to do at night on the ocean, you can find a better spot to do it than right here. So I'm guessing the main reason they're out there is because we're here. Those law-abiding sneaks are probably paparazzi hoping to catch my guests taking a skinny-dip in the drink."

All of this was mildly interesting but, to a hungry man, hardly a substitute for grilled lamb.

"I suppose you're wondering why we're out here when the food's in there?" Stew asked, reading my mind.

I shrugged.

"I want to hear about you and Charbonnet."

"Why?"

"He's like those punks on the ocean," Stew said, his lip curled. "An opportunist taking advantage of a situation. He's a minor partner in Golden Bear, the company that's producing my next movie. He seems to think that gives him the right to sleep with my daughter."

He paused, evidently expecting me to respond. I couldn't think of a thing to say other than TMI, so I remained silent.

"The guy's successful," Stew continued. "I'll give him that. He's got a bunch of the town's top restaurants, and I hear he's about to follow Wolf Puck to Vegas and points east. Probably be putting one up a block away from you in Manhattan."

Just what I wanted to hear.

"He's a black hat, Billy," Stew said. "I knew it the first time I saw him, with his fucking whiskers and black leather. Not that I'd write anybody off just because they're a poster boy for male menopause. He's too old for Dani. Too volatile. I've seen the way he treats his people. To top it off, the son of a bitch is a player. Dani's just twenty-two, and she's already one down. I don't want her making another mistake."

The mariachis picked up their instruments and started working on a festive little number that they took inside the house to entertain the diners. I shifted my feet and said, "What makes you think marriage is in the air?"

"I don't know for certain. I guess they could be just, what's the term, fuck buddies. That's bad enough."

"What's Dani say?"

"Christ, Billy. I haven't talked to her about it. I've bought so many wedding rings myself, I qualify for the discount price. If I tried to give her advice, she'd probably laugh in my face. But, damn it, she's my daughter."

"Maybe her mother—"

"Gloria and I don't talk . . . much.

"Here's the deal, Billy. A couple years ago, Dani quit school and ran off to marry a prick named Wilt Kirkendahl. I wasn't happy about her settling for life with a goddamn stuntman, which is not a profession that cries out stability or longevity. But I figured what the hell. She's happy.

"Six months later, she's at the door with an eye the color of an overripe banana. Turns out Kirkendahl's an abusive drunk. Gee, what a surprise. It took this peeper I hired less than a week to get enough on the weasel I was able to present him with an option—agree to a divorce or have a vacation on me at Pelican Bay State Prison. That worked out fine."

"I'm guessing you put your peeper on Roger," I said.

Stew nodded grimly. "The only thing he came up with was from a long time ago. Some dame he was banging got herself killed. For a while Charbonnet was a suspect. But he had an alibi. Other than that, nothing. In '94, he married a Vegas showgirl and divorced her a year later. I can't fault him for a waltz I've danced myself. For the last decade and a half, he's tapped a long line of beautiful women, which would be peachy, except that his current tap is my daughter."

"The odds are he'll be moving on eventually," I said.

Stew turned his back to the ocean and stared at me. "I was hopin' you'd know something about the bastard that might end it sooner than later."

This was definitely not anything I wanted a part of. "I wish I could help you—" I started to say.

I paused, because Stew was now looking past me, his eyes open wide in surprise.

I heard and felt the vibration of heavy footsteps on the deck, moving toward us.

"Blessing, you worthless piece of shit!"

I spun around to see Roger Charbonnet rushing toward me, drunk and dangerous. "What lies is this bastard telling you, Stew?"

"Take it easy, Charbonnet," Stew said.

"What did you tell him?" Roger demanded. His face was now showing splotches of purple.

"I were you, Roger," I said, "I'd cut way back on the tequila and the jalapeños."

"You son of a bitch."

He made a fist and drew it back. Just as he unleashed it at my head, I ducked and tossed my margarita into his face.

Trying to block the drink, he pulled the punch and almost hit himself in the forehead.

I wish I could say that I'm a lover, not a fighter, but that's only partially true. I am definitely not a fighter. I headed for the door. Guests were gathering there, eager for tomorrow's morning dish material.

Out of deference to my host, a Hollywood hero, I tried not to run.

Stew was calling out to Roger, urging him to "stop behaving like a raging lunatic."

Since that's exactly what Roger was, he paid no attention. Instead, he lumbered across the deck. At me.

Roger was as close to rabid as a human can get without the help of an infected animal. While I'd always considered myself the loser in our confrontation long ago, I realized at that moment that something—my celebrity, maybe—must have been ringing his chimes for years.

And now he was going to make me pay.

He'd be on me before I hit the door, so I checked my surroundings for an alternative to flight. A baseball bat would have been nice. But, alas . . .

Roger paused, glaring at me. Red-eyed and snorting. I swear I saw drool dripping from his nose and lips. Keeping our eyes locked, I began edging toward the door.

I took a sideways step, and my foot hit a wet spot near the pool. I stumbled backward to the deck just as he was almost on me. His fist sailed through the empty space that a second before had been occupied by my head. The momentum of the unsuccessful punch carried him forward, over me. The tip of a shoe caught my right ankle, and he sailed over me, barely missing the pool's concrete edge before disrupting the beautiful blue-green surface of the water with an inelegant belly flop.

"You okay?" Stew asked as he helped me up.

My butt hurt, and my ankle felt like it'd been caught in a bear trap. "Define 'okay,'" I said.

Roger was making a lot of noise, flapping around in his sodden leather and screaming that he couldn't swim.

"You damn fool," Stew shouted. "Just stand up. You're in four feet of water." Turning to me, he asked, in a much quieter tone, "What 'lies' did he think you were telling me, Billy?"

I shrugged. "You'll have to ask him. But I'd wait till he calms down a little."

Roger was now standing chest-deep in the pool. He wiped water from his eyes and spun around, searching the crowd. He stopped when he saw Dani standing by the pool, giving him a look of dismay before turning and walking inside the house.

Roger blinked, then began his jerky search again until he found me. "Blessing, you fucking coward," he yelled, moving toward a metal ladder. "I'm gonna kill you."

"Don't worry about that drunken jackass," Stew said as we watched Roger slip from the ladder and fall back into the water. "Once he manages to get out of the pool, if he doesn't behave himself, it'll be my pleasure to give him one right between the horns."

"Good luck with that," I said. "I'll be limping off now. Lovely party, Stew."

## Chapter
# EIGHT

Back at the villa, I devoured a Wolfgang Puck pizza that I'd found in the freezer and was depositing the plate and utensils in an otherwise-empty dishwasher when Des and Fitzpatrick floated in, smelling of booze and . . . chlorine?

"How was dinner?" I asked.

"Uh, okay," Fitz said. He seemed pale, even for him. And a bit unnerved.

Des said nothing. He focused on the bottle of Elevage Blanc that I'd opened earlier and resampled with the pizza, grabbed it, and headed out of the kitchen.

"He okay?" I asked Fitzpatrick.

"Gimme a minute," he said, and followed Des from the room.

It was more like five minutes when Fitz returned with a bottle of Jameson fifteen-year-old Irish whiskey. I'd kept busy by locating and heating a Toaster Strudel, assuaging some of my caloric guilt by purposefully ignoring the icing packet.

Without a word, he walked to the counter, poured himself a cup of coffee, and brought it and the whiskey bottle back to the table, where I was scarfing down my strudel. He uncapped the Jameson. He held it over my cup and, when I shook my head, reversed and poured a healthy tot of what may be the world's best sipping whiskey into his coffee. I tried not to wince at the sight of him taking that first gulp.

"Rough night?" I asked.

"Wojus, I'd call it."

"What happened?"

He gave me an odd half smile. "Case o' mistaken identity."

"Somebody take Des for Rod Stewart?" I asked.

"Not exactly," he said.

I stared at him, waiting for the story.

He shook his head. "Tales out o' school."

I took a bite of strudel.

Fitz brooded for a minute or two, then said, "Mr. Max Slaughter is a bloody horse's ass."

"How so?"

Evidently unhappy with the whiskey-coffee ratio, he added another inch or so of Jameson. "Slaughter and that gofer of his, Trey, pick us up in a limo and take us to a pub in downtown L.A. named O'Doul's. The joint was more Oirish than Irish. Strictly plastic Paddy. All bloody green an' white. The Brothers Clancy singin' from the speakers. Cheesy paper-doll shamrocks and wee folk strung from the rafters.

"The barman, who's never even seen the Isle, gets out a tiny camera and makes a thing of getting Des to pose for some snaps, durin' which he lets slip that Max owns the bloody place. Assumin' that Max is usin' him for free publicity, Des proceeds to down one pint of plain after another. This leads to him gettin' his back up and callin' out some boyos who'd been sittin' peacefully at the bar. Before there be wigs on the green, Max and this Trey herd us out of there, headin' to Hollywood for grub.

"In the limo, Des's black mood does a sudden roundabout. Now he's on the pig's back."

"Say what?" I interrupted.

"He's happy. Ready to celebrate. Which, at that moment, means downing most of a bottle of the bubbly. By the time we pull up at the restaurant, he's rubber, and me and Trey have to steer him in.

"The chow parlor is called In the Dark. Ever hear of it, Billy?"

"One of those restaurants that claim you get a truer dining experience by eating in pitch-black?" I ask.

"Bang on! Max says it's to give us a taste of the *O'Day at Night* set. He's got this wizard of a lighting designer on the payroll who's usin' darkness and shadow to come up with a look that's different from the other talk shows. The stagehands are gonna be runnin' around in head-to-toe black outfits, so they can move props and do stuff without the camera seein' 'em."

"Great," I said. "I'll look like the invisible man."

"Huh? Oh, I get ya." He grinned a bit sheepishly, the way some whites do when a black man makes a joke about his color. "Well," he continued hurriedly, "no matter what reason Max gives, I figure the choice of restaurant is one more piece of evidence that he has his head up his arse. Anyway . . ."

He seemed to hesitate, then took another mouthful of his doctored coffee. He swallowed it slowly, gazing across the kitchen at nothing in particular.

I prompted, "Anyway . . . ?"

"Oh. Yeah, well, the lights go off and, soon enough, the food is served, a good thing, 'cause by then I'm so starved I could eat the lamb o' Jesus through the rungs of a chair. It's not easy gettin' food to your mouth in the dark. An' the business about tunin' up your taste buds is bullshit."

He drifted off again, lost in some thought that, judging by his face, was none too pretty.

"Fitz?"

He shook his head. "Sorry, Billy," he said, standing. "I gotta . . . I dunno, get some sleep or somethin'."

I watched him waddle off, a bear-man with more on his mind than he cared to share with me.

I deposited the remains of my strudel in the disposal, poured off his Irish coffee, rinsed off the cups and plate, and put them in the dishwasher.

I exited the main building through the rear door

and was on the path to the guesthouse when I heard Des call out, "G'night, Billy."

He was sitting on the beach in his boxers, his body as pale as milk in the moonlight.

I walked toward him feeling the grit of the sand under my shoes. "You ought to put on a robe," I said. "Aren't you cold?"

"Freezin' my arse," he said, his teeth chattering. "It's a Catholic thing, Billy. Penance for your sins."

"Penance is ten Hail Marys, not pneumonia."

"You don't know my sins," he said. He turned to look out at the dark sky and ocean, frowning as if searching for the horizon line. When he lifted the wine bottle to his lips, there was enough moonlight for me to see what appeared to be blood crusted on his knuckles.

"Anything happen tonight I should know about?" I asked.

"What's me flannel-mouth friend been tellin' ya?"

"Not much," I said. "You guys went to a pub and had dinner in the dark."

"That about sums it up," he said.

"Doesn't quite explain why you both smell of chlorine," I said. "Or why your knuckles are busted."

He looked at the hand holding the wine bottle. "In that feckin' joke of an eatery, with the lights off and me in my cups, I musta dusted 'em on somethin' rough," he said, then returned to his contemplation of the darkness.

"Yeah, well, it's late," I said. "I guess I'll go hit the hay."

"Sleep well," he said.

*Probably better than you,* I thought.

# *Chapter* NINE

I awoke from a dream of Nat King Cole singing "Frim-Fram Sauce" to discover it had been prompted by my cellular's ringtone repeating itself.

"What the hell?" I said into the phone, squinting at my watch. "It's too damn early."

"Nine-thirty-six," Wally Wing said.

"Six-thirty-six here," I said.

"Excuse me," he said. "I guess you aren't the guy used to getting up at five for your morning show."

"What do you want, Wally?"

"To congratulate you on demolishing that prick at Stew Gentry's party," he said.

"How . . . ?"

"You've gone viral on the Internet."

I was wide awake. I'd been so caught up in the mystery of Des's night that I'd forgotten about my dustup with Roger Charbonnet. Evidently the shadowy figures lurking just off the beach at Stew's had been busy with their cameras.

"How . . . bad is it?" I asked.

"Bad?" Wally said. "You look great. Very heroic. It's the other guy, the hothead L.A. chef you tossed in the pool, who looks like a donkey. What'd you do to piss him off?"

"Just being my own sweet self," I said.

"Well, Harry's gonna want all the gory details for the book. You and he connect yet?"

The connection had been made, I told him. That seemed to satisfy him enough to click off and let me get back to sleep.

But I couldn't sleep.

For one thing, I was curious to see the footage.

It was on YouTube, my phone's small screen providing a picture that was a little dark, a little grainy. But it was recognizably Roger and me going through our dance. The distance had been too far for the mikes to pick up any conversation except for Roger's yelled threats.

At the time I'd been too full of myself to realize how lucky I'd been. Roger's physical and mental abilities had been dulled by drink, and he'd fallen into a pool, thereby hindering him from simply getting up and tearing me apart like a barbecued chicken. The reality of the situation was that he was a very large, dangerous man who'd hated me years ago and had even more reason to hate me now, especially since our little tango had turned him into a worldwide joke.

Shortly after nine o'clock Pacific Coast time, Gretchen Di Voss called from Manhattan, asking if I was all right after my "fight."

"You boys and your macho games," she said, and segued into the real reason for the call. She wanted me to host a few *Wake Up* segments using the network's West Coast facilities. "The viewers need to be reminded that you're still a part of the show. And that you'll be appearing with Des during his opening week."

"What type of segs are we talking about?" I asked.

"The sort of things you've been doing every morning. Interviews and the like. I'll talk to Trina about it, and she'll work out a schedule with Carmen." Trina Lomax was the executive producer of *Wake Up, America!* Carmen Sandoval was the vice president of network news and entertainment on the West Coast.

"Who knows?" Gretch added. "It may even make sense to keep you out there awhile. Maybe even permanently."

She clicked off without assuring me that she'd been joking.

I was starting to get that not-one-of-my-better-days feeling. Since the phone was still in my hand, I dialed a 212 number. The first ring was cut short by the crisp British accent of my ultraefficient assistant, Kiki Owens.

"What's the word?" I asked her.

"Wow, Billy, I guess it's still the Wild West out there."

"I'm more interested in what's going on where you are. I know what's happening here."

"So does the world, judging by the emails and phone calls. All wanting to know when their new favorite action hero will be returning."

That explained Gretch's request for West Coast segments. I told Kiki about them and that I'd be juggling those assignments with rehearsals for *O'Day at Night* and conferences with Harry Paynter.

"You're not good at parceling your time, Billy," she said.

"We'll see."

"I'm ready to help," she said. "I can be packed in a moment's notice."

"It may come to that. But right now I need you right where you are."

"Stew's beach house looked very . . . nice in the video."

I flashed on the fact that Stew had taken her to dinner last year when he was in NYC on a promotion tour. "Just your average twenty-five-million-dollar shack," I said. "Nothing special."

"What's his current status, Billy?" she asked, suddenly very serious.

"I think he's getting ready for a new movie," I said.

"Bastard. You know what I mean."

"He didn't seem to be with anybody at the party," I said.

"Interesting," she said.

"Aren't you almost engaged to that nice guy in ad sales?"

"Let me know if you need me out there," she said brusquely, and broke the connection.

Before I put the phone down, Stew called. I half expected him to mention Kiki, but that didn't happen. Instead, he asked how I was holding up. I told him I had a few bruises but was otherwise fit.

When I mentioned the Internet coverage of the party incident, he spent a minute or so cursing the boat paparazzi. Then his mood brightened. "After you left last night, Dani and Roger had a little talk. I didn't exactly have my ear to the wall, but from the way he stormed out of here, I think she's gonna dump the son of a bitch."

"I suppose Roger will add that to my scorecard, too," I said.

"Where's all the animosity come from?" Stew asked.

"Too long a story from too long ago."

"Well, the man's not the kind to forgive and forget, that's for sure. Watch your back, amigo. But if you feel you don't have enough excitement in your life, drop on by. I'm rarely busy, but if I am I'll always give you a drink before kicking you out."


I shaved, showered, and tended to my bodily necessities, noting the pain points at the base of my spine and my anklebone. From time to time, the "Dah-dah-da-dah-da, dah-da-dah-dah-dah-da" ringtone sounded in the bedroom.

There were six messages left, five of which I ignored.

Harry Paynter picked up on the second ring.

"Come up with a title?" I asked.

"Uh, no. Well, maybe *Sound of the Assassin*?"

"Might work for the audio version," I said.

"Well, that's not why I called. It's about the punch-out you had with Roger Charbonnet. That's literary gold, Billy. Two culinary masters duking it out like the *Iron Chef* ninjas of old. And all of it taking place at the Malibu beachfront mansion of a mega-superstar."

"There's only one problem," I said. "What's the first rule of Fight Club?"

" 'You do not talk about Fight Club,' " he replied, repeating the quote made famous by the Brad Pitt–Edward Norton cult movie. "Touché, Billy. I dig. You don't want to talk about it. Fair enough. We'll just let everybody else talk about it. Whet their appetites for the book. This project is gonna rock."

I clicked the phone shut, wondered if there was even a remote possibility of that being true.


I'd finished dressing and was slipping my feet into my shoes when Des knocked on the door. To my surprise, he looked bright-eyed and spruced up in a black silk shirt and neatly pressed black slacks. The only outward remnant of his rough night was a flesh-colored adhesive that masked his damaged knuckles.

"I'm heading out now to meet up with a camera crew," he said. "We'll be filmin' the rest of the day and on into the night, gettin' footage to open the show and bookend th' commercial breaks. Fitz's got a coffeepot goin' in the villa, if you're interested."

"Thanks," I said. "I could use a cup."

"I guess I sounded like a mope last night, all that depressin' talk," he said. "Don't give it a second's thought, Billy. I was just bein' Irish. We got more mood swings than a ladies' baseball team."

He gave me a wide grin, turned, and departed, leaving me with, "And isn't it a grand day today?"

That remained to be seen.

\* \* \*

Again, the "Frim-Fram Sauce" intro. This time it was the coproducer of our cooking show on the Wine & Dine Net, Lily Conover, offering the suggestion that we pitch a new reality series, *Battle with Blessing,* in which I take on a new opponent each week. "In the pilot we could have you wrestle an alligator," she said, barely able to keep from giggling. Nice that I was bringing joy to so many.

As I was about to stroll over to the villa to investigate the coffee situation, Cassandra called to report on the day's luncheon business at Blessing's Bistro. It sounded fine to me, but she considered it merely adequate. She ended with the request that I "try to remain sober and noncombative, if not for your own sake, for the sake of the bistro that bears your name."

Fitzpatrick was in the kitchen, bent over the dishwasher, studying its operating buttons. He pressed one of them, then closed the stainless-steel front panel. He turned, saw me, and gave me a halfhearted smile. "Des ain't here," he said. "Workday."

"I know. He stopped by the coach house. Mentioned something about coffee?"

"Just made a second pot," he said, indicating the carafe sitting on the stovetop, as he sat down at the table. "An' there're some sinkers on the counter near the dishes."

Watching me fill my cup, he added, "I'm headin' out, too. Meetin' up with a couple local musicians. Slaughter says he wants a full, rich sound. Like he'd know that from hail hittin' a tin roof."

I plucked a chocolate doughnut from the box and

carried it and the coffee to a seat across from him. Wondering why I didn't just tape the doughnut to my waist, I said, "So you're not too impressed by our producer."

"When you got respect for the man callin' the shots, the load seems lighter. There's gonna be a lot of heavy liftin' on that set, believe me."

"Des seemed pretty chipper," I said.

Fitz nodded his shaggy head. "Man's got the constitution of a well-oiled machine," he said. Then he mumbled something half under his breath, a moment later adding, "Forget I said that, will ya, Billy?"

"Did you say anything?"

His smile wasn't quite hidden beneath his beard. "When I leave, you're gonna be stranded here without wheels," he said. "Want me to order up a limo?"

I thanked him for offering but assured him I wouldn't be needing a limousine.

"Well, I better get inta gear," he said, pushing his chair back and standing. "Have a good day."

He lumbered into the other room.

I chomped my chocolate sinker, washed it down with coffee, and pondered the words he'd mumbled barely loud enough for me to hear. After commenting that his best mate had the disposition of a well-oiled machine, he'd added, "And a heart to match."

# *Chapter*
# TEN

I'd left my annoying phone in the coach house.

In the brief period of time I spent at the villa, several calls had come in. None required a reply. I sincerely hoped that the next time I was attacked by a madman, it would be in a camera-free location.

When the ringtone sounded yet another time, I answered it with a gruff "What now?"

"H-hello . . . Is this Chef Blessing?" The voice was female, barely audible, and hesitant.

"I'm Blessing," I said. "Sorry if I startled you."

"I . . . I'm Whisper Jansen."

Whisper, a name both weird and aurally appropriate. "What can I do for you?"

"I-I'm Carmen Sandoval's assistant. At Worldwide West."

"Right. Gretchen Di Voss said I'd be hearing from Carmen."

"She's hoping you might be able to meet with her this evening? At five?"

"Sure. Where?"

"Here at WBCW. Do you have the address?"

I told her I had it. "How do I find her office?"

"We're on the second floor of the Harold Di Voss

Building. I'll come down to reception and guide you up."

I told her that would be fine.

By three-forty-five my Internet fame seemed to have dwindled to the point where nary a single self-styled comedian chose to bend my ear with an unfunny quip at my expense. I celebrated by taking a stroll to a car rental agency on the Pacific Coast Highway that I'd spied yesterday on the drive in.

What I'd spied, actually, was a bright red Lexus hardtop convertible that seemed to be crying out, "You're the only person on the West Coast cool enough to be driving me." But I did not indulge myself by renting it. Actually, someone cooler had beaten me to it. I had to settle for a second-best indulgence, the same car in gray.

It said to me, "Why settle for cheap flash, a confident man of action like you?"

After scraping away a millimeter of my Worldwide Broadcasting credit card's information strip, the rental agent escorted me to the sparkling-clean car, where he began uttering a litany of its special features. Only a few of them permeated the fog that develops in my head whenever anyone is speaking technology. "The Lexus model number something . . . blah-blah-blah . . . goes from zero to sixty in five-point-eight seconds . . . blah-blah-blah . . . electronically controlled transmission . . . retractable hardtop . . . blah-blah-blah . . . HDD navigation system with touch-screen capability—"

"Hold it," I said. "That last thing. It tells me how to get places, right? That's the one I want you to explain in detail."

Another twenty minutes and I was zooming south along the Pacific Coast Highway, with at least a rudimentary knowledge of the ways of the navigation system. The top was down, the windows down, the Shirelles were harmonizing on "Baby It's You" and other hits from a best-of disc, thanks to a golden oldies channel on Sirius Satellite Radio. I was beginning to remember what a dreamland L.A. had been before Victor Anisette fired me and Roger threatened my life.

The warmth of the afternoon sun and the cool ocean breeze combined to produce the perfect temperature. The sky was a soft blue dotted by puffy white clouds. And the Lexus obeyed my every whim as I guided it through the gathering going-home traffic. In New York, I had a driver, and if he wasn't available, I caught a cab or walked. It had been years since I'd been behind the wheel of a car, and never one that was such a pleasure to drive.

From time to time, the efficient but creepily unemotional female voice of the navigation system told me where and when to turn. Eventually, with the Santa Monica Pier jutting out into the ocean on my far right, the voice interrupted the Shirelles long enough to advise me to "turn left onto the I-ten."

I glanced at the active map on the dash, where a little bug—representing the Lexus with me in it—floated along like a mouthless Pac-Man. It showed that the Pacific Coast Highway melded into the Santa Monica Freeway, the I-10, and that all I had to do was keep following the road.

Easier said than done.

The traffic was the problem. A thick stream of it

flowed in from the south, slowing all the lanes to a crawl. It was some forty-five minutes of agonizingly slow progress later when my helpful disembodied female voice ordered me to take the Normandie exit. I traveled on that street until the Worldwide Broadcasting West lot showed itself and I was given the final audio benediction, "You have arrived."

Compared to the company's towering East Coast headquarters—a sixty-five-floor skyscraper in the heart of Manhattan known locally as the Glass Tower—its West Coast center was almost a groundhugger, at only five floors. But what it lost in height, it made up for with width, its offices and studios forming an *L* surrounded by what seemed like a never-ending lot jammed with parked cars.

In addition to the vehicles that belonged to company employees, there were a couple hundred more driven in by members of various studio audiences. While most of the network's filmed dramas and comedies were created on sound stages in its studio complex in the San Fernando Valley, the quiz and participation shows, such as *Take Your Pick* and *Are You Smarter Than a Runway Model?*, and some live telecasts, including news specials, were handled in the longer section of the *L*.

At that particular time of evening, parking spaces were as hard to find as unaugmented breasts in this godforsaken land.

I finally found a temporary home for the Lexus at the far end of the lot. When I arrived at the reception area of the Harold Di Voss Building, I was winded and perspiring from the cross-lot run but still, as Whisper

Jansen informed me in her sotto voce manner, fifteen minutes late.

She stood beside me at the elevator, petite with shoulder-length blond hair combed back from a pale, heart-shaped face that, while attractive, would have benefited from just a little more makeup and a little less anxiety. She was wearing a zippered beige blouse over loose-fitting jeans that she'd rolled to an inch or so above the ankle. Her tiny feet were encased in beige canvas high-tops with white rubber soles.

She chewed the inside of her mouth as we waited for the elevator to arrive. "Carmen was wondering where you were," she said, her voice rising to an almost audible pitch, her eyes shifting nervously to me and then back to the closed elevator door.

"There was a line of traffic coming in from the beach," I said. "And then I spent the last fifteen minutes driving around the lot, hunting for a parking place."

She seemed to sink within herself. "They were supposed to send you to the reserved parking, right in front."

The elevator arrived, unloading a group of mainly young office workers who were calling it a day. "I can state unreservedly that that didn't happen," I said. "I'm way over by the fence."

"I'm sorry," she mumbled. "Sorry you were inconvenienced. Carmen will say it's my fault."

She was silent for a beat. Then, as the elevator stopped at our floor, Whisper Jansen took a deep breath, straightened her backbone, and said, "Well, heck. It'll be just one more tirade."

"Tirade," I said. "An attack on a haberdashery."

Her giggle sounded more like a gurgle. "Daffy Definitions," she said. "I remember them from when I was a kid."

"Monastery," I said. "A place where monsters are kept."

Grinning, we exited the elevator, moved quickly past a receptionist, who was straightening her desktop, then down a hall with walls filled by framed portraits of WBC celebrities other than myself and into the corner office of network vice president Carmen Sandoval.

She'd been seated behind an ultra-contemporary desk—a *J* shaped sheet of smoked glass resting atop three rosewood blocks. She stood quickly, sending her black leather chair rolling back across the gray tiled floor. She was nearly six feet in her Jimmy Choo python-print espadrilles, shiny black slacks, and scoop-neck, long-sleeve blouse that picked up the same pattern as her shoes. She was almost too thin, but there was nothing weak or fragile about her. Her overlarge black-framed designer glasses were fashionable, highlighting periwinkle-blue eyes while also drawing your attention to a nose that had been cosmetically altered.

Like Whisper, she was pale. I'd heard that was a badge of honor on this sunny coast, where a tan was the mark of the frivolous or the unemployed. But because of her jet-black, close-cropped hair, her skin seemed almost bloodless, a notion enhanced by lipstick so dark it was almost black. Somebody should have told her that the vampire look was hard to carry off once you passed the forty mark.

She glanced at a steel-and-gold Breitling watch

that looked as big as a sundial on her thin wrist and curled down the corners of her dark red lips in a gesture of distaste. "Chef Blessing," she said, "I'm surprised that someone with your on-camera experience would treat time so cavalierly."

"Sorry I'm late," I said, "but I had to stop off for a piss. You know how that is."

Behind me, Whisper was having trouble subduing a gurgle.

Surprisingly, Carmen Sandoval seemed genuinely amused. "Considering the extent of your tardiness, I hope you took time to wash your hands." She thrust out a thin and chalky claw in a gesture of friendship that I accepted, even though her fingernails looked like they'd been tipped in blood. "Welcome to WBC West, Billy," she said. "I hope you don't mind the first-name informality."

"I prefer it."

"I was surprised to hear from Gretchen that this is your first visit to the studio."

"The last time I was on this coast, I wasn't working for WBC."

"Well, Vida can serve as your guide," she said, gesturing to the other side of the office, where a very attractive young sister sat on a plum-colored armchair, smiling at me. Even though Carmen was an undeniably commanding presence, I couldn't believe I'd failed to notice Vida Evans.

"Hi, Billy," she said. "Been a while." She moved into my arms for a very unbusinesslike hug.

"I gather you two have met," Carmen said.

We had. Several years before in Manhattan. We'd been seated at the same table at a blowout celebrating the sixty-fifth birthday of Worldwide's CEO, Commander Vernon Di Voss. Vida, then part of the team of reporters covering the White House, had flown in from D.C. with her husband, Congressman Harrison Oakley.

At the time I'd pegged him as a pompous, "I rose above my ghetto background to become a Princeton graduate" jerk who couldn't hold his liquor. He took offense at my making polite conversation with his wife, whom he was ignoring in favor of a sitcom starlet with a chest size higher than her IQ. As it turned out, good old Harrison was also a greedhead who, shortly thereafter, got caught in the blowback from the Jack Abramoff scandal. For his crimes, including lying to a grand jury, he went off for a year and a day to the Federal Correctional Institution in Cumberland, Maryland.

His conviction turned out to be a good thing for Vida, at least professionally (and I hoped personally). She divorced the bastard and, since his criminal behavior had seriously compromised her effectiveness as a capital reporter, she'd leapt at the offer of an early-morning newswriter and -reader spot at the network's owned-and-operated affiliate in Los Angeles.

In relatively few years, she'd made an astonishing series of career leaps until, finally, thanks to an Emmy nomination for her documentary *Crack in the Wall of Sound: The Phil Spector Story*, she'd settled in as a regular contributor to *Hotline,* the net's prime-time newsmagazine.

"Actually, we met only once," I told Carmen. "But the effect was profound."

I stepped back a few paces to observe Vida. "You were merely beautiful then. Now . . . wow!"

"Is it any wonder I jumped at the chance to spend a few days with this lovely man?" she asked Carmen.

"Whatever spins your Frisbee," Carmen said as she shoved papers into a briefcase the size of a garment bag. "It's past time I hit the road. Thanks to Billy's tiny bladder, I'll be spending the next hour or more creeping through going-home traffic all the way to Costa Mesa."

"You live in Costa Mesa?" I asked.

"Why would anyone live in Costa Mesa?" she replied, clicking the case shut. "I'm going there to see a revival of *Equus* at South Coast Rep. We're about to put the young male lead under contract and, thanks to the full-frontal scene, I'll never get a better chance to judge his talent."

She picked up the case and, apparently deciding it was too heavy for her, handed it to Whisper, who nearly threw her back out accepting it. The four of us took a crowded elevator down to the main floor. "Anything else you need, Billy," Carmen said, "don't hesitate to ask . . . Vida."

We watched her marching off past other exiting staffers, Whisper at her heels, struggling with the briefcase.

"Well, that was bracing," I said.

"Carmen is definitely one of a kind," she said. "I like working with her. This is Passive-Aggressive City. Passive to your face, doubly aggressive behind your back. Carmen gives it to you straight."

"So you're my guide, huh? Things that slow at *Hotline*?"

"Hardly," she said. "And this won't be all fun and games. Your producer in New York sent a laundry list of 'wants.'"

"Why don't we discuss them over dinner?" I suggested.

"I'd love to, Billy, but I, ah . . . have another commitment." She dug a card out of her handbag. "Call me tomorrow, any time after nine, and we'll set something up."

She moved forward, kissed me on the cheek, and said, "See you when I see you."

Who says romance is dead?

## *Chapter* ELEVEN

Carmen was right about the going-home traffic. It was even worse than it was on the drive in, the stop-and-go extending all the way to Malibu. It was after seven when my guidance system led me to a supermarket near the Sands, another forty-five minutes before I turned onto Malibu Sands Drive.

Lars and Manny were on duty at the gate. I'd met them earlier, heading out for my walk to the car rental agency. At that hour their khaki uniforms had looked neat and pressed. Now, like the guards themselves, they'd lost some of their starch.

Lars was in his forties, with a long, flat face

that resembled the character actor who'd played the Frankenstein-like father in *The Munsters,* Fred Gwynne. Watery blue eyes, mouth turned down at the edges, gray hair, judging by what I could see of it under his peak cap. Manny, whose name was Manuel, I assumed, was in his twenties, Mexican American, slightly overweight but muscled. He was there for the heavy lifting.

Neither man carried a gun, a good thing, probably, because when Manny first caught sight of me that afternoon, I'd had three strikes against me. I was a black man he didn't know traveling by foot inside his gated community. Fortunately, Lars had recognized me before Manny even had the chance to slide his nightstick from his belt.

But Manny and I seemed to be on good terms now. "Sweet wheels," he said, waving me through.

Security floodlights were brightening the area in front of Villa Delfina, illuminating two unfamiliar vehicles parked in the driveway, a pea-green Hummer that was about the ugliest SUV I'd ever seen and a dark blue Camry Hybrid. I anchored the Lexus between them, its proper gas-guzzling position.

I put the top up and used the little gizmo to close the gate. I struggled out of the car, plucked the grocery bags from the passenger seat, and took the walkway beside the villa, heading for the guesthouse. I was almost there when I saw Fitz galumphing past the pool in my direction.

"Yo, Billy," he called out.

I watched, bemused, as he approached. "Glad to see you, cobber," he said, breathing hard for such a short dash. "Please tell me it was you left the slidin' door open."

"I'm pretty sure I closed it, Fitz. In any case, I left before you did."

"Shite! I was hopin' you'd come back."

I shook my head. "What's up?"

"We, ah . . . somebody mighta been in the house."

"A break-in?"

"Well . . . yeah. I guess you'd call it that."

"What would you call it?"

"A break-in. I mean, it looks like that. The back door was open when we got here a few minutes ago. Only they didn't really break any lock or anything."

"Then how'd they get in?" I asked, the groceries starting to get heavier.

"Ah . . . maybe the door was unlocked," he said. "I ain't used to settin' alarms."

The sound of glass breaking inside the villa drew his attention. "Des is goin' fuckin' ballistic. I better get back."

"I'll catch up with you as soon as I put this stuff away," I said.


It took me only a few minutes to unlock the guesthouse, shove the perishables in the fridge, and glance around to make sure my valuables, such as they were, had been undisturbed. When I arrived at the villa, I found a visitor in the living room with a cigarette in her mouth, a dust brush in her right hand, and a dustpan in her left. In the pan were the pieces of what looked like a china cat. The woman turned toward me, cocked her head to keep the smoke from drifting up into her eyes, and said around the cigarette, "Welcome to the happiest place on earth. Oh, wait. That's Disneyland."

"This is fecking unacceptable, you brainless sot," Des shouted from somewhere up above.

"The second-happiest place on earth," the smoking woman said.

She was in her forties, light brown hair professionally styled and highlighted by streaks of blond and gray. A strong jaw, straight nose. Full lips colored a frosted pink. Big prescription glasses in black curved aviator-style frames with DG in prominent letters on the temples. Green eyes. Green blouse, more or less covering full breasts. White silk slacks covering long legs. Pink-tipped toes tucked into black sandals with thick platform soles.

She looked vaguely familiar.

"Hello," I said. "I'm Billy—"

"Blessing. Yes. I know. Excuse me a minute." She moved to a table, got rid of the dust implements, and plucked the cigarette from her lips with her left hand. She extended her right and said, "I'm April Edding. Parker and Bowen Public Relations. We're handling PR and publicity for *O'Day at Night*."

We shook hands. I gestured toward the broken cat and said, "It looks like you may have your work cut out for you."

"Oh, *this*," she said. "A minor show of pique. Hardly in the same class as tossing one of L.A.'s better-known chefs into a swimming pool."

"Touché."

"I was there," she said. "At Stew's."

"Yes. I believe I saw you. I'm sorry we didn't meet."

"Well, you seemed a bit occupied with Roger," she said. "Speaking professionally, if you must do something like that again, please continue to do it in front of paparazzi. It's publicity gold. Actually, I know the lady who handles Roger's PR. Regina Simons. I bet we could work out a smashing event in which you and he just happen to meet up again. Fan the media flames a little?"

"Try something like that," I said, smiling sweetly, "and I just might toss *you* into a swimming pool."

"I'm afraid that wouldn't cause a ripple, publicity-wise."

A thud almost rattled the overhead rafters.

"I'd better see what's going on up there," I said.

"We ladies love you action heroes," she said as I headed toward the stairs.

The guys were in a large room with windows that looked out at the beach and ocean. Judging by the various musical instruments resting in cases on the bed and on a chair near a mirrored closet, it was Fitz's bedroom.

The musician was zipping up an overnight bag.

Des was draped across the only other chair, his right hand wrapped around a bottle of what looked like schnapps resting on his flat stomach.

"What was the noise?" I asked.

"Billy, me lad," Des said, sounding surprisingly mellow. "Me faithful friend Fitz was just givin' me a display of his strength by slamming his luggage onto the floor."

Fitz sheepishly lifted a huge metal footlocker from

the hardwood floor and placed it into the closet as effortlessly as if it were a bag of goose down. He saw the gouge it had left in the hardwood and rubbed the rubber sole of his Nike over it. He seemed disappointed that it hadn't disappeared.

"Don't worry about it, boyo," Des said. "Gives the place character. The important thing is nobody has messed with the lock."

He looked at me. "It appears our concerns were for naught. Nothing seems to be missing."

"Good to hear," I said.

"You meet April?"

I nodded.

He straightened and stood with his liqueur. "The three of us are heading out to dinner. April says the place we're going, Frush, is *the* current hot place to eat. Come on along."

I recalled that Frush was one of Roger's restaurants. "Thanks, but I think I'll just fix something light and catch up on my z's."

"You can get all the sleep you need when you're dead," Des said.

I could have mentioned that that was precisely why I wasn't going to Frush. Instead, I asked what he thought of April.

"She seems to know what she's doing. She was a big help in findin' the locations where we filmed today."

"She's workin' on a *60 Minutes* segment for Des," Fitz added as we headed downstairs.

"Wouldn't that just piss Letterman off?" Des said with a grin.

Searching for a word that described their mood, I

settled on "semi-relieved." Only minutes ago, Fitz had been fully stressed and Des was breaking crockery and yelling. I wondered what was in that footlocker. Something the burglar had not found, if indeed there'd been a burglar.

"Everything safe and secure?" April asked, when we joined her.

"Best as we can tell," Des said.

"Maybe the wind blew the door open," Fitz said.

I looked at the sliding door, seriously doubting a breeze off the ocean could move a sixty-pound sliding tempered-glass-and-steel door sideways.

Fitz tensed suddenly and said, "The bloody game room!"

"Well, go check," Des told him, and Fitz ran off in that direction.

The comedian's interest turned to the subject of drinks before they left for dinner. April's request for white wine prompted a mild rant from our host about Southern Californians' preference for wine over hard booze that sounded suspiciously like a stand-up routine he'd used before.

When he hit his punch line—"so when I'm drinking something, I want it to be the product of clean, healthy barley, not grapes that've been stomped on by some Eye-talian broad with dirty feet"—I excused myself and moved away from their chatter to put in a call to Cassandra.

She answered on the third ring. "Snoozing on the job?" I asked.

"How well you know me, Billy," she said. "Actually, I was not expecting a call this late. I'd assumed you were losing interest in your little food stand. It's such a minor part of the expanding coast-to-coast Blessing empire."

"I've been a little busy here," I said, though I didn't feel an apology was necessary. "How'd my little food stand do tonight?"

She gave me a quick summary of the evening's business, which was very good news, then went on to complain about a waiter who'd arrived for work with a head cold. "I sent the idiot home immediately. They've all been warned. Everybody's so damned health-conscious these days. One loud sneeze from a food handler and this place is as empty as a bowling alley."

"There's got to be a better simile," I said. "Bowling is a popular sport."

"Okay, *you* come up with one."

"As empty as . . . a country-western concert at the Apollo?"

"Too strained," she said. "And too stereotypical. If that's all you've got . . ."

I was in the midst of concocting the perfect empty-room simile, involving the mind of a publicity-hungry reality-show reject, when I caught a whiff of something coming from the kitchen.

I sniffed again.

"My God, Billy, don't tell me you're coming down with something," Cassandra asked.

"No," I said, distracted now. "I'll call you tomorrow."

I was vaguely aware of the stream of profanities indicating that Cassandra was not ready to ring off, but by then I was snapping my phone shut.

"Anybody smell anything?" I asked the others.

"Yes," April said. "Something's cooking."

"I'm guessing none of you is prepping hors d'oeuvres?" I said.

Not waiting for the answer, I pushed past the kitchen door.

The cooking odor was strong now. *Meat,* I thought, *or possibly fowl.* There was also an acrid smell mixed in. Something burning. All of this was emanating from the electric range, where a digital readout indicated that the broiler temperature was 400 degrees, with twenty-seven minutes left before the cooking was complete.

I grabbed a kitchen mitt and opened the broiler. Sizzling noises and some smoke, along with a full dose of the unpleasant fragrance.

April was standing behind me as I pulled out the sliding tray.

"My God," she said. "Is that what I think it is?"

There wasn't much doubt. If you've seen one ugly gray rat simmering in its own juices, its fur singed and smoking, you've seen 'em all. Someone had decided to broil the rat, surrounded by potatoes and carrots and sprinkled with parsley. They'd even placed a cherry tomato in the critter's mouth.

# *Chapter*
# TWELVE

"What the hell!" Des had evidently just entered the kitchen.

"Well, Billy," April asked, "is this the way one cooks rat?"

"I'm not exactly an Iron Chef when it comes to preparing rodents," I said. "But I'm pretty sure that when they cook them in Vietnam and Thailand, they clean out the intestines, then deep-fry them. Whoever did this wasn't planning dinner, they were sending a message."

"What feckin' message might that be, Billy?" Des asked, as if daring me to reply.

I shrugged. "Could be anything from 'A rat for a rat' to 'Nothin' says lovin' like roast rat in the oven.' "

"Fitz, git yer bloody arse in here," Des yelled.

The big man entered with a worried look. "Somebody's been in the game room."

"Stop eyeballin' me, you bloody wanker," Des yelled, "and tell me if ya see anything warped in here."

Fitz looked from Des to April, then to me. I pointed at the rat.

"Sweet mother of God! A feckin' rat?" His head turned in Des's direction fast enough to cause whiplash. "What do you—"

"I'm bolting," Des said, heading for the door. "I don't stay in places where anybody can just stroll in and light up a ratter in my stove."

"Hold on a second," I said.

When he didn't, I rushed after him. "I'm pretty sure the message was meant for me," I said.

He halted and turned. "Okay, Billy, you got my attention."

I sensed rather than saw the others following us into the room. "As April will tell you, a fellow chef named Roger Charbonnet went a little postal at the party last night and came after me."

"Charbonnet is a well-known hothead," April added. "Billy cooled him off by tossing him into the swimming pool."

Des raised an eyebrow. "Well, Billy. A regular Jackie Feckin' Chan, are we?"

"All I did was duck."

"What set the bloke off?"

"A feud from way back," I said. "I'd hoped it was forgotten, but apparently not."

"Apparently," Des repeated. "And he's that big a nutter he'd bust into a house and cook up a rat?"

*Twenty-three years ago he murdered his girlfriend,* I thought. What I said was, "Yeah, Des, I think he's that big a nutter."

"Amazin'. This really is header heaven out here."

"How'd he get past the security guys?" Fitz asked.

"He could have been put on the guest list by Stew Gentry's daughter," I said. "He's been seeing her."

"Gentry's *daughter*?" Des asked.

"Yes. She lives with Stew," I said. "Des, this guy Charbonnet is my problem. I'll head to a hotel in the morning and make sure he gets word he chased me off. He won't be bothering you again."

Des strolled to the bar, poured a couple of inches of Jameson into a tumbler, and shot it. "Fact is, Billy, I was gonna tell Max that this crib wasn't what I wanted. It's too damn far from the studio. And my Irish hide takes to the sun like a fish takes to the desert. Next to me, David Caruso looks like bloody George Hamilton. I'd already decided to move inland, to Brentwood or Beverly Hills. This beach-blanket bullshit isn't for me."

"Could be a pricey mistake," April said.

"Not mine. It's the production company's responsibility." Des took another bite of Jameson, then turned to Fitz. "Pack up, bucko, we're boltin'." To April, he added, "Find us a fine hotel, will you, luv? Two suites. Tout de suite."

"What's the rush, Des?" I asked. "Sleep on it. Tomorrow, I'll take care of the problem."

"I'm not waitin' around to see if the nutter left us something a little more lethal than the rodent dinner. You worry about yourself, old lad. If you think you can keep the bogeyman at bay, the villa's all yours for the rest of the month. I know Max is on the hook for at least that. I'd rather think a pal was gettin' some use out of it."

"I feel terrible—"

"Hey. Get it straight, Billy. I wasn't gonna stick around here anyway. And it wasn't you cooked the rat." He grinned. "If it had been, the damned thing might be worth a taste. All I ask is you keep this episode on the down-low. This is not the kind of publicity I'm lookin' for. You clear on that, April? This rat thing never happened, right?"

"I'm not a novice at this, Des," she said.

"In fact, not to put too fine a point to it, let's make it one of your priorities to keep my off-camera activities out of the bloody tabs."

"As much as I love you," she said, "a lot of those cats are already out of the bag. Your East Coast PR reps have done an excellent job of getting you press for the show. And a lot of that, like the piece in *GQ* that just dropped, focuses on your 'dark Irish moods' and 'fondness for single-malt and married supermodels.' So . . . I'll do what I can. But if you want to keep your private life private, you'll have to monk up. There are too many paparazzi, professional and amateur, for you to think you can even cop a quick feel in public without it showing up on *TMZ* in high-def."

"Point made," Des said. "But keep my name off the hotel rez, okay?"

"How about . . . Daniel Knight Lewis," she said.

He smiled. "That's brilliant, darlin'."

With that, he rushed off to put the whip to his packing mule, Fitz.

April brought out her phone but paused before making the reservations. "Billy, how sure are you it was Roger Charbonnet who broke in here?"

"Absolutely."

"Then since it's your rat, do you think you could dispose of it?"

I nodded, but I felt a little odd about it, as if I was getting rid of evidence. Of course, the "crime" didn't seem all that serious.

You'd think, by now, I would know better.

# *Chapter*
# THIRTEEN

"Sorry to bother you, Stew," I said when he'd unlocked the rear door to his house. He was wearing a tan warm-up outfit and Ugg slide-ins, and I guessed he'd had his nightly workout and was hoping to settle down in front of the TV. Or in his case, with a book in his hand.

"What's up, Billy? You're frowning like a man who's been staring too long at the sun. Come on in."

I followed him into his living room, where he'd built a pretty good fire in the hearth.

"Get comfortable," he said, indicating the couch facing the warmth. Judging by the bottle of Rémy Martin XO and the snifter beside a stuffed chair, I'd interrupted him from a little flame dreaming.

By the time it took me to sink into the couch's soft leather with a sigh, he'd found a snifter for me and was moistening it with the cognac. "You're a little late for dinner," he said, handing me the snifter. "I eat early. Helps with the acid reflux. God, old age is fun."

"You by yourself here, Stew?"

"Nobody else." He made a little grunting noise as he dropped onto the chair. "Dani's having dinner with her mom."

"Roger's not here?" I wanted to make absolutely sure.

"That jackass was here earlier. I guess I was a little premature in thinkin' the romance was over. But he left hours ago." He cocked his head and frowned. "Why do you ask?"

"Somebody broke into the villa this afternoon and left a dead rat in the oven."

"A *rat*?"

"Set to broil."

"Fucking unbelievable. You think it was Roger?"

I shrugged. "You say he was here at the Sands. You saw how much he likes me. And frankly, I don't know anybody else crazy enough to bust into somebody's house with a dead rat. I don't even know where you'd find a rat."

"That part's easy. They're runnin' wild out here. But Jesus, Billy. If Roger is that twisted, I sure as hell don't want him anywhere near Dani."

"That's the main reason I'm here," I said.

And I told him everything I knew about the murder of Tiffany Arden, Roger's former girlfriend.

He leapt from the chair and stood towering over me. "Goddamn it, Billy. You sure took your own sweet time to clue me in about this."

"I'm sorry, Stew. But the fact is, no charges have ever been brought against Roger. And the only thing I know for sure is that his alibi was bogus."

"Well, excuse me if I'm behaving like an overprotective father," Stew said, "but if your silence had given Charbonnet the chance to harm Dani, I'd have gone after him with a gun and then come looking for you."

"Well, as long as I'm here," I said, getting up, facing him. "Take your best shot."

He glared at me, teeth clenched so tightly his jaw muscles knotted. Then he shook his head and walked away. "Let yourself out, Billy. I've got things to take care of."

He climbed the stairs quickly, putting as much distance between us as he could.

That was me, making friends wherever I went.

At the villa, Fitz was carrying two guitar cases toward the open front door. "April's looking for you," he said without pausing. "I think she's in the game room with Des."

She was.

"Where'd you run off to, Billy?" April asked. She was draped across a sofa with several typewritten pages on her lap. Des was sitting at a felt-lined poker table, patiently constructing a house of cards.

"Took a walk along the beach," I said.

"Vida's trying to reach you. Said you weren't answering your phone."

"I left it in the coach house. She say what she wanted?"

She smiled. "Not a midnight booty call, I'm afraid."

"Then who cares."

"Des is going to be filming stunts at the La Brea Tar Pits tomorrow at ten . . ."

"Can you bloody believe it?" Des said. "Ten o'clock. In the morning."

". . . and Vida would like you there, too," April

continued. "Something to do with a segment on *Wake Up, America!*"

The Tar Pits! Where Pleistocene critters once paused to drink the water resting on top of asphalt oozing up from the earth and remained trapped in the sticky goo until thousands of years later, when finally freed by archaeologists in fossil form.

"I guess I should call her," I said.

"You won't be waking her," April said. "It sounded like she was in a club."

"Good for her," I said.

Fitz joined us with the news that he'd fit everything into the Hummer and was ready to roll. April and I walked them to the pea-green monstrosity.

"Billy, me lad, you'll be stayin' in the guesthouse?" Des asked.

"I'll see how it goes," I said.

"Well, enjoy." He opened the passenger door, grabbed hold of the roof, and swung himself in. "But watch yer back, mate."

"Later, Billy," Fitz said, and hopped up and into the Hummer.

The engine turned over. The iron gate swung open. And they were gone.

"If Des refuses to use the rat as an excuse, Crockaby Realty is going to squeeze Max like a ripe orange," April said, as if the idea amused her. "You going to be okay by yourself? I can have a bodyguard here within the hour."

"There are security guards, and the alarm system works," I said. "You just have to turn it on."

She nodded. "Well, Billy, it's been a very . . . unusual evening." She opened the door to the Camry and, just as she was about to get in, added, "If you need to reach Des, he's at the Bev Wilshire, registered under the name of—"

"Daniel Knight Lewis," I said.

She smiled, got into the car. It started up and rolled off without a sound. Those sneaky little hybrids. Road ninjas. Definitely not pedestrian-friendly.

I was mentally nattering. Not a good sign. Nerves. Just going on like a . . . *Shut up!*

I waited for the gate to automatically close and lock, then went back into the villa and searched for the alarm system's instruction brochure. I found it stuck behind the main keypad to the right of the front door. Since it explained how to cancel an alarm, this was probably not the smartest place to keep it.

Making sure the front door was secure, I carried the instruction brochure and the half-full bottle of Jameson back to my little undefiled guesthouse, where I looked in every room and closet to make sure no homicidal chef lay lurking. After checking the window locks, I flipped through the brochure, learned how to bypass the motion sensor in the guesthouse, and, using the keypad in my little enclave, did precisely that before arming the rest of the system.

A little red light indicated all was secure. As comforting as that was, I still had a creepy feeling of uncertainty that I hadn't experienced since those childhood nights just after my father's death, when, even with my mother in the next room, the house had felt empty and threatening.

I exchanged my grown-up clothes for my jammies and got into bed with the Walter Mosley thriller and the bottle of Jameson, my substitutes for the teddy bear named Mr. Happy who'd helped me chase away the goblins and ghostles of the night all those years ago.

*Chapter*
# FOURTEEN

To say that the next eight days rolled by uneventfully might not be entirely accurate. True, I had no further contact with Roger Charbonnet, either up front and personal or via some ugly little prank. Nor did I hear another word from Stew Gentry, though I did see him windsurfing on one of the rare evenings I was able to fit in a walk along the beach.

Nearly all of my time was taken up with work.

I spent my mornings with Vida Evans and a bearded cameraman named Hamid Tarul, doing segs for *Wake Up*. Someone, possibly Vida but more likely Carmen Sandoval, had decided to use several of the city's more famous locations as the sites for my "Reports from L.A.," creating a forced serendipity with Des's spots promoting his show.

The serendipity began, as previously mentioned, at the La Brea Tar Pits, more specifically, at the Page Museum and adjoining park. There, Des, playing the new-to-L.A. hipster, goofed on the various outdoor exhibits—imitating the giant sloths, the prehistoric bear—before entering the museum and nearly leaping from his skin when the animatronic baby mammoth began to move and trumpet.

Meanwhile, I, and the morning show's viewers, were given a mini-tour of the exhibits by a charming young volunteer guide that somehow managed to include a bit of Des's clowning while condensing the usual two-hour-plus exploration to nine minutes, including one commercial interruption.

On subsequent days, we visited Chinatown, the Hollywood sign (where Des rode a cherry-picker, pretending to clean the letters), the back lot at Universal Studios, the Bradbury Building (the iconic movie location for hundreds of fictional private eyes, where our comic hero wore a snap-brim hat and trench coat), and, of course, Grauman's Chinese Theatre (where, against all advice, he lowered his pants and impressed his Jockey shorts–covered skinny butt in cement, a grim exercise that, even though carefully photographed, to no one's surprise wound up on YouTube rather than on the network).

As for my afternoons, they alternated between working with Harry Paynter on the book, which now had a tentative title, *Murder on the Menu*, and attending daily three p.m. meetings with the participants of Des's new show. The latter included the baby-faced head writer Gibby Lewis, whom I'd met on my first night at the villa; producer Max Slaughter, a gent bovine in body and serpentine in thought, with a Vandyke beard that turned his plump face a bit demonic; his omnipresent gofer Trey Halstead; Tessa Ruscha, the show's director, a formidable woman with a profile not unlike the comic-strip legend Dick Tracy, who, in flip-flops, towered over most of us;

and Tessa's efficient, no-nonsense floor manager, Lolita Snapps, a black woman in her forties with hair dyed the color of dull gold.

It was Tessa who, with Max's approval, had brought in the "cutting-edge lighting consultant" identified by the uni-name Pfrank. With his chalk-white skin, long, stringy jet-black hair, a beard stubble that resembled smudged ash, fingernails as long as a mandarin's, though not as clean, and teeth the color of lemon pulp, Pfrank presented quite a picture.

He seemed devoted to an unwavering wardrobe consisting of a Black Sabbath *Heaven and Hell* tour T-shirt covering his emaciated chest and black jeans wrapped around his pipe-cleaner legs. There were sparkling stones embedded in his earlobes, rings on his fingers, bands of metal and leather around his wrists, and Nikes the size of country mailboxes on his feet. A heavy chrome key chain drooped from a belt loop, eventually disappearing into his right pants pocket.

He also had heavily mascaraed eyes and topped the whole image off by speaking with a faux-British accent. In short, he was a low-rent modern-day Captain Jack Sparrow. All smarm and no charm.

"I felt it imperative that the *at Night* designation in the show's title be treated as literally as . . . well, Black Sabbath treated their album *Live Evil*," Pfrank informed me on the afternoon before the big telecast.

We were watching a complement of workmen put the finishing touches to six-plus months of extensive gutting and restructuring that had transformed what once had been the Margo Channing Playhouse, a midsize live Equity theater venue on Fountain Avenue in Hollywood, into the new Harold Di Voss Theater, named for Commander Di Voss's late father, Gretchen's granddaddy, who'd moved Worldwide from a fledgling network into what was at the time considered one of the big four of television broadcasting— NBC, CBS, ABC, and WBC.

Put together by a set designer named Giselle Cateline, the interior of the Di Voss Theater consisted of a high-tech, state-of-the-art television broadcast studio that seated one hundred guests. That was an audience approximately the same size as Craig Ferguson's on CBS.

The building now had everything a TV studio needed. Except width.

"That is why," Pfrank continued, "it was necessary we envelop the video mise-en-scène in a cloak of delicious darkness. And use what I call the 'night minions,' stagehands garbed head to toe in black."

Des had already told me about the minions and the mise-en-scène, only not in those particular words. But I wasn't sure what they had to do with the width of the theater. So I asked Pfrank.

"Didn't you read my interview in the *L.A. Times*? It explained everything."

"Missed it," I said.

Pfrank sighed. "Well, first you have to understand that there were budgetary parameters that necessitated the use of the existing theater shell. So Giselle realized that while there was the limitation of width, we could play a little with depth. Did you meet Giselle?"

"Afraid not."

"Oh, too bad. She's in Quebec now, working on a

feature starring the Academy Award–winning Ms. Sandra Bullock, no less. Giselle is—well, the bitch is brilliant, and I don't use that word very often."

"I should hope not," I said. "Feminists would have your guts for garters."

He flashed a Joker grin, then continued his natter.

"Giselle has created a fucking fabulous design that uses the stage depth to create three separate areas—a cozy conversation-space stage front, near the audience, a flexible performance space just past that, and a permanent-space stage left behind that for the musicians.

"And you know what makes it all work?"

"The director?"

He gave me a chalky, tolerant smile. "I'm talking about the set. The things that allow Giselle's design to transform an awkward, some might say impossible, space into television magic are wheels and . . . my darkness."

"Anyone ever tell you you're a very dramatic guy?" I asked.

"Are you calling me a diva?"

"Al Pacino is dramatic," I said. "You're a diva."

He mulled that over and evidently was satisfied to be mentioned in the same breath with Pacino. "Shall I continue?" he asked.

"Please."

"Well, everything is on wheels, soft rubber spherical wheels. The chair and couch used for Des's interviews can easily be pushed to stage right to allow the cameras access to the performance area. There's a scrim that will hide the musical group during those times when they'd be a distraction. It will simply be rolled away when it makes sense to put Mr. Fitzpatrick and his orchestra on display. The minions, of course, will be doing the moving, dressed in black, with my darkness design facilitating their complete invisibility."

"It seems a little tricky," I said. "Especially the timing."

"We're working on that."

"And about those wheels, what's to stop the furniture from sliding out from under people? I imagine Des could make a joke of it if he winds up on the floor, but what if it's a guest like Morgan Freeman or Hillary Clinton hitting the deck?"

"That won't happen," Pfrank said smugly. "The wheels are set in a springlike device. When weight is applied, they disappear into the base of the furniture, making it as stable as . . . Oh, I'm sorry, Chef Blessing. I'm going to have to leave you now. My assistant has arrived with our minions."

I watched him head toward a group of nearly a dozen men and women who'd filed in through the front doors. It wasn't hard to pick out Pfrank's assistant, who, except for platinum spiked hair, could have been his double. The so-called minions were mainly young and burly, the obvious exception being a tall male, at least a decade older than the others. He was wearing unusual octagon-shaped sunglasses in the minimally lighted theater, which suggested either an eye problem, an affectation, or a bizarre fashion statement.

Or maybe he was just warming up for Pfrank's glorious darkness.

All of the minions, I presumed, belonged to IATSE

(the International Alliance of Theatrical Stage Employees). I wondered what the local thought about its members working in the dark, wearing Pfrank's ninja costumes. Well, it wasn't my union. Not my problem.

Or so I thought.

# *Chapter*
# FIFTEEN

The workmen had just removed the protective plastic covers from the hundred or so audience seats. I tested one and found it surprisingly comfortable. I had about fifteen minutes more to kill before a scheduled luncheon meeting with the head writer, so I decided to give the seat even more of a test.

I leaned back and observed floor manager Lolita Snapps herd the camera operators around the stage area in preparation for tomorrow night's show. Pfrank returned with the stagehands in full ninja garb and turned them over to Lolita. Chairs and couch were placed in position on the stage, and Lolita arranged a full-on demonstration of ninjas rolling furniture and fast-moving cameras narrowly avoiding collision.

A lot of choreography to work out with the maiden voyage of this leviathan a little more than twenty-four hours away.

"Not exactly like watching Kobe sink one for the

Lakers, is it?" Gibby Lewis said, interrupting my reverie.

"But almost as graceful," I said.

We moved on, via his white Porsche Boxter (topless, of course), to Nate 'n Al in Beverly Hills, where, after introducing me to assorted celebrities and power brokers, and suggesting I join him in ordering the extra-long hot dog with grilled onions ("That's assuming you like hot dogs"), Gibby settled back in the booth. His baby face broke into a strange conspiratorial grin, and he asked, "So what are you doin' here, bubbie?"

"Say again?"

"Why are you here in L.A.? Des says you're some kind of network spy."

"He told you that?"

Gibby nodded. "He said he wasn't sure, so he invited you to stay out at his place as a kind of test, I guess. When you went for it, he figured you were the spy guy."

"It didn't occur to him that a guesthouse in Malibu, with a pool and the ocean, might strike me as an improvement over a hotel room?"

"What can I say? The Des man is paranoid, of course. We all are. But sometimes it's not without reason. So . . . are you?"

"A spy?" I said. Me, the James Bond of WBC. I kinda liked the idea. "Is there something Des is trying to hide from New York?"

"That he didn't tell me," Gibby said. "Just that I should watch what I say around you."

"But you're doing the opposite," I said.

Gibby sighed. "I write comedy. Just like Conan

used to write comedy before Lorne took a chance with him. But I make the clubs and the comedy stores. I'm good. You'll see tomorrow night. I'll be doing warm-up for the show. If, God forbid, Des doesn't work out, I figure it couldn't hurt to be a guy who goes out of his way to cooperate with New York."

"Noted," I said. "I'll be sure to include that information in my next dispatch."

That bit of sarcasm seemed to please him. He reached into the pocket of his jacket and removed a folded piece of paper. "Here's the intro we put together for you. That and the acknowledgments at the end of the show are pretty much all of your planned material. It should be a snap. Both of them are voice-over, so you won't even have to memorize it."

The hot dogs arrived while I was reading the intro. They were very big and very tasty. Conversation more or less ceased until they were resting uncomfortably in our digestive tracts. Then I took another, harder look at the material and said, " 'The Celtic Lord of the Laughs.' 'Lord of the Laughs.' 'Lord of the Laughs.' I suppose I can say that without tying my tongue in knots."

"It's pretty damn good, right? You get the reference?"

I stared at him. "I assume you're comparing Des to Michael Flatley."

"Who? No," Gibby said. "We're referencing the Lord of the Dance."

"That would be Michael Flatley," I said. "He created the show, choreographed it, danced it."

"Oh, yeah?" Gibby said. "I didn't realize the term

applied to anybody specific. That's good to know. What about the rest of the intro?"

"I don't know what this means, the part about Des trying not to be starstruck," I said.

"We wrote this killer opening bit to bring Des on," Gibby said. "The stage is gonna look like the night sky. You know, dark. Some stars blinking in the far distance. Closer up, there'll be foam stars about a yard wide hanging from the catwalk. Covered with glitter. Des is gonna make his entrance lowered from the catwalk, straddling a crescent moon and singing one of the standard moon songs."

I blinked. "How high up will he be on takeoff?" I asked.

"Twenty-five, thirty feet. I don't know. However high up the catwalk is. Oh, Jesus. I shouldn't have said anything . . . It's perfectly safe, Billy. It's a great opening. Des loves it. He wants to do it. Please don't fuck it up by scaring 'em on the East Coast."

"When I make my evening report, you mean?"

He shrugged and looked sheepish.

"Gibby, I'm not a company spy. I'm a cohost on the network's morning show. The reason I was sent here to be Des's first guest announcer is because Howie Mandell wasn't available. Howie isn't a WBC spy, either. Maybe an NBC spy. Anyway, if Des wants to play man in the moon, more power to him. Okay?"

"I guess," Gibby said, frowning.

He continued frowning while he paid the bill, which I made no offer to pick up. And his forehead remained creased during the drive back to the theater on Fountain.

I got out of the Boxter, but before he drove away,

I asked, "What's bothering you, Gibby? I told you I'm not a company spy."

"That's what's botherin' me, bubbie. If you really are just . . . on-air talent, then you sure as hell aren't gonna be doing *me* any favors. You probably got your own bid in on the gig if Des can't hack it."

"Gibby, I've never known anyone quite as clueless as you. About everything. I live in New York. I love the city. I have my own restaurant. I like working on *Wake Up, America!* I can't imagine what the network could offer me that would make me give up all that to come out here and try to host a late-night show written by somebody like you."

He gave me his idea of a wise-guy sneer. "Yeah, you say that now . . ." he said. He put the sports car in gear and roared off.

Watching him grow smaller and smaller, I wondered how far Gibby would go to get his own show. Would he, for example, write an entrance that put the star of the show on a flimsy piece of scenery thirty feet in the air in the hope that something just might go wrong?

I suddenly realized comedy is a lot like sausage: Everybody likes it, but nobody really wants to see how it's made.

# *Chapter*
# SIXTEEN

The chirping of the guesthouse phone woke me the next morning at eight a.m.

It was the cosmetically restructured Amelia St. Laurent of Crockaby Realty. In a voice considerably more arch than I recalled from our first meeting, she informed me that she would be showing the villa to prospective buyers in one hour—at precisely nine—and would greatly appreciate it if everything were "in apple-pie order."

Since a cleaning crew had removed all evidence of Des's and Fitz's brief occupancy, including any vestiges of the rat, and I'd done the dishes after the previous night's dinner, I assured her that the place would be spick-and-span. Unless I decided to bake an apple pie. In which case, would that not enhance its apple-pie order?

Our conversation ended on that note of high frivolity. I hopped from the sack, took a quick shower and shave, mopped up the bathroom, and deposited the towel in a hamper. I dressed. Made the bed. Hid my pajamas and dirty clothes in a drawer.

Finally, I removed the cleaner's wrapping from the tux I would be wearing on the show that night, to let the fabric breathe. I then stood back, surveyed my temporary abode, and judged it to be, like the villa, in, yes, apple-pie order.

Not wanting to be on the scene when Amelia made her pitch, I drove the Lexus down the coast highway to Patrick's Roadhouse, the legendary green eatery facing the Pacific on the Santa Monica–Pacific Palisades border that was better known for its patrons than its menu.

True to form, while dining on an acceptable breakfast of corned-beef hash and two eggs over easy, I counted, among my fellow customers, three bikers, two males and a female, who were nodding into their omelets, a pair of surfer dudes in rubber suits who seemed to feel that every noun had to be modified by the word "bitchin'," two guys in business gray suits who might have been accountants but more likely were junior agents, and Sean Penn, sitting alone with a book.

Hunger satisfied—did I mention the slice of Dutch apple pie?—I returned to the Lexus, which I'd street-parked on Entrada Drive, and was about to start it up when my phone serenaded me. Cassandra, calling from the Bistro.

"You've got a problem," she said.

I checked my watch. Nine-twenty. The lunch hour in Manhattan. There was considerable noise in the background. Conversations. Cutlery clicking against plates. "Sounds like you've got a good house," I said.

"We're at near capacity," she said. "The Bistro is not the problem. You should call your assistant."

"Kiki? Why?"

"She's totally pissed off at you. As I would be, if I were in her place."

I was having a little trouble sorting out this information. I try to keep my restaurant and television worlds spinning on different axes, and it always surprises me to discover they've collided. "I didn't know you and Kiki were friends."

"Billy, we get together once a month. Late lunches or early dinners. Usually here. You've seen us."

"I guess I have," I said. Though, obviously, it hadn't registered. "It just never occurred to me that you'd have much in common."

"Only one big pain in the ass, really. You. Our boss. You're pretty much what we talk about."

This wasn't the sort of thing I needed to hear long-distance. "I'm guessing these aren't complimentary conversations."

"They're the usual. We try to top one another with examples of how you take us for granted. Or ignore us. Or say you'll do something and forget. In general, how you behave like an asswipe."

*This is what being a bigamist must be like at the moment of truth,* I thought, and congratulated myself for not being even a half-bigamist.

"But what Kiki told me at lunch today extends way beyond asswipe behavior," Cassandra went on.

"Tell me what she said."

"She thinks that when you told her you didn't need her out there, you had an ulterior motive."

"And what would that be?"

"To keep her from becoming Stewart Gentry's new flame and, consequently, quitting her going-nowhere job as your assistant."

"So lemme get this straight," I said, feeling a sudden heat that had nothing to do with the Southern

California sun. "First, before getting that going-nowhere job, Kiki was the secretary to a crude, bust-out Broadway producer who wasn't even paying her half the salary she's getting now."

"How much *is* she getting?"

"That's beside the point," I said. "Moving on to her fantasy about becoming Stew Gentry's flame, that's crazy talk. She had one date with the guy a year ago."

"She called him."

"Yeah?"

"He said he'd had some serious disagreement with you. He wouldn't tell her any details, but she's convinced it was about her. She said he seemed very cool toward her and did not invite her to come out there for a visit, even after she'd dropped some pretty obvious hints. She's sure you're to blame."

I took a couple of deep breaths of ocean air, ionized with just a hint of brine. "What happened to the ad salesman she was seeing?"

"She says he's too nice."

"Too smart," I mumbled to myself, I thought.

"What?"

"My *disagreement* with Stew had nothing to do with Kiki," I said. "I have not uttered a word to him about her. If, by some magical quirk of fate, she were to become the next Mrs. Stewart Gentry, I would be overjoyed to dance at her wedding."

"Don't tell me. Tell her."

"The show debuts tonight," I said. "I'll be with it through the week, then I'll be flying back to reality on Saturday. I'll deal with Kiki then."

"If that's how you want to play it," Cassandra said, in her nettling passive-aggressive way.

"Why the hell should I have to defend myself for something I didn't do?" I asked.

"Do what you think best."

"Do you understand what a big deal tonight's going to be?" I asked. "Millions of eyeballs on the show. And a live audience. I'm never comfortable in front of an audience, even when I know what I'm doing. I'll be announcing the show. A voice deal. Not really my thing. And there's this crazy lighting guy who's got us performing in semidarkness. I have enough to worry about. I don't need to be worrying about my assistant's imaginary love life."

I was expecting her to make some reply, but there was silence from her end.

"No comment?"

"Break a leg," she said tersely, and clicked off.

## *Chapter* SEVENTEEN

The rest of the day went downhill from there.

I tried to chill out at the guesthouse, but Amelia St. Laurent had prospective buyers playing through on the hour.

I went for a jog on the beach and twisted my ankle.

While I was soaking the ankle to keep the swelling down, Harry Paynter called to say that Sandy Selman, the movie producer who was planning to bring our literary epic to the big screen, was demanding some kind of supernatural element. "He didn't come right out and say 'vampire,' but I know that's what's on his mind."

"Vampire?" I repeated. "That's crazy."

"The first thing you learn out here, Billy, is that everything is crazy. So there is no crazy. It's Sandy's nickel. He wants vampires, that's what we give him."

"How do you do that in a realistic way, exactly?"

"My suggestion?" Harry said. "We make our international assassins a romantic vampire couple."

"That solves the realism problem?"

"Sure. We're not talking Bela Lugosi. Nobody believes that bullshit. But young vampires getting it on—people buy that without blinking an eye."

"How exactly would they relate to our story? My story? Something I actually experienced?"

"This is just spitballing, but when our hero starts looking for something linking the victims, he discovers they've all bled out. Only here's the kicker, there's been no blood found."

"Yeah," I said. "And since our hero owns a restaurant, in the big climax scene, he can trick the vampires into thinking he's fixing them a midnight snack of blood-rare porterhouse steaks. But when he lifts the lid on the server, it's two *wooden* stakes. Which he drives into their respective hearts."

"Shit, Billy, that's gold, cinema gold. You've got a talent for this."

This was said without sarcasm. Without a hint of irony. Too sunny for irony.

"Thanks, Harry. I'd love to continue spitballing with you, but I've got a show tonight and lots to do."

"I understand, Billy. Hell, you're the man. You've cracked this story, really opened it up. My juices are *flowing*. I'm on this. Stakes for steaks. I love it."

I snapped the phone case shut and looked at my ankle. I decided it needed a little more soaking.

*Chapter*
# EIGHTEEN

"Moonlight madness and mirth at midnight. Tonight at the midnight hour. *O'Day at Night. Live* from L.A." That was pretty much the substance of the ads running in the East Coast media. Since the telecast would begin at nine p.m. Pacific Coast time, the "live" aspect would be missing locally, of course. The L.A. network affiliate, KWBC, reserved that family-hour slot for the ratings hits *Hot Bodies* (two wacky young coroner's assistants cut comedy capers in the morgue) and *Flaunt It!* (male and female runway models compete for the attention of single multimil-lionaires). Therefore, the hour would air nationwide (prerecorded in L.A.) a half-hour after the usual talk-show time of eleven-thirty p.m.

Actually, the show wouldn't be precisely live in

the East, either. It would be seen on a seven-second delay to allow the ever-watchful standards-and-practices folks to nip profanity and wardrobe malfunctions in the bud.

These particulars, as important as they might have been for the network and the show's producer, were of small consequence to me. As I aimed the Lexus in the direction of Hollywood that night, my main concern was that I arrive on time for the telecast. I was expected at least an hour before the show went on the air. Hearing tales of traffic congestion on the highway heading east from Santa Monica, I'd given myself an hour for the trip. So I touched down at a little before seven p.m., with more than enough time to relax alone for a bit in the dressing room I would be sharing with country-western singer Rennie Nolan.

Someone had been kind enough to stock the room with iced champagne and plates of caviar and crackers and, it being L.A., carrot sticks and celery stalks filled with feta cheese and something that was probably tabbouleh. Since the morning show was telecast live, I'd learned the hard way that you shouldn't drink fluids too close to showtime unless you want to suffer the torture of a full, unrelieved bladder. Ditto for eating. I'd fixed a tuna sandwich at two-thirty p.m., washed it down with bottled water, and kept dry and food-free thereafter. So I was thirsty and hungry, and the sight of that frosty bottle of champagne and caviar was too damn tempting.

I decided to stroll down the hall and pay Des a visit. I hadn't had a chance to talk to him since Gibby mentioned his belief that I was a company spy. This would be a good time to quash that notion.

With my tux in the hands of the wardrobe folks, who were steaming out the wrinkles, I rewrapped the elastic bandage on my ankle, slipped on the terry-cloth robe the production company had provided, and left the room. The door to Des's dressing room was shut. I was about to knock when I heard him speaking angrily and loudly enough for the words to penetrate the door.

"Cop on, ya eejit. The bloke's got nuthin'. An' you're shittin' bricks. Jasus, you make me wanna gawk."

I couldn't tell if he was talking to someone on the phone or in the room with him. No less curious than the next guy, I moved closer. I had my ear about a foot away from the door when:

"Nice legs, Billy."

I jumped back, my heart pounding with that just-been-caught beat.

Vida Evans was facing me in the hall. She looked beautiful, dressed in a sensational shiny aqua dress slit up the left side almost to her hip. A Versace, she would inform me later. Actually, the way she put it was: "This little Versace?"

"Vida," I said with a croak, almost running toward her and away from Des's door. "Hi."

"You're looking just a little . . . undone," she observed.

I tightened the robe, though she might have been talking about my awkwardness.

"I wasn't expec— What's up?" I asked.

"Just dropped by to say hello," she said. "And to tell you how much I enjoyed working with you on those spots. I hope we can do it again. You okay?"

"Sure. Just . . . before-the-show butterflies."

"I know the feeling," she said. "Well, I'll let you get back to . . . whatever it was you were doing out here in your robe."

"Taking a walk. That's . . . all I was doing. Are you sticking around for the after-party?"

"I . . . I'm not sure."

"Please," I said. "I promise to be a little more unflappable. We might even have a full-blown conversation."

She smiled. "I'll try to make it." Judging by the way she said it, I figured the odds at one hundred to one against. "In any case, Billy, break a leg."

"It's what everyone seems to want," I said.

An hour later, I was standing stage left, hidden from a rather noisy audience by one of Pfrank's scrim/light-cloaking combinations, while a sound tech adjusted my wireless lapel mike. He asked me to mumble a few words into it, stepped back, gave me a wink and a thumbs-up, and promptly disappeared.

I was feeling a little better than adequate for the job ahead. Not only was my mike working, my freshly steamed tux fit me perfectly, a symbolic emerald-green display handkerchief peeking from its pocket. The stomach butterflies had been replaced by an unhealthy but invigorating rush of adrenaline that was having the added benefit of deadening the pain in my ankle.

Onstage, in the spotlight, Gibby Lewis was desperately trying to warm up the crowd with a routine that might have had the late George Carlin groaning in his coffin. Hell, it might have had George Burns groaning. "First off, you've never heard of the disease," Gibby was saying, "because some advertising writer made it up. Ever see the commercial for Septumagic? It goes something like this: 'Are you suffering from nostril inflammation? Are your nasal walls falling down? You could have the pain, the social embarrassment of . . . *nasalitis*!'

"In the TV enactment, a young woman is sitting by herself in a very chichi restaurant with a schnozzola as red as a monkey's rear end. Camera pulls back to another table, where two upscale femmes are talking about her. 'Uh-oh,' one is saying, 'looks to me like Gladys could use a little Septumagic.' And the other one says, 'Yeah? Looks to me like she's due for another trip to Betty Ford.'"

Granted, it was a tough crowd, a lot of them in the biz. There were executives with the network and West Coast affiliates; talent agents and their clients, who were showing Des their support in the hope of reciprocity; and his comedian friends and competitors from Vegas and elsewhere. Judging by the reaction to Gibby's less-than-stellar material, he was getting through to about one-tenth of the audience. The others were talking among themselves or being distracted by the cameras and/or a scowling Lolita Snapps, in a white gown, sneakers, and a headset, looking a little like Dennis Rodman in drag as she managed the floor.

"And the small-print advice," Gibby went on bravely, "always delivered by a British lady at very high speed . . . 'Not recommended for anyone suffering from asthma or bronchial discomfort, ruptured mucous membranes, apnea, hoof-and-mouth disease. If profuse bleeding occurs, or intense sneezing, or if your nose remains engorged and stiff for longer than four hours, seek medical advice immediately.'"

Across from me, also hidden from the studio audience, Des, in a tux but with a black shirt open at the neck and a bright green cummerbund to indicate his swaggering nonconformity, was being helped onto the crescent moon by two ninja minions.

Onstage, Gibby was pointing to the applause signs.

We were less than a minute from magic time, and my throat was suddenly very dry.

With Des comfortably situated, facing the curved edge of the moon, riding it, cowboy-style, the ninjas began operating the winch device that gathered the cable, hoisting the contraption aloft. Des rose up to a height of twenty-five feet or more, his Irish mug expressionless. I wondered if he was aware of the precariousness of his situation. A fall from that height probably wouldn't be fatal, barring a broken neck, but it would certainly do damage enough to sideline his talk-show hosting for a while.

There was nothing wrong with Gibby's timing. As soon as Des and the swaying moon arrived at the catwalk, the writer warm-up thanked the unresponsive audience and hotfooted it from the stage. He brushed by me, trailing a familiar odor of fear and flop sweat.

I turned my attention quickly to Lolita, who was holding up a hand, indicating *Stand by*.

With my heart pounding, I waited and watched.

Only seconds more.

I took a deep breath and released it, saying a silent

prayer that I would remember the intro and get it out without a spoonerism. At those moments, I always thought of the legendary Harry von Zell flub, "Ladies and gentlemen . . . President Hoobert Heever."

Suddenly, in response to an order to Fitz's headset from the director's booth, he and the band began blasting out the catchy theme he'd composed, and home viewers on the East Coast were seeing the pre-recorded title sequence with Des romping about L.A.

When the music softened and segued into a few repeated bars, Lolita's big finger pointed at me like the barrel of a gun. My cue to get to work.

"Frommmm Hollywood . . ." I began, consciously channeling all the announcers I could recall, from Gene Rayburn to the subtly satiric delivery of *Saturday Night Live*'s Don Pardo. ". . . the Worldwide Broadcasting Company presents the debut of . . . *O'Day at Night* . . . with our special guests . . . Nashville's number-one singing sensation . . . Rennie Nolan . . . from the WBC megahit *Flaunt It!* . . . the beautiful Emmalou Adams . . . direct from the MGM Grand in Las Vegas . . . the hilarious Plimsol Brothers . . . and the mayor of the city of Los Angeles, Lucille Marquez."

The stage and the theater were suddenly enveloped in darkness, thanks to Pfrank's oddball visual concept.

There was an intake of breath from the surprised audience, but I was prepared for the blackout and didn't miss a beat. "And now here he is . . . the Celtic Lord of the Laugh . . . that irrepressible son of a *shamrock* . . . who's trying not to be too starstruck in Hollywoodland . . . Des . . . mond . . . O'Day-eee!"

A red dot appeared on one of the three cameras precisely at the same instant a spotlight captured Des up near the catwalk, straddling the moon. He looked surprised and startled, and pretended to lose his balance, wrapping both arms around the upper part of the crescent.

The studio audience responded with a universal gasp. Then some giggles. And as Des righted himself, grinning from ear to ear, arms extended in a "Look Ma, no hands" gesture, the applause and cheers rose energetically and on cue.

The image of a starry night sky was being projected on a backdrop and, with luck, the televised illusion would be of the comedian floating through the heavens on the crescent moon, dodging huge hanging stars while singing the Harold Arlen–Yip Harburg classic "It's Only a Paper Moon."

He was about halfway to the floor when the moon jerked and he was almost tossed off for real.

"Whoa," he interrupted the song to shout at the two black-cloaked stagehands nobody could see. "Take it easy, boys." He looked at the camera and added, "That's what you get, folks, for usin' stagehands sent over compliments of Jay Leno!"

There was a rim shot courtesy of Fitz's alert drummer, followed by laughs and more applause from the studio audience.

Des picked up the song again and, finishing it in time with his arrival at stage level, hopped from the unstable moon with athletic grace.

To the encouraging sound of whistles and shouts and more applause, he did a surprisingly professional pirouette and punctuated that with a low bow. "Good evening, good evening, ladies, gentlemen, and all the many alternative genders in between. Welcome to our first big show in this new *little* theater.

"You folks at home probably can't tell how small this building is . . ."

"How . . . small . . . is . . . it?" the band asked in unison, an homage to the late Johnny Carson that would, with hope, link Des to the forever king of late-night entertainment.

"It's so small, you can't even begin to Twitter or tweet. The best you can do is *twuh*. And my dressing room? The prison cells at Guantánamo Bay were bigger. Better furnished, too, now that I think of it.

"But we have the magic of television on our side. And that's no little thing. For example, all I have to do is point my finger and . . . bid-a-boom . . ."

Fitz and his band were suddenly illuminated, the former in a white tux and a green T-shirt, his musicians in green tuxes over white T-shirts.

". . . allow me to introduce you to me auld boyhood chum Fitzpatrick and his chart-bustin' band o' merry minstrels . . . Knackers!"

When that round of applause began to subside, Des pointed at me, and I was suddenly hit by a blinding light. "I think you all know my good friend from *Wake Up, America!,* that master chef, restaurateur, raconteur, and, for this week, my right-hand man. Billy Blessing!"

I bowed, not quite as deeply as Des, and smiled. As I walked toward him, the intricate set and lighting design passed another test. A leather chair and couch seemed to materialize, while shadowy stagehands scurried to the wings.

"What's *this* all about, then?" Des asked, indicating the furniture.

Going along with the bit, which was from the clueless comic/smart straight man playbook, I explained that the chair was for him and the couch for his guests.

"And then what? We just sit here?"

"You converse with your guests," I said. "Discuss important things, or entertaining things. What did you think you'd be doing out here for an hour every night?"

"Frankly, mate, I didn't have a plonker's plink."

The camera faded out on Des's amazingly pliable face holding on an exaggerated what do-I-know? expression while the audience reacted with laughter.

And . . . we cut to a commercial, with Lolita giving us a reassuring thumb-forefinger circle. Everything was okay.

So far.

My dressing-room mate, Rennie Nolan, was scheduled to be the first guest. But he was among the missing and, in a bit of panic improvisation, it was decided by the director in her booth that the Plimsols, a trio of high-energy comedy midget acrobats, be brought on early.

Dressed as leprechauns, they tossed one another around, staged fake fights, performed surprising gymnastics, and eventually dragged Des into their bang-ups, kicking him in the ankle, tripping him, and then, big finish, pretending to knock him flat, lifting him over their heads, and carrying him offstage to the tune of "When Johnny Comes Marching Home."

Rennie Nolan arrived during the Plimsols' segment, in leather jacket and jeans instead of formal wear, looking, frankly, stoned. But he'd remembered to bring his guitar, so during the three-minute commercial break, his makeup was blotted, his hair gelled, and his butt placed on a stool in front of the band just in time for Des to welcome him to the show. Our host then disappeared into darkness as Nolan began singing a cut from his new album.

Though the performance went reasonably well, all things considered, the singer's sit-down with Des was deadly. It began with Nolan dreamily announcing that he had recently become the spokesperson for FEC, the Fight to Eradicate Chlamydia. He then began to expound on "the pain and serious consequences of the disease" to our hypochondriac host, who began sliding back away from him until he was almost out of the frame.

"Ya know, ma fren', it is th' mos' common STD bacteria in the U.S.A. today," Nolan said, leaning forward into Des's personal space. "It's so damn destructive. And folks don' know they got it. Kinda gets up in there and plays hell with all the lady parts. And with men, hell, arthritis and—"

"Sorry to interrupt you, Rennie," Des said when he could stand no more. "You're doin' great work, bud, but we've got to sell a few things." He faced the camera and added, "Stick with us for more fun with the luscious and loquacious star of *Flaunt It!*, Ms. Emmalou Adams."

During the commercials, it took three ninja minions to "escort" a now rubber-legged Rennie from view, and a fourth to get Des an industrial-size bottle of antibacterial sanitizer.

Emmalou Adams had been watching the segment from the wings. After her introduction, which was delivered by our host with all the lecherous innuendo of a man who'd been playing Vegas for the past seven years, she walked onstage and allowed Des to do a paw-and-pet number a little to the left of even Gerald Butler. Taking her hand, he kissed each of its fingers and then led her by that hand to the couch, all the while seemingly transfixed by the dramatically low neckline of her tight blue silk blouse.

She sat down on the couch and, with no small malevolence, said, "You know, Des, considering your reputation as a player, you really should pay attention to all those scary things Rennie was saying about chlamydia."

It was the first time that night that I felt like laughing.

Des made quick, nonflirtatious work of the rest of their interview, dismissing her just before the commercial break with an obviously insincere, "Emmalou, I wish we had more time. Promise me you'll come back . . ."

As she rushed offstage, she mumbled, "Asshole," loud enough to be heard not only by me but by Mayor Lucille Marquez, who was standing beside me in the wings. The prim-looking politician's face broke into a grin. "I'm guessing that word will be getting quite a workout on this show," she said, watching Des strut around the stage.

After the break, I escorted her out to meet him.

She welcomed Des to Los Angeles and presented him with a key to the city and a scroll indicating that he was now an official Los Angeleno.

There was brief badinage about life in L.A. with, as planned, the mayor getting the last word. Suddenly frowning, she took the scroll back from Des, glanced at it, and relaxed. "Thank goodness," she said. "I was afraid I'd given you the one we forgot to present to Conan O'Brien."

Smiling to the audience, she departed to much applause. That left Des and me alone onstage to bring the whole thing to a close.

"I want to thank you, Billy, for makin' this special night even more so," he said. Then, following the direction of Lolita's pointing finger to camera two, he thanked the viewers for tuning in and invited them back to "our little after-hours club of fun and frolic every weeknight, same time, same WBC station.

"What a great and wonderful country America is," he continued, his pliable face registering humility, "where a hooligan from Dungannon can tell a few jokes and sing a few songs and wind up"—his face underwent the best effects-free transformation into evil lechery since Spencer Tracy segued from Dr. Jekyll to Mr. Hyde in a single take—"with as many birds as Mr. George Clooney and almost as much nicker as Mr. Bill Gates."

While he'd been delivering this insincere au revoir, the half-moon had descended behind him. He stepped back and stared at it for a beat. He was supposed to say, "Looks like my ride is here," and hop aboard the crescent, floating upward, reprising "Paper Moon."

Instead, he turned to me. "Billy, why don't you take the trip, mate, while I head out to the nearest pub?"

This bit of improv caught me off guard. Was I supposed to get on the damn thing? Or insist he do it? Or what the hell? All I got from Des was a demonic leer. I looked to Lolita, but the floor manager shrugged, obviously as puzzled as I was.

Des's next move clarified the situation. He faced the studio audience and asked, "You folks want to see me ould flower Billy takin' a moon dance, right?"

There was the expected outpouring of encouragement. Lolita gave me a big thumbs-up.

Having no other choice, I approached the wooden moon warily. I saw that some kind soul had fitted it with a narrow padded bicycle seat. Somehow that didn't ease my apprehension. As I straddled the damn device and lowered my butt to the seat, I couldn't help but wonder if Des didn't have another surprising bit planned. Like maybe a "company spy" taking a bone-breaking fall that would guarantee a fair degree of publicity for the show.

With a jarring jerk, the moon started its rise. I got a firm grip on the front of it and looked over at the stagehands working the winch. Make that stage*hand*. Only one of them. Des had had two, I was certain. What was the deal? The hoist seemed to be working smoothly, but it was a little disconcerting to realize I was being short-staffed.

Backed by Fitz and the band, Des was singing his own lyrics to Harold Arlen's melody: "It's Billy Blessing's moon, hangin' out in a cardboard sky . . ."

The higher up we went, the less I cared for the situation, especially when my right shoulder brushed against one of the hanging stars. I wouldn't be lowered to the stage until the credit crawl ended. How long did that take? Sixty seconds? Ninety?

My flight stopped with the top of the moon inches away from the catwalk. I looked down. I knew I was just a shade more than twenty feet from the stage, but it seemed twice that far.

There was an odd whirring sound coming from somewhere below, and I thought for a second it had been the winch. But that had been silent during my rise, and it was not in use now. I looked at Lolita, who was giving Des a speed-up arm swing. She didn't seem to have noticed anything off. At that moment I could no longer hear the sound. I wondered if it could have been an anxiety-induced form of tinnitus.

Des was finishing his serenade. I told myself that had to mean the show would end any second.

". . . but it wouldn't be make-believe, if you believe in me," the comedian sang. He bowed, basked in the applause, waved both hands in a farewell gesture, and said, over the noise, "G'night, mates. Believe!"

*Okay, it's a wrap,* I thought. *Back to earth for Billy, safe and sound.*

That's pretty much when the bomb went off.

I'm guessing, because I was momentarily transported to a much less troubled dimension. A second before that happened, I witnessed a bright light, and I think I heard the explosion. When I returned to reality, people were screaming and the moon and I were in a wild spin, banging against the hanging stars.

But we stayed aloft, thanks to what I later discovered had been an automatic locking device on the winch controlling the cable. I grabbed a star and used it to slow the moon's spin. Through the smoke and the floating debris, I saw that my solo ninja had been knocked flat on his or her back. Others were down. A camera operator. Lolita.

There was no immediate sign of Des. The stage where he'd been standing was ruptured and charred, a large section of concrete foundation showing through the damaged tile.

The audience members had rushed away from the stage area and were climbing over one another to get through the exit doors. I leaned forward, put my head against the plywood moon, and closed my eyes. All I had to do was stay calm and wait for the shouting and the panic to subside. Some thoughtful soul would see me and lower me to the ground. As best I could tell, my damage was slight.

I opened my eyes again to make sure about that. Only then did I realize that the moon and I were covered with bits and pieces of Des O'Day.

## Chapter
# NINETEEN

"What the heck is he doing back there?" I asked.

I was sitting on a stool in the wings, not far from my least favorite prop. A white-gloved coroner's technician was using king-size tweezers to pick things from the wooden moon's surface. Another tech was standing behind me, using the same instruments on my head and neck.

Hence my question.

"He's gathering body particles," the homicide detective said. "They'll take all those little bits back to the lab and try to put Humpty Dumpty together again." He was leaning against a wall across from me. He was older, grayer, and had put a few pounds on his wiry frame, but I'd recognized him the moment he entered the studio. Detective Pete Brueghel. One of the cops who'd investigated Tiffany Arden's murder twenty-three years ago.

The recognition had been mutual. I could see it in Brueghel's ever-alert brown eyes. "How're you feeling, Mr. Blessing?"

"Not exactly my best." The tech's tweezers were like a hungry bird, pecking at my scalp. I turned to him. "Long as you're drilling holes, could you fill 'em with hair follicles?"

"You're lucky the explosion wasn't more powerful," the detective said. "The real damage was limited to a small area of the stage. Mr. O'Day seems to be the only fatality. Ms. Snapps and a cameraman named Assunto got shaken up pretty bad, along with five other members of the crew. The paramedics are checking them now, along with half a dozen audience members who got trampled trying to get out of the building."

"What happened, exactly?" I asked.

"I was hoping you'd tell me."

I gave him all I had: riding the moon up, relaxing when the show seemed to be over, then seeing a bright light like a camera flash going off in my eyes, followed by a roar and a brief fade-out. Then waking up to smoke and bad odor and screams coming from people rushing out of the building.

"Tell me about the bad odor," he said, getting out a small notepad and a pen.

"I don't know. Smoke. And something even more unpleasant."

"Burning flesh?"

"Jesus. Maybe. And . . . a metallic odor, too. Like when a laptop overheats."

He nodded, scribbling on the pad. Then those intense eyes were back on me. "How'd you get down?"

"One of the nin— The stagehands saw me up there, got the winch working, and lowered the moon to the floor."

"What was it you started to say and then changed your mind? Nin?"

"The stagehands were dressed in these black outfits. In my mind, they're ninjas."

"I saw the outfits," the detective said. "They wear something similar in those Cirque du Soleil shows in Vegas, so you can't see them picking up after the performers."

I wondered if that's where Pfrank got the idea. "You spend much time in Las Vegas, detective?"

"Not so much anymore," he said. "I had family . . ."

The technician stopped pecking at me. "All finished," he said. He promised to send a medic over to dress my cuts, which were not serious but numerous and had to be cleaned and treated.

Brueghel waited for him to leave, then asked, "Any idea why someone would want to demolish Mr. O'Day?"

"I'm sure Conan O'Brien would have a few thoughts on that if we were talking about Jay Leno."

"Do you know of anybody who felt O'Day had screwed him over?"

"If that was the case, I imagine we both would have heard about it by now."

A tall black woman wearing a fitted dark blue suit and a badge entered the stage area, looked around, spied us, and headed our way. Brueghel introduced her as his partner, Mizzy Campbell.

"A few words, Pete?" she said.

"Sure."

They moved beyond earshot, huddled for a minute or two, then returned.

"Mr. Blessing," Detective Campbell said, "I understand from the show's director that Mr. O'Day did a little improv shortly before the explosion. Is that correct?"

"Yeah. He went off script. He was supposed to get on the moon and sing his farewell as he was floating away. Instead, he got me to do it. Shamed me into it, actually. We were on a live telecast, and I couldn't very well refuse."

"Any idea why he changed things?" Detective Brueghel asked.

"No." Then I remembered something. "The device nearly bucked him off at the start of the show. That could have spooked him."

"But the switch was a last-minute decision, right?" Detective Campbell asked.

"It was a surprise to me."

"Then if things had gone as planned and O'Day

had taken the moon ride, where would that have left you?" Detective Brueghel asked.

I stared at him, suddenly realizing where they were headed. I guess I'd subconsciously been blocking it.

"You would have been standing precisely where Mr. O'Day was, right?" Detective Campbell asked.

I nodded.

Detective Brueghel applied the icing on the cake. "Then, Mr. Blessing, I suppose we can assume you were the intended victim."

# *Chapter*
# TWENTY

Detective Brueghel accompanied me to my dressing room at the rear of the building, where he waited for me to shower away the remaining bits of Des's flesh and blood. The hot water offered some comfort, but it was temporary. And it called attention to my own cuts and scratches, leaving them stinging and bleeding.

When I was dressed, a paramedic arrived and took care of my wounds. He didn't think any of the cuts needed stitches. He taped one on my neck and two on my left hand. The ones on my forehead, cheek, and the back of my head were scratches, better left to "breathe." He doubted any of the cuts would result in permanent scarring. "But you might want to get the opinion of a specialist," he said.

At my request, he also took a look at my sprained ankle and taped it professionally.

When he'd finished and moved on, the detective said to me, "You know, I meant to look you up last week, when I heard about you and Charbonnet having that tussle. I don't suppose it had anything to do with the Arden case?"

"That was a long time ago," I said, sniffing. There was an unpleasant odor in the room.

"But not forgotten. And not solved." He stared at me, as if that was my fault. "What was the fight about?"

"Roger was drunk." I spotted the source of the malodor, got up from the chair, and limped to the table containing stale champagne, wilted carrots, and ripening feta cheese.

Brueghel watched me dump the offending items, then said, "There were a lot of people at the party. Why'd he go after you?"

"Just lucky, I guess," I said, limping back to the chair.

"I don't get you, Blessing," the detective said heatedly. "Somebody tried to kill you tonight. According to all accounts, Roger Charbonnet took a swing at you last week. That makes him a standout suspect. But instead of helping me get the son of a bitch, you make little jokes. What's going on?"

The honest truth was that I had no idea what was causing my reluctance to put Roger on the spot.

"You have any reason to think Charbonnet *wasn't* responsible for the bombing?"

"No," I said.

"Then work with me, for Christ's sake."

I nodded. "Roger went a little postal at the party because he thought I was talking about him."

"Were you?"

"No."

He smiled. "You're a professional interviewer, right?" he asked.

"That's part of what I do."

"Then you know how hard you have to work when people answer with just 'yes' and 'no.'"

"Another thing my profession has taught me: Be careful when you're accusing somebody of criminal behavior. Too many lawyers in the world."

"There's nobody here but you and me. Just tell me what you think. Did Charbonnet murder Tiffany Arden?"

"I believe he's capable of it. I've seen his anger."

"At the party, you mean?"

"And back in the day." As soon as that popped out of my mouth, I realized I was going to tell him about Roger confronting me with his gun and threatening to kill me if I didn't leave Los Angeles.

The detective's reaction was as expected. "Goddamn it, Blessing. What the hell were you thinking? You should have come directly to us."

"I went directly to you about Roger's broken alibi," I said. "We all know how well that worked out for me."

Detective Brueghel was silent for about a second. "Okay. I'll give you that one. But you come out here last week. You find out this . . . sociopath has been harboring a twenty-three-year-old grudge against you, and *still* you do nothing about it?"

"Like what? He took a drunken swing at me, and he wound up in the pool. What exactly do you expect me to do with that, even if I could link it to a murder that's over twenty years old?"

"I'm going to link it to a murder that happened two hours ago," he said. "But two hours or twenty-three years, the dead . . . they're depending on *me* to find justice for them. And I'll do it, no matter how long it takes." His eyes were moist. He blinked, and a tear worked its way down his face. "It's my calling. The blue religion."

*Whoa.* This guy was either a true believer or a megalomaniac. And I didn't know of too many true believers in his profession. Good cops, sure. But homicide dicks who cried for the dead? Not too many of those. At least not in my hometown. In L.A. . . . ?

He stared at the floor for a few seconds, then blinked and rolled his head in a circular motion, prompting little popping sounds from his neck. "Don't mind me," he said. "I can get a little carried away."

I nodded, as if I understood.

"It's not just the dead I serve," he said. "Whoever rigged that explosion is going to come at you again. I wish I could offer you some kind of police protection, but those days were over even before the latest budget cut. Does Charbonnet know where you're staying?"

I told him about the break-in at the villa and the dead rat left in the oven.

He shook his head. "There must be a reason you were holding back that little event. Maybe you have a death wish? Or maybe you just don't trust me, or cops in general?"

"It's nothing like that," I said, though he'd been close to the truth with the question about my trust issues. For much of my earlier life, I'd considered police the enemy. I no longer believed that, but old habits die hard.

"Well, the guy hates you. He's a chef. Somebody breaks into the place where you're staying and cooks a rat for you. More than a coincidence, right?"

"Right."

He asked for the address. When I told him, he said, "Isn't that near where you and Charbonnet had your party fight?"

"A few houses down."

"A gated community?"

I nodded.

He got out his cellular phone and called Detective Campbell. He instructed her to send a forensics team out to the villa. Checking his watch, he said, "Tell them to wait for us at the gate. No, cancel that. They should follow us out. I want to make sure the gate-keepers don't interfere."

Detective Campbell evidently said something that reignited his anger. "Goddamn it. What next? Homeland Frigging Security?"

He snapped the phone shut and put it away. "The FBI has arrived, arrogant and an hour late. As soon as they force my guys to stop working long enough to fill them in on everything, they may want to talk with you."

"Should I stay here and wait?"

"Your choice. As far as I'm concerned, you can forget I mentioned it."

So I wasn't the only one guilty of being uncooperative.

"About the villa in Malibu," I said. "A real estate agent has been showing the place to prospective buyers."

"Great," he said, meaning just the opposite. "Wouldn't want to make it too easy. Well, I know the fingerprint I'm looking for. It'll match one we've had on file for twenty-three years."

"If you and Detective Campbell are driving out to the villa, I'd like to come along and get my stuff out of there."

"Not a good idea. Charbonnet knows the property. He's had access. And he knows you're still alive. The villa is the last place I want you tonight, even with Detective Campbell and myself on the scene. We've got work to do, and worrying about your safety would only slow us down. Find yourself a hotel room and try to get some rest."

"Okay," I said. "But I'll have to go out there and pack up tomorrow."

"Yeah. I guess you'll be needing your razor, fresh clothes, and the rest. If you want, I could throw your stuff into a bag and have it when we meet."

"I appreciate the offer, but I'd rather do my own packing," I said.

He withdrew a small white card from his shirt pocket, scribbled something on it, and handed it to me. On its front was an embossed detective shield and his name, office and email addresses, and office phone number. "That's my cell number on the back.

Call me when you want to get your gear, and I'll drive out with you."

"It might be early," I said. "I'm going to try and catch a flight back to New York tomorrow."

"No flight," he said, getting that dedicated look again. "I want you out here. I can make it official, put you in custody as a material witness. That might not be a bad idea, with our deadly friend on the prowl."

"No. Don't do that," I said. "How long are we talking about?"

"I can give you a better idea tomorrow, after I see what we have on Mr. Roger Charbonnet. You using a limo?"

"A gray Lexus convertible. In the lot next door."

"Leave it until I get one of the bomb squad guys to check it out. It's probably blocked in, anyway. It's a mess out front. Fire trucks. Police cars. Media. Show that card to a patrol cop and tell him I said he should find you a ride."

He took a few steps toward the door and stopped. "I almost forgot, there are some women from the network in that booth the director uses. They've been waiting to talk to you. Maybe one of them can give you a lift to a hotel? Be careful, Blessing. Start acting smart."

As far as I was concerned, smart was taking the next flight out to New York City.

# *Chapter*
# TWENTY-ONE

Thanks to my nicks and scratches, I looked like my barber was Sweeney Todd. They stung. I was tired. And thirsty. And as always, I was hungry. More than that, I had zero interest in meeting with "women from the network." That would most likely be Carmen Sandoval and her attentive slavegirl Whisper Jansen. And probably Vida Evans. Dedicated network employees, eager to discuss Worldwide's response to the tragedy. That was the last thing I needed after experiencing what I could accurately describe as the worst night of my life.

Knowing the company mind-set, I suspected the first question could easily be a paraphrase of the old joke about Mrs. Lincoln: "Other than that, Billy, what did you think of the show?"

I'd have to meet with Carmen et al. sooner or later. But later was better.

I rolled up the probably ruined tux I'd been wearing and stuck it into my overnight bag, along with the other utensils I'd needed for the show.

I'd learned through experience to turn off my cellphone before leaving the dressing area. You don't want an incessant ringtone annoying people backstage. I clicked it on and quickly scrolled through the calls it had registered. Apparently, once you've survived a fatal explosion, it seems everybody wants to talk to you. That included, among others, Cassandra, Carmen, Vida, Harry Paynter, and Kiki. Even Stew.

I'd return the calls later, when I'd settled in at a hotel. I slipped the phone into my pocket, picked up my overnight, and left the room.

Standing in the hall, I steeled myself and headed for an exit.

The LAPD had slapped an official yellow keep-out tape across the entrance to Des's dressing room. Though the tape was adhering to the closed door, one end of it was torn and hanging free.

Somebody had broken the police seal.

Just as I was contemplating this breach of the law, the door opened and Fitz exited the room.

"Billy!" he said, jerking in surprise. "Jasus. You nearly put the heart crossways in me."

He was still wearing his white tux pants and green T-shirt, but he'd dumped the coat and hat. I didn't see any cuts or abrasions, but his eyes were red, and he had, past the slightly matted beard, the pasty-faced, frazzled look of a man who'd been through the mill.

He was carrying something. A bulging soft leather man-purse.

"Aw, but it's awful, ain't it?" he said. "Des . . . poor goddamned Des."

"Poor Des, indeed."

"You look like you took some damage," he said.

"Nothing too serious. What about you?"

"The blokes and me, we were pretty far back from the blast. An' that screen in front of us . . . it blocked the soot and crap that was flyin' about. I jus' keep wishin' . . . aw, hell, if only he'd listened to me."

"Des? If he'd listened to you about what?"

Fitz shook his head. "Nothin'. Not important now." He was starting to edge away.

"The police talk to you?" I asked.

"Oh, yeah. Tall black lady. Detective . . . Campbell. It was kinda weird."

"Weird how?"

"I figgered the chin-wag would be all about Des. And there was a lot of that. But she also wanted to know about *you*."

I suppose that figured, since Brueghel believed I'd been the target. "What kind of questions?"

"How long I'd known you. Did I know any of your friends? Had anybody been askin' me about you? Like that. T'wasn't much I could contribute. Like I told her, we just met last week. Ah, Billy, I better be runnin' . . ."

"Running because of that?" I asked, pointing to the broken tape.

He stared at me. "I didn't harm nuthin'."

"What's in the bag?"

He hesitated, then sighed and said, "Medicine."

"Drugs?"

"Nuthin' heavy. Jus' some oxy, Percocet, Ecstasy. A little pot. Some white."

The man was carrying a portable drugstore. "Just light stuff like that?"

"Yeah. Still, I wouldn't want people sayin' Des was, you know, an abuser."

I considered asking him what he planned on doing with the stash, but in truth, I just didn't care.

"You're not gonna play the informer?" Fitz asked.

"Just because you broke a police seal to remove drugs from a murder victim's room?"

Even half hidden by beard, his face registered dismay.

I shook my head. "I won't say anything unless the detectives make it an issue. And that doesn't seem likely."

"You're a good egg, Billy," he said, relieved. "I better get out of here with this stuff."

He headed toward the rear of the building.

"Hold up," I said. "Where are you going?"

"To the alley exit," he said. "I sure as hell ain't gonna carry this past a line of coppers."

He started walking again, and I was walking with him. It felt like the thing to do. The other direction seemed a little crowded.

"What makes you think there won't be police in the alley?" I asked the big man.

"'Cause I just came in that way. Nary a one."

He was right. The alley was clear, except for his Hummer, parked with the engine running. As he was about to get in, he asked, "You headed out to Malibu?"

"No. I'm staying in town."

"Need a lift, then?"

"Thanks, Fitz. I'm okay," I said. The way the night was going, I didn't want to risk riding in a pea-green Hummer with a scofflaw Irishman behind the wheel and a bag full of illegal drugs resting between us.

"Later, then," Fitz said, and rolled away down the alley, heading east. I walked off, heading west.

# Chapter
# TWENTY-TWO

I followed the alley to Cahuenga Boulevard and headed south to Fountain to see for myself how bad things were in front of the theater.

It was worse than I'd imagined. A great clog of humanity and noise and bright lights, featuring police and parked patrol cars, emergency vehicles, paramedics and EMTs, media and TV news vans, a bomb squad transport, pedestrian gawkers, and street people. A bumper-to-bumper traffic line crept by until it reached Cahuenga, where, faced with nothing more to see but several blocks of dark industrial buildings and a black man standing on the corner with an overnight bag, the vehicles drifted off into the night.

I spied my lovely leased Lexus—try saying that five times in a row—sitting nearly alone in the lot. Most of the others had been removed before the drivers of a Channel 12 news van and an LAPD patrol car decided that they needed a parking space more than we unlucky few would be needing an exit for our cars.

Considering Brueghel's warning, maybe *lucky* was more accurate in my case. Any bomber expert enough to demolish only one single victim on a small, moderately populated stage could probably wire a device to a car in jig time.

I considered and then decided against bumming a ride in a patrol car. Going back to the theater would mean risking a meet-up with Carmen and Whisper or, worse, the FBI. It wasn't that far a walk to Sunset, where, if there were no cabs, I'd at least find a restaurant or bar where I could drink or eat or, better, drink and eat, then call a cab.

I was about a quarter of a block away when I heard a car behind me. Moving slowly along Cahuenga. I quickly scanned the buildings to my right, searching for a nice narrow pathway to race down on my sprained ankle.

The car stopped. Its driver tapped the horn.

I didn't turn to look. Instead, I walked faster. Limped, actually. Limped faster.

The car started up again, engine roaring. It was a pale blue Mercedes-Benz with a black convertible top. Not new. Probably not worth more than sixty grand. It cut into the driveway in front of me.

I was about to do a bolt when I saw Vida behind the wheel. She bent across the seat to pop open the passenger door. "Get in, Billy. This isn't Manhattan. People don't walk here. Definitely not at night."

I tossed the bag behind the seat and got in, giving her a grateful grin. My ankle was grateful, too, temporarily rid of all that weight. But my butt was telling me that I was sitting on something other than Mercedes leather.

Vida watched me with a raised eyebrow as I groped between my legs. When my hand emerged with an iPhone, I hoped still in one piece, she said, "Sorry, I'll take that."

She put the instrument in a little black beaded bag,

saying, "What a horror show that was. The explosion was bad enough, but the panic. People screaming and crawling over one another. Hitting and kicking. A woman I respected, a VP at Sony, was smashing people with the spiked heel of her Roberto Cavalli."

She stared at my face. "A detective told us you were okay. But I see cuts."

"Scratches. I'm okay."

She continued to study my face. "Don't you have a car?"

"In the lot next to the theater, trapped."

She put the Mercedes in reverse and backed out into the street, then roared forward toward Sunset. "You have to tell me where we're going," she said.

"You wouldn't be hungry, by any chance?"

She smiled. "Oh, wouldn't I?"

Her suggestion was Meals by Genet, a small establishment with an exterior resembling an unassuming French café. But before you leap to any conclusions about the menu, as I did, I should add that this Genet is a local chef and caterer, and not the late French existentialist and ex-con playwright. And the restaurant is located on a block of South Fairfax Avenue known as Little Ethiopia, or as some purists would have it, Little Addis Ababa. Tucked between an eclectic home-furnishings shop and an adult day-care facility, it shares the neighborhood with other restaurants, markets, coffeehouses, and stores selling various products, predominantly imported from the horn of Africa.

The restaurant's dining room is elegant, softly lit, and, when you're lucky enough to be accompanied by a smart, beautiful woman, extremely romantic. And the food? Well, the first bites were so delicious they almost made me forget that I was accompanied by a smart, beautiful woman. But not even manna from heaven could pull that off.

I watched Vida glide past the other late diners as she returned from the powder room. She was quite a vision in her aqua dress, and I told her so. "You are an instant reminder that there is still romance in the world," I said. "Especially in that dress."

"This little Versace?"

"It's a knockout," I said. "But it's gilding the lily."

"My goodness, Billy. That kind of talk, combined with food and wine, can lead to . . . almost anything."

"I like this version of you," I said. "During all the days we worked together, you seemed a little . . ." I was searching for a word.

"Distant," she said. "Cold. Unapproachable. Bitchy. Stop me before I begin to hate myself."

" 'Businesslike' is how I'd put it," I said. "But 'unapproachable' works, too."

" 'Businesslike' is a good one, Billy. These days, I live by a specific set of rules. One of them is: When I work, I work. When I play . . ."

"As I recall, I asked you out to play once or twice."

"As I recall, I said I was busy. Which I was. You gave up pretty quickly."

"I didn't want to be a bore."

"That should be the least of your worries." She took a sip of wine and changed the subject. "Now, does this or does this not meet your restaurant criteria?"

I had asked for a place where the food was tasty and the décor tasteful. And possibly more important, one that was off the *TMZ* grid, where we wouldn't be bothered by young geeks in baggy pants and backward baseball caps, sticking cameras in our faces and shouting, "Tell us about the big blowout, dudes."

"You know damn well you knocked it out of the park," I said.

She smiled. "This is very naughty of us. Carmen wanted desperately to talk to you about the show tomorrow night."

"The show? How can there be a show without a star? Excuse me for going all Monty Python on you, but the show is dead. Kaput. Finito. It's an ex-show."

She shook her head. "This parrot is alive. New York has decided that the show must go on. They're doing the Craig Kilborn thing. Remember when he pulled the plug on *The Late Late Show*? CBS held several weeklong on-the-air tryouts for the host slot, and Craig Ferguson got the nod. That's worked out very well."

"They got lucky," I said. "Ferguson's a natural. And the name, *The Late Late Show*, stayed the same. WBC won't even have that much continuity. It'll mean starting from scratch. New name. New host. Probably new theater. New everything."

"That's what Carmen wants to talk to *you* about," Vida said.

"Me? They're not thinking about me hosting the show?"

"Not host. Just to continue as announcer until a host is found."

"That could take forever," I said, trying not to panic.

"There are a lot of very funny people who'd jump at the chance," she said. "It shouldn't take that long."

"I've got too much going on back in New York."

Some of my desperation must have surfaced, because she said, "Okay. My bad. I didn't mean to spoil the moment by mentioning the show. Erase. Rewind. Beep. We're back to being just a couple on a first date, checking each other out and enjoying an excellent meal."

"I'll drink to that," I said, lifting my wineglass and trying to subdue my apprehension. The "first date" concept intrigued me. It suggested more to come. Even more dates. And as I already mentioned, the meal was splendid, too much so to be soured by thoughts of late-night television. Or murder.

There were many Italian dishes on the menu (supposedly a nod to Italy's short rule of Ethiopia in the thirties), and I'm sure each of them was excellent, but I could get my pasta fix almost anywhere. It wasn't often I had the chance to glut myself on *yebere siga tibs,* a mound of tender steak chunks sautéed in Ethiopian butter, onions, green chilies, and several unidentifiable but heady spices and served on a pancake-like bread called *injera.* At Genet, it's accompanied by a pot of *awaze,* a hot chili purée that will leave you with tears in your eyes and a smile on your face.

I should mention that in lieu of eating utensils, you're provided with extra *injera.* You tear off a piece and use it to scoop up the food. It may sound messy, but it isn't. On the other hand, it adds a certain sensuality to the meal. Especially when you've moved on to a second bottle of Picket Fence pinot noir and your tablemate suggests you sample each other's dishes.

I waited for Vida to remove a few cubes of my steak, then watched her close her eyes as she savored their taste. We both took a drink of wine, and I tried some of her *dorowot,* a sort of chicken stew with a sauce of . . . what the hell was it? Maybe ginger, clove, and a few other things, none of them obvious and all mingling to form something beyond description.

I grinned at Vida. She grinned at me. We took another sip of wine.

# *Chapter*
# TWENTY-THREE

We closed the place down.

Sitting beside Vida in her Mercedes, parked behind the building, I realized I was more than slightly wine woozy. I suggested to her that since things seemed to be going so well, perhaps we should leave the car and call a cab to make sure the evening stayed in the positive column.

Her reply was to lean in to me for a surprising passionate kiss.

"Positive enough?" she asked when we finally came up for air.

"I meant—"

"I know what you meant, Billy. So I ask you: Was that the kiss of someone who was too fried to drive?"

"I'm not the best judge of that," I said. "Maybe one more test?"

Her reply was to start the car. She did it efficiently and without a moment's falter, a further demonstration of her sobriety. "I had a total of two glasses of wine tonight," she said, steering us onto Fairfax. "I keep track of these things. For example, I clocked you at a bottle and a half."

"Point taken." Forcing myself to stop staring at her lovely profile, I saw that we were driving north toward Sunset Boulevard. *Heading where?* I wondered. Definitely away from where she knew my car was parked.

Crossing Wilshire Boulevard, we passed the classic building that was once the city's most famous May Company location. It appeared to have been taken over by the County Museum. From the corner of my eye, I saw Vida glance at the digital time readout on the dash.

She increased our speed.

"In a hurry?" I asked.

She smiled. "Why waste the night on the road," she said, "when we could be sitting on my deck in the hills, having a cup of coffee and enjoying the city lights below?"

I didn't think I'd ever been asked a more rhetorical question.


Her home was a Spanish bi-level with a red tile roof on one of those bewilderingly meandering little streets high above Sunset. Vida gave me a mini-tour through a smartly appointed living room, small enough to be considered cozy, a tiny formal dining room, and a modern kitchen, where she got the coffee started.

The deck she'd mentioned was off the living room, a solid redwood structure with a gas barbecue and redwood chaises that offered a breathtaking view of the city lights below. So she lost a point for going gas rather than charcoal but scored highly in all other categories.

The night was chilly, however, and it took only a few minutes for comfort to trump aesthetics. Back inside the house, she led me up a short flight of stairs to a visually oriented den/office that I guessed was where she spent most of her home time.

She parked me on a soft, white U-shaped sofa that faced a humongous television screen and, promising a swift return, wandered off to what I guessed was the bedroom area. With coffee mug in hand and visions of Vida slipping into something comfortable in mind, I took a walk about the room, noting several awards— a news Emmy among them—resting on a stone mantel above a wood-burning fireplace that looked like it had never been used. Two bookshelves, recessed into a wall, held back issues of *Time, Newsweek, Entertainment Weekly, Variety, The Hollywood Reporter,* and *Emmy,* neatly stacked.

There was a desk, actually a slab of soft yellow Formica anchored atop a pale wood filing cabinet on each end. On the desk were a closed MacBook, a cordless phone, an iPad, several large mugs filled with pens and pencils, clippings from the *L.A. Times*—one about a child mauled by a formerly harmless border collie, the other listing the names of reporters fired from a local television station—and a plastic jewel box containing an audiobook version of one of Eric Jerome Dickey's sexy thrillers.

"Let me see," Vida said, walking into the room.

She was not talking to me. She had a cellphone pressed to her ear. She had not slipped into anything more comfortable than her little Versace.

"Okay, I'm trying it."

She picked up the TV remote and brought up a silent HD picture of a guy in a newsroom, wearing a starched shirt with the sleeves rolled up. "Just a sec," Vida said.

She did a little surfing before settling on a clear but not HD image of a woman sitting at a desk with a phone to her ear. I knew her. I had, in fact, been in love with her once. Gretchen Di Voss.

"Good," Vida said. "Let me turn up the sound."

On the giant TV Gretchen cradled her phone and said, "I see you, Billy, but you're almost offscreen. Would you mind sitting on the sofa?"

I gave Vida a woeful look and mumbled, "Traitor." Then I sat on the sofa.

"Am I coming through clear, Billy?"

"Loud and clear." I looked for and found the small camera eye perched on top of the giant screen. "What's the deal on this two-way TV, Gretch? Is there a Di Voss interoffice channel no one told me about?"

"It's simple, everyday Skype," Vida said, "transferred to the big screen."

"It's late, Billy," Gretchen said, "and—"

"Wow, you're right. It must be after four in Manhattan."

"What it is is crunch time. So let's not screw around. What happened is a tragedy. Our star was murdered. Other employees were injured. As far as I can tell, the investigation into the bomber's motives is at a standstill. There's a rumor, true or false, that the mayor may have been the real target."

I wondered where that came from. Was Brueghel trying to make Roger think he was safe? Safe enough for him to screw up when he came for me again? That led to another question: Was Brueghel keeping me in L.A. to lure Roger into making that second try?

I was distracted from that disquieting thought by Gretchen asking Vida if there had been any more news from the LAPD.

"I . . . I haven't had a chance to—" Vida started to reply.

"Billy, are those cuts on your face?" Gretch asked.

"Scratches. I'm all right."

"No trauma? The company will provide you with whatever care is necessary."

"I think I'm okay on the trauma score, too."

"The effects don't always show up right away. But you'll have to be the judge of that. The reason for this call is that I need you to stay with the show. Not forever. Probably not longer than a few weeks."

"Gretch, this is—"

"Let me finish, Billy. Then you can have your say. WBC is committed, contractually, to our affiliates and to our participating advertisers, to provide a show in that time slot. That advertiser commitment includes a specific number of viewers. If we were to discontinue the show, or if we fail to attract that minimum viewership, we will forfeit a great deal of money. That could have a devastating effect on our whole operation."

"So put on your show," I said. "Why do I have to be a part of it?"

"Because right now you and Fitzpatrick form the still-beating heart of *O'Day at Night*. I . . . *we* are convinced that you both will put eyeballs on the show."

"Great. We can wear 'I Survived the *O'Day at Night* Bombing' T-shirts," I said.

"If you want to, I'll have some printed up," she said. "I reached Fitzpatrick, and he has agreed to remain. With most of his band."

"Won't that be enough of a beating heart?"

"The thing is, viewers like you, Billy. They find you friendly and sympathetic. They'll be tuning in to see you. Which means they'll also be sampling the guest hosts. We'll get a much better idea of who to anoint. I don't understand your reticence."

"Hello? I've got a restaurant to run. Not to mention *Wake Up*. And the cable show."

"The morning show can wait. We can do repeats of the cooking show. And as far as the Bistro goes, I was there last night, and Cassandra had the place spinning like a top."

Having run out of all the other reasons for me not to do the show, I decided to tell her the truth, sort of. "Gretch, I don't want to do the show because I'm afraid."

"Please, Billy, stage fright?"

"Hell, yes. Frightened that the stage could blow up again! Suppose that was only the first bomb?"

Gretchen and Vida, at opposite ends of the country, stared at me with identical expressions of surprise.

Gretchen was the first to speak. "Why would you think such a thing?" she asked.

"Listen to our newscasts," I said. "Hate's very big right now. Suppose some crazy has a hate on for WBC."

"The police must be looking into that possibility," Vida said. "Did they mention it to you?"

"No. But it's not like they go jabbering about their plans to every handsome chef they meet." I couldn't tell them what Brueghel had been jabbering about. They were, after all, in the news business. If word of my involvement—or worse, Roger being a suspect—broke before Brueghel gave the go-ahead, there'd be two people wanting to kill me in L.A.

"That reminds me," Vida said. "There's that bunch of freaks who did everything they could to stop the renovation. The Save the Margo Channing Theater Society. They protested, picketed, even tried to get the building declared a historic monument. They went totally aggro when Carmen sicced the cops on them. Came back that night and spray-painted graffiti all over the front of the theater. I could see them thinking they could stop the show with a little boom, then overdoing."

"There are so many disturbed people today," Gretchen said. "Especially out there. Maybe we should hire that fellow who took care of Tonette when her fiancé was giving her all that grief. You remember, Vida, the pretty-boy investigator who wore those ridiculous, loud Hawaiian shirts and had an office full of Disneyland junk."

"Hard to forget a hottie like that," Vida said. "Man talked a good game, but it was his buddy with the funny tattoos who got the job done."

"What's the situation with the FBI?" Gretchen asked.

"They were there," Vida said. "I got the feeling they were willing to take a step back and let the LAPD run with the investigation."

"I suppose we should do the same," Gretchen said. "Regarding your fears, Billy, beginning tomorrow afternoon—I guess it's actually *this* afternoon—you'll be doing the show from a studio on the WBC lot. So right away, the security will be tighter. We can even add an extra guard or two on site. It won't be a big deal getting audience members to pass through a metal detector. It's not like they're paying customers. And our insurers will be telling us that's something we should have had in place at the theater."

"Okay, Gretchen," I said. "But I beg you: Don't keep me out here longer than a couple of weeks."

She smiled. "Thank you, Billy. The contracts will be on Wally Wing's desk by noon. I'll be talking to Carmen about beefing up the security. Is there anything else?"

"Who's going to be hosting the show?"

"The comedy writer. What's his name? Gibby Lewis."

Interesting. Des's demise couldn't have worked out better for the writer than if he'd planned it.

"Gibby, huh?"

"You say that like it's a mistake."

"No. I was just . . . no." There was no reason for me to rain on Gibby's parade.

"Max seems to think he can do it. And if he doesn't work out, we'll just replace him."

"It's your sandbox."

"I didn't mean to sound harsh. The late hour. The lack of sleep. Take care of yourself, Billy."

The image of Gretchen faded and the screen went to black. Vida clicked off the TV and said, "Well, Billy, shall I drive you to your car? It's probably freed up by now."

"It's . . . not working."

"What do you mean? We can call Triple A."

"It's . . . well, the detective in charge of the investigation wants to make sure it's safe to drive."

She frowned. "He thinks what, that it could blow up?"

"Maybe, but he's just being cautious. It was parked near the theater."

"A bodyguard might be a good idea."

"No. Really. No bodyguard. I may change my mind if they do find . . . anything in the car."

"Then I should drive you home."

"Actually, there could be a bomb out there."

She stared at me. "Lame, Billy. Almost high-school lame."

"It's not a line. I can stay at a hotel, I guess."

"At this hour? I wouldn't put a dog in a hotel at this hour. Get your little bag and come on."

I picked up my overnight bag and followed her down a hall to a nice peach-colored room with windows that looked out on the city, a dresser, a chest of drawers, and a king-size bed.

"You wouldn't have pajamas in that bag?" she asked.

"No. Just a razor and a toothbrush and a tuxedo that I'll never wear again."

She opened a drawer near the bottom of the chest and withdrew a dark green box with a Polo horsey logo. She opened it and removed a pair of black silk pajamas that she tossed on the bed. "They may be a little large," she said.

They still had tiny white tags attached. "These are new," I said. "And they look expensive."

"I'm glad they'll be getting some use. They've been in that drawer awhile."

"It's a shame to wear something this nice and just go to sleep."

"Give it a rest, Billy," she said. "Literally."

She opened a door that led to a black-and-white tile bathroom. "All the comforts of home," she said, and left me to my room with a bath.

I splashed some water on my face, brushed my teeth, and put on the silk pajamas, which were only one size too big. Not the worst thing for pajamas. I turned out the light in the bathroom but left the bedroom table lamp on. Then I pulled down the oatmeal-colored covers and slid into the bed.

It was one of those Posturepedic numbers, slightly hard but with a pliable top layer that conformed to your body, a bruised and bomb-weary body. I lay there, wondering if the night was over or if there might be more to come.

Just as I was drifting away into sleep, I felt the bed move slightly, then realized Vida was lying beside me. She was wearing a very thin, see-through gown, and there was a lot to see through it. She rolled toward me and, holding my face in both hands, kissed me hard.

I put my arms around her and pulled her on top of me.

There was one little problem. She was also on top of the covers. We stayed like that for a minute. Then I said, "It's nice and warm under here."

"I bet it is," she said.

"I think you should join me."

"I want to."

Then she rolled away and got up from the bed. "But not tonight."

"Why not?"

She paused at the door. "It's just our first date," she said. Then she added, "Sleep well," and was gone.

I lay in priapic misery, thinking, *I never saw that coming*. But the whole night had been like that, chock-full of things I never saw coming.

# *Chapter*
# TWENTY-FOUR

"There were hundreds of prints at that multimillion-dollar joint where you're staying," Detective Brueghel informed me on our drive to Malibu the next day. "But none of them Charbonnet's. Still, we're checking 'em all. Maybe we'll get lucky and find a perp he hired to plant the rat."

"Roger was at Malibu Sands that afternoon."

"I know. The security guards showed us the log.

They didn't note or remember anybody entering with him. But he drives a Rolls. Lots of room for a guy to hide behind the front seats, and a vehicle that expensive intimidates even real cops. I'm sure those bozos didn't bother to give it a second's glance."

For the next few minutes, we drove in silence. I watched sun-dappled gulls swooping low to the choppy, bottle-green Pacific. With just a flick of their wings, they soared up into a cloudless blue. The birds reminded me of discarded wrappers picked up from a grimy Manhattan sidewalk and sent skyward by a sudden blast of subway-stirred air. The sad thing was that I missed even the litter of New York.

Nostalgia? Or depression? Maybe both.

Another glum mood. Another day.

I had woken just before nine, feeling a little let down to discover I was all alone in the hillside house. Alone but not forgotten. Before heading to work, Vida had left enough Starbucks French Roast heating in the carafe for two cups, along with Pop-Tarts resting beside the toaster. The latter were filled with grape goo and had sprinkles, neither of which I fancied. But the thought was kind.

Vida had also left a hastily scribbled note: "Want to chance a second date? Call me." She added a P.S.: "The front door locks itself."

"P.P.S.: You have a cute snore."

My phone call caught her on her way to Yorba Linda, a coastal city some forty miles southeast of L.A. It was famous for being the birthplace of Richard Nixon and, more recently, the discovery of what the media had labeled "Satan Prep," a private school that was, per the *L.A. Times,* "rumored to be staffed by demon worshippers who forced their young students to commit acts of depravity."

Vida told me she'd covered the story for *Hotline* when it broke. She and a cameraman were headed back because after more than a month in prison, the supposedly satanic teachers were finally getting their day in court. Vida was hoping to interview them and their families, their accusers, and folks on the street who, she said a bit gleefully, "must be bummed at what the whole thing is doing to the city's rep as one of the safest (and wealthiest) in the U.S."

I told her that sounded like she'd be there for a while.

"Why? What's on your mind?"

"Dinner tonight."

"Tonight probably won't work," she said. "What about Saturday night?"

"What about Thursday night? Or Friday?" I asked.

"Saturday's our best bet," she said. "Besides, you won't be doing a show. We could have a nice dinner at my place at a normal hour."

"I'll miss you, but Saturday it is."

"I'll make it worth the wait," she said.

We ended on that pleasant note. Then I made the mistake many gamblers do. Instead of quitting while I was ahead, I decided to answer some of the calls that had come in last night.

Wally Wing, once he'd breezed through a perfunctory inquiry about my post-bombing physical condition, began to chastise me for not letting him renegotiate the details of my updated *O'Day at Night* contract. "I'm sitting here getting sick to my stomach looking at this . . . *thing* Business Affairs calls a con-tract," he said, and went on from there. I hung up, freeing Wally to do his thing with the Business Affairs pirates at WBC.

Next I called Kiki, expecting the worst—a show-down about my imaginary objection to her imaginary romance with Stew Gentry. Instead, it was a different complaint. She'd watched the show and had stayed up all night worrying about me. Why the fuck hadn't I called?

I apologized humbly, then said, "About you and Stew . . ."

"Cassandra told you, huh?"

"She mentioned you think I—"

"I'm going to stop you right there, Billy. I'm mor-tified that I said those things. I was feeling very vul-nerable at the time. And maybe a little tipsy. I know you better than to think you'd interfere with my hap-piness just to keep me working for you."

"I'm glad to hear it," I said.

"Then you forgive me?"

"Of course. And you can do me a big favor, Kiki. Please spread the news of my good health to all my friends on the morning show. And my non-friends."

"Will do. But I'm going to call Stew first," she said. "He's very concerned."

"You talked to him today?"

"Yes," she said brightly. "We've been . . . talking. In fact, he invited me to spend the first week in Sep-tember with him in Spain. Just before he starts a new movie."

"Ah," I said. "Glad that worked out for you."

"No fear. I'll use my vacation days."

My next call was to Cassandra, who surprised me with an initial display of compassion. "Oh, God, Billy. I'm so happy you're okay. I actually stopped off at Old Saint Pat's this morning and lit a candle." I thanked her for doing that. Then I mentioned that I was going to be staying in L.A. a little longer than anticipated.

"Of course you will," she'd replied. "And let's see: What would be keeping you there? The bombings? The earthquakes? The dry winds that suck all the moisture out of your body? Or could it be brain-dead bimbos doing all the sucking?" And she was back in form.

Brain-dead bimbos, especially the sucking variety, were odd subjects to be on the mind of someone who'd visited Old Saint Pat's that very morning. But I didn't bring that to her attention. Instead, I tried to repeat all the reasons Gretchen had given me last night for staying. I even passed along Gretch's compliment about how splendidly she, Cassandra, was running the Bistro.

"About that, Billy. I was not hired to run this place by myself. If you're going to be continuing your . . . dalliances in movieland, I want an assistant."

*Oooooh. Good one.* A new employee meant paperwork, insurance, at least a minimum salary. "I'll be here only a few more weeks," I said.

"And then you'll be off somewhere else. I could put an ad in the paper today."

"Why don't I just give you a raise instead?"

"How much?" she asked.

We settled on a figure that was less than half of what an assistant's assistant would cost.

* * *

I was putting my razor and toothbrush back into my overnight bag when Brueghel called to say that no incendiary device had been found in the Lexus. "Where are you right now?"

"At a friend's."

"Why don't I swing by and pick you up? We can drive out to get your things, and then I'll drop you at your car."

Which was why I was in his Ford Crown Victoria, heading for Malibu Sands, on a cloudless, sunny day, thinking wistfully of dirty old New York.

"Charbonnet doesn't have such a good alibi this go-round," Brueghel said with a rare grin. "Claims that at the approximate time Des O'Day went misty, he was at his place, waiting for a lady to show."

"What's her name?" I asked, wondering if it might be Stew's daughter, Dani.

"Zeena Zataran or Cataran or Trashcan, one of those cable reality-show hotties. She was at his place in Brentwood when I dropped by at around one last night. In his hot tub. Naked, of course. Looked like she had cantaloupes floating in front of her. Shameless little female. Asked me if she could stay in the tub while we talked. I had no problem with that.

"Didn't have much to say, though. Just that she got a call from him around nine-thirty. He wanted to know where she was. She told him she was at a party at the Chateau Marmont, helping to launch a new brand of vodka. He reminded her that she'd agreed to have dinner with him at his place.

"She told him she didn't remember making the

date. In any case, her agent had booked her for the vodka gig. But the party was winding down. If he was still in the mood for a booty call, she could make it to his place a little later. She just had to spend a few more minutes with the dudes who were paying her ten grand to show up at their lame party."

"What time did she get there?" I asked.

"She thinks it was somewhere between ten-thirty and eleven. Charbonnet was waiting with a shaker full of sour orange daiquiris, her current favorite."

"So it would have been tight, making it to Brentwood from the theater by ten-thirty. But doable."

"That's my take," the detective said. "The girl said she thought he was at his place when they spoke at nine-thirty, that there was geezer jazz music he likes playing in the background. My guess is he was sitting in his car outside the theater, playing the radio, when he called."

" 'Geezer jazz music,' " I said. "She sounds like she's easily bored, self-absorbed, and spoiled by celebrity. The perfect match for Roger. Was he naked in the hot tub, too?"

Brueghel didn't think the question was frivolous. "He answered the door dry as a bone and fully dressed," he said. "Which I found interesting, because it suggests he might have been expecting somebody like me to drop by.

"Of course, he pretended to be surprised. And he did this other thing, a little too clever by half. He pretended he thought I was there for another go-round on the Arden case. He asked if I was 'digging through those old bones again.' "

"Nice choice of words to describe the woman he swears he loved."

"Exactly. I explained I was digging through new bones that had belonged to Desmond O'Day. He said he knew who O'Day was and he thought he'd met the comedian once, in Vegas. But he hadn't heard about the murder. Or the bombing. And he didn't know why I was bothering him about it at one in the morning. He had absolutely no reason for wanting the comic dead.

"That's when I told him about O'Day changing places with you at the last minute."

"And his reaction to that?"

Another rare smile. "He said he now understood why I was there. And the interview was over. If I wanted to talk with him further, his lawyer would have to be present."

"And that was that?" I asked.

"Well, I—" He paused to pull his cellular phone from his pocket. It must have been on vibrate, because there'd been no ringtone. "Brueghel," he said.

He said "Yeah" a few times, interspersed with a "You're sure?" He ended with an "Abso-fucking-lutely we go for it. But wait for me."

He slipped the phone back into his pocket; said, "Hold on"; and, without hesitation, made a U-turn on the Pacific Coast Highway that was no doubt as surprising and frightening to other motorists as it was to me.

"What's happening?" I managed to get out, once my heart had started beating again.

"No need for you to pack and move out now," he said, his eyes shiny with excitement.

"Why not? And where are we headed?"

"To something a chef like you will appreciate, one of those increasingly rare events where justice will be served with all the trimmings."

*Chapter*
# TWENTY-FIVE

Our destination was a house on Carmelina Avenue in Brentwood. Actually, calling it a house was a little like calling Moby Dick a fish. It was a big, sprawling affair, set far back on the lot and separated from the street by a stone fence and foliage and palm trees and, from what I could see of it standing beside Brueghel's Crown Vic, a lush garden.

It was just a few blocks away from O. J. Simpson's old place, a connection brought to mind by the scene before me. That would be Roger Charbonnet, hands cuffed behind his back, being perp-walked from his home by Detective Mizzy Campbell and two uniformed cops. They hurried him past the arriving media mob and his grim-faced neighbors to one of several parked police vehicles.

Brueghel stood off to one side, obviously enjoying the moment. Then he strolled back to where he'd insisted I remain, beside his car. "Better twenty-three years late than never," he said.

The detective was speaking in a normal tone, and,

with the press shouting questions and the general hubbub, I doubted Roger could have heard him. But he turned his head suddenly in our direction and saw me.

He glared, did that flaring-nostril thing, and stood otherwise frozen until one of the cops used a head push to coax him into the patrol car. He sat in an awkward position, with his manacled hands behind him, as the cop slammed the door. He continued to stare at me through the side window until the vehicle drove away.

"Time to roll, Blessing," Brueghel said, as the gentlemen and ladies of the press, having lost their main attraction, began to fan out in search of someone of lesser interest to harass.

He backed the Crown Vic away from the approaching horde, made another of his famous U-turns, and took off down the avenue.

"Media got here pretty fast," I said.

"Sometimes they fill a need," he said. "Especially when there are certain scenes you want captured. So you can cherish them forever."

He made a few turns until we were headed back in the direction of Hollywood.

"Were you expecting an arrest today?" I asked.

"No. But sometimes you get lucky. Or maybe God provides the luck."

"What exactly did He provide?"

"In this case, I'd say it was a combination of arrogance and overconfidence. Maybe Charbonnet didn't think we could get a search warrant so quickly. Or maybe he assumed we were so stupid we'd ignore all the crap he had in his garden shed out back."

"What did they find?"

Brueghel gave me a sharp look. "You're an okay guy, Blessing. But you are a member of the tribe."

I blinked, not certain I'd heard him correctly. "Say what?"

"The tribe," he repeated. "The media."

"Oh."

"If the chief wants you guys to know the details of Charbonnet's arrest, he'll hold a press conference."

"'You guys'? Do I look like Brian Williams to you? Maybe Woodward or Bernstein? I'm asking you not as a member of the *tribe*. I'm the guy Charbonnet tried to light up, remember?"

He nodded. "Hell, I don't suppose it's gonna be any big secret, anyway. They found the materials used to make the bomb in Charbonnet's shed."

"Dynamite?"

"Nothing so hard-core. An empty container that smelled of bleach, distilled water, imitation salt, and camp-stove gasoline."

"How do you make a bomb out of that?"

"Well, you need a container, a scale, a battery hydrometer, all of which were in the shed," Brueghel said.

"Okay. You get all that stuff, then what?"

"Then you punch up any one of a couple dozen websites that tell you how to make the bomb."

"How difficult is it?"

"I'd say if you can cook a soufflé, making a plastic explosive from bleach should be a breeze."

"And these materials were still on his property?" I asked. "After your visit last night?"

"Like I said, arrogance. Probably figured we'd

think they were just household items. In any case, he screwed the pooch and left them there long enough for us to find 'em. And the DA told Mizzy to bring him in."

Roger was arrogant, yes, but stupid? Or careless? For that matter, was he enough of a nutburger to mix up a bomb, put on a ninja suit, and sneak into a theater with it, just to get rid of yours truly? Well, maybe. In any case, the idea of him being behind bars certainly appealed to me. And when the detective deposited me at the parking lot next to the renamed but now boarded-up Di Voss Theater on Fountain, I was feeling almost upbeat about extending my L.A. stay.

"You're sticking around awhile, right, Blessing?" Brueghel asked from the car. Reading my mind, apparently.

"A couple of weeks," I said. "Why?"

"The DA assigned the case may want a sit-down with you," Brueghel said. "You'll have to come back for the trial, too, of course. But that could be as long as a year from now."

Brueghel's eyes seemed to lose focus, and he mumbled, mainly to himself, "Charbonnet's going to have a lot of time to think about his sins. To sit in his tiny cell, where he'll be visited by Tiffany and Des O'Day and who knows how many of the departed he's wronged over the years."

The detective was creeping me out a little. "I'll be at the trial," I told him, backing away. "Thanks for the lift."

"Justice demands you be there, Blessing," he said, focused on me again. "You understand what I'm saying?"

"Sure," I said, hoping he wouldn't question me on it.

"In addition to what you can tell the jury about your run-in with Charbonnet a few weeks ago, I expect the prosecutor will use your testimony to try and introduce information about the Tiffany Arden murder. Specifically, that Charbonnet's alibi was bogus."

"His lawyer won't object?"

"Once the truth is said, he can object all he wants. The jury will have heard."

"Good point," I said, backing away farther.

"Tiffany Arden will be in that courtroom, you know, just as she has been with me for twenty-three years." He was drifting away again. "She and all the other victims whose killers have never been made to pay for their crimes. In my dreams they circle around me like a whirlpool, dragging me down . . ."

He shook his head suddenly. If the motion had been an attempt to clear his mind, it didn't quite work. "Remember, Blessing, Tiffany is still here with us. With me. And, I think, with Charbonnet. And none of us will be free until he joins the six-four-eight."

"I don't know what that means, the six-four-eight," I said.

"The six hundred and forty-eight prisoners on death row in the state," Brueghel said.

He put the Crown Vic in drive and roared away, leaving a three-foot-long trail of rubber on the asphalt.

An interesting guy, the detective. An honorable cop. A dedicated and dogged cop. But when the Good Lord was serving the entrées for a sane and happy life, Brueghel must have wandered off the buffet line to search for clues.

Chapter<br>**TWENTY-SIX**

"Listen up," Max Slaughter ordered from his position at the head of the table. Actually, it was a round table, following the example set by the planners of international sit-downs seeking to avoid the problem of choosing one attendant poobah over the others to sit at the head (or conversely, the foot). But television rehearsals are not known for their diplomacy, and anywhere the portly producer of the newly rechristened *The Midnight Show* chose to deposit his pear-shaped rear end automatically became the head.

To his left was his gofer, the pale, deadpan assistant producer, Trey Halstead. Beside Trey, Whisper Jansen was leaning forward, her scrubbed, unadorned face frozen in concentration as she aimed a Sony TG1, billed as the world's smallest camcorder, at the producer, hoping to capture every syllable of his words of wisdom for her boss, Carmen Sandoval, and, after that, posterity, I suppose.

Next to her, Fitzpatrick slumped, his beard pressed against his chest, looking as if he'd had another rough night and exuding a boozy-sweaty musk that had prompted me to move my chair as far away from his as I could without bumping into our director, Tessa Ruscha.

Her sullen silence made me wonder if she was catching a Fitz whiff, too. Or maybe she was reacting to the not-so-funny two-lesbians joke Gibby Lewis was telling to a stand-up pal of his named Howard something, who was helping him with the opening monologue.

Howard laughed like a howler monkey even before the punch line, but the joke definitely wasn't playing too well with floor manager Lolita Snapps, who'd been damaged in the bombing and was shaking her bandaged head at the comic's choice of material.

If our final table mate had heard any of Gibby's utterances, she wasn't showing it. April Edding, whom I'd met at the villa the night of the rat, rested languidly on her chair, eyes active behind her large aviator glasses, as she studied her iPad.

"Zip it, Gibby," Trey Halstead said, identifying the room's main disruptive element and, from the look on our new, possibly temporary star's pliable mug, making an instant enemy. Not that Trey cared. The pale young man's only concern seemed to be satisfying Max's every whim. Any other thoughts or deeds he kept under wraps.

"First, in case some of you may not have heard, I have some good news," Max said. And April's attentiveness was suddenly matching Whisper's and Trey's. "The police have caught the bastard who murdered Des. Not some druggie or fruitcake, as you may suspect. A well-known restaurateur, Roger Charbonnet.

I *know* the guy. I've played cards with him at Hill-crest."

"Christ, I know him, too," Gibby said. "What was the deal? Why'd he do it?"

Max shrugged. "Cops haven't said. Or what led them to him."

"There's going to be a news conference any minute," April informed us. "I've been checking my *L.A. Times* alerts. Nothing yet."

"Keep us posted," Tessa said. "We all want to know what's going on."

I considered enlightening them. "It's all because of me," I could have said. But in spite of the occupational road I'd taken, I wasn't really that "it's me" guy. In fact, I should have known better than to even harbor that thought. I'd seen enough evidence of mental telepathy to believe in it.

"Billy."

It was April who'd called my name. She was staring at me, smiling. "I must be slow today," she said, holding up her iPad. "*The Smoking Gun* made the obvious connection."

"What?" Max asked. "Lemme see."

"The fight at Malibu," April said. "Remember. It was all over the Internet. Billy tossing Roger Charbonnet into the pool." By now, I had given up playing the "didn't toss him in the pool" card.

"That's right," Gibby said, staring at me, mouth hanging open in a mixture of surprise and amusement.

They were all staring at me. And not in a totally friendly way. With the exception of Gibby's pal, they'd all been affected by the explosion, and they no doubt felt I'd been hiding something they deserved to know—why Roger had gone from iron chef to behind-iron-bars chef.

*What the heck.* Brueghel said the news would be out soon enough.

"The detectives believe Roger Charbonnet meant that bomb for me," I said.

"It wasn't . . . Des wasn't . . . ?" Fitz sputtered, trying to process what I'd just said.

"At the villa, the rat!" April exclaimed. "Tell them about the rat."

"By all means," Max said.

"Somebody broke into Des's place, where I've been staying, and left a rat cooking in the oven," I told them. "I thought it was just a bad joke. I should have taken it more seriously."

"That can't be," Fitz said, shaking his shaggy head in obvious confusion. "The rat was . . ."

"Was what?" I asked.

He stared at me, glassy-eyed. Then he got it together. "Don't mind me," he said. "I'm about as sharp as a beach ball today. Still bolloxed from last night."

That's when the ringtones started.

First was "Ode to Spring" on April's iPhone. She answered, said a few words I couldn't hear, and signed off. "Police Chief Weidemeyer is meeting with the press at the new headquarters at First and Spring."

Max ordered Trey to turn on the TV set in the corner of the room.

Trey was complying when the lilting sounds of "Frim-Fram Sauce" issued from my pocket.

"Enough with the goddamn cellphones," Max

yelled. "Turn 'em off. This is supposed to be a rehearsal."

My caller was Carmen Sandoval. "Hello, Billy," she began.

"Carmen, I'm sorry," I said, "but Max wants us to turn off our phones."

"Tell him to go fuck himself."

I passed the word on to Max.

"Give Carmen my best," he said.

"Okay, back on again," I said.

"Bravo. Are you on, too, Whisper?"

I looked across the table and saw that Whisper had a phone to her ear. "Yes, I am, Carmen," I heard her say through my phone.

The network veep summarized the *Smoking Gun* announcement in a few succinct words before asking me if the website was correct in assuming I was Roger's intended victim.

"It looks that way," I said.

"When I have more time, Billy, I would love to know why you've kept this information from the news-gathering network that's paying you so handsomely. But right now, there are more important things to cover.

"You are about to be besieged by every media outlet in the free world. I'd like to remind you that as a WBC employee, you owe us a certain exclusivity on this fast-breaking story."

I was not at all certain that was true. But if I wanted to continue working for the network, there was little point in discussing it.

"When we're through talking, I want you to turn off your phone. Avoid the other media at all cost. If any of them manage to get past the gate, call security immediately.

"Now, Whisper, I'll be phoning Wanda in D.C."— Wanda Lorinski was the producer of the network's half-hour *News Tonight!*—"to tell her Billy has confirmed the *Smoking Gun* rumor and that we, by that I mean you, Whisper, will have him ready in a studio here for a Q-and-A with Jim, as early in tonight's show as Wanda can arrange." Jim McBride anchored the nightly news half-hour from the nation's capital.

"While I clear things with Wanda, please inform Max that he'll have to shift things around on tonight's show to make room for a more in-depth Billy interview. I'll make sure that it will be plugged on the news."

"Ah, about Billy's *Midnight* interview?" Whisper asked, lowering her tiny voice even more than usual. "You don't want Gibby to do it, right?"

"God, no. He'd pause mid-question for a fart joke. Get Marcus Oliphant."

That was a name from the past. Marcus Oliphant had been the late-news anchor for the net's L.A.-owned-and-operated station KWBC back when I'd lived in the city.

"But watch out for the old boy," Carmen cautioned Whisper. "Telling him he'll be guesting on a network show is liable to give him wood."

"I'll phone him," Whisper said, without a hint of irony.

The conference call was over. Never once was I asked if I *wanted* to talk about my history with Roger Charbonnet in front of 8.5 million viewers.

"We have to rush, Billy," Whisper said as she circled the table. "We've less than twenty-seven minutes to get you sponged and in the chair."

As we headed to the door, Max bellowed, "Where the hell are you going, Billy? This is a rehearsal. There's blocking . . ."

Whisper, her voice reedy but clear, evoked the name of Carmen, mentioned my *News Tonight!* appearance, and promised to have me back within the hour.

"No later," Max said, trying to save face.

But Whisper wasn't finished with him. "Oh, and about tonight's show," she said. "You'll have to make a change in the lineup."

"At this hour, that's fucking impossible," Max said, his face reddening. "Forget it."

"Carmen will be very disappointed," Whisper said.

For a second or two, Max pursed his lips and relaxed them, staring at the table in front of him. Then he stopped that and asked, "What is it she wants, exactly?"

"A longer interview with Billy. Conducted by Marcus Oliphant. It'll be promoed on the evening news."

"Makes sense, I suppose," Max mumbled.

I could feel him glaring at our backs as we left the room. Closing the door behind us, I asked, "How often does Carmen put you in the middle like that?"

"This was the first time," Whisper said, with more than a hint of wonder. "She likes to order people around herself. And now I know why. It's fun."

# Chapter
# TWENTY-SEVEN

The Jim McBride interview went smoothly enough. Fortunately, the press conference at LAPD headquarters had provided an abundance of footage in which Police Chief Clarence Weidemeyer, the latest in a revolving door of short-termers to occupy the position, explained the official theory: "We have arrested local restaurateur Roger Charbonnet in connection with the explosion that claimed the life of comedian and television talk-show host Desmond O'Day and destroyed portions of the Harold Di Voss Theater in Hollywood. It is our belief the explosive device was, in fact, intended to kill another performer on Mr. O'Day's late-night show, William Blessing, whom Charbonnet considered a rival."

For the most part, all I had to do was agree with Chief Weidemeyer's report. There was a moment when McBride asked me about the source of Roger's antipathy. To avoid getting into a discussion about who may or may not have murdered Tiffany Arden, I had to twist my answers so much I almost fell off my chair. McBride sensed my discomfort and moved on to another question.

The *Midnight* interview was another matter altogether.

In the first place, the whole show seemed off. Gibby's opening monologue was neither clean enough to pass Bill Cosby's standards nor vulgar enough to be distinctive. Most of it was of the "I shouldn't even be doing this!" variety, none of it capable of eliciting more than a few errant chuckles from a studio audience that expected more, having been put through a tougher security check than it takes to get into the Pentagon.

Due to the low wattage of our celebrity guests—a TV hero from the seventies who was running for governor of Arizona, a starlet who took time from plugging her upcoming movie and her "naughty new website" to teach Gibby how to tie a knot in a cherry stem with his tongue, and Gilberto, the new Guatemalan singing sensation—my interview was kept till last.

By then the show seemed to be dragging on longer than the Academy Awards. Even more vexing, when the time finally came for our dog-and-pony routine, Marcus Oliphant seemed to think he was auditioning for *60 Minutes*. Or maybe FOX News.

"Tell us how you felt, Billy, when the universe suddenly exploded in a white flash of destruction and death?"

I stared at him, trying not to focus on how the thick pancake makeup was making his age-wrinkled face resemble a raised relief map of the Great Smoky Mountains. "A little like I feel now, Marcus," I said. "Only not as vulnerable."

His questions, though overly dramatic and verbose, were on target enough to get me to respond with a detailed account of the minutes leading up to the explosion.

"But how fortunate that was for you, up there above the chaos and madness. Tell us exactly what you were going through."

"I was pretty uncomfortable, hanging twenty feet in the air. Des was singing. I remember thinking that when he finished his song I'd be lowered to the ground, so I was wishing he'd hurry it up. And . . ."

At that point, I realized I'd forgotten something about last night. Something possibly important that I should tell Detective Brueghel. Making that mental note, I committed one of television's cardinal sins. I froze on camera. Not for very long, but enough to cause Marcus a few anxious moments. His eyes were starting to bulge, and he was turning pale under all that makeup.

Lolita, standing just to the left of the camera, reacted to the sudden silence by whipping her bandaged head in my direction. She placed a cupped hand behind one ear and wiggled it, glaring at me.

"And"—I repeated, trying to recall where I was in the answer—"Des stopped singing and said his good-bye to the audience. And that's when the explosion took place."

"You were knocked unconscious?"

"I think so," I replied. "A lot of things were happening all at once."

"And Desmond O'Day died?" Marcus said.

"That would be an understatement," I said.

"You two were close, you and Des. I believe you were living together."

*Huh?* "Hey, Marcus, just because two guys barbecue a few steaks in their bathrobes, it doesn't mean . . ." I stopped because the perplexed look on Marcus's face reminded me with whom I was dealing. "Actually, to answer your question seriously, Des and I first met less than two weeks ago on a flight out here from New York. He mentioned that there was an empty guesthouse on his property and asked if I wanted to use it during my short visit. So I guess you could say we were living together.

"Des seemed like a nice enough guy, and his death is certainly a tragedy. But we were not what I would call close friends."

"Uh-huh. Well, let's move on to the presumed villain of the piece, Roger Charbonnet. He hated you for something that happened in the past. Tell us about it."

It was a very broad question that required a slippery answer. "You'd have to ask him why he hated me, if indeed he did."

"Can't we assume that? He tried to kill you."

"Maybe we should let a jury decide what Roger Charbonnet did, or tried to do," I said.

"The evidence seems pretty conclusive. But you're correct, Billy. Innocent until proven, and all that that implies. So how do you suppose the *killer* managed to get the explosive into the theater?"

I was a little surprised to realize I had an answer. That rear door that, for some reason, wasn't as guarded as it should have been when Fitz and I made our exits. But it was another strike against the network's security arrangements, so I answered, "I wouldn't want to speculate."

"According to the *L.A. Times* website, Char . . .

the *killer* was disguised as a stagehand," Marcus said, "wearing a black bodysuit similar to that worn by the legitimate stagehands. Those outfits were unique, weren't they?"

I went into a semi-elaborate description of the ninja suits and how they fit into the set and lighting designs of the show. The designs and the black suits were not being used in the show's present iteration.

"The situation was made to order for him, wasn't it?" Marcus said. "He puts on the suit and becomes . . . the invisible man."

"That's a likely assumption," I said.

"Oh, it's more than that," Marcus said. "He was definitely dressed in the black bodysuit."

I gave him a patronizing smile. "Unless there was an eyewitness or a confession, I don't see how even the savants at the *L.A. Times* could know without doubt what the killer was wearing."

"The police found the black bodysuit at Roger Charbonnet's home," Marcus said. "He'd tried to hide it in his closet."

As surprising as that revelation was, I remained aware of the little red light on the camera and refrained from letting my jaw drop, at least not too far. "Well, let's hear it for the police," I said, before getting another of Lolita's "Speak up" signals.

"It's believed the bomb was some form of homemade plastic explosive," Marcus said. "Possibly as small as a cigarette pack or a man's wallet. Did you see anything like that?"

"No," I said, not daring to challenge him on the "It's believed." I hadn't heard a thing about what the bomb had looked like. The info had probably been in that same damned *L.A. Times* report.

"If it was that small, it seems logical he had hidden it under his clothes," Marcus speculated. "He had access to the stage area. Am I right that there were strips of tape to indicate where you—or as it happened, Des O'Day—were supposed to be standing at the close of the show?"

I answered in the affirmative.

"Then it was just a matter of the killer walking out and leaving the bomb near the tape strips," Marcus concluded.

"It could have happened that way," I said. I didn't really think so, but this wasn't the ideal time or place to hold a discussion of how the bomb was positioned or triggered.

"Well, I'm sure I'm speaking for all of us when I say, of Desmond O'Day"—he turned to face the camera—"good night, sweet comic prince. May flights of angels sing you to your rest. And to our own Billy Blessing, *bravo*, sir. Blessed are we to have you with us still."

Lolita was giving him the "hurry, hurry" arm windup.

"This is Marcus Oliphant, discussing last night's tragedy with one of its near victims, WBC's own Chef Billy Blessing. Stay tuned. There's much more to come on *The Midnight Show*."

# Chapter
# TWENTY-EIGHT

The hour ended not with a bang or even a whimper. More like a thud.

Specifically, it ended with Gibby's decision to replace the final joke he'd told at rehearsal with one about a guy whose golfing partner drops dead from a heart attack on the twelfth hole. You probably remember it. Back at the clubhouse, somebody asks him what happened after that. "Not much," he replies. "From there on in, it was pretty much the same. Hit the ball, drag Charlie. Hit the ball, drag Charlie." In itself, a good joke. Old but good. It would probably have prompted a wave of laughter at almost any time other than immediately following a discussion involving the death of the show's previous host.

Oblivious to his lapse in sensitivity, Gibby was thrown off cue by the lack of audience response. Still, he gamely waved the show's few lingering participants back onstage for a group good-bye. Then he performed what he hoped would become his under-the-credits signature, a standing backflip, ending with a semi-grotesque little-boy grin and a wiggling-fingers wave.

As soon as the camera's red light went off, he rushed to the wings. I had him pegged as the kind of despotic twit who'd start blaming everyone in sight for the shambles he himself had made of his first show. Instead, he brushed past us and went directly to his dressing room without a word.

Marcus Oliphant turned to me with a surprised look on his pancaked face. "Did you see that?"

I nodded.

What we had both seen was Gibby Lewis, not only looking like an unhappy baby but crying like one.

Twenty minutes later, he knocked once on my dressing room door, opened it, and came in. I was on the phone, talking with Detective Brueghel. I'd called to tell him about hearing a whirring sound just before the explosion, and he'd insisted we get together immediately. Since I had no more information, I was about to ask him why a face-to-face would be necessary. But Gibby picked that moment to barge in.

His eyes were red, his cherubic face blotchy. He was still wearing his on-camera suit, but he'd removed the tie and his shirt collar was unbuttoned. He flopped onto the only other chair in the small room and glared at me, nodding his head, tapping his foot, and showing just about every known sign of impatience.

I asked the detective where he wanted to meet, told him I'd get there as soon as I could, and clicked off the phone.

Gibby immediately lapsed into "Give it to me straight. Am I fucked?"

I stared at him, not quite sure what he was asking

or how I was supposed to answer. I decided to wait him out.

"I know the show was a monu-fucking-mental disaster," he said. "I mean, after tonight, forget *Cop Rock*. Forget the Iraq War even. Are they gonna can my ass, Billy?"

"What have you heard?" I asked.

"Max says it's not his call, that the decision will come from the East Coast. That's why I'm asking you."

"How many times do I have to tell you I'm not New York's rep out here? They've already got someone they rely on, a vice president with a nice, big office in the main building. Carmen Sandoval. You may have noticed how just the sound of her name causes Max to deflate."

"Aw, shit. Carmen is not a fan," he said gloomily. "Max had to do handsprings to get her to give me a shot. I really fucked the duck tonight. I just didn't . . . I couldn't get a fix on the studio audience. I couldn't get into the zone.

"No! You know what it was? I lost faith. That's it. I lost faith in the material and was trying to edit on the fly. That takes real cool and real smarts, and, let's face it, I'm not a guy gets too intellectual, you know?"

Why couldn't he have lived up to my expectations and been a blame-everybody-else weasel? Then I could have just given him the usual three-word suggestion of what he could do to himself and walked away. Instead, he was wallowing in self-pity and self-recrimination, which, while not exactly my favorite traits in an adult, tapped into one of my less protected pockets of sympathy.

"Gibby, at our lunch you mentioned Conan O'Brien. Like you, a comedy writer moving up to show host."

"So?"

"Remember what his first shows were like?"

He brightened a little. "Yeah. You're right. They were awful. Even as bad as ours, maybe."

"And he kept improving."

"Yeah. He improved so much, he wound up getting booted off *The Tonight Show*."

"But now he's thirty million dollars richer and he's got a show on TBS," I said. "People love CoCo."

"You're right, Billy," he said. He lowered his head in a gesture of faux humility. "Do you think you could mention the bit about me being the new Conan to your contact at the network?"

I sighed. "I'll add it to my morning report," I said, hoping it would satisfy him and get him to leave.

"You're a mensch, Billy," he said. "And your segment with the alter cocker? The only part of the show that didn't suck."

"Thanks, Gibby."

He stood and started for the door. Then he stopped and turned, looking as despondent as he had when he'd entered. "Shit, I was fucked from the git-go. If Carmen was expecting the show to be any good, she'd have had April go full-out on the publicity."

"What makes you think April didn't?"

"Did you see anybody shooting backstage promo footage for the website?"

"No."

"She had a guy doing it for Des's debut. I saw him. I realize Des had the big contract and I'm just trying to prove myself. But how much would it cost to have a publicity guy with a camera?"

"Ask April about it," I suggested. "Maybe somebody was there and you didn't notice."

"Yeah, I'll do that," he said. "Ah, well, fuck it. It's only a career."

When he left, the atmosphere in the room brightened considerably. I felt so relieved to be rid of him that I did not give his story about the backstage photographer a moment's thought.

My foolhardy lack of awareness didn't end there.

I completely overlooked the black BMW sedan that had to have been waiting for me as I exited the lot.

## Chapter
# TWENTY-NINE

It wasn't until I'd started on my way up Calvin Coolidge Drive that I noticed the car, and only then because ignoring it was impossible. It was the only other vehicle on the winding drive, and its headlights flashed in my rearview mirror at every twist and turn.

Even then I didn't suspect it was following me.

Brueghel's house was near the top of the drive. A work in progress. Just half of the front of the small cottage had been recently painted. The gate was new, but the wood was bare and, even in a city with mini-

mal rainfall, cried out for some kind of stain or var-
nish.

As I entered through the gate, the BMW drove
past, traveling neither fast nor slow. *Nice car,* I
thought. But I never quite understood why people
liked those dark tinted windows.

I turned and followed a short brick walkway to
the front door of the house, passing a paint can that
rested on a patch of scrub grass that constituted the
front lawn. The lid of the can was missing, and the
paint had solidified around a brush that Brueghel or
somebody had left in it. I wondered how long ago
he'd been called away from working on the house
and how long it would take him to get back to it.

In response to the buzzer, a light went on over the
front door and, after a second or two—the time it
would take to press an eye to a peephole—the detective was framed in the doorway, wearing a blue
warm-up outfit. He gave the surroundings a quick
scan, then invited me into a tiny entrance area that
smelled of turpentine, though I saw no evidence of it.

There were baseball caps, a hat, and several jack-
ets, of cloth and leather, hanging from pegs on a
wooden block bolted to the wall next to a closet
door. A handsome bleached-pine floor seemed to run
throughout the house.

"Have any trouble finding the place?" he asked,
leading me down a short hall to a living room that a
neatness freak would call messy but that struck me as
comfortable.

"Nope. My rental's GPS led me right here."

"Good. How about a beer after that drive?"

"Sure," I said, wondering, not for the first time, what I was doing there.

He disappeared for about as long as it took me to move a stack of paperback mysteries from a chair and sit down. He returned with a frosty bottle of Cerveza Pacifico in each hand.

"Maybe you'd prefer a glass?"

I told him I didn't, and accepted the offered bottle. He clinked his against mine, and we both drank. The icy beer was just a few degrees shy of a brain freeze and had a nice sharp edge.

"I'm out of limes," he said.

"You drag me all the way up here and you don't even have limes?" I said.

It took him a second or two to realize I was kidding.

"What can I say, Blessing? I'm not used to playing host."

"I'm surprised you suggested we meet here at your house," I said. "Don't you guys usually draw the line between your work and your home?"

"Ordinarily I'd have suggested a bar," he said. "But knowing how you hoard information, I don't see you blabbing my address to just anybody on the street. And the fact of the matter is it was too late for me to get a sitter for the kid."

Only then did I notice the little transformer toy resting on the floor near the dark TV set. "A boy?" I asked.

He nodded. "Just turned four. A real handful. In his bed, hopefully asleep."

"I didn't take you for a married man," I said.

"I'm not. Little Pete's mother and I never . . . well, she's out of the picture now."

He raised the beer bottle to his lips. I waited for him to either explain why she was out of the picture or to move on to another topic. When he remained silent, staring at the floor, I, used to filling in awkward silences while on camera, said, "A homicide detective raising a young boy. Can't be easy."

"No. I wouldn't call it easy. But it has its moments." He smiled. "And Pete's making a better man of me. At least this guy who's a pretty good observer of human nature thinks so."

"A fellow detective?"

"No. He writes books. Ever heard of a crime novel called *The Manicurist?*"

"Of course," I said. It had been a bestseller. The story of a tough L.A. homicide detective on the trail of a serial killer who murdered hookers and then painted their fingernails pale green. "Wait a minute. Don't tell me . . . ?"

His grin turned sheepish. "Yeah. He kinda based his fictional story on my investigation and capture of a whackjob the media named The Hairdresser. I don't know if there was much about that case on the East Coast, but out here it was a big deal. Anyway, he's writing a sequel. And since I've got Pete now, in the new book his detective is becoming a single father, too. He says it'll make the character more unique and more human."

"So your son living here is a recent development?"

"A few months," he said. "But I didn't ask you up here to talk about me."

He took a slow sip of beer.

"If it's about the whirring sound I heard before the explosion," I said, "I don't know what else I can tell you."

"That was helpful info, and I'll pass it along to the techs who are trying to identify the device and its triggering mechanism. But that's not why I asked you here, either. Something's come up I didn't want to get into on the phone."

"Yeah?"

He stared at me for a beat, as if he were contemplating several approaches to the something that had come up. He settled on: "Charbonnet wants a sit-down with you."

I think I showed great restraint by not doing a classic spit take. Instead, I asked, "Why?"

"His attorney, Malcolm Darrow, who's pretty damn sharp, by the way, said he didn't know why. He was just passing along his client's request."

I placed the beer bottle on the floor and stood up. "Tell Mr. Darrow I'm sorry, but I've had more than enough meetings with his client."

"Sit down, Blessing. Finish your beer and hear me out. Please."

Reluctantly, I sat down. I said, "It's not hard to figure out why you'd want me to meet with Roger. You're hoping he'll blow up and do something stupid, like cave in my head with a chair."

"Maybe not that, exactly," he said. "There's no chance of him harming you. In fact, I can't see a downside to your meeting with him. But it could result in him spilling something that will help our case."

"Don't you have enough evidence now to put him away?" I asked.

"You never have enough," he said. "The ghost of the O.J. trial will be haunting us for a long time."

"This won't be anything like the O.J. trial," I said.

"Oh, really? Let me bring you up-to-date. The lovely Miss Zeena Zataran has now definitely remembered, without a doubt, that she'd made a date with Charbonnet that night for eight o'clock and failed to notify him about her conflicting vodka party commitment. So he'll say he was expecting her. Ergo, the 'I was at home' alibi is looking better.

"And she's positive he called her from his home at nine-thirty. She even recalls a chime going off from the clock in his living room."

"What about all the junk you recovered from his place?"

"That's the O.J. touch," Brueghel said. "There's a rumor going around that one of the investigating officers may have had a hidden agenda that drove him to plant that 'evidence.' "

I leaned back in the chair. "The officer being you," I said. "And the hidden agenda being your previous failure to nail Roger with the death of Tiffany Arden."

"You got it. Before little Pete became a part of my life, this kind of crap would have driven me nuts. Now I just look for other ways of getting the job done. Will you talk to him, Blessing?"

"Let me sleep on it," I said.


If the BMW followed me out to Malibu, I didn't notice it.

*Chapter*
# THIRTY

I woke shortly before ten a.m. the next morning. The villa had seemed sinister and intimidating the previous night, but now, under a blue, cloudless sky with a balmy breeze wafting from the ocean, all was right with the world.

Except for the messages that had been collecting in my voice mailbox.

The first call I'd ignored when I turned off my phone last evening was from the defense attorney Brueghel had mentioned, Malcolm Darrow. His voice was confident, no-nonsense. A deep-timbre voice worthy of another, more famous Darrow, named Clarence. I wondered if the name had influenced his choice of profession or if the profession had influenced his choice of name. In either case, he'd left his number at five-fifty-seven p.m.

Two hours later, at roughly eleven p.m. Manhattan time, Cassandra had provided a report on the status quo of the Bistro that, minus the snark, seemed satisfactory, especially since she'd not requested a return call.

Stew's daughter, Dani, had left a voice mail at ten-oh-five p.m., requesting a callback.

Malcolm Darrow had left his second message a couple of hours before I awoke.

Shortly thereafter, Amelia St. Laurent had left word that she would be showing the estate today. She said she'd canceled yesterday's tours "out of respect for Mr. O'Day's untimely passing." To alter the late comedian Fred Allen's line: You can fit all the integrity in Hollywood into a gnat's navel and still have room for a kumquat and a real estate agent's heart.

At precisely nine, Whisper had called to remind me that rehearsal for tonight's show would be at two p.m. She'd added, with a hint of wonder, that the overnight ratings had been good enough, especially in the key eighteen-to-forty-five-year-old demographic, for Gibby to remain on as host for this week and possibly even the next. She suggested I ignore some of the hypercritical comments on the Internet.

No problem there.

I had no intention of phoning the lawyer and, though mildly curious about why Dani had called, felt I could let that slide for a while. The fact is, suddenly I was feeling glum, and I knew why. Though I hadn't really expected Vida to call, the fact that she hadn't dimmed the day a little.

Well, as we all know, there's nothing like a big breakfast to lift one's spirits.

Thanks to a trip to the nearby supermarket, that dream was to be fulfilled. I brewed an extra-strong pot of French roast coffee, toasted four pieces of sourdough bread, which I buttered while still hot, and fried a rasher of bacon, resting the resulting strips on a paper towel to dry and crisp. I then performed a bit of stovetop magic with four eggs (but using only two of the yolks: See, I can be healthy), several hunks of jack cheese, and minced mushroom. Veggies, healthier, still.

I loaded a tray with the finished omelet, the sides, and a jar of homemade raspberry preserves, and carried it out to a table on the deck. There I sat, facing the Pacific, allowing myself to be mesmerized by the gentle surf while enjoying the fruits of my stovetop labor.

I was having a third cup of coffee, amusing myself with the fantasy of the liquid somehow dissolving the breakfast cholesterol and calories, when my eyes were drawn to a familiar tall feminine figure in a familiar white bikini, running full-out along the waterline in my direction.

When she saw me, Dani Kirkendahl made a right-angle turn and, slowing to a jog, crossed the sand toward the deck. She'd been running long enough for her skin to be glistening, but she wasn't even breathing hard. "Billy," she said, as I rose to greet her, "I didn't think you were . . . I called you last night."

"Can I get you some coffee?" I asked, as she took a chair. "Or water?"

"No. I'm fine."

"I apologize for not getting back to you. I slept in this morning, and—"

"It's okay," she said. "I understand. I know you must be . . . I mean, after that horrible night. I hate to bother you, but it's important."

"Is it about your dad?" I asked.

"Dad? No. He's . . . fine. It's about Roger."

I suppose my face must've reflected my thoughts.

"Oh. I don't blame you," she said. "I mean, he

certainly has . . . anger issues. And he's told me you guys have a long history."

"Did he mention any details about that history?"

She hesitated, then broke eye contact, looking off down the beach. "Some." She turned back to me. "I'll say to you what I said to him. Whatever happened is between the two of you. Leave me out of it."

"So you guys are still an item?"

"An item? You mean like boyfriend-girlfriend? Eeewwww. Billy, the man's ancient. He's Dad's age. Well, maybe a few years younger, but still . . ."

"I'm sorry," I said. "I just assumed . . . Well, what *is* your relationship?"

"We're friends. Platonic friends. There are such things, you know."

"Really? And what are your thoughts on unicorns? Or Bigfoot? Or, God help me, vampires?"

"You're being cynical."

"It's not cynicism," I said. "I'm sure *you* think your relationship is platonic. But what about Roger?"

"He feels the same. Women know when a man is coming on to them." She smiled and added, "When you and I first met and you helped me to my towel, you were sending out a vibe. But it went away when Daddy appeared. Right?"

An interesting question.

I've never put much faith in platonic relationships, probably because I am convinced that, barring conditions such as premature sainthood, narcolepsy, or debilitation, anyone is capable of being seduced by anyone they perceive as sexually alluring. When I first laid eyes on Dani, I was wide open to that possibility. Did that change when I learned she was Stew's twenty-two-year-old daughter? Looking at her now, sitting across from me in her white bikini, I doubted it. I have to admit, though not with pride, I was even considering the possibility that she was fishing to find out if I *was* interested.

She was, therefore, mistaking the myth of platonic relationship for the reality of a little thing called self-control. If she hadn't discovered the difference by now, I was not about to bring it to her attention, by word or deed. Instead, I made a lateral shift in the conversation.

"I don't suppose you came over here to discuss platonic relationships," I said. "What's up?"

"Roger wants you to meet with him."

"Old news," I said.

"Oh. His lawyer talked to you?"

"No, but not for lack of trying. Did Roger happen to mention why he wants a sit-down with me, of all people?"

"They haven't let me talk to him. It was the lawyer who asked me to ask you. He said Roger needs your help."

"Then we must be talking about some other Roger. The actor Roger Moore, maybe. Or Roger Rabbit. Some Roger I'd actually want to help."

"Don't be that way, Billy. He's my friend. And he's not a murderer."

"Not a murderer. Got it."

"Please talk to him," she said.

"Why? How could I help him, even if I were so inclined?"

She shrugged. "All I know is he believes you can."

"How long have you known him?"

"He says we met a long time ago, when I was just a kid, having brunch with my parents in one of his restaurants. I don't remember that. The first time I can recall was at Santa Anita maybe two years ago. I was with Wilt, my ex, and Mom and her boyfriend of the moment. Roger stopped at our box to say hello to Mom. He was very charming. He gave us a tip on a race that actually paid off. I didn't see him again until just after my divorce."

"That was this year?"

"About six months ago. I was really down, and Mom took me out on a shopping binge. We had lunch at Bagatelle, Roger's place off Rodeo Drive. He joined us for dessert, and when Mom got one of her right-now-or-never calls from a prospect, he offered to drive me back here. Since then, we've spent a little time together."

"But you've really only known him for six months," I said.

"We talk, Billy," she said. "I know more about him than I know about Dad. You asked how much he's told me about his history with you. I know about the murder at Chez Anisette and that you think he killed that woman. He said he didn't, and I believe him."

"That's the thing about sociopaths. They may be crazier than hell, but they can still be believable."

"Roger's not crazy," she said.

"Okay, let's assume for the moment that he didn't kill Tiffany Arden. Or set off an explosion that took the life of Des O'Day. How sane can he be if he'll break into somebody's house to cook a rat in their oven?"

She blinked. "R-roger did that? Well, he . . . probably meant it as a joke. You guys were still in your twenties . . ."

"This happened just days ago, right after he attacked me at your dad's party."

"Here?" she asked, looking at the villa.

I nodded.

"Well . . . just because you found a . . . This property had been vacant for a while, and the whole area is a haven for rats. Even the Colony. We have to set traps all the time. One may have crawled into the house and—"

"And hopped into a pan, surrounded itself with carrots and potatoes, turned on the oven, and cooked itself? With a cherry tomato in its mouth?"

"What makes you think Roger did it?"

"Who else? And he happened to be here at Malibu Sands at the time. Visiting you. He could have done it before or after the visit."

She looked disheartened. "It still sounds like a joke," she said. "And it doesn't mean he killed anybody. In fact, it might mean just the opposite." The thought excited her. "He knew how easy it was to break into your house. If he'd wanted to kill you, he could have put his dumb bomb right here under your bed. Why would he have gone to all the effort of sneaking into a studio full of people?"

"That would be a valid question," I said, "if Roger were rational."

"You're the one being irrational."

I really wasn't up to reminding her about the damning evidence that the police had found at Roger's. I stood up and began placing my breakfast dishes onto the tray. "The day is slipping away," I said. "And there are things I have to do."

"I guess meeting with Roger won't be one of them."

"I didn't say that," I told her. I might have, if it hadn't been for that damn white bikini she was wearing.

<br>

*Chapter*
# THIRTY-ONE

Brueghel's pitch the night before, about the evidence losing its luster, had spooked me. Of late, the odds were at least two to one against an L.A. jury convicting a celebrity murderer suspect. If my sitting down with Roger could in some way help to balance those judicial scales, how could I refuse? And let's face it, I was more than a little curious about what he could possibly have to say to me.

As soon as I'd sent Dani on her way, I called the detective and asked him to start the ball rolling. I explained that I'd be tied up after two p.m. that day but would be free the following morning.

Less than an hour later, while I was amusing myself watching Amelia St. Laurent lead a straw-thin, shaggy-bearded fiftysomething member of British rock royalty and his actress wife around the property, Brueghel called back. Could I make it to Men's Central Jail on Bauchet Street in downtown L.A. in forty-five minutes?

"You tell me," I said. "I'm out at Malibu."

"Drive fast," he said.

The MCJ, maintained by the L.A. County Sheriff's Department, is said to be the world's largest jail. For one or two very personal reasons, even the world's smallest jail would be near the top of my avoid-at-all-cost list. So it was not with eager anticipation that I deposited the Lexus in a public lot on the corner of Vignes and Bauchet and walked toward the lobby of the twin towers.

Brueghel was waiting just past the door with a man whom he introduced as Malcolm Darrow. Though I had mused on the lawyer's surname, I was not expecting him to look quite so similar to the legendary Clarence. He couldn't have been more than forty, but the image he conveyed was of an older man. His three-piece suit, though no doubt expensive, might as well have been off-the-rack department-store material, the way it was wrapped around his ample frame. He wore a vest pocket chain, the likes of which I'd seen only in black-and-white movies, and a starched collar/narrow bow tie combo that went back even further in history.

His receding hair had strands of both white and black, and a hank of it flopped down on his very high forehead in a manner that resembled Clarence's. And come to think of it, Oliver Hardy's. His shiny pink face was strengthened by high cheekbones and a slightly jutting jaw. Thin brows, arched in arrow points, gave him an air of permanent awareness. His eyes were as pale blue as a frozen pond. And my guess, about as deceptively treacherous.

"A pleasure, Mr. Blessing," he said, staring at me unblinkingly, as if I were a beetle on a pin. He shifted a battered cordovan leather briefcase from his right hand to his left so we could shake. "Good of you to come."

That point was debatable.

"We'd better get to it," I said. "I have to leave in about an hour."

"Then I'll be heading back to the office," Brueghel said.

"You're not joining us?" I asked.

The detective glanced briefly at Darrow. "Wouldn't want to intrude," he said. He nodded to us both and walked away.

The lawyer's pale eyes followed him to and through the exit, then turned my way. "Shall we?" he said.

There were three chairs and a table in the meeting room, all industrial gray metal. The single door was metal, too, painted a pale green like the walls. An old-fashioned buzzer was attached to the door frame at chest level. Except for the door, the walls were solid and went straight to the white ceiling without benefit of decorative molding. There was no two-way mirror behind which bored cops might observe our conversation.

In this age of technological miracles, I suppose there may have been a hidden camera or microphone. But I couldn't see any, and Darrow struck me as the sort of barrister who'd bring the house down if such a device were discovered.

He sat next to me, placed his briefcase on the floor between us, and frowned at the empty chair across the table.

"How far away is his cell?" I asked.

"Not that far. Roger is in a private custody unit, designed to keep high-profile prisoners away from the unnecessarily inhumane, toxic atmosphere of the general prison population."

"That toxic stuff sounds like something your great-uncle Clarence might have said."

He smiled. "He and I are related only by political and philosophic bent. I share his belief that people are not in prisons because they deserve to be. They, like the five thousand poor souls in this facility, are behind bars because of circumstances beyond their control. An accident of birth. A mental aberration."

"Would Roger Charbonnet be an example of the latter?"

He gave me full benefit of those arched brows and icy blues. "Roger Charbonnet is an innocent man."

"The police have turned up a lot of evidence to the contrary."

"As the greater Darrow once noted, 'The police are the real criminals.'"

So Brueghel had been right about a planted-evidence defense. Considering the amount of it, that was probably the only way for the lawyer to go. Still, even though the average citizen's paranoid distrust of authority seemed to be on an alarming upswing, judging by the vitriol permeating the Internet, playing to that struck me as not only desperate but disruptive. I didn't like it. And I wasn't all that crazy about Malcolm Darrow.

I watched him tug a round gold watch from his vest pocket, glance at it, and tuck it back in place.

"I understand your being simpatico with Clarence Darrow," I said to him. "But isn't the suit, the vest, the pocket biscuit, and the hairstyle carrying that a little far?"

That earned me a shark's grin. A lawyer's grin. "When you appear on your cooking show, Mr. Blessing, or on the cover of your cookbooks, do you not wear a chef's white jacket and toque?"

"Jacket, yes. Toque, never."

"The jacket gives you the instant recognition of being a professional, an expert. You dress the part you play in life. In the dim, dark days when I was a very young lawyer competing against graduates from schools more prestigious than mine, I decided to take full advantage of my surname. Let them wear their Ivy League suits like a banner. I dressed the part of a Darrow. My suits and bow ties and pocket watch were and are instruments of what they now call 'product branding.' But I'm curious, Mr. Blessing, as to why you seem so averse to wearing a toque."

There was no harm in telling him the truth, that I thought it made me look too much like the guy on the Cream of Wheat box. I was about to do so when the door opened and a guard entered with Roger Charbonnet.

The room was small, and the looming six-foot-three presence of Roger in a bright orange jumpsuit seemed to bring the walls and ceiling closer in. His brief jail time had changed him. Hands cuffed in metal, he had a wild and dangerous look about him, enhanced by a drastic case of bed head and eyes red-rimmed and frantic enough to belong on Dracula's dog. His stubble had grown past the fashion-statement length.

And unlike my über-chef buddy Mario Batali, orange just wasn't his color.

He glared at the guard, then at his lawyer, and finally at me. He nodded his head. "I knew you couldn't stay away."

The guard dragged the empty metal chair out from the table, scraping its legs against the floor tiles. He used a key to unlock Roger's left wrist, then, when Roger sat and dutifully moved both arms behind the chair, ran the empty cuff and chain through the metal spindles and reattached it to his right wrist.

Satisfied that his charge was pretty well chairbound, the guard stepped back.

Roger continued to stare at me, nodding. I wondered if I was being set up as a witness for an insanity plea.

Darrow thanked the guard in a manner that was also a dismissal.

The guard didn't move.

"We can handle it from here," Darrow said.

The guard raised an eyebrow, as if in disagreement. He and the lawyer had a brief, rather low-key, face-off, at the end of which he said, "I'll be right outside. Hit the buzzer when you're through." He glanced at Roger. "Or if you need me."

When the three of us were alone, Darrow asked Roger if he was being treated well.

Keeping his eyes on me, Roger replied, "I haven't slept since I got in here."

"I'll get them to give you something to help with that," the lawyer said.

"Blessing's going to be all the help I need. Right, Blessing?"

I looked at Darrow.

He said to his client, "We'd better get down to business, Roger. Mr. Blessing only has a few minutes."

"Right. Right, right," Charbonnet said. "Busy man. Down to business." He flared his nostrils and took on that bull-like presence he'd shown me at Stew's. I supposed that Roger could stand with the chair and charge at me, for whatever that would get him. In any case, I slid my chair back a few inches and began to speculate on how fast the guard would respond to that buzzer.

"The bottom line, Blessing, is that I had nothing to do with that fucking bomb, and I don't know how all that crap got on my property. I mean, obviously it was put there to frame me. The only person I can think of who hates me that much is that whacked cop. Not even you hate me that much."

"I don't hate you," I said.

"Roger, perhaps we should—"

"I'm getting down to business, like you said. Okay?" He leaned forward as far as he could with his wrists secured behind him. When that proved too uncomfortable, he slumped back and said, "For the last twenty four hours I've been thinking about this. And it doesn't scan. There's something I'm missing. Like I say, the cop hates me. But how the hell could he have collected all that stuff, the dynamite and whatever, and then put it in the shed so fast?"

204

Darrow leapt to his feet. "That's enough," he said firmly. "This is not a topic for discussion."

Roger gave him a quizzical look. "Whose meeting is this?"

"Yours, but—"

"Mine. I know what I'm doing, Malcolm. Just chill."

The lawyer sat down again, slowly.

"Let's see now. Where was I? Brueghel getting the explosive stuff to plant. Let's say he went out to buy it. A lot of people know him by sight. He's supercop, for Christ's sake, the detective who caught The Hairdresser. When that writer, whatever the fuck his name is, came out with his book, he and Brueghel were on TV every time I turned it on. If somebody sold him the dynamite, they're gonna remember."

"Roger, I have to insist—"

Charbonnet ignored him. "So assuming he was the one who planted the evidence, it seems to follow that he didn't just go out and buy it the day before it turned up in my shed. You with me, Blessing? Brueghel had the bomb ingredients at hand. Which would also mean that he's got to be the one who made the bomb and blew up the studio."

Okay, so Roger was now officially running for mayor of Crazy Town.

"We should end this," Darrow said. "Roger, you're not yourself . . ."

"You don't stop interrupting, Malcolm, I'm gonna get my good friend Elmer the guard to kick your uptight ass out of here," Roger said. He hit me again with those bloodred eyes. "Well? What do you think?

Did the asshole detective want to put me away so bad
he tried killing you to do it?"

What did I think?

There seemed to be two possibilities. Roger had
won the mayor's race by a landslide. Or, as I suspected, he was faking it.

In either case, he'd made a serious mistake, as his
lawyer had correctly realized. I'd be taking at least
one useful bit of info away from the meeting. Even
while feigning the loonies, Roger had admitted that
the detective's fame would have made it impossible
for him to purchase the evidence to plant without
being noticed.

"Well, Blessing, would he have hated me that
much?" Roger stared at me expectantly.

"No," I said. "I don't believe Brueghel would try
to blow me up just to have an excuse to put you in
prison."

He nodded again. "It's a stretch, I admit," he said.
"But who else would want to frame me? This guy's
been on my ass for twenty-two years. Nothing proac-
tive. Nothing to merit a harassment complaint. But
he keeps popping up in my peripheral vision. Having
lunch in one of my restaurants. Or parked down the
street near my house. The movie ends and the lights
go on, there he is sitting five or six rows away. I'm at
my tailor's, standing on the box, and I see him in the
mirror, looking at swatches. That goes beyond dedi-
cation. That's insanity. Or am I wrong?"

"It's pretty weird," I had to admit. "But not in-
sane. And insanity is what it would take to commit a
murder just so you could arrest a murderer."

"So lemme get this straight," Roger said. "Victor

lies about my alibi, so I'm a murderer. Brueghel spends the last twenty-two years stalking me, but he's sane. You've got a weird fucking logic working for you, Blessing."

I looked at my watch. It was nearing one-thirty. Almost time for me to leave, thank God.

Darrow had been paying attention. "We're running out of time, Roger. Could we move on from Detective Brueghel to the original point of the meeting? The one you and I discussed?"

Charbonnet glared at his attorney, then turned to me with a look that was almost plaintive. "What he's talking about is . . . The only reason I'm being accused of killing a guy I never met is because a woman I loved got murdered twenty-three years ago. You understand what I'm saying?"

"Not really."

"Okay. Let me put it this way. I didn't kill Tiffany. And if I didn't kill her, then I sure as hell didn't set off any bomb to try and kill you."

"Roger, I don't understand what you want from me. I'm not going to be on your jury."

He looked at Darrow.

"What Roger is having a hard time saying," the attorney told me, "is that he needs your help."

"My help with what?"

"Proving his innocence."

I wondered again if there wasn't a camera hidden somewhere in the room. That ubiquitous entrepreneur Ashton Kutcher had to be lurking somewhere nearby, ready to punk me.

"Why would I want to do that?" I asked Darrow. Roger spoke before the lawyer had a chance.

"Let me ask you something, Blessing. Man to man. Back in the day, what was your deal with Tiffany? Were you giving her a little poke every now and then?"

I stared at him, changing my opinion. Maybe he wasn't faking craziness after all.

"Naw," he answered his own question. "Nothing like that. I doubt you even liked her. I cried at her funeral. What about you? Did you even go to the funeral?"

"I went."

"Well, good. Good for you. But the fact of it is she was just a broad you worked with who had the bad luck to get in the way of a meat tenderizer somebody was swinging. Right?"

"What's your point?" I said.

"Back then, you must've realized that by putting the cops on Victor and me you'd blow your job at the restaurant and maybe end your career before it even started. All for a dead woman you barely knew. Why would you do that?"

"I worked with her for nearly a year," I said. "For part of that time, she was living with a good friend of mine. But I didn't go to the police because of her. I'd have done the same thing if the victim had been a complete stranger."

"Exactly," Roger said, leaning forward on the table eagerly. "That's why I wanted you here, Blessing. You're the only guy I trust to do the right thing. The only guy I trust with my life."

Kutcher had to be nearby.

"Don't get me wrong," Roger continued. "I hate your ass. You set that cop on me, and I'll never forgive you for that. But I know why you did it. You thought it was the right thing. You truly believed I killed Tiffany."

"I still do."

He surprised me by calmly asking, "Why?"

"You know as well as I. Because Victor Anisette lied about you being with him the night of the murder."

"Okay," he said. "I'll give you that. Victor lied like a rug."

"Roger, for God's sake . . ." Darrow cautioned.

"Relax, lawyer, we're just guys talking." Roger refocused on me. "So Victor lied. What else have you got? Witnesses? Evidence? Even material that couldn't be used in court? Anything?"

I was a little shocked to realize I had nothing else. "If you were . . . if you are innocent," I said, "why did Victor think he had to provide you with an alibi?"

"Because I asked him to," Roger said.

"Why?"

He cocked his head to one side and grinned at me. "Suppose I not only answer that question to your satisfaction but also prove I couldn't possibly have killed Tiffany. Then will you help me get out of this stinking shithole?"

# *Chapter*
# THIRTY-TWO

I leaned back in my chair and stared at Roger. He did not wither under my glance. In fact, he seemed as bemused as a man can be with his arms chained behind a chair.

"I'd be more inclined to believe whatever you're about to tell me," I said, "if you hadn't threatened me with a gun back in the good old days."

"What can I say? I was an asshole."

" 'Was'? Just last week, you tried to deck me while my back was turned."

"I was angry and a little drunk. I thought you were telling Stew that same old bullshit about me murdering Tiffany."

"I wasn't."

He shrugged. "So I'm still an asshole. That doesn't carry a prison sentence."

"In your case, maybe it should."

"You know, Blessing, if you're wrong about me, there's a dynamiter walking free out there who wants you dead."

Was he being purposefully disingenuous by continuing to mention dynamite, or was he actually ignorant of the composition of a bleach bomb?

"My guess is, the dynamiter is precisely where I want him," I said.

"Come onnn. Do I strike you as the kind of guy who'd build a bomb?"

"I don't know that much about you, Roger."

"You're not thinking straight," he said. "A: If I'd wanted you dead, why in God's name would I think of dynamite when there are so many simpler and less-dangerous-to-handle weapons? And B: If it had to be dynamite, why would I risk blowing myself up when I could hire an expert?"

I'd been trying to keep a straight face, but some uncertainty must have slipped past my filter.

Encouraged, Roger unloaded one more argument. "Assuming I thought so little of my own safety, would I have kept all that crap in my shed for the cops to find? Especially after Brueghel's visit the night of the crime?"

"Okay," I said, with the weariness of a man beaten down by what had at least the appearance of logic. "Tell me why you couldn't have killed Tiffany."

He took a second or two to shift his concentration to the earlier crime, then replied, "I have a real alibi I've never been able to use."

Apparently convinced he'd hooked me, he leaned back in his chair and waited for me to ask what that real alibi was. I hadn't seen a smile that smug since Bruce Willis won his first Emmy. I'm not a big fan of smug. I looked at my watch, yawned, and said, "It's a little late, folks." I turned to Darrow. "Will you buzz for the guard, or should I?"

"Okay, Blessing," Roger said. "I was at Palm Springs when Tiff . . . when she was killed."

I frowned. "That's your alibi? I was at the restaurant that night, remember? When I left at about eleven, you were still there with Tiffany and Victor."

"Yeah," he said, "but just after you guys took off, Tiff started getting on my ass. Finally, she told me to go fuck myself. That didn't sound like much fun, so I decided to fuck somebody else."

"Palm Springs is a long way to go for a booty call," I said.

"You go where the action is."

"It's what, a two-and-a-half-hour drive?"

"Maybe the way you do it. In that beautiful little Vette I had, at that time of night, I made it in just under two hours. We hit the sheets right away and kept it going all night long."

"Too bad there wasn't an Olympic category," I said. "So let me guess why you couldn't use this marathon boink for an alibi. The guy didn't want it known you were his gay lover."

"Fuck you, Blessing. It was a woman I was with. But before I say any more, you've got to promise me something."

I stared at him. "What?"

"That you won't mention anything about her to the crazy cop," he said. "Even if I wasn't fond of her, I wouldn't want that asshole to mess up her life."

I thought about it. "What good is the alibi going to do you if nobody in authority knows about it?"

"You'll know about it. That's what I'm going for here. Promise me you'll keep her identity a secret."

I shrugged. "If that's the way you want it . . ."

"And it's a little late to be asking, but I'd appreciate it if you also didn't tell Brueghel what I said about

Victor lying. The old man had a stroke a couple years ago, and he's still in pretty bad shape. But that hasn't stopped the fucking cop from dropping in on him every now and then to give him a hard time. Brueghel may have even caused the stroke."

"I don't see what the point of this meeting is, if I have to censor everything that has to do with establishing your innocence," I said.

"Humor me, please?"

"It's your freedom," I said. "So what's the story on your booty call that I'll be keeping a secret?"

"Like I said, she's a good woman. Back in those days, she was quite a beauty. She'd made that New York supermodel–to–Hollywood starlet move. When that didn't work, she got married, and that did work, for a while, anyway. I picked her up one night in Dan Tana's. She was at the bar, crying into her martini. Over a couple of Tana's red-sauce specials, she told me she and her old man were having problems. He was gone a lot, leaving her alone with too much time on her hands. She wanted to work. He wanted her to be a housewife. Ordinarily, I stay clear of married broads, but Glory's special. And twenty years ago, well, any guy would have found her irresistible."

"What about Tiffany?" I asked.

"Well, that was the thing," he said. "Glory and I weren't in love. In lust, maybe. We didn't get together all that often, maybe four or five times total. She had a husband, and I had Tiffany. The night I drove to the Springs was the first time I'd seen her in months. Her marriage was headed for the rocks, but she still had some hope for it."

"So rather than destroy what sounds like the ideal

American marriage, you got Victor to lie," I said. "You're a regular Sir Galahad, the white knight of sleazy affairs. Can I go now?"

"You don't believe me?"

"It's not much of a story, Roger."

"I got there at around one-thirty and stayed the whole night. Even if the murder took place at one, no way could I have made it to the Springs before two thirty, even by plane. Talk to her. Talk to Glory. She's been divorced for a long time. She'll tell you the truth."

"How would I know the truth from a lie? I don't suppose you have a canceled charge receipt from Palm Springs? Or anything like that?"

"Just Glory," he said. "Talk to her."

The lawyer snapped open his briefcase and withdrew a sheet of paper that he handed to me. It had a neatly printed name, cellular phone number, a phone number at the Bank of California with extension, home, and email addresses.

"Gloria Ingram," I read.

"You say that like you don't know the name."

"Should I?"

He stared at me for a beat, then said, "Guess not. L.A. always seems like a small town to me. Everybody knows everybody."

"I'm just a visitor, myself."

"Yeah, well, anyway, she's expecting you to call."

"And then what?" I said. "Suppose I wind up believing her, and you? How does that help you?"

"I trust you to do the right thing," he said. He turned to his lawyer and gestured with his head toward the door.

"What right thing?" I asked.

Malcolm Darrow stood and headed for the buzzer. Watching him press it, Roger said, "Once you're convinced that I'm no killer, I know you'll do everything in your power to see justice done."

The door opened, and the guard checked the room before entering. He marched to Roger, freed him from the chair, and recuffed him.

"Do the right thing," Roger said, as the guard led him away.

He seemed sincere, but as I joined the lawyer at the door, I asked, "Was that some kind of racist razz, him repeating that Spike Lee movie title?"

"Oh, I think not," he said. "Although with Roger one can never be quite certain."

## *Chapter*
# THIRTY-THREE

On my way from the lockup, I finally became aware of the black BMW. It was resting in a no-parking zone, engine running. The windows were too dark to see anything except vague outlines of a driver. His window had been lowered an inch or so to allow his secondhand smoke to add to his exhaust's pollution of the atmosphere.

He was a few cars back in the gathering traffic as I headed away from downtown L.A. toward the

WBCW lot. But somewhere along Third Street, the BMW disappeared. And by the time I passed through the network's east gate, I'd convinced myself that I'd let my imagination get the upper hand.

I discovered an empty parking space and powered off the car at precisely two p.m., the time scheduled for the run-through and camera blocking for that night's show. But those things rarely began on the dot, so I figured I'd have time to dial Brueghel and fill him in on the twin towers meeting.

As I'd promised Roger, I omitted the subject of the infamous twenty-three-year-old alibi. I also made no mention of his appraisal of the detective's mental state and the theory that insanity had probably induced Brueghel to turn bomber.

The detective remained quiet until I'd stopped talking, then said, "You sound like you're wavering, Blessing."

"Say again?"

"I get the impression you're starting to believe Charbonnet's bullshit. Did that insidious bastard turn you?"

The question stung, mainly because I *was* starting to doubt Roger's guilt. "I'm trying to keep an open mind," I said, too defensively. "I don't know why he'd have left all that evidence on his property, especially after he knew you suspected him."

"These guys like to flaunt it. Sometimes they actually want you to catch them. You honestly think there could have been somebody else who planted that crap to frame him?"

"It does sound far-fetched," I said.

" 'Far-fetched'? It's pure fucking fantasy. That

would mean some unknown party, who has it in for you, also knows enough about Charbonnet—mainly, that he's capable of murder—to pick him for the frame. Is that in any way possible?"

"You tell me. You're the cop. But he and I did have a well-publicized scuffle last week."

"You embarrassed him at a party," Brueghel said. "If that were motive for murder, this city would look like Tombstone. This fictitious mystery bomber would have had to know that Charbonnet killed his girl-friend twenty-three years ago to make him worth framing. And that he hated you for trying to bust his alibi. So we're talking about somebody who was around then. Maybe even involved. Can you think of anybody like that?"

I could. But it wouldn't have been very diplomatic to remind him that he filled that bill. Instead, I asked, "What about Victor Anisette?"

"Anisette? That old bastard and Charbonnet are partners in the restaurants and they're thick as thieves. It's a father-and-son deal. Anyhow, I can assure you that Anisette didn't set off any bomb. He suffered a massive stroke. Can't even go to the toilet on his own.

"Anyhow, I don't have time for this kind of mental masturbation. Stay strong, Blessing. Charbonnet's the guy, and he's where he should be. Now, if they can only find a jury that doesn't have its head up its ass, maybe we'll see justice done."

We ended our pleasant little chat on that note of hope. And I jogged off to Stage 7, where I found the usual suspects seated at the round table—Gibby; Max and his assistant, Trey; Whisper, with her Sony cam-corder; Fitz, a little less hungover than the previous day; Tessa, our director, bigger than life; Lolita, her head still bandaged and unbowed; April; and the show's new head writer, whose name I'd discovered was Howard Seymour.

They were all gawking at me. And I noticed an unfamiliar face turned my way. It belonged to a dour, bald-headed man, probably in his sixties, with skin the color of dust.

"We've been waiting for you, Blessing," Gibby said. "Why ya late? McDonald's run out of burgers?"

He was evidently expecting this witty comment to be rewarded with gales of laughter. But he was the only one laughing. He faced his coworkers. "It's the old fake excuse," he tried to explain. "You know. 'I'm late getting back from lunch because they ran out of burgers at McDonald's and I had to go somewhere else.'"

When there was still no reaction, he continued, desperate now, "Don't you get it? They never run out of burgers at McDonald's, which is why it's such a dumb, obviously bogus, excuse. That's what makes it funny."

Ignoring Gibby, Max asked, "Why *are* you late, Billy?"

Squeezing a chair between Lolita and Fitz, I said, "They ran out of burgers at Jack in the Box."

This time there was laughter. But not from Gibby, who whined, "Why the hell is that funny? Jack in the Box? That's funnier than McDonald's?"

"Shut up, Gibby," Max said. "Billy. These rehearsals are crucial to the success of the show."

"I'm sorry, Max," I said. "Won't happen again."

"Now I'll have to repeat what I already informed

the others. Your participation in the show is changing. Explain it to him, Trey."

The assistant producer turned his pasty face toward me. "Last night, Billy, your Q-and-A with Marcus Oliphant was very popular. The usual ratings pattern for late-night shows finds viewership dwindling in proportion to the lateness of the hour. This is the result of older viewers, the less-important over-forty-nines, opting for sleep. But there is some fallout for the eighteen-to-forty-nine demographic, too."

Gibby was leaning back in his chair with his eyes closed. Fitz was slumped forward, staring at his overhanging stomach. The rest of the table seemed to be equally disinterested in Trey's information. Maybe because it was the second time they'd heard it.

Or maybe it was just Trey's monotone delivery.

"Our show kicked off with an eighteen-to-forty-nine average of one-point-three-five million," he was saying. "This is superb, considering the overall decline in commercial TV viewership, the number of talk shows at that hour, and the fact that most of them began twenty-five minutes before ours. Part of our success can be attributed to curiosity, people wondering what we were going to do, post-tragedy. This was especially notable in those time zones where *Midnight* is broadcast live."

This was like the song by Kesha, "Blah, Blah, Blah."

Beside me, Fitz mumbled something to himself and shifted on his chair.

"But here's the odd thing, Billy," Trey continued, undaunted. "Your Q-and-A aired at approximately twelve-forty a.m. Instead of falling off by that late hour, the ratings peaked at one-point-three-eight mil for eighteen-to-forty-nine viewers, and one-point-six-one mil for the twenty-five-to-fifty-four seg. Some of that can be the result of mainly positive Internet chatter that began after the show aired in earlier time zones and its effect on West Coast viewers. Even so, it's safe to say that viewers are tuning in to *Midnight* primarily to hear news about the tragedy from the horse's mouth, so to speak."

"Very flattering, Trey," I said. "Much better than being compared to the other end of the horse."

"That would be Marcus Oliphant," Gibby said, proving he could get a laugh every now and then.

Beside me, Fitz exhaled loudly. I wondered if he might be unwell.

Trey continued on with his dry recitation. "This positive result has prompted two things. Carmen has arranged for a Des O'Day memorial section to be added to the WBC website. It will honor his memory and also serve as an up-to-the-minute account of information pertaining to the bombing. The latter will consist primarily of the network's Twitter releases.

"Of more relevance to the show itself—and to you, Billy—we'll be devoting the last fifteen minutes each night, at least for the next few days, to a discussion of the crime and its aftermath. You will host the segment, Billy. And there will be an appropriate title, something on the order of the Blessing Report, for which we have April to thank."

The publicist gave him a wintry smile of acknowledgment.

"Suppose there is nothing for Blessing to report in the Blessing Report?" I asked.

Max said, "We're asking interested visitors to the website to submit their questions. How many do we have so far, Trey?"

The assistant producer flipped through his notes frantically and came up with the answer. "Over a thousand, but there is a high degree of repetition. Staffers are sifting through them, and we should have some for you to address tonight."

"I assume I can select the questions myself?" I asked.

"Absolutely," Max said. "Judging by the ratings and the amount of hits your segment has scored on Hulu, I don't give a shit what you do with the fifteen minutes, as long as it puts eyeballs on the screen."

"Max also feels that it would diminish the importance of the Blessing Report if you continue to announce the show," Trey said. "Therefore, we've added Quentin Utach to the team."

The newcomer, who resembled the Crypt Keeper, nodded his head and offered what was almost a smile.

I returned that with a genuine grin. I was happy to relinquish that duty. I turned to Trey and asked when I might see the questions.

Max replied before Trey had a chance. "We've arranged for an expert to join you tonight. Dr. Benjamin Dover."

"Ben Dover?" I asked. "There's a guy who took a lotta crap in high school. Other than the punch-line name, who is he?"

Max responded with a sharp "Trey?"

Responding to his master's voice, the good dog Trey dragged a briefcase from the floor and split it open on the table. From it, he withdrew a hardcover book.

Suddenly, Fitz's cellphone beeped.

"Turn that off," Max ordered.

Fitz looked at the phone and stood. "I gotta take this."

"Goddamn it!" Max shouted, as the big man strolled off with the phone at his ear.

Trey stared at Max, waiting for instructions.

Finally, sighing in helpless frustration, the producer waved a hand and Trey presented me with the book.

The dust-jacket art was a garish Southern California coastline scene consisting of an orange sun in a bright red sky above a sinister purple ocean and a white beach. A naked female corpse lay beside a solo palm tree. The title read: *The Barbarous Coast, a Benjamin Dover Novel of Suspense by Benjamin Dover.*

"Don't tell me you've never heard of Dr. Dover?" Trey said.

I blinked at the book.

"Dr. Dover," Max said, "is a retired psychologist who consults with the LAPD on murder cases. Actually, he does most of the solving, but he's too humble to take the credit."

"I'm guessing from the repetition of his name on the cover that he's not above taking some of the credit," I said.

"The books are fiction," Trey said. "But they are based on the doctor's investigations."

"He doesn't make many TV appearances," Max said. "Just the ones with heavyweight hosts, like Bill

Maher and Ryan Seacrest. We're lucky to get his services. He says he's fascinated by this killer, Charbonnet. He's anxious to get your take on it, Billy."

"Call it a hunch, but my take is that Roger Charbonnet will sue our collective asses off if we label him a killer on the show. There's a whole thing called a trial to go through first, not to mention a verdict."

"Good point," Max said. "In any case, at least skim the book so you'll sound knowledgeable when you plug it."

I stared at the novel. "Is there anybody on this coast who doesn't write books?"

Whisper raised a tentative hand. "I'm writing a spec script for the *MILF and Cookie Show*," she said.

"You need any help with it, honey," Gibby said, "just drop by my dressing room. I'm one of the leading authorities on MILFs."

"As much as I love useless badinage," Max said, "we've got a dozen trained cats arriving in less than an hour, and I would dearly love to get at least one run-through before we break out the litter boxes. Thanks primarily to Billy's tardiness, we are now . . . how long behind schedule, Trey?"

"Seventeen—" Trey began. He was interrupted by Fitz, who returned to stand at the table.

"I . . . um. They're releasin' Des's remains."

"In what? A cigar box?" Gibby said, chuckling.

Fitz shot him an angry stare that froze the grin on his baby face. If looks could kill, Gibby would have been dead on the spot.

No one else said a word.

"So I'll be takin' him back home on the weekend," the Irishman said.

"Home?" Max said. "What home?"

"Dungannon. We'll be holdin' funeral services there."

"The hell you say," Max exclaimed. "You've got a show on Monday."

"I been meanin' to talk to you about that. I've already discussed it with my guys. I'm through here. I was only doin' the show for Des."

"You've got a contract."

"You're payin' me more than the job is worth. People who tune in, they don't care if it's me leadin' my crew or a guy with a banjo."

Clearly, he was singing Max's song. The producer turned to Trey. "How soon can the talent coordinators find a replacement?"

"Soon enough, I imagine. Lot of hungry musicians out here."

"Great," Gibby said. "It's not like we don't have enough problems with this fucking show. Now we'll have second-rate music, just so a bunch of fucking mackerel-snappers can put a pine box in the ground."

He was looking at Max. He didn't see Fitz rushing toward him until the big man lifted him out of his chair by his shirtfront. "Ya mingin' maggot. I'll show ya how we snap."

He shook him like a maraca, then slapped his face with the back of his free hand. "Snap!" he shouted.

Fitz repeated the word and hit him on the front swing.

Gibby's eyes were wide, the pupils rolling around like plastic buttons. Fear had turned his face ghostly white, but the slaps were rouging his cheeks. He was starting to resemble a kid's doll. Or maybe a plump Pee-wee Herman.

"Snap!" One final backhand, and Fitz dropped the comedian onto his chair. "Dribble one more word and I'll rip out your yockers and stuff 'em down yer trap."

While we were all trying to figure out what "yockers" were, Fitz wheeled around and glared at us, his eyes red with fury. "Anybody else got somethin' clever to say about poor Des or the true faith?"

Judging by the stunned silence, none of us did.

Fitz stood there a moment, then slumped. He shook his big head. "I . . . I beg your apology," he said. "I didn't think I still had the violence in me. If you want me to be stayin' with the show till the weekend, Max, I owe ya that much."

"I think we'll be okay, buddy," Max said, with surprising calm. "But I appreciate the offer."

Fitz nodded. He raised an arm in a halfhearted wave to the rest of us, turned on his boot heel, and left the room.

"Christ," Gibby whined in what seemed like honest confusion. "What the fuck did I say, anyway?"

Max stared at him for a beat and suddenly broke into a laugh. As his laughter grew, the others, experiencing something of the same tension release, joined in. Even Gibby, whose soft face was still a bright red from the slaps.

Eventually, the laughter stopped. Wiping his eyes with a handkerchief the size of a tablecloth, Max said to Trey, "Go to the office and tell the talent assholes to find me a new bandleader. Also, find out what we're paying the current band crew and see if we can't get replacements who'll work for scale."

Trey was out of his chair and halfway to the door when Max stopped him. "You better reschedule the singer booked for tonight. Let's keep the music to a minimum till we figure out what to do about it."

"Ferguson doesn't even have live music," Trey said.

"It's something to consider," Max replied.

"We'll need a replacement act for the singer," Trey said.

"I got a guy," Gibby said. "One of the great Vegas lounge acts. He's here in town. I just saw him at Nate 'n Al."

"Who?" Max asked warily.

"Philly Slide."

"He still alive?"

"Philly's . . . not that old," Gibby said. "He's younger than Rickles."

"I got paintings by Goya younger than Rickles," Max said. "My grandmother's younger than Rickles. The trick is to find somebody older than Rickles."

"Abe Vigoda," Gibby said.

Max nodded. "Okay. Call Philly. And tell makeup to do something about your face. You look like Holyfield after Tyson head-butted him."

It seemed as if we'd be there for a while. I cracked the cover on Dr. Dover's new thriller.

# Chapter
# THIRTY-FOUR

By five, they'd somehow managed to make it through the scripted part of the show. I was occupying one of the audience seats, alternating my perusal of Dr. Dover's convoluted tale of madness and murder with glimpses of Gibby in a dog suit playing with the trained cats, when April took the seat beside me.

"What have I missed?" She was staring at Gibby in the dog suit, lying on his back on the floor with a cat resting on his stomach. "Or shouldn't I ask?"

"He's hoping to see how many times he can say 'pussy' on network TV," I said.

"I'll put out a press release," she said. "Title it 'Pussy Galore.'"

"Actually, the feline fashion show is pretty amusing. I'm not sure why the big G's wearing the dog suit except that he seems to like it."

"It does humanize him," she said. "But I'd better go get him to take it off. A photographer from *Entertainment Weekly* will be here in half an hour, and I think sport jacket and slacks would be more appropriate."

I returned to Benjamin Dover's book.

I'd skimmed about twenty more pages when Max arrived beside me and asked me to move over one seat.

"Damn rows are too close," he said, squeezing into the seat I'd been using. "Need the aisle for my legs. How's the show look?"

"The cat segment is pretty funny."

"Gibby still lacks confidence. But I think he's got the potential of turning into a meat-and-potatoes guy like Jay. Old school. I've always been partial to the real stand-ups. Johnny Carson. He was the goddamn champ of 'em all. Alan King, Buddy Hackett, Jan Murray, Jack Carter. Hell, I'm old enough to remember Myron Cohen. Those guys always delivered."

"Letterman's pretty good," I said.

"The critic's choice? Too sarcastic, too smug. Above it all. Dick Cavett without the warmth. Middle America doesn't give a shit about him. But Middle America loved those other guys, and so did the hipsters. Seinfeld's like that. Man, if we coulda gotten Jerry to do the show. But why would he? He's got enough dough to buy the network. And he's too loyal to his buddy Jay to go up against him. He even trashed Conan."

"Des didn't strike me as old school," I said.

Max was silent for a few seconds. "No. If anything, he reminded me of Richard Dawson. You remember . . . the Brit who hosted *Family Feud*?"

"Sure," I said.

"Des wasn't even on my list, but Trey really pushed him. Got me to sit down and look at a couple of his sitcom eps. I saw he had presence, rolled right over the headliners. His reel was damned impressive, too. Held his own with Jay and Dave during guest spots. Seemed a little too angry-young-man in his early appearances. Then he mellowed a little, started making jokes about himself. But between you and me, Billy, he was not a nice man."

"No?"

"Nastiest drunk I've ever had to deal with."

"How so?"

Max scanned the area to make sure nobody was within earshot and lowered his voice. "He nearly killed a pathetic creature up at my place one night."

"An animal?"

"A human being, if you could call it that. A tranny he picked up at this stupid fucking restaurant where you eat in the dark."

I remembered Fitz telling me about the restaurant. That had been our first night at the villa. After I'd left Stew's party. "Des had a thing for transsexuals?" I asked.

"Hardly. This one really was special. Had me fooled, too, and usually I can spot 'em a mile away. Des had been drinking heavily, and when we hit the restaurant, he spied what we all thought was a hot blonde going in with a bunch of her girlfriends. Des did his thing, finally convinced the blonde to join us.

"So while Fitz, Trey, and myself are trying to enjoy the experience of sightless dining, Des is enjoying the experience of the blonde going down on him. But that's not enough. He convinces the blonde to come with us to my place, where I've got several real bimbos waiting.

"All is fine for a while. Then there's the big moment when it's 'everybody in the pool.' The blonde says no. But Des insists. And that's when he discovers she's a he. Me, I would have laughed it off as a life lesson. But Des goes all Chris Brown on the blonde. I mean, really tearing into him, her, whatever.

"If it wasn't for Fitz and Trey, he would have killed the poor son of a bitch. I really believe that. As it was, if you remember that LAPD picture of Rihanna, the tranny was much worse. It cost the budget of the show nearly thirty grand to put him back together. And until the bandages come off, we won't know how much more."

"I'm surprised you were able to keep it under wraps."

"That's April. She's the best in the business."

"There must have been other incidents," I said. "I wonder who swept those under the carpet."

"This time it was a mix of booze and the white stuff," Max said. "Fitz told me Des usually stuck to one or the other. Hell . . . I shouldn't be telling you this stuff."

It wasn't the first time I'd realized there was something about me that got people to open up. It had proven useful when I'd been on the con with my mentor Paul Lamont. It proved a lifesaver with the judge who went easy on my sentence after I got caught. And it comes in handy even now, interviewing celebrities who are usually on guard around the media.

"Don't worry, Max," I said. "I'm not a network spy, and I'm not going to go running to Perez Hilton."

"Well, what the fuck. The dude's dead, anyway," he said, pushing himself up out of his seat with a grunt. "And Gibby's a lox. And we'll be damn lucky if the show improves enough to even make it on the bubble."

\* \* \*

I still had a chapter or two to go on *The Barbarous Coast* when Trey arrived with the doctor-author, a trim, handsome man, both aesthetic- and athletic-looking, wearing a midnight-blue blazer over a pale blue polo, faded denim pants, and white sneakers. His grip was firm but refreshingly noncombative. However, he did have a probing stare that ranged between unnerving and downright creepy.

"As I believe I mentioned," Trey said, "Dr. Dover is a special consultant with the LAPD, as well as the author of a dozen bestselling novels based on his cases."

"Seventeen, actually," Dover said. "But who's counting?"

"Billy, these are some questions emailed to the website." Trey handed them to me. "You and Dr. Dover can use them or not. I'd better get moving. Fitzpatrick's officially off the show, and I've got to make sure there's a replacement." He bowed out gracelessly, bumping into a seat and nearly falling.

Onstage, they were getting a sound check on Philly Slide, a fiftysomething Vegas lounge comic with dyed mahogany-colored hair and a gray sharkskin suit that was so shiny it was causing a flare-up on camera. He would be doing some supposedly hilarious movie and TV reviews tonight. If that worked, he might become a regular guest.

Judging by the fun he was having at the sound guy's expense—moving his lips while remaining silent, then suddenly shouting into the lavalier mike—

he'd be lucky if anything he said on tonight's show would be heard.

I suggested to Dover that we find a less distracting place to talk about what we were going to talk about. We wound up at Café International, the Worldwide commissary that, since it offered no dinner food other than self-microwaved frozen burgers and pizza, was about as empty and quiet as a church on Super Bowl Sunday.

We settled for two small bottled waters. Dover glanced at the book I'd placed on the table. "You're reading *Barbarous Coast*. What do you think?"

A writer has to have a great deal of self-confidence to ask that question. I wasn't sure my skimming gave me the right to be too judgmental, so I said, "The title seems familiar, for some reason."

He smiled. "That's purposeful. Tests have proven that people are more apt to embrace the familiar. It's one of the reasons why there are so many television series and movies that remind us of shows from the past. The film people call it pre-awareness. So though I wouldn't dream of copying another writer's plot or characters, which would be plagiarism, I often use familiar titles, which is perfectly legal. As for *The Barbarous Coast*, the great Ross Macdonald coined the title several decades ago. But who remembers that, really?"

I'd have to tell Harry Paynter about that. We could call our book *The Maltese Falcon*. Better yet, *The Girl with the Dragon Tattoo*. "I appeared on your show *Wake Up, America!* once," Dover said. "I was on tour with *The Lad in the Lake*, my first book."

"I must have been on assignment," I said.

"It was eighteen years ago," he said. "Before your time. I suppose I was something of a success, since they've asked me back often. But the East Coast really doesn't do it for me. It's too mired in Old World tradition. Much too twentieth century, if you know what I mean. And I'm fortunate enough not to need the publicity."

Grandma said, "If you can't say anything nice. . . ." So I said nothing.

"Might I call you Billy?" He was staring at me again. I was reminded of a phrase from my comic strip–reading days: "Mandrake glared hypnotically."

"Of course," I said, using a sip from my water bottle as an excuse to break eye contact.

"I suppose we should talk a little about Roger Charbonnet," he said. "An amazing character."

"You know Roger?" I asked.

"Not personally," Dover said. "But I've observed him. His narcissistic personality, his arrogance, his problems with substance abuse."

"I don't understand," I said. "If you don't know him, I assume that means you haven't examined him. How can you diagnose—"

Dover cut me off with "I've seen him in action. My significant other, Raven, and I eat out often, so I've observed him at his restaurants, strutting like a peacock. Dressing down his staff. He even had the chutzpah to ask Raven for a date, with me sitting right there. And, of course, I've seen the YouTube footage of him attacking you at the party and your tripping him into the pool. Very macho, Billy."

"I was lucky," I said.

"I think we make our own luck. In any case, a

professional therapist such as myself can glean quite a bit from merely observing a subject. And from what I have observed of Charbonnet's antisocial behavior, he exhibits all the signs of someone capable of murder."

I wondered how much of that observation had to do with Roger hitting on his "significant other." I said, "There's still that boring old traditional thing about a man being innocent until proven guilty."

"Oh, please," Dover replied with an eye roll. "You can't really believe this guy is innocent? My sources at the LAPD—and they are rock-solid, owing to the numerous cases I've helped them close—have not the slightest doubt about his guilt."

"Would Pete Brueghel be one of those sources?"

"No. I've never had the pleasure of working with Detective Brueghel. Stabler and Stabler published *The Manicurist,* and I'm published by Nobel House. So if we were to work a case together, there'd be a conflict over the eventual book rights."

*Wow. Publishing trumps justice?*

"Life gets complicated out here," I said.

Dover was giving me that whammy-eye thing again. "Since Detective Brueghel is in charge of the investigation, you must have some idea of his feelings on the subject of Charbonnet's guilt."

"He believes he's arrested the right man," I said. "But even the experts can be wrong."

"Not if they're genuine experts," he said.

"How many years were you in practice as a forensic psychologist?" I asked, blinking under his gaze.

"Actually, my practice was devoted mainly to child psychology."

That was a surprise. "Children. Murderers. Seems like a stretch."

"Murderers were all children once," he said. "Actually, my work with the LAPD began with a homicide involving one of my patients. A twelve-year-old boy, suffering from a form of social anxiety. He was kidnapped from the family home in Bel Air. No ransom demand was made, and, a week later, the boy's body was recovered from the Oneonta Slough, just this side of the California-Mexico border. The case was the basis for my debut novel, *The Lad in the Lake*."

"They ever find the kidnappers?"

"No. But I'm fairly certain I know who was behind it and why. As soon as the investigating detective, Terrance Koenig, confided in me that the victim's father was not just mournful over his son's fate but was visibly nervous and seemed to be hiding something, I made a connection. The father was the manager of Movieland Motors, a dealership specializing in top-of-the-line classic cars. I suggested to Terry—whom I've accepted as a close friend, by the way, in spite of his sexual bent—that he should ask the man if he'd sold a Lightweight E-Type Jaguar within the last year.

"When the father replied that he couldn't recall, I knew I was on the right track. I doubted he'd forget such a sale. There were only a dozen Lightweight E-types produced. Terry found the sale on the dealership's books, and that was that."

"That was what?" I asked. "I don't get it."

"Because I've given you an incomplete puzzle. It's the way we authors build suspense, holding back key information until the end of the story. Here's the thing I remembered that broke the case. I'd read an item in *The New York Times* a week before the kidnapping. A young man named Luis Martinez had died in a car accident in Baja. He'd been a wild kid, and probably stoned to the eyebrows, when he drove his sports car through a guardrail and wound up drowning in the Gulf of Mexico."

"And his car was a Lightweight E-Type," I said.

"Exactly," Dover said. "Purchased the previous year, while he was attending UCLA."

"I'm wondering what it was about the accident that made the *Times* cover it."

"Well, that's the thing, Billy. It became newsworthy when some smart reporter realized that Luis was the only son of Alfredo 'Guapo' Martinez, then the leader of the Palmador Cartel. Do you know that shortly before his arrest seven years ago, Martinez made the *Forbes* billionaire list?"

"I missed that one," I said. "So Guapo had to find somebody to blame other than his son? And he picked the guy who sold junior the car?"

"That's what I deduced," Dover said. "It had not been a kidnap for money but an act that a deluded father believed to be biblical, an eye for an eye. Hence the drowning. In any case, it turned into the perfect literary property for me. My next two cases also involved youths. But when I submitted book three, my agent informed me that if I wanted to break through to the bestseller lists I'd have to expand my horizons. So I offered my consultant services on major crimes in general. I suppose you could say that my years as a child psychologist were altruistic and my forensic psychologist years have been egoistic, not to mention very remunerative."

Well, altruist or egoist, he was my expert for the night. So we hunkered down and for the next hour and forty-five minutes tried to figure out how we would fill the segment. The questions from the website—ranging from "What did it feel like to see the British guy get blown to shit?" to "How'd the killer dude throw the bomb at the Irish dude without any of the other dudes seeing him?"—were basically useless.

Instead, we addressed the information that had been released to the media. Dover understood that I knew more than that and did his best to coax it from me. I, in turn, hoarded my secrets, keeping them from his very professional questions and searching gaze.

We developed a fairly effective give-and-take that I hoped would continue under the scrutiny of, by Trey's approximation, somewhere between a million and a half and two million viewers. But before that could take place, we in the greenroom, like the brave viewers at home and in the studio, had to endure Quentin Utach's very dramatic opening welcome and intro to Gibby, who then delivered a monologue chock-full of quips about drunken starlets and reality series grotesques and political scandals.

Dover, being both intelligent and something of a pretentious asshole, thought the whole thing was ghastly. Being something of a pretentious asshole myself, but also understanding the work and struggle that goes into any TV show, I was a bit more tolerant.

I sat there, watching the large flat HD screen, ignoring the doctor's acerbic critiques, and hoping the show's other guests-in-waiting—specifically, the

Vegas comic—would do the same. Actually, Philly Slide seemed to be on his own trip and ignored us entirely.

Dover actually laughed in spite of himself at the fashion felines.

Philly Slide leapt to his feet during the ensuing commercials. Something about him seemed off. He was sweating profusely and mumbling.

At Utach's introduction, he rushed from the room and, what seemed like seconds later, appeared on the big screen, standing in front of brief clips or stills from the movies and TV shows he was mentioning. He began with some amusing riffs on actors such as Clooney and Matt Damon, in their just-released *Ocean's Fourteen,* but he seemed a bit nervous.

The nervousness increased, and he eventually broke down in the middle of his review of the new Tarantino movie, a contemporary thriller based on *The Golden Stallion,* a Roy Rogers Western from the 1940s.

Gibby rushed onstage to rescue his old friend, pretending Slide's weeping and pleas for help were somehow part of the routine. Regardless of what I thought of our host, it was a courageous act, and he pulled it off, more or less, allowing Philly to regain enough control to take a bow.

Live TV.

During the commercial break, Dover and I took our places at the conversation nook. While the sound guys miked us, it was impossible not to hear Slide asking Gibby to forgive him.

"I shoulda told ya, Gib. I been in rehab at Stepping Stones for the last six weeks. I thought I was straight. But the pressure . . ."

Gibby hugged him. "Just get well, boychik," he said.

I suddenly realized he wasn't quite the ego-involved weasel he'd seemed to be. I'd been wrong about him. I wondered if I'd been wrong about Roger, too.

*Chapter*
# THIRTY-FIVE

The first edition of the Blessing Report seemed to pass even quicker than its actual thirteen and a half minutes. I began by eliciting the doctor's opinion on the sort of sociopath who'd plot a complicated assassination like the one that took Des's life. His response was more or less as it had been during our pre-show discussion.

"From the little I know of the man they arrested," he added, "he would seem to fit that profile."

"So far, he's just a suspect," I said. "I know you've worked closely with the police on numerous occasions, Dr. Dover. Any suggestions for them?"

"This is a very unusual act of homicide," he said. "Not merely premeditated but elaborately so. I imagine the detectives should be wondering why the killer wanted the crime to be telecast. And why did he use an explosive when there are so many other weapons available today?"

"What do you think?" I asked him.

"The venue indicates a certain flamboyance. It's the act of a show-off or a showman. The explosive adds to the display. It's Hollywood's influence. Thanks to computer graphics, unless a contemporary action film destroys a city, nobody takes it seriously. I think this killer wanted his victim to go out with a bang, literally. A shooting or a poisoning wouldn't have been dramatic enough. And a shooting would have made it particularly hard for the killer to get away clean."

"Right," I said. "By using an explosive device and a timer, he might have been in Pasadena when the murder took place."

"Have the police identified the device?" the doctor asked.

"As far as I know, not yet," I said. "I'm just assuming there was a timer."

"Well, if true, might I suggest detectives look into their suspect's television setup at home or in his restaurants. With a plan this complex, I'd be surprised if the killer wouldn't have wanted to see it play out. That means he's probably got a satellite receiver that picks up shows as they're being telecast to the East Coast."

"Clever," I said.

"It's what I do."

From the corner of my eye I saw Lolita standing beside camera two, grabbing air with one hand, a sign that it was time to wrap up the interview.

I thanked the doctor, held up *The Barbarous*

*Coast,* and urged viewers to pick up a copy at their neighborhood bookstore. I ended by mentioning the Desmond O'Day memorial section of the network's website, where tonight's Blessing Report would be available for viewing.

Since the very gray Quentin Utach was handling the announcing chores, I was free to go. So I accompanied Dover to the parking lot. At his Lamborghini, we shook hands. He invited me to have dinner at his home on Sunday, noting that his significant other, Raven, was a third-generation luthier who made Celtic harps and loved playing for guests.

As appealing as was the aspect of Sunday dinner and a harp recital at Chez Dover, I regrettably declined, claiming a previous engagement. If things went as I planned, that wouldn't be a lie. With visions of Vida and me spending a languorous weekend, probably my last, at the Villa Delfina, I headed off in search of the biggest, baddest fast-food emporium I could find.

"Fatburger. The Last Great Hamburger Stand," the sign read.

To a man who hadn't eaten since ten that morning, the bright yellow-and-red banner was like the North Star to a lost sailor.

I surveyed the menu printed over the counter and made a modest selection: a Triple King and, to wash it down, a Maui-Banana shake. If I'm going out, I'm going out with a full, contented belly.

My driver in New York, Joe Yeung, won't let me eat in my own car. He claims the crumbs attract vermin, and he's probably right. But I was on the final frontier. I planned to kick it, SoCal style. Top down, loud music, zooming down the Pacific Coast Highway under a starry sky with a burger in my face.

Alas, the Fatburger Triple King was the sandwich equivalent of Trump Towers, literally as high as the shake. Nor was it what you'd call self-contained. There was no way to eat it, keep an eye on the road, and avoid dropping bits and pieces of the burger, bathed in special savory sauce, on my lap.

Courting minor back strain, I carried my supper to a table.

I was the only customer dining in. Showing remarkable restraint, I got out my cellphone, reactivated it, and checked the calls.

Savoring the first bite of the night, I saw that there were three messages. The earliest was from Cassandra, requesting a callback. The machine had logged it at a few minutes after nine, Pacific Coast Time. After midnight in New York. It was then close to one-thirty there. Since she hadn't demanded a return call, I figured it could wait until the morning.

I gnawed the Triple King down to Double King size.

The second message was from Fitz, left at nine-thirteen.

"Uh . . . me, Billy. I'm an eejit, phonin' you while the show's on. Call me soon's ya free." He reminded me of his cellphone number.

Holding the monster burger in my left hand, I awkwardly thumb-dialed the musician. After a half-dozen rings, my call was directed to voice mail. I wondered if Fitz had decided to fly out that night. Maybe he was in the air.

I did a little more damage to the Fatburger, which was now seeping through the once-neat napkin panty.

Message three was left at a few minutes after ten by the demon writer Harry Paynter. "What the hell you doing with that hack Dover, bro? That guy couldn't write his way out of a . . . out of a . . . I don't know, into a whorehouse with a hundred-dollar bill taped to his dick."

My classy collaborator seemed to be speeding on more than just anger.

"It's not me gives a shit," he continued, motor-mouthing. "I didn't even see the goddamned *Blessing and Dover Show*. I'm too busy under the gun, working on the outline. Fuckin' Sandy calls me and wants to know what's going down. Sandy Selman, bro! The guy providing the moolah. He thinks you've sold us out to Benjamin 'I'm a fuckin' *New York Times* bestseller' Dover. Sandy wants to know what's what, bro. He wants a face-to-face. Call me tonight. I'll be up till two at least, working on this fucking thing. Benjamin Dover? I can't fucking believe it."

*Wow,* I thought, people take their writing seriously out here. No wonder the publishing houses on the East Coast think Southern Californians don't read books. They're too busy writing them.

I could have phoned Harry back, but why? Better to wait until tomorrow, when he might even be sober. In any case, I wanted to finish the Fatburger while it was still deliciously warm.

That accomplished, I ordered a side of onion rings. I carried them and what was left of my shake to the Lexus, lowered the top, and settled on a jazz FM station broadcasting from Manhattan Beach. Nibbling, drinking, with the clear, starry night sky high above and the late great Art Blakey and the Jazz Messengers playing their soundtrack song from *Les Liaisons Dangereuses* loud enough to be heard above the wind, I roared down the nearly empty Pacific Coast Highway toward Malibu, satisfied and at peace with the world.

A self-delusion, soon to be corrected.

## *Chapter*
# THIRTY-SIX

" 'Oh, Danny boy, the pipes, the pipes are calling,

" 'From glen to glen, and down the mountain side.' "

The a cappella voice was as clear and pure as a mountain brook, and it might have brought tears to my eyes, if I'd been awake.

" 'Tis I'll be there in sunshine or in shadow,

" 'Oh, Danny boy, oh, Danny boy, I love you so!' "

The problem was: I was awake, and the singing continued.

There was enough moonlight for me to see Fitz sitting on a chair in the corner of the bedroom, cradling a bottle of whiskey in his arms like a wee one, faith 'n' begorrah, and singing like a doomed angel.

The guy was like a male Susan Boyle, an incredible voice coming from an unexpected source. I waited for him to finish the song before saying, "That was beautiful, Fitz. Not sure about the time or the place, though."

"I'm sorry, boyo. I didn't think I could wait for you ta rise on yer own."

"It was a kinder wake-up than water in my face," I said, reaching for the light switch.

"Don't do that," he said. "The darkness suits my mood."

I maneuvered my watch into a patch of moonlight. Nearly three a.m. "So, ah, what the hell are you doing here?"

"I . . . got something to tell ya. But first I want you to tell *me* somethin'."

"Name it."

"Who's causin' the trouble, Billy?"

"Al-Qaeda, last I heard."

"I'm tryin' to have a serious con . . . versation, damn it." He punctuated that with a swing from the bottle. "Tell me who's my enemy."

"Could you be a little more specific?" I threw the covers off and rolled out of the bed, toe-searching the rug for my slippers.

"What went on after I walked out on the show? Who was it left the table after me? Gibby? Max?"

I thought back. It was twelve hours ago. "I don't remember seeing anybody leave but you," I said.

"Bullshite! Somebody had to make the call. Pass the word I was headin' for home."

"What makes you think so?"

"I was runnin' free till then. Now I got a shadow."

"C'mon, Fitz. You're letting your imagination—"

"The hell you say! He's been ridin' my arse since I packed up and left the lot. Got himself a gray Mercedes sedan, he does."

"Fitz, there are more gray Mercedes sedans in L.A. than there are in Stuttgart."

"But how many of 'em are driven by a man with a milk-eye?"

The moonlight painted his bearded face a bluish white. He took another pull on the bottle.

" 'A milk-eye,' " I repeated. Next he was going to start talking about the Thirty-nine Steps. "You might want to ease up a little on that sauce."

"Don't fuckin' talk down to me, ya bastard!" He leaned forward, glaring at me. "Now I'm startin' to wonder if it coulda been you ratted me? That'd be a real kick in th' bollocks."

"Why would I have done that, Fitz?"

"Because of yer . . . Naw. Of course ya wouldn't have." He slumped back. "Forget I let the words pass my lips. You're a good man." Another slug of whiskey.

" 'Oh, Danny boy . . .' Des hated th' feckin' song. Don't know why."

"I gather Des hated a lot of things."

"What might ya' be referrin' to?"

"The transvestite he nearly killed."

"Ah. And where'd you hear about that? From that fat bastard Max or his milksop Trey, I suppose. Well, yeah, that was a terrible thing Des did. Brutal. And he paid the price, didn't he?"

"You're saying that and the bombing were connected?"

"On'y in the vast scheme o' things. You believe in the Good Book, Billy?"

I assumed he wasn't referencing one of Benjamin Dover's novels. "I believe in a lot of the things in it."

"An eye for an eye?"

"I'm more in the turn-the-other-cheek camp."

"Eye for an eye," he said again, and suddenly lurched to his feet. The whiskey bottle hit the carpet with a dull clunk. He didn't seem to notice. "Gotta get movin'. Places to see, people to do."

He staggered to the door.

"Hold on, Fitz," I said. "You said you had something to tell me."

He seemed puzzled.

"Was it about Des's murder?"

He winked and tapped the side of his nose. "That's it. The razzers got it all arse-back'ards."

"Explain."

"There are things we do in the name o' love an' country. . . . Des was a pretty serious boyo when we was younger. Believed in the good fight. Damn the Brits!"

He smiled at some vague memory. But the smile didn't last.

"The thing is, mistakes are made. Terrible mistakes because of things you put in play. Take the night Des nearly did for the he-she . . . Bet you never imagined it was you put the guilt on Des that made him fall back on his booze and pills."

"What the hell are you talking about?"

"Nothin' you meant to do, I'm sure. But I knew soon's you said it, we were gonna be in for a rough night. The bullshite in the Oirish bar did nothin' to aid the situation . . . and then Des took all his fear and frustration out on that poor poof."

"What was it I said?"

Fitz shook his big head. He staggered toward the door again.

"Don't just walk away."

"I gotta get movin', Billy. It was a risk I took comin' out here. I don't think Milk-Eye got wind of it, but ya never know. And there's somethin' more I got to do."

"Where are you going?"

"You're better off not knowin'. You're safe now, Billy. Be happy. Stay well."

He headed out.

I hopped from the bed and ran after him. "Just talk to me in plain English," I shouted.

He replied with a drunken chuckle. "Ah, the plain English," he said. "Fuck 'em. An' fuck this nightmare town. I'll be on the next flight out. Be gone all th' way to . . . *Slán abhaile.* Safe home."

"Safe? You won't even make it to the airport in your condition," I said. "Get some rest. There's an extra bed here, or you can sleep in the villa. There'll be flights later in the day."

"Like Des would say, I'll sleep when I'm dead, Billy. *Slán.*"

And he was gone.

# *Chapter* THIRTY-SEVEN

If there was a way of returning immediately to sleep after being awakened and brain-teased by a drunken, paranoid Irishman, I was not able to find it. I lay abed for the next hour or so, trying to puzzle through his ravings. I got it that he believed Des was the intended victim on the night of the bombing and that it had been payback for something the comedian had done in the past—an eye for an eye. What I didn't know was if Fitz had had any legitimate reason for his belief. Or if his comment about me saying something that sent Des on a guilt trip had any basis in reality. If so, what the heck had I said?

Somewhere around five or six I must have drifted off, because when I opened my eyes again, the room was filled with sunlight and Fitz's odd visit seemed less important and more lunatic. And yet . . .

I showered, shaved, and dressed. I fixed coffee and drank a cup while I put together an egg-bacon-toast breakfast and ate it. I washed the dishes. I did all those things mainly by rote. My mind was primarily occupied in trying to recall every word I'd spoken to Des before he and Fitz took off that first night. I remembered them playing the videogame with Gibby.

Des had seemed more interested in the game than in anything I was saying.

Finally, I gave up. I poured another cup of coffee and took it and my cellular out to the villa's patio.

I paused briefly to enjoy the sun, the cloudless sky, the mild surf. Then I phoned Cassandra.

"Oh, hello, Billy." Her voice was full of faux gentility. "How lovely of you to return my call AT THE BUSIEST TIME OF THE DAY!"

I checked my watch. Nine-forty-two. Twelve-forty-two in Manhattan. I heard lots of noisy luncheon chatter in the background.

"Busy is good," I said. "You called last night?"

She lowered her voice and said, "I have to replace Margaret."

"Why?" I asked. Margaret Leifer was a seemingly pleasant and efficient middle-aged lady who'd been our cashier for about five years.

"Call you right back."

The phone went dead.

I placed the cellular on the glass-top table, leaned back, and closed my eyes. I did not open them until the phone made its music. I picked it up and said, "So what's the problem with Margaret?"

There was a momentary silence, then a very crisp, very British, very feminine voice asked, "Is this Mr. Blessing?"

"Right. Sorry, I was expecting a call . . ."

"Mr. Malcolm Darrow calling. Wait one, please."

I was put on hold, something that ranked just a notch below arrogant British receptionists on my things-I-don't-need-in-the-morning list.

"Mr. Blessing," lawyer Darrow began without social preamble, "Roger was wondering why you haven't contacted Gloria Ingram."

"Well, let's see. I had a business meeting, a rehearsal, a show. Then, before I knew what was happening, I'd frittered away the whole day. I can send you a fax on that if you're not taking notes."

"A fax will not be necessary," he said. "I was just speaking with Ms. Ingram. She's at work and available. I believe you have her number, but if not . . ."

"I've got it. Thanks," I said. "I'll give her a call."

"That would be excellent," he said.

My next call was not to Ms. Ingram.

"So many busy signals," Cassandra said. "Thanks for fitting me in." There was no longer the sound of a chatty, happy lunch crowd in the background.

"Where are you?" I asked.

"Your office. It's very unpleasant, Billy. Dusty and musty."

"Put the cleaners on it, for God's sake."

"I don't have time to watch them when they're in here."

"Nobody watches them when I'm there," I said. "We've been using the same cleaning crew since we opened. I think we can trust them to dust my office."

"Really? Then let me tell you about trust."

"First tell me about Margaret."

"It's the same story. You know she got a divorce from Otto last month?"

"I'm not that up on Margaret's private life." My attention was drawn to a familiar surgically rearranged figure in the far distance, heading my way across the sand. The pride of Crockaby Realty, Amelia St. Laurent. I considered going back inside the guesthouse.

"Margaret and Otto had been married for twenty-three years," Cassandra said, as if that were a record. "She told me she grew tired of him, but, actually, it was because of Heinrich."

"Heinrich being . . . ?"

"Margaret's twenty-seven-year-old boy toy."

"Not exactly a boy." Ms. St. Laurent paused to observe the home to her right.

"Man toy, then. Or more to the point, she's his mommy toy."

"Bottom-line it, Cassandra, in the middle of your *busiest* time of day. Why fire Margaret?"

"I thought I made that clear," she said. "She's smitten with Heinrich."

"So . . . ?"

Ms. St. Laurent had resumed her march. I stood, picked up the coffee cup, and walked to the guesthouse.

"Heinrich is an identity thief," Cassandra said.

"You know this for a fact?"

"Oh, yes," she said. "A.W. looked into it." A. W. Johansen, Cassandra's paramour, was in charge of the East Coast office of a top security agency. "He said Heinrich's MO is seducing lady cashiers, bank tellers, and the like, any female who can provide him with credit card information."

"Last I looked, there was a law against such things."

Just as I entered the guesthouse, Ms. St. Laurent was marching toward the villa's sliding glass doors with a ring of keys in her hand.

"A.W. says you have to catch Heinrich with the goods," Cassandra was saying. "Otherwise, he could say he simply had a jones for frumpy women. Oops, strike that, Billy. Matronly women. I'm trying not to be overly critical."

"Since when?"

I entered the kitchenette and plucked a nice red apple from a now-empty bowl.

"Anyway, we could wait until he sweet-talked Margaret into providing him with our customers' credit card information. But that would mean Margaret would be arrested, too. So I want to fire her instead."

"Margaret's been honest up till now," I said. "What makes you think she'd turn crook for Heinrich?"

"Haven't you been listening, Billy? She left her husband of twenty-three years for the creep."

"Good point," I said, replacing the apple, saving it for another day.

"This way, with her out of a job, Heinrich will drop her like a hot rock. She'll be heartbroken. But she won't be in prison. She may even go back to Otto."

"You're a combination Solomon and Ann Landers," I said. "Do what you think best."

"Don't I always?" she said. "And Billy, in the future, please don't wait forever to return my calls. It's so simple, even for someone like you, who keeps fighting technology. Your phone has a touch-screen capability. You see my number on the recent call list. You press my number. My phone rings. We talk."

"I know about the touch screen. It's just that it was very late—"

"I don't think you do know about the touch screen. Otherwise, you'd be more careful."

"Come again?"

She hesitated a moment. "The touch screen. It's possible to engage it accidentally. Something in your pocket presses against it. Or someone bumps into you in a crowd. It's called 'ass dialing,' as in your ass presses the dial and—"

"I get it. So?"

"I've . . . overheard you . . . once or twice."

"The damn thing can phone somebody without me knowing?"

"Well, you should be able to hear it dialing," she said.

"Unless I've got the volume turned down. What have you overheard?"

"Nothing that interesting. I heard you at a meeting a couple of days ago. Mainly other people I didn't know talking. Got bored and clicked off. I should have mentioned this before. It's the sort of thing that could have embarrassing consequences."

"You think? I need a new phone."

"Touch screen is a popular feature," she said. "You may have to just be more careful."

That was her exit line.

I stared at the phone, the list of numbers on the touch screen, and wondered which, if any, I may have unknowingly allowed to listen in on my life.

Too late to worry about that now.

Now I needed to put the traitorous phone to use.

Gloria Ingram answered on the third ring. Her

voice had a measured, unaccented sound that I associate with people who speak professionally.

After the awkward amenities, she said, "As I told Roger, I have no objection to talking with you about the night of Tiffany Arden's murder, but it has to be off the record. I'm employed by the Bank of California, a company not known for having a broad-minded nature, even in times of plenty."

I assured her that our conversation would be kept private.

"Then suppose you tell me exactly what you want to know," she said.

"Would it be possible for us to meet?" I asked.

She hesitated, then asked, "When?"

"Are you free for lunch?"

"Actually, no. I'm on something of a deadline. But I can spare you a few minutes. I assume it won't take longer than that."

We settled on an appointment at eleven. I bid her good day and clicked off the phone, making sure I'd be able to hear it if it decided to make any calls.

I was pouring a third cup of coffee when someone began pounding on the front door.

"Mr. Blessing!" Amelia St. Laurent's voice was just a few decibels shy of glass-breaking.

I was heading toward the door to open it when she barged in, tottering a bit on her platform wedges. "What in God's name has been going on in the villa?" she demanded.

"Good morning, Ms. St. Laurent," I greeted her, settling on a world-class passive-aggressive approach. "Care for a cup of coffee?"

"What went on here last night? The villa's a disgrace."

"That's news to me."

"Mr. Fitzpatrick didn't mention it?"

That one caught me off guard. "What makes you think Fitzpatrick was here?" I asked.

"The security guards still have him listed as an occupant of the villa," she said. "According to the log, he arrived at two a.m. and left at three-fifty-two. You didn't see him?"

"I went to sleep at a little before midnight," I said. "What's up at the villa?"

"It's an unholy mess. I came here this morning to prepare a home down the beach. When I saw that Mr. Fitzpatrick had been here at such an odd hour, I figured I'd better check to see if he'd disturbed anything. Thank God I did. I've a cleaning crew at the other home. I'll have to deploy some of them here. Prospects are due in less than an hour."

"Show me the damage," I said.

I followed her from the guesthouse through the sliding glass door and into the villa. The living room looked pristine. What I could see of the formal dining room looked just fine.

Amelia St. Laurent was clip-clopping toward the den. "Just look in there," she said. "I won't. The sight absolutely makes me sick."

She was overdoing it a bit. There was a strong smell of whiskey in the room that I traced to a bottle of Bushmills resting on its side in a puddle of its former contents. Other than that, the furniture had been moved around. The leather couch was several feet from the wall, with a throw rug wrapped around one leg. The giant TV screen was slightly askew. One of the leather chairs had tipped over backward.

It looked as though there'd been a struggle in the room. But it may have just been Fitz hunting for something. Maybe one of those bags that he or Des had left behind.

If that was the case, he'd been on a fool's errand. The police gave the place a thorough vetting after Des's death. It was doubtful they'd have missed a bag full of drugs.

"Well?" Amelia St. Laurent was waiting just outside the room.

"It's a mess," I allowed. "How's the rest of the place look?"

"Passable," she said. I took that to mean it hadn't been touched. "This is all very annoying. I'll be talking to Mr. Halstead at your network about this. It was my understanding that while you would be staying in the guesthouse temporarily, the villa would be unoccupied. Would you have any idea if Mr. Fitzpatrick plans any other visits?"

I shrugged helplessly.

"Well, I shall have to deploy some cleaners from the other job. Rest assured, I shall charge your network for their services."

I gave her my blessings.

# *Chapter*
# THIRTY-EIGHT

The address Gloria Ingram had given me was in the ultra-ritzy Holmby Hills, a gated estate with rolling lawns, fish ponds, tennis courts, a pool complete with cabana, and gardens filled with rainbow-colored buds, all failing to soften or beautify a two-story granite monster of a mansion. I parked the Lexus at the end of a gravel drive, behind two large Carrying the World vans.

Gloria Ingram was standing at the door to the ugly mansion, overseeing movers in white jumpsuits as they toted furniture from the house to the vans. She was a tall, patrician woman in her forties. There was something familiar about her. Roger had said she'd been a model and a starlet before her marriage.

She gave me a cool, professional welcome and explained that her work consisted of preparing foreclosed properties for sale. "The so-called owner of this mausoleum blew the country, sticking the bank with a twenty-nine-million-dollar mortgage he'd barely dented." She added wearily, "We'll be lucky if we get twenty-six-five."

As she led me into the house and a marble reception area, two men were removing a huge painting of voluptuous nude ladies cavorting rather naughtily on black velvet. They were followed by two of their associates carrying a portrait of Elvis with angel wings. A third painting rested against a marble wall, Satan behind the wheel of a speeding Maserati, leaving a trail of hellish flames in its wake. Where, I wondered, was the painting of the dogs playing poker?

"Was the mortgage walkaway a pimp?" I asked.

"A television evangelist," Gloria replied. "Not to say you were wrong. As you can see, he had lovely taste. Usually we prefer to present a property furnished. But in this instance, I'm quite sure that would not have helped the sale."

I followed her through rooms that showed the touch of a decorator with either an absolute lack of taste or one hell of a sense of humor. I particularly liked the mink-covered beanbag chairs in the main living room and the red-and-black sitting room with clear-plastic furniture.

"Satan's Maserati was hanging there," Gloria said, pointing to a red wall. "The painters are coming in tomorrow to reclaim the room from the eighth circle of hell."

"What exactly did this evangelist evangel?" I asked.

"The power of the pill," she said. "I gather his communion wafer was an amphetamine-laced cookie that convinced his followers they'd been miraculously healed. Alas, the district attorney proved to be something of an agnostic, and, fearing a forced relocation to a much rougher congregation, the divinity Dr. Feelgood departed in haste. So here I am."

Indeed, she was. "I know we've never met," I said.

"But I get the feeling I've seen you before. In a film? Or on TV?"

"You're talking about my previous life. That was long ago, Mr. Blessing. And believe me, there was nothing memorable about it. Come. We should have our chat in the kitchen. It's the only room in this horror that doesn't cause your eyes to bleed. I'm leaving it as is, so we won't be disturbed by the movers."

Apparently, the evangelist's only evidence of taste was in his palate. The kitchen was elegant and well designed. Gloria Ingram told me he'd hired a promising young chef from Esplanade, one of the Coast's top restaurants, and given him complete control over the room.

Gloria didn't remember the chef's name.

"What happened to him?" I asked, while she poured thick black coffee into two refreshingly plain mugs.

"The chef? He's working for Roger now. That is, he's working at La Maison Rouge."

She placed the silver pot on the countertop and sat on a stool beside mine. "Roger was a little vague about this . . . What shall I call it? . . . Interrogation?"

"What did he tell you?"

"That you'd be asking me about that night, and I should tell you the truth. He believes you have some influence over the detective who arrested him."

"He may be overestimating that influence."

"I'm a little unclear on why you're trying to help him."

"I'm not sure," I said. "I guess it's because I may have caused him a lot of grief over the past twenty two years because of a misunderstanding. If that's the case, I owe him a lot more than spending a few minutes in the company of a beautiful woman."

The blush made her seem ten years younger. "Well, you'll have to help me with this. How do I begin?"

"Start with what you remember about the night."

"I should explain something, otherwise . . ." She stopped speaking and stared at her coffee cup.

I had a little time.

I sipped. The coffee was good and strong. Starbucks Dark Roast, I was guessing. Sommelier, barista. Very close . . .

"I've never thought of it as being adulterous," she said. "But I *was* married at the time. My husband and I . . . It wasn't an ideal situation. He'd spent nearly a year making a crappy cops-and-robbers movie in Canada. And he was off again, to Moab, Utah. I was young. And being human, had needs that . . . were not . . ."

She blinked, sniffed, and straightened on the stool. "It had only been a few months since Connie . . . since we lost Connie. Our daughter. Actually, my husband's daughter from a previous marriage. But her death had taken its toll on both of us, and, eventually, our marriage became part of that loss."

"I'm sorry."

"Water waaay under the bridge," she said. "Anyway, to get to what you need to know, Roger and I spent all that night in a house my husband owned at the Springs. I was pretty sure Stew used to bring his bimbos there, so it seemed appropriate for me to use it to entertain Roger."

"Stew? Stew Gentry?"

"Sorry, that was indiscreet of me. Do you know

him? Oh, God, of course you do. It was at his party that you and Roger . . ."

"Yeah," I said. "I like Stew."

"He is likable," she said, "just not terribly faithful."

I suddenly realized why she'd seemed so familiar. "You're Dani's mother," I said.

"Yes."

"Your daughter is a knockout."

"And bright. And athletic. Oh, God, aren't I the doting mom?"

"Not without cause," I said.

"Mr. Blessing—"

"Make it Billy. Please."

"Billy, I hope you won't take this the wrong way, but I'm suddenly feeling very uncomfortable about all this. I'd appreciate it if we could just wrap it up."

"Of course. Only a question or two more. Are you absolutely certain Roger couldn't have left while you were sleeping, driven to L.A. and back before you woke?"

"Not possible. We . . . stayed up through the night. We made love. We talked. We laughed. Dawn was breaking before we fell asleep. At around two the next day, we finally left the house in search of food. We were in the car when we heard about the murder. Roger went off his head. Almost drove us into a streetlamp. I thought he was going to rip the steering wheel from its post. It took all my strength to pry his fingers from it.

"Later, when he finally calmed down, he realized he'd be needing an alibi. And that was a problem. Stew is a sweetheart in normal circumstances. But if the affair had gone public, he would have assumed I'd seduced Roger to spite him. I was afraid of the consequences. You don't want to get on Stew's bad side."

I'd seen that myself, close up.

"So Victor Anisette was asked to fill in for you in the alibi department," I said.

"Victor volunteered eagerly," she said. "You understand, we had the advantage of knowing that Roger was innocent."

"How close are you and Roger these days?"

"I'm not lying for him, if that's what you're asking."

"No. I just wondered if you still had much contact with him."

"We're old friends," she said. "We still meet for the occasional lunch or dinner, and, if I desperately need an escort, he's on my list. But that weekend at the Springs was the end of our . . . affair. There's nothing kicks the pins out from under a romance quicker than almost getting drawn into a murder investigation."

"Did Stew ever find out about you and Roger?" I asked.

"God, no. The fact that both Roger and I are still alive is proof of that," she said.

"You mean that literally?"

"Of course not. Stew's not capable of murder, though he'd probably like people to think he is. That macho thing. He does hold grudges, however, in case you planned to tell him about that night."

"Why would I?"

She shrugged. "I don't know you or what kind of friend you are to Stew. You might think he should be told. But it wouldn't be good for him or me, or Dani. And it wouldn't do much for your friendship, either. He'd never forgive you."

"I wasn't planning on mentioning it," I said. "Did you know he had a background check done on Roger?"

She froze. "When was this?"

"When Roger started going out with Dani," I said.

She laughed. " 'Going out'? That's priceless. But it's so Stew. Always worried about the wrong things."

"Roger strike you as Mr. Right?"

"Hardly. But why wouldn't Stew ask Dani about their relationship instead of . . . ? Well, he is what he is."

I wondered if it wasn't she who should have that talk with Dani. But it was none of my business.

She slipped gracefully from the stool. "Will that about do it?"

I stood. "Thanks for seeing me. I hope it wasn't too . . ."

I stopped talking because I'd lost her. She was staring at something behind me, hugging herself, as if caught by a sudden draft of frigid air.

I turned to see an amazingly old man, his frail, twisted body seated on a wheelchair so streamlined and full of bells and whistles it might have come from the latest Michael Bay movie. He was even more interesting than the chair. Bald, except for a few long strands of yellow-tinged white hairs pasted to his scalp. His left eye was closed in what appeared to be a permanent wink, and his nose and chin were just an inch or so from an embrace.

He was wearing a bowling shirt of pale blue and white stripes with the team name "Frush Strike Kings" on the right pocket. Spindly bare arms were crossed over his sunken chest. Matching bare legs dangled from white baggy shorts. The toes of his bare feet were constricted and pawlike. His flesh was bottle-tanned. Too even and with a hint of green in the mix. He looked like a Southern California surfer dude version of Ebenezer Scrooge.

In any less bizarre company, his "assistant" would have commanded my attention first. She could have been in her early twenties, a cap of gamine-cut red hair surrounding a pretty face with the standard Irish green eyes and full lips and freckles. The freckles extended at least as far as the deep V-neck of a thin, starched white short-sleeve shirt that came within a few threads of transparency. Her white slacks were so form-fitting that it was not until the white soft-sole shoes that I realized she was wearing a nurse's uniform, albeit a fetishist's version.

"Hello, Billy," the old man said. Only his lips didn't move and it sounded more like "Her-row, illy."

I stared at him and saw, hidden in that aged, Punchlike, semiparalyzed face, a hint of the arrogant, energetic man I'd known twenty-two years ago.

"Hi, Victor," I said. "How's tricks?"

His reply was wet and slurry.

"I'm sorry, but I didn't get that."

The nurse wrinkled her nose in annoyance. "He said he hoped he wasn't intruding."

I turned to Gloria. She was staring at a corner of the room.

Victor Anisette lifted a withered arm off his chest.

His fingers were like a spider's legs wiggling in the air until they came in contact with the nurse's thigh and began to rub it in a circular motion. The fact that she was not repulsed suggested she'd grown used to the familiarity.

He issued another comment, indecipherable to me but not to the nurse. "He says Roger asked him to stop by, to make sure you got everything you needed."

"Roger's a very thoughtful guy," I said.

"I'd better get back to work," Gloria said.

"'Onc go. I lih looking ah ya lo'e tes.'"

"He says, 'Don't go.' He likes looking at your lovely tits," the nurse translated.

Gloria did not bother to reply. She gave them both a wide berth as she left the room.

"So haugh'y . . . for a slu."

"He says she's so—"

"I got it," I said. "Nice seeing you, Victor. Kinda made my day."

I started to go.

"Wai'!"

I stopped, stared at him.

"Yah gnna hel' Haya?"

"'You going to help Roger?'"

"I doubt I can," I said. "I don't think he killed Tiffany. But I don't know if what I think will matter to the police."

"Onna her."

"'Wouldn't hurt,'" the nurse translated.

"No hah elly a hah ah he yee?"

I looked at the nurse for assistance.

"'No hard feelings after all these years?'"

I smiled at the old man. "You tried to destroy my

reputation and end my career before it started," I said. "It probably shows a weakness of character, but I still hate your guts, Victor."

The half-frown on his partially mobile face might have seemed more sincere if he weren't caressing his nurse's buttocks. "Uh a aye you uh han hu ake huhan ah ha hel."

"He says he gave you the chance to make something of yourself."

I laughed. "That's very good spin, Victor. Stay healthy, now."

He burbled something else as I left the room, but I wasn't curious enough about it to spend another minute with them. I collared one of the movers and asked where I might find Ms. Ingram. He gestured upstairs with his thumb.

She was in the master bedroom, supervising the removal of a mirror from the ceiling over the huge, round bed. "Are they gone?" she asked.

"Maybe leaving," I said. "I'm not sure."

She moved to the window. I joined her and saw that it looked out over the front of the house, including the drive. The nurse was pushing Victor in his wheelchair toward an immaculate vintage silver Rolls-Royce Wraith parked behind my rental. It was a glistening machine with cream side panels and gangster whitewall tires.

"I had nothing to do with him coming here," she said.

"I picked up on that," I said.

We watched the nurse open a rear door. As she

lifted Victor from his chair, he pressed his face between her breasts. The nurse didn't skip a beat. She swung him onto the backseat of the Rolls as if he were made of straw, buckled him in, and slammed the door on him.

She got behind the wheel and, with little effort, made a U-turn and drove away.

"What a loathsome creature that man is," Gloria said.

"You're preaching to the choir," I said.

She asked me the same question the old man had: Was I going to help Roger? I gave her the same answer, then asked, "Why would Roger send Victor here, knowing how you feel about him?"

"I've never given Roger reason to think I feel any way about Victor, pro or con. They're partners and friends, though I can't imagine how Roger puts up with him. They're so different in every way."

I thought they were as alike as cuff links, psychologically and philosophically, but I kept that to myself, preferring to part on, if not exactly a friendly note, at least a polite one.


Before driving off, I phoned Detective Brueghel and was directed to his voice mail. I left a request for a callback, pocketed the phone, and put the car in drive. As I departed, I glanced back and saw Gloria still at the window, looking off into the distance, as if trying to convince herself that Victor was truly gone.

# Chapter
# THIRTY-NINE

Having lunch in Hollywood isn't exactly a problem, unless you're an easily recognizable figure currently involved in a front-page murder investigation. That rather limits your choice of restaurants. I had no desire to dine in any of the flash places where the paparazzi roam, but I wasn't sure if I'd be able to finish a meal in peace in even the less-celebrated venues.

I decided traditional was my best bet and headed to Hollywood Boulevard and Musso & Frank. Neither the grill nor the menu had changed much in twenty-two years. Just the personnel and the prices.

I settled into a dark red leather booth, my back to the rear door, the main entryway, and managed to polish off a pounded steak with country gravy, lyonnaise potatoes, creamed spinach, and two glasses of iced tea, with just one tourist couple stopping at the table to gawk. And that was only until I looked up and winked at them.

Sated, and having nowhere else to go, I arrived at the Worldwide lot twenty minutes early for the afternoon meeting. I sat in the Lexus with the top up and the AC on high, wondering if I should go in or just fly back to Manhattan and pretend the trip had been a dream, like that infamous season of *Dallas*.

Detectives Brueghel and Campbell made the decision for me.

Their black Crown Vic entered the lot, drove right past me, and slid into a no-parking space about ten vehicles away.

I closed down my AC and engine and met them on their way to the main building.

"What's up?"

"Damn it, Blessing," Brueghel said. "Why don't you ever answer your goddamned phone?"

Thanks to Cassandra's heads-up, I'd turned the thing off rather than risk inadvertently bugging myself. "Sorry," I said.

"I been trying to reach you for the last hour," he said. "No good deed . . ."

"You have to excuse him, Mr. Blessing," Detective Campbell said. "Man hates to be wrong."

"Not wrong," he snapped. "But even if I am, my wrong doesn't make you right."

Detective Campbell giggled at that. She was much more attractive in giddy mode.

"What's going on?" I asked, as we entered the building.

"My partner had to kick Charbonnet loose," Detective Campbell said.

"Why?"

"'Cause the prick . . ." His sentence drifted into an undecipherable mumble.

"The prick what?" I asked.

"He didn't do it," Brueghel groused, and, ignoring the approaching elevator, pushed through the door leading to the stairs.

Campbell and I followed.

"What happened?" I asked her.

"Couple things. First, we finally got the report on the explosive used. It was a little more sophisticated than a Clorox bomb. Not much, but enough to make the stuff we found at the Brentwood house useless as evidence."

We were double-timing it up the stairs, Brueghel nearly a level ahead and widening the gap. "There's more," Campbell said, not even breathing hard, "but we should wait for Pete to give that out, him being the lead."

She was grinning.

"You're getting a big kick out of his discomfort," I said.

"Pete's the best partner I've ever had, and he's an excellent detective. Except when he's got Charbonnet in his sights. I've been telling him all along he's been misreading this one."

Carmen was not alone in her office. Whisper was seated on a chair to her right. Max and Trey were standing nearby, shaking hands with Brueghel. After an introduction to Detective Campbell, Carmen gave Brueghel the floor.

A scarlet flush was spreading upward from his neck, and his jaws were clenched so tight that little knots protruded from the sides of his face. "There have been . . ."

He paused, his right hand going to the back of his neck. I was concerned that he might be experiencing a seizure of some kind. But he just made a head roll accompanied by neck pops and launched into his announcement. "As I mentioned on the phone, Ms. Sandoval, Chief Weidemeyer, ah, *suggested* this heads-up because your network is directly involved in our investigation. We're doing it in the spirit of mutual cooperation. The chief will be making an official statement to the media in just about two hours. I want to make it clear that this is off the record."

"Our evening news anchor, Jim McBride, is flying in from D.C. to attend the chief's briefing," Carmen replied. "That will be the source of our coverage."

"I assume that pertains also to Ble  Mr. Blessing's appearance on *The Midnight Show*?"

Carmen hesitated, then nodded.

"Fine." The detective and his partner exchanged glances, and he continued. "We have become aware of certain facts regarding last week's fatal explosion that have made us reopen the investigation.

"Initially, because the explosive had been ignited on a section of the stage where Mr. Blessing had been scheduled to stand, we had assumed that he, and not Mr. O'Day, had been the intended victim. Our primary investigation . . . proceeded from that assumption, the result being the arrest of Mr. Roger B. Charbonnet, a suspect who not only had a history of . . . animosity toward Mr. Blessing but was in possession of materials used in the creation of a bomb."

Campbell had an unreadable smile on her face.

"This morning, however, we have learned considerably more about the explosive and the device used to trigger it, information that indicated our original assumption had been in error. It appears more likely that Mr. O'Day was the assassin's target. Consequently, we have released Mr. Charbonnet and refocused our investigation."

"What'd the techs tell you about the bomb that changed your mind?" Max asked.

Brueghel's face registered only a hint of annoyance at being interrupted. He was doing his best to maintain his good-cop mode. He got a small spiral notepad from his inside coat pocket, flipped a single page, and read, "It was a 'cast-loaded composition B burster' about the size of a couple of cigarette packs." Closing the notepad and putting it away, he continued, "The materials we found in Mr. Charbonnet's shed could have created a bomb but are not consistent with this particular one."

"There's something I've never understood, detective," Carmen said. "The theater's stage was built on solid cement. For the bomb to claim Mr. O'Day, it must have been in plain view. But no one remembers seeing anything unusual, not even something as small as a couple of cigarette packs."

"Right. Well, a tiny piece of plastic, found in the rubble, helps to explain that, ma'am. It was identified as a portion of a wheel, one inch in circumference, from a kid's toy called a Zapmobile. It's like a little automobile with a wireless control. We think it had been rigged to hold the explosive. When Mr. O'Day took his final position on the stage that night, the killer sent the Zapmobile in his direction and then used another wireless device to detonate. The whole operation could have been done in less than thirty seconds."

I remembered the whirring sound I'd heard. And there was something else that seemed relevant. A comment someone had made? Maybe on that night? I couldn't get a fix on it.

"That's the main reason we released Mr. Charbonnet," Brueghel was explaining. "The killer had to be present and could see, without doubt, that Mr. O'Day would be his victim. To our knowledge, Mr. Charbonnet had no motive for killing Mr. O'Day. The focus of our investigation now is to find out who did."

"We will assist you in any way we can," Carmen said.

Max turned to Trey. "You're the expert on Des," he said. "Maybe you should sit down with the detectives, give 'em whatever you've got."

"Actually, I provided Detective Campbell with my files on Des and all the other members of the cast and crew days ago."

"Oh?" Max turned to look questioningly at the detective.

"Mr. Halstead has been very cooperative," Campbell said.

"I'm surprised to hear you were looking into Des's background before today," Max said. "How long have you had the information about the bomb?"

"As Detective Brueghel said, we just found out about the bomb today. While our primary focus has been on persons of interest with motive to do harm to Mr. Blessing, it was Mr. O'Day who died in the explosion, and we could hardly ignore the possibility he might have been the intended victim. I've been working on that possibility."

"Come up with anything?" Carmen asked.

"Tons about his career as a performer, beginning with his first paying job on the radio in Dublin. That was in 1997. Before that, not much. Born in Dungannon on January seventh, 1972. Father and mother were both merchants. Now deceased. No siblings. Attended Saint Mary's University in Belfast but dropped out after a year for some unknown reason. That's about it."

"You should talk to Jimmy Fitzpatrick," I said. "They grew up together."

"That's where I got what little information I have," Campbell said. "I've spoken with him a couple of times. He's pretty vague. Or maybe he's been stonewalling me. I tried reaching him today, but his phone's off. What time does he come in?"

"He's not coming in," Max said. "He walked out on the show yesterday. After manhandling our star."

That caught Brueghel's interest. "He was violent?"

Max turned to Trey. "I'd say so, right?"

"Yeah," Trey said. "Definitely violent."

"I want to know more about this."

Before either Max or Trey could put Fitz even further under the bus, I said, "Fitzpatrick told Max he intended to take Des's remains home to Ireland for burial," I said. "Gibby made some pretty insensitive jokes about the body parts and then called Catholics mackerel-snappers, and Fitz slapped him around a little."

Brueghel nodded and seemed a little less intrigued. He turned to his partner. "They released the body?"

She nodded. "Mr. Fitzpatrick asked me to let him know, and so I did. Yesterday. But as of an hour ago, the remains were still unclaimed."

"And Fitzpatrick's not picking up his phone,"

Brueghel said. "Anybody here have any contact with him after the . . . slapping incident?"

"He dropped by my place last night," I said.

Once again, I was the center of interest.

"And . . . ?" Brueghel asked.

"He'd been drinking and seemed a little . . . stressed."

"Jeeze, Blessing, don't make me drag it out of you. Details, please."

I was beginning to feel like those mastodons who'd paused to take a sip of water and wound up trapped in the La Brea Tar Pits. Ever since I'd arrived in L.A. I'd been stuck and slowly sinking. Opening up with everything that Fitz had told me would only put me in deeper.

But I realized now he hadn't been raving. He probably did have a good idea why Des had been killed. Even more disquieting, if he was right about that, who's to say he wasn't right about somebody connected with the show being involved in the murder? Or that the somebody had sent a milk-eyed man to stalk him? These were things Brueghel should know.

"Is that it, Blessing? You're clamming up?"

"No," I said, and told him the salient parts of my late-night visit.

## *Chapter*
# FORTY

"You didn't consider any of that significant enough for a call?" Brueghel asked.

"He was drunk as a skunk, singing songs and speaking in riddles. So no, my feeling was he was talking through his beard. And just a reminder, Roger was still in jail, and you were convinced *he* was the killer, so you would have agreed with me."

Brueghel's frown deepened. Any more and his brows would completely overlap his eyes. He turned to the others. "Don't suppose any of you know of a man with a milky eye? I guess that might be a cataract."

They didn't.

"That's utter nonsense about someone on the show being involved in Des's murder," Max said. "Nobody had even met him before he was signed. And that was only a few months ago. Right, Trey?"

"As far as I know, Des spent surprisingly little time in Southern California."

"Could there be a reason for that?" Brueghel asked. "Maybe somebody out here he didn't want to see?"

Trey shrugged.

"Once he arrived, was there any kind of incident or problem?" Brueghel asked.

I looked at Max, and he looked away. He and Trey had been eyewitnesses to the beating of the transvestite. But they evidently were not going to mention it. Maybe that was the correct choice. The only certain result would be the transvestite winding up at the top of the detective's list of suspects. And he'd already been through enough.

"Blessing," Brueghel said, startling me out of my reverie. "About the mess in the house out in Malibu, did it look like it had been caused by a struggle?"

"That or a drunk floundering around by himself."

"But the realtor put a cleaning crew on it. Probably not much to see, Mizzy, but still we ought to drive out there, look around. And we need to get a handle on this Fitzpatrick. Find out where he is. Here. In Ireland, or wherever."

Max glanced at his watch. "If that's it, we'd better move on to our staff meeting," he said. "Thanks for the update, detectives."

"We should probably stop by that meeting on our way out," Brueghel said. "Check in with the rest of your people. Maybe they've bumped into the guy with the milky eye."

"As you wish," Max replied.

"I appreciate your cooperation."

The daily meet had been relocated to the executive conference room, down the hall from Carmen's office. The multiwindowed space was bright and airy, and the chairs cushioned, all of which seemed to lighten the atmosphere. Until the detectives began asking questions about Des and Fitz and the milky-eyed man.

Though Brueghel did most of the initial talking, the staffers seemed more responsive to Campbell. It appeared that while he'd been involved in his pursuit of Roger Charbonnet, she'd had meetings with many of them, investigating what was then the less likely scenario of Des being the intended victim.

Brueghel was quick to read the room and smoothly deferred to his partner. The two detectives spent nearly half an hour with us, mainly answering questions. If they got any information in return, I missed it.

What I did notice was Gibby's thoughtful silence, which struck me as being slightly out of character.

When they departed, Max gave us a pep talk about putting our concerns regarding "this regrettable situation" on hold. In the grand tradition of our industry, the show must go on. "Our responsibility is to entertain. Let Billy deal with the harsh reality in his segment.

"By the way, Billy, Jim McBride will be your guest tonight. You guys can kick around the *official* LAPD announcement.

"Okay, kids, I'll see you on Stage Seven in fifteen minutes."

Chief Weidemeyer held his press conference at precisely four that afternoon, timed to make the early newscasts on the West Coast and the late news in the East.

I watched the East Coast feed of the complete seventeen-minute conference with Carmen in her office. I discovered she had a habit of snorting derisively. When the chief told the members of the media about the unique bomb-delivery device and purposely left the toy's brand name unmentioned, she let out a snort. When he spoke of the 180-degree shift in the homicide investigation, he made it seem more like a breakthrough than the correction of an initial deductive misfire. Another snort.

He began his wind-down with a substantive comment: "The popular musician known by the name Fitzpatrick, a close friend of the victim's, is currently being sought. If anyone has any knowledge of Mr. Fitzpatrick or his current whereabouts, please contact the LAPD. I should emphasize something: Mr. Fitzpatrick is not a suspect." Snort. "We do believe, however, that he may possess information that would assist our investigation.

"Other than that, I can assure you that the investigation is on course. We are making excellent progress, and we expect to make an arrest shortly. Thank you."

I snorted with Carmen on that one.

Chief Weidemeyer clearly hoped to exit on that note, but the noisy crowd wasn't finished with him. The newsies wanted more sound bite material on just about everything, and their questions, once begun, were relentless, repetitive, and overlapping. They boiled down to: Was Fitzpatrick missing? What was it he knew? Did they suspect he might be dead? Did they know why Des O'Day had been murdered? Whom did they suspect, if not Fitzpatrick?

The chief's face remained unreadable throughout. He seemed to be staring just over the heads of the crowd, as if counting the windows in the building across the street. Finally, he'd had enough. He bent slightly to get closer to the mike, cleared his throat, and repeated, "Thank you."

That didn't stop the flow of questions, but he no longer seemed to care. He gathered his notes, paused to whisper something to the public information officer, and made his getaway. The perky public-relations lady, who seemed to enjoy confrontation, assumed the role of blocking guard for the chief and responded to questions with the usual canned nonanswers designed to close down a conference.

That's when I noticed Jim McBride plant himself directly in the chief's path, ready with a question. He opened his mouth just as the chief's female flying wedge moved in on him, a perfect smile plastered on her perfectly made-up face.

Jim suddenly buckled, and the chief and his entourage squeezed past his bent body.

"The bit about Fitz means that the detectives reported our meeting to the chief," I said.

"That should make it fair game for the show tonight," she said. She stood, an indication that she was no longer fascinated by my presence. "I assume you and Jim will get together as soon as he arrives from the conference."

"Right," I said, backing toward the door. "It looked to me like the chief's PIO nearly knocked Jim on his ass."

"Kneed him in the balls, if I'm any judge," Carmen said.

\* \* \*

The rehearsal for the last *Midnight Show* of the week was in full swing when I slipped onto a seat in the nearly unpopulated audience section of Studio 7. A black-and-yellow-haired member of the Asian group No Fangs was goofing on Gibby mercilessly, pretending to teach him hip-hop while getting him into positions that defied gravity and inevitably resulted in his hitting the deck with a thud.

Gibby was supposed to be holding his own verbally with the No Fangser, but he seemed a little distracted. One of the comedy writers was standing by, feeding him lines that he kept fumbling. Somehow that made it more amusing.

Suddenly, I got a whiff of camellias and felt a warm body pressed against the back of my head. Graceful hands covered my eyes.

"Guess who?"

"Hmmm. Give me a hint. Ebony or ivory?"

"Definitely ebony."

"Jennifer Hudson?"

"No," she said.

"Beyoncé?"

"No," she said again.

"Then you must be *my* dream girl," I said, taking her hands in mine, pressing my head back, and looking up at Vida smiling down at me.

She circled the seat, trailing her fingernails across the back of my neck. I rose as she brushed past me to take the adjoining seat.

"How was Yorba Linda?" I asked.

"You first. On the drive in, every news station was blowing up with stories and speculation about you and Des, and new evidence in the investigation."

"You probably know more than I do."

"Oh, sure. You're not going to hold out on me, Billy?" she asked.

"Ah, if only that question were sex-related."

"With me, baby, news is sex."

"I hope that's a joke."

She smiled to show me that it was. "Okay," she said. "If you won't tell me yours, I'll tell you mine. Satan has officially left Yorba Linda. The woman who started the whole mess broke down this morning under some very tough questioning by the teachers' attorney. She admitted she *may* have been mistaken about what her son said in his sleep re: the school celebrating a devil mass."

"How old is the kid?"

"Four."

"And she still monitors his sleep?"

"My guess is she'd chew his food for him if he'd let her. The real story, and the one I'll be reporting, is that a teacher at the school had incurred mommy dearest's wrath by laying hands on her precious son. The teacher, a twenty-five-year-old pregnant lady, had pulled the monster boy off of a little girl after he'd knocked her to the ground and was kicking her."

"Sounds like Mom was looking for Beelzebub in all the wrong places."

"You got it. Her brat acts up, and her reaction is to spread a lie that sends five innocent, dedicated teachers, one of them with child, to prison for over a month."

"But the bad genie is back in the bottle?" I asked.

"Pretty much. The DA is afraid of looking like the idiot he is and hasn't quite given up the fight. But his case is dissolving as we speak, and it appears the teachers will be exonerated."

"That kind of toxic cloud doesn't blow away all that easily," I said. "There'll be quite a few empty desks in those classrooms for a while."

"I know. But at least the teachers will be spending tonight in the comfort of their own homes. And I'll be spending tonight in mine. Alone, unless I can find somebody who's free for dinner."

"Short notice," I said.

"Boeuf bourguignon," she said. "I use a recipe in a cookbook by my favorite TV food expert."

"I'm flattered."

"You? I was talking about the Muppets' Swedish Chef."

"Oh. But you'll be serving real F-O-O-D, right?"

"As real as a clogged artery."

"The earliest I can get there is ten-thirty," I said.

She stood. I stood. "It'll take me that long to do justice by the Swedish Chef," she said. She leaned against me suddenly and kissed me, her tongue darting between my lips. As I raised my arms to pull her closer, she slipped away.

"Don't be too late," she said, "or I may have to start without you."

I watched her as she strolled gracefully toward the exit.

When she was gone, I turned and found Gibby staring at me from the stage. He gave me a wink and a thumbs-up, then began a series of pelvic thrusts, humping the air.

Ever the class act.

I turned to go in search of Jim McBride, who

should have made it back from the press conference an hour ago.

"Hold up, Billy," Gibby shouted.

I watched him grab a towel from the back of a chair and walk toward me, blotting his perspiring face.

"I . . . need some advice," he said, lowering his voice.

"What's the gag?"

"No. No gag. I'm seriously freaked."

He looked it, and he wasn't that good an actor. "How can I help?"

"Today, when the cops mentioned—"

He was interrupted by McBride, lanky and as immaculately dressed as always, calling out, "Billy B. Great to see you in the flesh, as it were." He approached us slowly and carefully, wincing with each step.

I introduced him to Gibby, who thanked him for guesting on tonight's show. Then, inching away, Gibby added, "I, ah, better get back. Billy, can you spare a couple minutes later, after the show?"

"Sure," I said.

"He seems a little nervous about something," McBride said, as we watched the comic heading for the set. "They dumping him?"

"Not that I've heard," I said, turning to McBride. "You look a little nervous yourself," I said.

"That's pain, brother. At a press conference today, the chief of police's PR lady kneed me in the 'nads."

"I saw it happen on the tube. You got in her sight line. She was a beauty, by the way. Roger Ailes should hire her for FOX News. They have a thing for hot women."

"Hot and mean," Jim said with a wide grin. "Just like we like 'em. Except for their politics, of course. So what's our plan here, Billy? I understand we've got twelve minutes to fill. Do we do this *60 Minutes* style, write down a series of talking points, each stopwatch-timed, each feeding off the other until we arrive at a final conclusion that has a kick harder than an LAPD PR flack? Or do we go to plan B and find us a couple of comfortable chairs in whatever passes for a green-room here in lotusland and chat about the good times and then, when we get the red light, wing the whole damn thing as smoothly and effortlessly as the old pros we are?"

"I vote for plan B," I said.

## Chapter
# FORTY-ONE

I won't say we were Emmy material, but we whipped through the recent developments of what was now considered the Des O'Day murder in just under eight minutes and finished up with Jim, whose news-anchor persona is smooth, efficient, and buttoned-down, displaying his off-camera charm and wit reminiscing about a murder case he'd covered early in his career.

After our segment, Whisper conveyed a late supper invitation to Jim from Carmen. He turned to me. "You joining us?"

"Not that I was invited," I said, "but I've got a previous engagement."

"Yeah? Starlet?"

"Better than that," I said.

On my way to Vida's, I stopped at a twenty-four-hour liquor store and was pleased to find, hidden among its otherwise uninspired wine selection, several bottles of Adelaida HMR Estate Paso Robles pinot noir. I purchased one—well, two, actually. It was, after all, the beginning of the weekend.

Whistling a merry tune, I carried my purchases back to the Lexus and discovered that someone had stuck a folded ad flyer under its driver's-side wiper. Still whistling, I removed the paper and surveyed the parking lot for the nearest trash bin. Too far away.

The Lexus's automatic wireless unlock did its thing. I opened the door and eased behind the wheel. I placed the wine bottles gently on the passenger seat, then transferred them to the rubber floor mat. Finally, I unfolded the sheet, preparing to give it a cursory glance before balling it and tossing it beside the wine bottles, to be disposed of later.

It consisted primarily of a very familiar design. "I (Heart) NY," bold, black letters surrounding a red heart. Beneath it, a copy line read: "Live It Up in the Big Apple!"

Someone had added, in hand-printed block letters, "Or die in L.A."

I refolded the sheet and stuck it in my shirt pocket.

Then I twisted on the car seat and took a hard look at my surroundings. There appeared to be nothing terribly sinister about the liquor store's narrow, brightly lighted parking lot. Still, I didn't feel quite panicked enough to do anything more than get the hell out of there.

My finger was an inch from the Lexus's starter button when the concept of a car bomb came to mind.

No, I told myself. A bomber, even a demented one, would not have bothered to put a warning on my windshield if he intended to send me to New York in little pieces. I pressed the button, and the car started as safely as always.

I rolled the Lexus out into the street.

Half a block behind me, a car left its curbside parking spot. The black BMW.

I speeded up. So did the BMW.

Up ahead was Melrose Avenue, which I knew would be bustling with customers of the late-hour boutiques and restaurants and clubs. I eased into the traffic. The BMW fell back a little but remained on my tail.

What to do? I could think of only one thing. I got out the cellular and was about to phone Brueghel when the black car made a right turn and apparently left the chase.

I drove another few blocks to make sure. No black BMW.

I'd seen enough movie thrillers to consider the possibility of a two-car shadow. With that in mind, I made an abrupt right turn onto a less-traveled side street. I drove it all the way to Santa Monica Boulevard. Nobody followed.

I remembered how paranoid Fitz had sounded with his story of a milk-eyed man in a gray Mercedes. I'd made that flip comment about the number of gray Mercedeses in the city. Weren't there just as many black BMWs?

The threatening note made my concern a little more credible. But as a scare tactic, it was a pretty lame effort. And shaking Brueghel's tree with it would only set him off on an I-should-never-have-set-Charbonnet-free rant and tie up the rest of my night.

On the other hand, I had a beautiful woman waiting to feed me dinner. I had two bottles of very good wine. And tomorrow was a work-free Saturday.

No contest.

Vida's house was filled with the perfume of beef braised in red wine. She'd transformed her small dining room into a romantic candlelit cloister. If that weren't intoxicating enough, she was wearing what looked like two sarongs, a black one with shiny golden suns that covered her from waist to ankle, and the other, a bright red, draped around her upper body, leaving her bare midriff to fend for itself. It seemed to be doing just fine.

She gave me a quick kiss and slid dreamily away, leaving me with the taste of grapes on my lips.

"A confession," she said. "The Swedish Chef didn't say what to do with the leftover wine, so I've been drinking it. And I feel wonderful."

God bless the Muppets.

I was feeling pretty wonderful myself.

We drank. We ate. We talked and laughed, and

eventually arrived at the moment when I was to discover the parameters of a second date with Vida.

She stood, swaying slightly, and began walking around the room, extinguishing the candles. "Safety first," she said.

"Excellent motto," I think I said, rising to help.

Somehow we snuffed all the little flames without setting ourselves on fire. At least not literally. Vida moved closer, pressed against me, and we were about to kiss when she pulled away.

"Something's coming between us," she said. She reached out, playfully plucked the New York flyer from my shirt pocket, and danced away with it into the living room.

*Damn. Please don't read it. Please don't read it.*

She stood by a lamp, reading it.

"What is this, Billy?" she asked, her sexy-happy mood doing a 180.

"Just a brochure," I said. "I Love New York."

"You understand this is somebody telling you to get out of town, right?" She sounded like she was now Ms. *Hotline.* "Who gave it to you?"

"I found it under my windshield. It's nothing to worry—"

"You didn't happen to see who put it there?"

"No."

"Notice anything else? Somebody sitting in a car, maybe?"

"No. What are you getting at?"

"Maybe a black BMW parked nearby?"

I guess my expression must have given her the answer, because before I could open my mouth, she was running toward the front door. She fumbled it open and rushed out. Almost immediately she returned, grabbed what looked like a walking stick from a stand beside the door, and ran out again.

By the time I got going, she was racing down the sidewalk toward a black BMW parked just behind my Lexus near a streetlight. "Damn you, Brute," she was screaming as she brandished the walking stick.

The driver's door opened, and a black man stepped out. He had a stubbly mustache that matched the hair on his head. He was six-foot-two or -three, no wider across the shoulders and chest than a fully padded football player. But he wasn't wearing padding, just muscles under a tight black T. And, oh, yes, a gun in a polished shoulder holster.

He was watching Vida's advance with alarm. He kneed the door shut and went to meet her.

"Hold on, now, baby. Don't go flyin' off the handle like you do," he advised.

She took a swing at him with the stick. He easily avoided it, then wrapped her in his arms so that she couldn't make another try. "Somebody's been slurpin' the vino," he said.

"You bastard," she shrilled, struggling. She was not a small woman or a weak one. But her efforts were useless against his bulging arms.

"Tell me what's wrong," he said with surprising calm.

"You . . . betrayed me."

The words surprised him. "I betrayed *you*?"

"I trusted you," she said, crying now. "You betrayed that trust."

"I never would," he said.

"You're hurting me," she said.

He relaxed his hold, and she suddenly broke free and took another swing with the stick.

He dodged, then grabbed her again and forced the stick from her hand.

She pulled away from him and raced past me and into the house. I don't even think she saw me.

The big man walked toward me. "I guess we oughta take this off the street, huh?" he said.

It wasn't a threat, exactly.

As I fell in step beside him, heading for Vida's, he said, "My name's Brutus Mackey." He offered his hand.

I shook it and replied, "Billy Blessing."

"I know. I'm a big fan of your cooking show. I'm kind of an amateur chef myself."

I indicated the weapon he was carrying. "LAPD?"

"Private," he said.

"Vida asked you to watch out for me?"

"Do a guardian angel. Bodyguard you from a distance."

We found Vida sitting on the sofa in her living room, crying.

"I should never have called you, Brute," she said. "That was my miscalculation."

"I don't understand, baby," he said, sitting beside her. I noticed she did not pull away.

She thrust the "I Love NY" flyer at him. "You're gonna tell me you don't know about this?"

He took the flyer and read it. "This was under your windshield wiper, right, Billy?" he asked.

"You oughta know," Vida said. "You put it there."

"You think I'd play that way?" he asked her. "Well as you know me?"

"I think you're bullheaded enough to still believe we can work things out."

"You got that right. But why would I bother trying to chase this man away when I know he's not gonna be around long enough to give me any serious competition?"

"What do you mean?" she asked.

"Billy's a New Yorker. He lives and works there. He's got a restaurant there. Friends. And you're L.A. all the way, baby. Just like me."

She turned toward me. I couldn't quite read her look. Maybe she was asking me to contradict Brutus.

More likely, she was saying goodbye.

I bent down and picked up the flyer, put it back in my pocket.

"A white dude left that," Brutus said, "wimpy, khaki pants, T-shirt type. Five-nine or -ten. Brown, maybe dirty blond, hair. Didn't get a good look at his face. Somebody was chauffeuring him in a gray C-three-fifty sport sedan. Too dark to make out the plate number."

"That C-three-fifty thing. It's a Mercedes, right?"

"Yeah," Brutus said with a smile, as if any fool should know. "A Mercedes."

"Why didn't you just tell me it wasn't you left that note for Billy?" Vida asked him.

"Like you gave me a chance to, baby," he said.

They made a cute couple. I headed for the door.

"Billy, I . . ." Vida began.

I held up a hand. "One thing about us New Yorkers," I said. "We learn to roll with the punches."

Brutus asked if I wanted him to continue guardian angeling me. I told him it wouldn't be necessary. I'd be taking the threatening note to the police in the morning.

"Let them handle it," I said.

He said he'd be available to provide them with a description of the wimp.

I left the house, shutting the door behind me.

I hoped Brutus wouldn't be too upset when he discovered I'd broken in his new silk pajamas.

*Chapter*
## FORTY-TWO

Considering how the night was going, I was not surprised to find the security kiosk unattended at Malibu Sands and five cars lined up at the blocked entry, honking their horns.

A gray-haired man in a starched white shirt and plaid Bermuda shorts got out of his Audi, ducked under the bar, and went in search of the missing guard.

More honking.

I leaned back against the Lexus's headrest, stared up at the winking stars, and thought about heading for Manhattan. The threat had nothing to do with it. Well, maybe a little. But even if there wasn't some homicidal lunatic on the loose, I'd still want to leave.

I was, to quote the immortal words of Billy Joel, in a New York state of mind.

The aging preppy returned with an apologizing guard who looked like he was still in his late teens, gawky and with acne in full bloom on his cheeks and the portion of his forehead not covered by his cap.

I gathered that the line consisted mainly of the guests of a resident named Halliday who was hosting an over-the-hill shindig party at his place. The guard clutched his clipboard as he searched for names and waved the other cars through. When I finally arrived at his window, he said, "Sorry about the wait. Name, please?"

I told him. He checked his list and seemed perplexed. He raised his eyes and looked at me for the first time. Then he did a perfect double-take. "You're not going to the Halliday party," he said. "You're the guy on TV. Lars, the day guard, said you were staying here. I'm Rambo."

Of course he was. This was, after all, the land of citizens whose parents had named them Moon Unit, Kal-el, Free, Banjo, and even an Audio.

"You manning the booth alone tonight, Rambo?" I asked.

"My buddy really let me down. Usually it's not a problem if he wants to screw around on a Friday night, but with this party . . . and people complaining about the noise. I can't be in two places . . . Well, the party can't last much longer."

"Good luck," I said.

"And you have a good night, sir."

A good night was not what I was having.

The Halliday party must've been pretty big. The

strains of old-school rock and roll rattled through the conclave. And both sides of the private road were lined with the guests' vehicles.

I maneuvered around a powder-blue T-Bird that was blocking a portion of the villa's drive and parked. I closed the gate and strolled toward the guesthouse.

The villa was shadowy and, in my current mood, gloomy and a bit sinister-looking. The ocean was black and uninviting. If anyone complained about the sounds of music and laughter, it would not be me. The first thing I did when I entered the guesthouse was to throw open the windows for an unfiltered sound sample of upbeat human activity.

The party was being held near the other end of the gated community, where the beach began its curve. I had a good enough view of it to see that Halliday was an unstinting host. He'd put in a lighted dance floor on the sand where couples boogalooed and twisted to a band that was much better than their matching Hawaiian shirts indicated.

You might think that a bunch of elderly boomers writhing to the music of the sixties beside the ocean, like a *Beach Blanket Bingo* movie gone gerontic, might add to my feelings of depression and alienation. But it had just the opposite effect. These people, whoever they might be, were doing what you were supposed to do on a Friday night. They were having fun.

I took off my jacket, dutifully removing my wallet, the wireless Lexus key, and my cellular phone.

I carried the phone to a table and sat. The band was playing The Foundations oldie "Build Me Up Buttercup." I watched the distant dancers for a minute or two, then clicked on the phone to check my voice mail.

As usual, Cassandra had called with a brief report on the week's overall business. It was, in a word, satisfactory. No further news about Margaret the cashier, which meant that she was no longer seated at the register or that she'd dropped her identity-thief boyfriend. In either case: problem solved.

The second message was a surprise: Roger Charbonnet thanking me for helping to spring him from the lockup, which I hadn't. He invited me to a celebratory party the following night at his restaurant Frush, which was in Malibu near the Sands. I doubted I'd go, but one never knew. Had the invitation been for that night, I'd be on my way.

The third message was a guilt-tripper that added to my general malaise: Gibby, whining that he'd been waiting for me in his dressing room for nearly twenty minutes. I had, of course, forgotten my promise to meet him.

Message four, also from Gibby, was pretty hostile. The general theme was that he didn't need my help. He'd make his own decision. He suggested I could perform a certain sex act solo, a request no more possible than my performing that same act with Vida.

I went to the kitchen and found a bottle of Merlot purchased earlier in the week at the supermarket. I uncorked the bottle, sniffed it, then poured an inch into a glass. It was not quite up to the wine I'd bought for dinner, the last of which Vida and Brutus had probably polished off before they . . . But why go there.

I turned out the lights and carried the wine back

to the table, poured three inches into the glass. The musicians were jamming on "Johnny B. Goode." It was a little too bouncy, but the dancers seemed to like it.

I toasted them.

Then I toasted the band, even though they'd lapsed into what sounded like a medley of department-store melodies. I recognized one of the tunes as "Love Letters in the Sand," so maybe they all had a beach theme. Or a Pat Boone theme. I toasted Pat.

I was into my fifth or sixth toast when the musicians moved on to a melody that was still popular in my youth, Johnny Mathis's great love ballad "Chances Are." If there is one song you don't want to hear, drunk and alone in the dark at two a.m., watching somebody else's party, it's "Chances Are."

That was followed by "The Party's Over," the inevitable time-to-go-home song. I could barely hear the leader of the band thanking Mr. Halliday for asking them to play "for these nice folks." Then he and his group packed up within a minute and a half and were out of there.

There were some malingerers, but eventually even they accepted the fact that, as Fats Waller once sang, all the jive was gone. Soon the portable beach pavilion was deserted.

I toasted the end of the party.

And then Halliday, that cheapskate, decided to stop keeping the beach aglow.

The resulting dark and empty coastline was doing nothing for my mood. I squeezed the last dregs of wine from the bottle. It was time for me to retire.

I knew I should get up, get undressed and into my

PJs. But thought I'd rest my head down on the table for just a minute. Maybe . . .

I was on that wooden moon again, high in the air, watching the little people run around below. The band was playing "Who Wrote the Book of Love?" and I was thinking, *They didn't put vampires in that book. Why mine?*

The people down there were dressed in ninja outfits without faces.

"You see, Blessing, you son of a bitch," Gibby was shouting at me.

He was standing on the end of the crowd of ninjas, wearing a dog suit without the head. He was pointing a paw at a ninja who held a camera in his hands. Only it wasn't a camera, exactly. He pointed it at Gibby, and it emitted a glowing bolt that knocked the comedian off his feet.

"Stop it, you fucker," he yelled. But the ninja moved closer, bending over Gibby as he writhed on the floor. Suddenly, Gibby reached up and yanked the ninja's hood from his head.

The man had white hair. He turned to look up at me, and I saw that one of his eyes was clouded over with a film of mucus.

"Help me, for Christ's sake," Gibby screamed. "Help me."

And I was suddenly awake, bathed in sweat and dizzy as a bat.

"Drunk and disoriented," I croaked. "The end of a perfect week."

But it wasn't quite the end.

"Help—"

Was that real? Or more of the dream?

I blinked and stared through the window.

There seemed to be . . . something on the beach. Two men struggling?

I pushed myself from the chair and stood, woozily, trying to stop the world from spinning. I staggered to the door, opened it, got through it.

"Hey!" I called.

Was that a figure running away, or the shadow of a giant bird flying past the moon?

I paused, grabbed the doorjamb to steady myself.

Was someone lying in the shallow surf?

Too far to tell.

I staggered from the guesthouse and moved slowly across the sand, trying not to fall. I was either in a very real dream or a very dreamy reality.

I moved past several homes, including Stew's, all silent as tombs. Bad simile, all things considered.

It was a man! Lying facedown in the surf, his head at a strange angle. What was the deal? You weren't supposed to move someone with a broken neck. But if their face was in water?

I fell to my knees and slowly and carefully began to turn the body. My plan was to do no more than get his face out of the water, but he flipped over on his back.

Gibby.

I blinked again. How could it be Gibby?

Before I had any time to puzzle it out, a powerful arm circled my neck and squeezed. I panicked. Wriggled. Dug my fingers into the guy's wrist. Kicked back with my feet. Nothing.

The pressure increased. I couldn't breathe. I knew about the hold he was using. It was called a blood choke. An NYPD cop had demonstrated it on me one morning on *Wake Up*. It was compressing the jugular vein or maybe the carotid arteries and depriving my brain of oxygen or blood, or both. Done right, it puts you to sleep. Done wrong, it's the big sleep.

I felt a pounding in my ears. Then that stopped and I couldn't hear anything. I experienced a sinking feeling, as if my body was melting into a puddle.

Then . . . I felt nothing at all.

# *Chapter*
# FORTY-THREE

There was that song again. It seemed to be playing over and over. I got it! The guy didn't want french-fried potatoes or red, ripe tomatoes . . . just frim-fram sauce with the ausen fay and chafafah on the side.

*Holy hell!* Would it never cease?

Without opening my eyes, I reached out a hand and grabbed the cellphone from the bedside table.

"Yeh?" was all I could manage.

"Billy?" Cassandra asked.

I opened my eyes to the guesthouse bedroom. It was bright with morning sun. I was in bed, all tucked in. I saw the clothes I'd been wearing hanging neatly on the back of the open closet door.

"Billy?" she asked again.

"Ah. I'm gonna have to call you back." I clicked the phone shut on whatever she was saying.

I swung out of bed, hungover but not hungover enough to forget a couple of things that had happened just before the lights went out. Gibby lying dead in the surf. And . . . my hand went to my throat . . . someone choking me.

But my throat didn't feel raw or even a little damaged. And never mind my still being alive, why had the strangler carried me back to the guesthouse and put me to bed?

I staggered to the window. Not much beach activity. The surf had flowed in. And caught something! There was definitely something out there in the shallow water.

Gibby!

I stumbled down the stairs, each step like a knife being shoved into my skull. I fumbled the door open and ran out across the sand.

The closer I got to Gibby, the less it looked like him. Finally, I realized it wasn't even a man. It was a huge piece of driftwood. I ran up and down the beach for a while, but the closest thing I could find to the dead comedian was the hunk of wood.

Could I have been so wasted the night before that I fantasized the whole thing?

Breathing heavily, head ready to burst, and full of sudden self-doubt, I plodded back to the guesthouse. I almost made it.

"Mr. Blessing!"

"Good morning, Ms. St. Laurent," I said. "You'll have to excuse me. I'm not feeling . . ."

I stopped because she was gawking at me, jaw dropped. "What in the world?" she said.

With her were two sour-faced young women I assumed were prospective buyers. It was hard to see them fitting in with neighbors like Stew or the party-thrower Halliday. They were wearing torn tees, grungy jeans, battered Doc Martens, and more embedded metal than was dug out of Legs Diamond. I knew them. Marty and Circe Wynott, a pair of performance artists known as Split and Splat. They'd been on *Wake Up, America!* plugging their album, *Splisterhood.*

They were staring at me, too. Registering more disgust than surprise. "Ew," they said in harmony.

"This is not Saint Tropez," Amelia St. Laurent said haughtily.

I realized at that precise moment I was wearing only my boxers. And they were a little askew. "Sorry, ladies," I said, straightening my shorts. "It's been a pleasure, but I must be getting back to the guesthouse. It's much too breezy out here."


Brueghel sounded as if he regretted having given me his cellular number. "Let me get this straight. You *think* you saw some guy kill Gibby Lewis last night out at your place? What's there to think about? You either saw it or you didn't."

"It wasn't at my place," I said. "I mean, it was *near* my place. Fact is, I wasn't exactly sober . . ."

"It's Saturday, Blessing." He lowered his voice. "I promised the kid I'd spend the day with him. Don't yank my chain, huh?"

"It's just . . . the killer was choking me, detective. It was so real I can still feel it. But there's no sign of it having happened. No rawness. No bruising."

"You don't always get that with a choke hold," he said. "What else do you remember?"

"Nothing. Until I woke up in bed."

"You think what, that the killer put you to bed? Fuck you, Blessing." He added, away from the phone, "Forget you heard that, son. Go watch *SpongeBob* while I finish up on the phone.

"What do you want from me, Blessing? You can probably find the nearest AA meeting in the phone book."

"Gibby's not answering his phone," I said. "I thought maybe you could try and locate him. Make sure he's okay."

He hesitated. "Yeah. I can do that. Uh, you sure you actually saw Jimmy Fitzpatrick night before last?"

"Yeah, I'm sure," I said. "I had a little too much to drink last night, but I'm not an alcoholic."

"Fitzpatrick didn't happen to mention the flight he was taking?"

"No. I think he said he was taking the next available."

"He was booked on an Aer Lingus at nine-fifty-one yesterday morning. It would have been tight if he planned on picking up his buddy's remains. But he didn't do that, and he missed the flight."

"Maybe changed his mind?"

"Maybe. But we found his rental Hummer in long-term parking at LAX. And that's the only airline ticket we've come up with. So here's my problem, on my daddy day with my boy. I'm trying to solve the murder of the original host of your goddamn TV show. I've got the bandleader from that show apparently missing. And now you call to tell me you *think* the new host of the show has been murdered."

"I can still feel that choke hold," I said.

"Damn it. I'll be there in an hour."

"Should I—"

"Don't do a fucking thi—oh . . . *SpongeBob* isn't on? Okay, I'll be right there, son." Then, readdressing me, "An hour."

He arrived with Campbell. He was wearing denim pants and a gray T-shirt with the faded full-figure image of Clint Eastwood as Dirty Harry Callahan on the chest and the caption "Make My Day" on the back. She was wearing spandex workout gear. Both wore black LAPD caps and guns on their hips.

I was looking a little less official in a tomato-red Izod shirt, khaki golfing shorts, and flip-flops.

Beach activity had picked up. There were walkers, swimmers, surfers, kids playing and building sand sculptures. A windsurfer was being blown at a fast clip along the gently ruffled water. Too far out to be sure, but I thought it was Stew.

My neighbors were curious and not exactly pleased to see us as I led the detectives to where the driftwood still rested in the surf.

"You sure it was here?" Campbell asked.

"In this general area," I said.

We were standing in front of a multimillion-dollar two-story, where what looked like three generations of a family, maybe twenty of them, from grandparents to toddlers, were seated at a long table on a redwood deck, having an elaborate brunch and trying to pretend we didn't exist.

"Not exactly murderer's row," Campbell said.

"If there was evidence of a crime, the tide's washed it away," Brueghel grumbled. "And, oh, yeah, Blessing, did you happen to know there was a big blowout here last night? Forty, fifty cars in and out. Security has some of them listed but probably missed a few. Take quite a while to make sure somebody didn't slip in with the partygoers."

*Especially with the gate being understaffed,* I thought but did not mention. It would only make Brueghel even more sour.

We traipsed back to the guesthouse, where we trailed sand over the floor.

The detectives poked about.

Returning from the upstairs bedroom, Brueghel asked, "When you *think* you found Gibby Lewis's body, did you have to step in the surf?"

I closed my eyes and tried to remember. "I think . . . Yes! I'm sure. My shoes should be—"

"They're bone-dry, not a trace of sand," he said. An accusation. "Get some sleep, Blessing. We'll let this one slide. Everybody has a rough night every now and then, right, Mizzy?"

"No. Not everybody," she said.

They departed, convinced I'd wasted their time with a drunken fantasy.

I went upstairs to convince myself. I picked up the shoes. They were as dry as a desert wind. But they seemed a little stiffer than I'd remembered. Like they would be if treated to a fast dry near a fireplace or even in an oven. Not exactly the shiny clue I was hoping for. But something.

Why would the killer have gone to the trouble of drying my shoes and all the rest? I immediately concocted a totally paranoid scenario. He'd realized I smelled like a winery and took the chance I'd been so drunk I wouldn't remember or wouldn't believe what I'd seen. And even if I did believe it and tried to tell someone, that person would take me for an inebriated asshole.

Until it became clear that Gibby was among the missing. Then what? Maybe I'd be blamed for the murder?

That whole concept fell apart the moment I realized how much simpler it would have been just to keep choking me. The killer had to get rid of one body—probably out in the ocean. Why not two?

I put the shoes back.

The shirt I'd been wearing last night was draped over a hanger.

If my head wasn't throbbing, I would have slapped it. I'd forgotten to show the detectives the warning note that had been left on the Lexus. It was something real and maybe even worth their drive out.

I removed the sheet from my shirt pocket. I unfolded it and experienced a sinking WTF sensation.

The paper was blank.

I'd been as sober as an Amish picnic when I found it under the car's windshield wiper. Vida had seen it. So had Brutus. He'd even seen the guy who left it.

I got out the phone, then stopped.

I really didn't want to talk to Vida. Nor did I want

Brutus back as my guardian angel, though that was probably foolish pride disabling my usual caution. I wasn't afraid. The killer had had the perfect opportunity to put me away, if that's what he'd wanted. Instead, he'd opted for a lot of bother.

It didn't occur to me that his decision might be subject to change.

*Chapter*
# FORTY-FOUR

What to do?

I was like a man with ADD on a coffee high. The guesthouse was too confining. I took my nerves out for a walk.

Even more people were enjoying the sun, sand, and surf. Some offered a friendly nod; others purposely avoided eye contact. Just like walking up Fifth Avenue, except for the friendly nods.

I paused at the driftwood and walked into the surf to get closer. I tried to budge it, but it seemed to be lodged in the sandy bottom.

"That'd make a lousy fire," Stew Gentry said, walking toward me. He'd probably just returned to shore with his windboard. He was slipping a plain white tee over his head.

"I don't remember seeing it here yesterday," I said.

"It probably wasn't here. The ocean is always bringing us little gifts like that."

I joined him on the dry sand.

"How's it going, Billy? You look like you mighta had a rough night. Were you at Halliday's?"

"Not at Halliday's," I said, "but it was rough."

"Best thing for that, come on in and have a brew."

The words made my stomach flip over. "A little early," I said.

"Coffee, then," he said. "I was a little rough on you last time we talked. Have a cup of coffee and I'll have some humble pie."

I followed him up the beach to his property. His rolled sail and board rested beside the wooden walkway. As we passed the infamous swimming pool, I could almost hear Roger screaming at me.

Stew was at the back door, brushing sand from his bare feet. I removed my flip-flops, slapped the sand off them, then brushed my feet and slipped them back on. You can never get rid of all the sand. It's part of the price one pays for beachfront living, along with distance to town and incredibly high taxes and devastating storms that destroy your house.

Just call me Mr. Buzzkill.

The interior of the house looked pretty much the same. Spacious and woodsy and masculine. "Park it on the couch," Stew said, heading for the kitchen. "I'll get the coffee."

He disappeared past the swinging doors.

I went to the chocolate-colored leather couch and parked on it, facing a cold, white stone fireplace.

Before too long, he returned with a tray filled with a silver coffeepot, two cups, a pitcher of cream, a sugar bowl, napkins, and a plate on which rested an assortment of cupcakes the size of softballs.

"I'm gonna go get out of these wet trunks," Stew said. "The cupcakes are part of my apology. The black-and-white is really good."

He took the stairs two at a time. I poured a cup of coffee, ignored the cream and sugar, and tried to ignore the cupcakes, but they kept calling to me. The black-and-white one was tasty. Even better, it was soft enough not to aggravate my headache.

I picked up my coffee cup and began strolling around the large room, checking out the mounted antlers, the long snakeskin, the oil paintings, and the glass cabinet with its display of handguns and rifles and shotguns. Eventually, I made my way to the round table with the green felt cover, on which rested Stew's photos in standing frames.

I'd looked at them before, but this time my attention was drawn to a snapshot that had been taken on the rear deck some years ago. Four people in swimsuits, smiling into the sun. Stew, a much younger version of Gloria Ingram, and a couple a few years younger than she. The girl was pretty, petite, with fair skin and a generous mouth. She looked enough like Stew that she had to be his daughter, the one whose death marked the beginning of the end for his marriage to Gloria. The boy seemed shy and a bit nerdy. He was staring at the blond girl with total adoration.

I picked up the framed photo to make sure I wasn't letting my imagination fool me. No mistake.

The boy was a collegiate edition of Max's assistant, Trey Halstead.

"'Photographs testify to time's relentless melt.'

That's a Susan Sontag quote." Stew was standing near the staircase, freshly dressed in white slacks and shirt, and staring at me with mild curiosity. He crossed the big room, using that unique high-right-shoulder lope I remembered from his movies.

"I guess Sontag must have spent a lot of her later years thinking about photography," I said.

"When you love somebody, you do tend to share their lives." He took the frame from me, studied the photo. His face was expressionless, but his eyes were shiny, and he was probably as close to tears as movie heroes were allowed. " 'Time's relentless melt.' Damn if that doesn't hit the nail right on the head."

"I didn't know you and Trey were friends."

"Since he was a baby. Boy grew up next to us. That was when we lived in San Marino. His daddy was a photographer. He took that picture. Gone now, poor fella. He knew his business, sure enough."

He replaced the frame on its exact spot on the table. "Funny about that photo of the four of us. As many times as I've lost myself in it, I never see anybody but Connie. She was beautiful, wasn't she?"

I nodded. There were a thousand things going on in my head. Connections being made. Conclusions being drawn. Or was I leaping to them?

"Something botherin' you, Billy? Spit it out."

"Connie and Trey were close?"

"Planning to marry when she graduated in two years."

"How long ago was the photo taken?"

"Twenty-four years, seven months, and eight days. Connie was home from Skidmore that summer, the best I ever spent. You sure you don't want a brew? I think I could use one."

"I'm fine with my coffee."

"The coffee. Yeah, I should probably go with that, too. Let's you and me palaver, *amigo*." He delivered that last line sarcastically, a mockery of his movie image.

I hesitated. Part of me wanted to run out of the house. Another part thought that part was being foolish. By then the schizo discussion was moot. His arm was around my shoulders, and he was herding me toward the coffee.

He indicated I should take the couch, while he sat on a chair to my left. "How'd you like the cupcake?" he asked.

"Good."

"Don't go reading too much into that picture, Billy."

"It's worth at least a thousand words," I said.

He picked up one of the remaining cupcakes, broke off a piece, and ate it. "When I was a boy, I used to read mystery stories," he said. "I was particularly fond of the whodunits. Ellery Queen, Nero Wolfe, Sherlock, of course. I even made a whodunit, maybe forty years ago. Some too-smart screenwriter ripped off a book by a novelist named Donald Westlake. Turned it into a Western and decided to sell it as an original script.

"Hell, I'd never heard of Westlake. Nor had the studio's story people, the producers, or the horse's ass directing the film. Problem was, there was a very unique twist in the story. And shortly after the film was released, we all became very aware of Mr. West-lake. And his attorney." He chuckled.

It was the kind of amusing vignette he'd told when I'd interviewed him on the morning show. Now it seemed a little off point.

I stood up. "I'd better be going, Stew."

"Just settle down, now, podnah. What's your hurry?" He glanced at his watch. "Dani'll be back almost anytime now, and we'll all go have ourselves a nice seafood lunch at Beau Rivage. Meanwhile, lemme finish up on my little parable. Okay?"

Actually, it wasn't okay. Not even close. But I looked at this man I thought I knew, sitting there, calmly nibbling on a cupcake, waiting to take his daughter to lunch, and I decided I might as well hear him out.

I sat down.

He smiled, took a sip of coffee to wash down the cake. "So, to return to this Western whodunit tale I've been apparently boring you with, our director decided he was too hip to use that time-honored scene where everything gets explained. He felt the script's twist was so good, it wasn't needed. 'We've knocked their socks off with this gimmick,' I remember him braying. 'They won't even miss the explanation until after they've left the theater. And by then, who the fuck cares?'

"That was the biggest financial turkey I ever unleashed on the moviegoing public. And that includes the stinker I just finished that they're now spending millions of extra dollars on, hoping a conversion to 3-D is gonna turn it into a silk purse.

"My point, Billy, is we all want explanations. So

why don't we start with your explanation about what
you think that picture means?"

I said nothing.

"C'mon, Billy. Something's made you jumpy as a
cat, and we can't straighten this out until you tell me
what's going on up here." He pointed to his well-
groomed head. The gesture may have been innocent,
but it looked suspiciously as though he was pointing
a thumb-and-forefinger gun at his temple.

He was older than me, but he was bigger, and in
way better shape. I doubted I could make it to the
door, even if I tried. And I still wasn't convinced I was
in trouble. So what the hell? I might as well find out.

"It's a little surprising to discover that you're only
one degree of separation from Des O'Day," I said.

"Hell, thanks to Clint, I'm also one degree away
from Kevin Bacon. So what?"

"There's not much chance Kevin Bacon killed
your daughter."

"Wh-hoa there! You lost me round that turn."

"How'd Connie die, Stew?"

He was silent for a beat. "You tell me."

"It happened less than a year after that picture
was taken."

"How d'you know that?"

I didn't want to bring Gloria into the conversation, so I asked him a question instead. "She was on
a trip to Europe, right? No. You said she was gradu-
ating in two years. Junior year abroad?"

"Ellery Queen's got nothing on you, Billy."

"Studying in Ireland?"

"Goldsmith's in London."

"How'd she die, Stew?"

"You're the—how do they put it?—the amateur sleuth. You tell me."

Fitz had told me Des had been serious when he was younger and he'd done something for love of country that had gone bad. Then there was Dr. Dover's story about the vengeful father. An eye for an eye. A drowned son for a drowned son.

"Did she die in an IRA bombing?" I asked.

Stew gave me a wistful smile that I didn't think had any relationship to what he was thinking. "In the Mill Hill section of London, Miz Thatcher's parliamentary constabulary. They were sending the prime minister a message. Connie was spending a few days with a girl she'd met in one of her design classes. They went out to breakfast at a place British Army soldiers frequented.

"The fragile things on which our lives depend." His eyes filled with tears, but he held on. "Those were the days when you had some control over your privacy. And a macho superstar such as yours truly wasn't looking for pity from his fans. So to the rest of the world, Connie was just a college kid from Southern California, one of three civilians who died in the explosion. Today there'd be pictures on the Internet of me being held down by a couple of Teamsters and getting tranked by the location nurse after hearing the news."

He took a deep breath, then let it out slowly.

"All a long time ago," he said.

"How'd you find out Des was involved?"

"Trey. I hadn't seen him since Connie's funeral. About seven or eight months ago, he called, out of the blue, I thought, and suggested we have dinner. Turned out he'd spent a lot of loot on investigators over the years, and one finally came up with a list of the four Mill Hill bombers. Three had died in the Troubles. The survivor, Desmond Rafferty, had been booted out of the IRA shortly before the peace accord. He'd reinvented himself as Desmond O'Day, a comedian who'd migrated to the States and was appearing in a sitcom shot on the East Coast."

It occurred to me that, like Des, I'd engineered my own reinvention. I'd walked out of those prison gates with a new skill set, new ambition, and, within a few weeks, a new name. But even if there'd been a reason to mention this to Stew, he was too deep into his own story to have paid it much mind.

"Trey asked me what I thought about Connie's killer leading the good life in New York. I must admit I told him I wished I could get my hands on the mick bastard. To my surprise, he said he could arrange that.

"I started backpedalin'. I said it was macho bluster, that I really didn't give a damn about the asshole. Twenty-three years was a long time. And it wasn't like he'd aimed a gun at my baby and pulled the trigger. He was fighting a war, and Connie just happened to get in the way.

"But Trey was deep in vengeance valley. He said he had no interest in anything but avenging Connie. He had no personal life, no desire for fortune or fame. And he'd wound up in a position to get O'Day to come to him. Then he'd make the man pay.

"I told him he was on his own. Next I knew, the papers are talking about O'Day doing a nighttime TV show from out here, exec-produced by Max Slaughter and line-produced by Trey. So I sat back and waited to see what would happen."

"Accessory before the fact. And after."

"Oh, hell, Billy. I didn't know for certain what Trey had in mind. And I sure as hell felt no obligation to warn the Irish prick."

Stew's story was pretty convincing. I knew that Trey had sold Max on hiring Des. But I also remembered something else he did. "If you weren't involved in Trey's murder plan, why'd he pick a house for Des barely a grenade throw from yours?"

"That's something you'd have to ask him. Maybe he figured my being that close to the guy, seeing him in all his glory, might change my mind. It didn't, but . . . I have to fess up. I did leave a rat in his oven."

"That adds breaking and entering to the accessory charge."

"I hope you're toying with me, Billy. It was a joke, for Christ's sake. I was joggin' by and saw the damn back door hanging open. If Rafferty or O'Day or whatever the hell he called himself was stupid enough to go off and leave his door open, I figured I might as well poke around a little.

"I found a stash of pills and cocaine in the party room. Typical. I could have made an anonymous call to the cops, but, like I said, I wasn't looking for any serious payback.

"So I tossed his stash in the ocean. And I took his broiling pan back to my place. I found a nice juicy rodent in the walk-in traps they've got all round the palms and fixed up a little dinner surprise."

"It scared the crap out of him," I said. "So much so, he immediately moved out of the villa."

He smiled. "So the little rat chased the big rat away."

"He was scared of you, Stew. According to his friend, Fitzpatrick, on our first night out here, when I passed along your party invitation, it sent him into a dark mood that ended with him getting drunk and nearly killing someone."

"Sounds like the kind of guy who made a lot of enemies," he said. "Maybe it wasn't Trey took him out. I'd be surprised if your cop friends didn't wind up with a list of suspects long as your arm."

"My cop friends."

"The two detectives who were prowling the beach with you. What brought 'em out here, anyway?"

He popped the remains of his cupcake into his mouth.

"I asked them to come. Last night—"

I was interrupted by door chimes.

"Hold that thought," Stew said, and hopped from the chair. He was halfway to the front door by the time I stood.

I'd barely made it around the couch when he said, "Don't run off, Billy. I want you to meet an old friend."

A tall man with gray hair was standing in the open doorway. He was wearing odd octagon-shaped sunglasses. I'd seen them and him at the theater the day before the explosion. I was pretty sure that if he took the glasses off, there'd be a milky film over at least one of his eyes.

"Meet Doc Blaney. He's the troubleshooter you went to in the old days when the job was too shady for Pellicano to handle." Anthony Pellicano, the so-called "private eye to the stars," had recently been convicted on charges of wiretapping and racketeering, among others.

"Then it'll be four of us for lunch at Beau Rivage?" I asked.

Stew smiled. "Trey should be arriving shortly," he said. "Fact is, we'd been plannin' to just rustle somethin' up here."

"And Dani?"

"She's in Coral Gables. I got her a script-girl job on a TV pilot."

"So it was all a lie?"

"I'd prefer to call it acting."

"What's goin' on, Stew?" Pellicano's moral inferior asked.

"Billy brought the cops out here today," Stew said with a hint of regret.

Blaney removed a gun from beneath his rumpled jacket. "Told you we shoulda just wasted him last night. Dumping two is as easy as dumping one."

"Billy's a friend. I was hoping he was so drunk that . . . Hell, in the light of day I can see it was a dumb idea."

"Like I told you before, simple is better. You can fuck yourself up trying to be too clever."

"That's one of the problems with spending a lifetime pretending," Stew said. "The movies I make, the plans always work out in the end."

"This sure isn't any movie," Blaney said.

"No. But it will work out. Only not so nice for you, Billy."

I guessed they were not planning for me to be around to see this flick released on Blu-ray or DVD.

*Chapter*
# FORTY-FIVE

Trey arrived within the hour. By then, Blaney had cuffed my right wrist to the leg of a table in the kitchen. Stew had slapped together a pile of sandwiches for us. Roast beef, honey-cured ham and Swiss cheese, and for Trey, who was one of those meatless half-vegans, a tuna melt on rye.

They had theirs with soft drinks. I ate mine, single-handed, with a wheat beer while they discussed my fate.

The early part of their conversation concerned my "cop friends."

"What'd you tell 'em about last night?" Blaney asked.

"That I saw Gibby Lewis being murdered."

"Shit," Trey said. "I told you this would happen, Stew."

"It's just a hiccup," Stew said. "On Monday, when both Lewis and Billy are no-shows, things will get a little frantic at the network. Eventually, the police will be notified. The lead detective —what's his name? The one who caught The Hairdresser?"

"Brueghel," Blaney said.

"Right. He'll zoom here and find that Billy moved out the night before. That's why we've got to keep him alive. So that the security guard can see him drive away with all his crap in the car.

"Brueghel will still dig around out here like a hound hunting truffles, but there are thirty-seven homes in the Sands, not including the villa. I'll take those odds."

"He won't have to dig too deep to make the connection between you and Des O'Day," I said.

"Let him. I got an alibi for that night, podnah." He smiled. "I was with my good friend Doc."

Blaney smiled, too.

"But Blaney did kill Des," I said.

"That's the beauty part, Billy," Stew said. "By him being my alibi, I automatically become his. We both slide."

"Why'd Gibby have to die?" I asked.

"Tell him, Doc," Stew said. "That one's on you."

"I, ah . . . It's my eye thing," Blaney said. "I spent a lot of time in the sun, growing up. It kinda fucked up my eyes. It's why I wear these glasses during the day. But after dark, I can't see worth shit with 'em. That night in the theater, just as I'm getting ready to operate the fucking overcomplicated trigger device, I look up to see the schmuck staring straight at me. I tell him some bullshit that I'm a photographer and it's a camera I'm carrying, and between that and the fact I'm hidden by this black outfit head to toe, I figured all was copacetic.

"But last night, almost midnight, I'm relaxing in my hot tub with a friend and the phone rings. My office number. It's the schmuck. He says he recognized me by my eyes.

"A few years back, I did some work for a friend of

his, a cheeseball comic named Philly Slide who needed somebody to throw a scare into this bimbo who was squeezing him. Lewis tells me Slide confided all this to him just after I put the fear in the broad so bad she went running back to Bumfuck, Kansas, or wherever she was from. At the time, Slide also mentioned my . . . eye ailment which is how Lewis made the connection.

"So he's blabbing to me about all this, and I'm thinking about how I'm gonna have to kill him when here comes the fucking unbelievable part. He offers me a hundred grand to appear on his show in disguise and tell the world who hired me to off O'Day. That's more than Stew paid me to do the job.

"Lewis swears he'll never give me up afterward, even if they throw him in the slams. It'll only add to his fame. He'll write a book about it. He's got it all figured.

"It's too loony to be a setup. I mean, the schmuck is a witness to murder. He goes to the cops, they're not gonna play games like this. They're gonna drag my ass in and then do their best to make me give up names."

He turned to Stew. "Not that I ever would. Anyway, I can't see a downside in meeting the schmuck. If the cops are behind it, I'm nailed anyway. If he's for real with his offer, I can get all or part of the hundred grand and . . . kill him. It's a win-win.

"At my suggestion, we meet in the parking lot at Du-par's in the Valley. I get him into my car. Check for a wire, though I know fucking well there will not be one. Then bounce his head off the dash and stick him in the trunk."

"And you bring him out here," Stew said, obviously miffed.

"Like I told you, where else? My 'friend' is at my crib. I don't know where Trey coops. I got to find out if the schmuck's told anybody about me, and I figure this place is nice and secluded."

"With the party of the year going on," Stew said.

"How the fuck was I to know that?"

"There are a million places where you wouldn't run the risk of the guy breaking away and running for it. The place where you disposed of the body, for one."

"Stew, ease off, huh?" Trey whined. The peacemaker. "We're all in this together."

"Yeah, Stew. Don't forget, if we hadn't listened to you, right now we'd be looking forward to a nice, enjoyable Saturday night. Instead, we'll be heading back to the fucking dump."

"You'll be heading back," Stew said. "Like last night."

"It's a different situation from last night, Stew," Doc said. "I drove in with Gibby in my trunk, and I drove out the same way. No prob. But this guy is gonna have to be seen driving his car out. So it's a three-car, three-person job, like Fitzpatrick was."

*Poor Fitz,* I thought. *Didn't make it to his safe haven.*

"Okay," Stew said reluctantly. "But I'm not going to be the guard dog again. You can hold the gun on Billy, Doc. I'll drive your car out."

"That won't work. You don't look nothing like me."

"I'll wear your glasses."

"I don't wear 'em at night. And I don't like other people wearing 'em. It's called conjunctivitis. Look it up."

"This is fucked," Stew said. "All I wanted to do was blow that homicidal mick to hell. That was a just act. That was setting the record straight. This other stuff, it's murder, boys. And it doesn't seem to end."

"This is definitely the end," Trey said.

"You said that about the musician."

"We had to do that, once we realized he knew about you and Des. But you can't call this murder. It's more like . . . I don't know, collateral damage."

Stew glared at him, eyes blazing. "That's what they called Connie's death."

Trey lowered his head and seemed to melt into his chair.

They were quite a trio. Larry, Moe, and Curly given a David Mamet update. But they'd killed three people, and, unless I was very, very lucky, I'd be number four.

## Chapter
# FORTY-SIX

It was near midnight when we got rolling.

They spent the time arguing, eating, watching one of Stew's movies on a big screen in his den. *High Timber* was the title, in case you were wondering. Not the film ripped from the Westlake novel. All agreed it was one hell of a flick. I thought it may have been just a tiny bit too heavy on exposition. Kind of like what I had just endured.

At ten the four of us slunk along the sand under the cloak of darkness to the guesthouse, where they put on latex gloves and paper booties, provided by Blaney, before entering. They cuffed me to the bed's headboard, without much conversation, then removed all my stuff from the closet and drawers. They carefully folded my clothes and placed them and my other possessions into my bags.

I asked why they were being so neat, and Blaney explained, "If the cops ever do find your body and the luggage, it'll slow 'em down a little if they think you did your own packing."

Ah, that's where they slipped up. Little did they know, I'm a lousy packer. I had them right where I wanted them.

"Look around," Blaney said. "Make sure we got everything."

"What about his computer?" Trey asked. "Shouldn't we make sure he didn't put anything on it that could cause trouble?"

"Good call," Blaney said. He pulled the laptop from a bag and took it into the bathroom, where he began banging it against the tub.

When he tired of that, he returned with the poor thing's case dented and cracked. He dropped it onto the bag.

"That looks dumb," Trey said.

"His car is going to take a real long fall," Blaney said. "Things break."

"You oughta distress the bag, too, or it won't look right. And the computer could still work."

"Fuck it," Blaney said, and slammed the bag shut.

Eventually, they were going to kill one another. But probably not soon enough to do me any good.

They spent the final hour sullenly eating and drinking the remains of my larder, allowing me a final hunk of Jarlsberg Swiss and a cluster of red grapes. They cleaned everything and, like the good departing guest they assumed I was, left the house keys in their box on a table near the door.

At the Lexus, Blaney popped the trunk and they laid in the luggage. Then Trey departed.

Blaney watched Stew remove the handgun from his belt and get into the Lexus behind the front seats. There was not a lot of room. Whoever designed the floor space had not had the body of a big, raw-boned man in mind.

Stew grunted, twisted, tried to find a position at least partially comfortable, and failed. "Trey had better stop for the switch as soon as we make the turn," he told Blaney. "Otherwise, I may shoot myself."

He did something that I assumed was releasing the safety and pointed the weapon at me as I got in behind the wheel.

"Trey should be in his car by now," Blaney said to me. "A Prius. He'll make his exit. Give him a minute, then you leave. I'll be following."

I watched him open the metal door and depart into the night. The door swung shut behind him with a clang.

"Get going, Billy. And don't do anything stupid,"

Stew said, his voice sounding as if the seat were talking to me.

"Or what? You'll shoot me?"

"You and the security guards."

"What's a few more murders, right?" I said.

That shut him up.

I started the car. Through the bars of the gate, I saw a silver Prius ambling past soundlessly, headed for the security kiosk.

I backed until I hit the beam that slid the gate open, then continued backing into the lane. I put it in drive and crept forward until I could see the taillights of the Prius. When they disappeared I counted to fifty, then got moving.

The youthful Rambo was on duty with a guard only a few years older, probably the one MIA the previous night. He was the personification of the surfer dude, tanned, lanky, and slightly spacey. Unlike Rambo, he was hatless, the better to show off his long, curly blond locks. He gave me a funky salute and almost crooned, "Have yourself a merry evening, sir."

"Thank you," I said. Then, following the script, I added, "As Rambo can tell you, my name's Blessing." Hearing his name, Rambo joined us, waving. "I'm moving out of the Villa Delfina tonight. Please make a note on your log that I left the keys in the guesthouse for the realtor."

"Sure thing," the blond said.

"Pleasure meeting you, Mr. Blessing," Rambo added.

And thus ended my Malibu stay.

\*    \*    \*

"That was nice," the car seat said.

Round the bend, the silver Prius was parked by the side of the road. I pulled up behind it.

"Oh, man. I hope that means I can get out of this vise," Stew said.

I did not reply. I just remained behind the wheel as I was told.

Before too long, Blaney's Mercedes parked behind me, and he got out.

He'd taken off his glasses.

He walked to the other side of the Lexus and opened the passenger door, and I got a good look at those cloudy eyes. Pretty damned unnerving.

"You can come out now, Stew," he said. "Unless you like it back there."

"Take this fucking gun," Stew said, holding the weapon up. When Blaney complied, the actor extricated himself from the well, accompanied by a series of moans, grunts, and curses.

"Now what?" he asked.

"You sit right down on the passenger seat and keep Blessing obedient while he drives."

"I'm not doing that again. While I was shepherding the musician, I kept thinking: *What do I do if he runs a red light or signals a cop in some other way? Do I shoot him? And then what? Shoot the cop?* Forget it."

"What do you suggest?"

"You take the passenger seat, and I'll drive your car."

"Nobody but me drives my car," Blaney said.

"Why don't we just call this whole thing a mistake?" I said. "I'll go find a hotel."

"Let Billy drive the Prius," Stew said. "Trey can carry the pistol."

"Forget Trey," Blaney said. "I don't think he's ever held a gun in his life. Here's the deal. Trey leaves the Prius where it is. We'll drop him off here after we're done. He drives the Lexus, and I drive my car with you and Blessing in back."

Carpooling can be murder.

# Chapter
# FORTY-SEVEN

"Where is this so-called dump?" I asked, as our caravan of two rolled south on the PCH.

"Doc's private burial ground," Stew said. "How many stiffs you put in there, Doc?"

"Shut up that kind of talk," Blaney growled.

My nose itched, and I reached for it, forgetting that my right wrist was cuffed to the metal handle above the right door. It took me only a few seconds to remember my left hand was free. It's called flexibility. "How long a drive will it be?" I asked.

"A couple hours," Stew answered. "Maybe longer. Depends on traffic. What difference does it make?"

"The longer it takes, the longer I live."

Blaney was a good wheelman. There wasn't a lot of traffic, but he took it easy, keeping the big car cruising at the legal limit. For obvious reasons.

"Nice car," I said.

"Damn right."

"What year Mercedes?"

"'08."

"What do you call the gray color?"

"Gray."

Point made.

After about fifteen minutes of silence, Blaney clicked on the radio. A late-night DJ was introducing Jerry Goldsmith's score for the movie *Wild Rovers*.

He quickly changed the station, coming in on the middle of Def Leppard's "When Love and Hate Collide."

"Fuck you, Doc," Stew said. "Go back to the other station."

"My car. My music," Blaney replied.

We headed east along the Santa Monica Freeway. So far, it had been a familiar route. But eventually we moved beyond that. "Where are we, exactly, Stew?"

"East L.A. You wouldn't like it here, podnah. Trust me."

"What the hell was that?" Blaney asked suddenly. He turned down the radio.

"What was what?" Stew replied.

"A beep."

"How should I know? It's your car. Your fucking music. Your fucking beep."

Blaney turned the radio off. "It was an electronic beep. Didn't you hear it?"

"No."

"You did check Blessing for a wire, right?"

"A wire? You nuts?" Stew replied. "He was wading in the water when I grabbed him."

"I definitely heard a beep. Check."

I used my left hand to lift up my shirt, exposing an impressively handsome, subtly muscled brown chest with not a sign of a wire.

"Clean."

"Check his shorts," Blaney demanded.

"You check his shorts," Stew said.

We approached a green sign that stretched across five highway lanes. We took the lane marked 605 North.

"Where does this lead?" I asked.

"Right past El Monte, considered the end of the Santa Fe Trail by its natives—very few of them black, by the way, Billy."

"Then where?"

"Damn if you don't sound like a kid on a family outing," Stew said. "The next big town will be Azusa."

"Then Cuc-amonga?" I asked.

Stew smiled, evidently remembering the old Jack Benny gag routine. He'd probably seen it during its first run. "No. We won't be makin' it to Cuc-amonga this trip."

Somewhere in the Azusa area, Blaney left the freeway and headed up a winding road, going north, according to the little lighted compass on his rearview mirror. "What do they call this?" I asked, gesturing with my free hand toward the craggy moonlit landscape.

"Podnah, you are looking at the San Gabriel

Mountains. And we are now in the Angeles National Forest, the wild and woolly edge of Los Angeles. *Newsweek* magazine called it the Prime Evil Forest. Acres of pot. Human bones. Wild critters. Predators of every stripe."

"Welcome home, boys," I said.

"You don't hear that beep?" Doc shouted.

"In your head," Stew said, looking at me and making a finger-circle, "this guy's nuts" gesture near his temple.

"What do they call this street?"

"Chico Canyon Road. Doc'll be taking a dogleg soon onto a skinny little path. Don't ask me its name, because I haven't a clue. May not even have a real name. It leads to a generally unknown ridge to one of the steepest cliffs in this part of the US of A. Take one step too many and you go down, down, down, past inaccessible canyons and ravines untrammeled by living human toe. Right, Doc?"

"Not listening."

"Then why'd you answer?" Stew chuckled.

So nice to see his good humor was returning.

"That where Gibby and Fitzpatrick now rest?"

"Along with some of Doc's other patients."

"There's my blue rock," Blaney said. He swung a sharp left onto a road that looked more like a tar-covered bike path. The Mercedes-Benz took the humps and potholes in stride.

We drove upward for at least fifteen minutes. The higher up, the lower the temperature. In my shorts, T-shirt, and flip-flops, I was getting downright chilly. It didn't help that the fog, merely wispy when we entered the mountain range, had quickly thickened to the density of a cumulus cloud. A giant, damp, cold cumulus cloud.

The Lexus, with Trey at the wheel, was maybe two car lengths behind, but, with the fog and a moisture that coated the rear window, I couldn't see much more than its headlights. Beyond that, the road looked dark and empty.

That could be a problem.

"Can you see where you're goin,' Doc?" Stew asked.

"That a comment about my eyes?"

"It's a comment about the fog."

"What fog?" Blaney said, and laughed.

Everybody was so jolly, now that Billy was about to be thrown into a bottomless ravine.

"You sure this . . . whatever it is, has no name?"

"Doc?"

"The road?" Blaney asked. "Yeah, it's got a name. Dump Road." He laughed again.

It was like Comedy Central in our sleek death car.

"Hey, Stew!" I said. "Knock, knock."

He looked at me, half grinning. "Okay. Who's there?"

"Three dead bodies in a ravine, covered by insects, flesh being ripped away by birds of prey and vermin."

He scowled. "Not funny, Billy."

"My point exactly."

"Just passed the yellow rock," Doc announced. "Won't be long now."

"As the mohel said, putting away his knife."

"You know, Billy, you're pretty damned weird," Stew said. "But I gotta give you props for holding up."

"That's how I roll."

Blaney stopped the sedan, turned off the engine, and killed the lights. "We're close enough," he said. "Don't want to push our luck in this fog."

He reached into his shirt pocket and removed something. He reached back with it. The key to the cuffs.

Stew took it with his free hand. He hesitated, apparently wondering if he could unlock the cuff left-handed. Then, having switched the gun and key, he paused again, trying to figure out how to get the key to the lock without moving close enough for me to make a grab for the gun.

Blaney watched him until he could stand it no longer. "Give him the goddamn key, Stew, and let him unlock it himself. If he tries anything, shoot the bastard. I'm gonna bring the Lexus up."

He threw open his door, letting in a wave of cold, wet fog before slamming it again.

On the long drive to Dump Road, along with the other things I was hoping to achieve, I'd tried to figure out my options once we'd arrived at the live-or-die moment. I was limited by the fact that there were only four objects in play on the backseat. Stew and myself were two. He was bigger, stronger, and more athletic. My being more alluring to the opposite sex didn't count. No way could I overpower him.

Object three: the gun. I refer you back to the over-powering thing. That left me with object four: the set of handcuffs.

My original plan involved distracting Stew when he tried to unlock the cuffs. I had one very powerful distraction. But my having control of the key was a major improvement. Still, I thought I'd use the distraction anyway. It couldn't hurt. Unless it compelled him to shoot me.

He held out the key.

"What made you decide to frame Roger?" I asked, taking the little metal object.

"That cop, Brueghel, showed up the day after the bombing," Stew said. "Scared the shit out of me, but he just wanted to ask about the fight you and Roger had. I could tell from the questions he asked, he thought the bomb had been meant for you. And for some reason, he really wanted Roger to be the bad guy. So I figured why not make him happy? Doc did the black-bag job at Roger's."

I turned until I was facing the right door, blocking my action with the key. "I thought you might have had another reason for throwing Roger in the fire." I was having trouble with the key. I always do. "A personal reason."

"You mean Dani?"

"That's what I mean."

"There wasn't anything there. She told me . . . convinced me there was no sex going on."

The double lock clicked, and the cuff's jaws popped apart, freeing it from the door handle. "I hope not," I said. "He was her real father."

There was a moment of total silence in the car. Well, not total. Just the barest discernible beep was coming from the right pocket of my pants. Blaney must have had the hearing of a dog or a teenager.

"What the fuck did you say?" This was Stew in his Owen Wister "Smile when you say that" Western gunfighter mode.

I kept facing the window, believing he considered himself too heroic to shoot a man in the back.

"Think about it, Stew. Does she look like you? Brunette hair. High cheekbones. Green eyes?"

"That . . . That doesn't . . . You don't know . . ."

"You were on location in Canada, making a cop movie," I said. "Gloria and Roger were in Palm Springs making a baby. You do the math."

He was breathing like a fat man who'd just run up a flight of stairs. "You . . . You're . . . Roger's a lying fuck if . . ."

"I didn't hear about it from *him*," I said, hoping Gloria would forgive my betrayal of confidence.

He screamed, and I felt his hand digging into my shoulder, trying to turn me around. I did turn, quicker than he'd been expecting, and using the handcuffs like brass knuckles, did my best to mess up his multimillion-dollar profile.

His gun exploded, punching holes in the car door and shattering the window. By then I was scuttling past his legs, heading for the opposite door. The noise had been so loud it left my ears painful and barely working.

My punch had busted his nose, but it hadn't put him out. The pain distracted him enough for me to crawl past him and get the door open. Another shot went through the top of the car as I tumbled out onto my bare knees.

"What the hell's goin' on up there?" Blaney yelled from somewhere in the fog.

I wasn't sure I could stand, and I figured I'd be less apt to get shot if I stayed down. I belly-crawled away from the Mercedes and into the mist. I had no idea where the cliff's edge might be, and the fog had grown even thicker. I couldn't see more than a foot in front of me.

It became a case of crawl a little, reach out and test for terra firma, crawl a little more.

I heard angry voices behind me. Blaney screaming about the damage to his car. Stew yelling that he wanted to cut out my heart. Poor Stew—he'd brought a gun to a heart-cutting contest.

I removed my cellphone from my pants pocket, held it to my ear. "Somebody, be there, please," I said softly.

It was silent. Dead. Except for the tiniest beeps from its inner mechanisms. My heart sank.

At the guesthouse, I'd seen the cellular and grabbed it when the gang was busy arguing and emptying out my closet. Remembering Cassandra's instruction about the ease of returning calls, I'd found Brueghel's number on the list, turned the sound down as far as it would go, and called him. Then I'd put the phone in my pocket.

I'd hoped he'd had access to his phone. I'd hoped he'd been able to hear our conversation well enough to get the drift of what was going on. Along the drive, I'd had other hopes. That turning down the incoming sound had had no effect on the transmitting sound. That we weren't traveling in a dead zone. That Brueghel wouldn't be too late to save me.

Finally, I'd hoped that if nothing else worked, I'd die from fright or heart failure or flying seagull, anything, before I hit the bottom of the ravine.

That last hope had returned, growing stronger with every moment of cellular silence.

*Damn!* I would have slapped myself behind the head if this had been a sitcom. The volume was turned down. I turned it up from zero and heard "—ing, this is Mizzy Campbell. Can you hear me?"

"Sweetest sound I ever heard," I said.

"Great. We're trying to find you. Unfortunately, we've been unable to locate your unnamed road, and the fog is not cooperating. Did you see anything that might help us find the road?"

"It's a narrow macadam," I whispered. "I didn't see it, but the driver, Doc Blaney, said it was marked by a blue rock. There's a yellow rock farther up."

"Thanks. We couldn't hear Blaney very well. Just you and Gentry. What's your situation?"

"Facing death would cover it."

I heard Brueghel grumble something.

"Pete says for you to hang in there."

Heart-stoppingly close behind me, I heard Trey yell, "It's coming from over here."

I saw his outline in the fog.

I dialed down the phone's volume and replaced it in my pocket. Then I crawled onward, finger-testing the ground in front of me.

Never look back is the advice of choice.

I looked back. Two vague outlines.

Onward.

My hand swept emptiness.

I was less than an arm's length from the edge of something. My worst-possible-scenario outlook told me it had to be the first step to eternity.

I felt the edge and backed a little.

"The flashlight's no damn use," Blaney yelled to

my right. "It doesn't cut through. We need, I don't know, a blower of some kind."

I moved left quietly, on elbows and knees. Maintaining arm's distance from the edge, I was struck by the fear that I was on an outcropping surrounded by empty space on three sides. That stopped me.

I flattened on the ground, determined to stay there until the detectives found me, or Blaney and his cohorts found me, or the cows came home. I was cold and damp. My knees were scraped raw. And to top it all off, I had to pee.

It wasn't pleasant.

"Well, look what I found."

It was Blaney, standing beside me, pointing a gun at my head. "You are so going down," he said.

I pushed up into a sitting position. That's all I did, I swear to God. I'm not sure how Blaney interpreted it. A threat, I guess. He took a backward step . . . and wasn't there anymore. Just like Wile E. Coyote.

The scream that followed was loud and had an echo effect. It lasted for a surprisingly long time, growing softer and softer until it was no longer audible. In my mind, he's still falling.

I wasn't going anywhere.

I hugged my legs, trying to keep warm. I rocked back and forth. I don't know why. After what seemed like hours but was probably only a couple of minutes, I got out the phone and turned up the volume. "You there, Campbell?"

"We're here," Brueghel said. "You in a safe place?"

"Relatively."

"How many in the gang?"

The gang. "Was a gang of three. Now two."

"Good work. We're sitting on the two. Where are you?"

"You tell me."

"Okay. Stay. We'll find you."

"No. I'm too near the edge. Just start honking a car horn. I'll find you."

Maybe I could have stood up and walked. But I'd developed an affinity for the ground. With my knees stinging, I crawled toward my own personal foghorn.

Eventually, I saw headlights adding a ghostlike quality to the fog. I got to my feet and staggered toward them.

Campbell was leaning against the rear of the Mercedes, her phone to her ear. Stew and Trey were lying on their stomachs at her feet, their hands cuffed behind their backs.

"That you, Blessing?" Stew asked, twisting his head to look up.

Blood caked the side of his no-longer-handsome face, and his frantic eyes reminded me of a prairie dog's I'd seen in a cage too small for him.

"You were lying to me, right?" he asked. "Glory didn't really tell you that?"

"I've never even met the woman," I said.

# Chapter
# FORTY-EIGHT

Somebody in the hotel must have tipped the media I was there. After the first dozen calls, beginning at five in the morning, the zero hour, apparently, for lean and hungry freelance journalists, I disconnected the room phone. Management was kind enough to provide a security guard to stop their more aggressive brethren and sistren from knocking on my door.

My cellphone, once it had been fully charged, was my own responsibility. No longer a fan of "Frim-Fram Sauce," I put the instrument on vibrate and, depending on the ID, either ignored the call or pretended to humbly accept effusive praise from friends and associates who'd been misled by the elaborately spun reports of my heroic capture of the killers of Desmond O'Day, James Fitzpatrick, and Gibson Lewis (carefully doled out in the early hours by April Edding and her publicity crew).

Cassandra had been surprisingly impressed, suggesting we frame and mount *The New York Times* account of my bravery and hang it at the Bistro's front door beside a long-standing lovely restaurant review by Ruth Reichl in *Gourmet* when it was a magazine as well as a website. Wally Wing, who was calling himself my manager as well as agent, saw even bigger business opportunities, thanks to my new fame. A restaurant chain. Several movies. Books. A show in prime time.

"Hell, Billy, I think we're ready for our own videogame."

"Baby steps, Wally," I replied. "We can discuss this rationally when the fairy dust has blown away."

"When do you return to Fun City?"

"With luck, tomorrow."

Gretchen Di Voss called to congratulate me. She and several other executives, including her father, had had an early meeting to discuss the fate of *The Midnight Show*.

"It's a goner," she said. "Unlike the people who refuse to believe in global warming, we recognize a disaster when it's staring us in the face. Even if the show hadn't been struck by so many tragic events, the talk-and-entertainment competition is simply too great. I mean, just look at Leno's new numbers. Temporarily, we'll be filling the time slot with repeats of two sitcoms from our premium cable channel, *Nasty Nancy* and *The Boy with the Magic Ding-Dong*. Since they'll be on after midnight, we won't even have to do much editing.

"In the fall, we're starting a full hour of news hosted by Vida Evans. She's raring to go."

"I'll bet."

"She, ah, suggested you for her cohost. Any interest?"

"Oh, gee . . ."

"You'll be here, in New York. She'll be out there. With your recognition factor going through the roof, I think we can kick *Nightline*'s ass."

My recognition factor. My fame. Such ephemeral bullshit. All I wanted was my old life back. I liked getting up early and being part of the *Wake Up* team. I liked doing the cable shows and having enough time to at least say hello to the customers who were keeping the Bistro going.

But the news hour might be fun.

"We can talk about it when I get back," I said.

"Excellent. Meanwhile, Billy, bravo. You did a brave and wonderful thing."

I clicked the phone shut and looked down at my bandaged knees. "Bravo," I said. "You guys did all the work."

The phone vibrated. Harry Paynter. Not today, Harry. Maybe I'd return the call tomorrow, if I had time.

Before another call came in, I dialed Gloria Ingram. She seemed surprised to hear from me and, surprising me, said she was glad I called. She hoped I could tell her why Stew had wanted to kill Des. When I did, she seemed relieved.

"Did you know Des?" I asked.

"No. I don't think I ever even saw him perform. But Stew . . . well, I never knew what was going on in his head. I'm just glad . . ."

She let it trail off, but I understood what she was glad about. That none of it had anything to do with her.

"Could I ask *you* a question?" I said.

When she agreed, I did.

She hesitated briefly, then told me what I wanted to know.

I thanked her and wished her well.

As soon as I clicked off, the phone vibrated.

"Hi, Vida."

"My God, Billy. Stew Gentry and that weasel Trey. And you nailed 'em, single-handedly. It's an incredible story."

"The detectives helped," I said.

"Don't start that Mr. Modesty bit. It doesn't become you. Flaunt it, baby."

"Maybe I'll get a T-shirt made. On the front: 'Guess Who Solved the Des O'Day Murder?' On the back: 'Me.'"

"You're the most amusing man I know," she said. Then, lowering her voice just a hint, added, "I got some wonderful news today."

"Really?"

"They're putting a current-events show in the *Midnight* slot. And guess who's hosting?"

"Couldn't happen to a more deserving person."

"Thank you, sir. Ah, Billy, I think you may have gotten the wrong impression about Brutus and myself. We're not . . . committed."

"No. That would be Stew and Trey."

"Romantically committed," she said. "You know what I mean."

"Yes." And I knew what she was about to say.

"Anyway, I thought it might be nice to celebrate your amazing accomplishment tonight. Over dinner and . . ."

"I wish I could. But I'm kinda tied up."

"Oh. Then tomorrow night, maybe?"

"Bad timing. I'm heading back East tomorrow."

"Darn. I'd love to see you. There's something we should talk about."

"Personal . . . or business?"

"Oh, hell. I'd like you to cohost the show with me."

"See how easy and painless that was? And a dinner wasn't even necessary."

"You'll do it?"

"Let me mull it over. I'll get back to you early next week."

I hadn't been lying to her about having something else to do that night.

At eight-thirty, Pete Brueghel and I were headed out on what I hoped would be my last trip to Malibu for a long while. Our destination was the restaurant Frush, where Roger Charbonnet was celebrating his release from the lockup.

Brueghel and I looked rather dashing, I thought, in Hollywood-casual slacks and sport coats. Ties neither required nor expected.

"I don't get why you insisted I come along to the prick's get-out-of-jail party. I'm the guy who put him in jail."

"There's your reason. In a way, you inspired the party."

He rolled his eyes.

"Okay," I said. "I need a wingman."

"Seriously, what are we doing?"

"Enjoying ourselves for a change. All work and no play . . ."

"This is not my idea of play, Blessing. My idea of play would be putting the cuffs on Charbonnet in the middle of the party and perp-walking him past all his sleazy friends back into the lockup."

"The night is young," I said.

He gave me a hopeful look and increased our speed.

"By the way," he said, "there's a pilot who thinks he can put a copter down on the floor of that ravine. If the DA can find a forensic team willing to be his passengers, he might just have everything he needs to put Gentry and Halstead away forever."

"You really think that'll happen?"

"If the only victim had been O'Day, the guy who helped blow up the Gentry girl, conviction would be a tough call. But you throw in Lewis and Fitzpatrick and we're talking a slam dunk. Especially with you in the witness box."

The thought of having to return for the trial made me wince. "I don't suppose the prosecutor and the defense attorney could question me via Skype?"

"Not likely, unless—goddamn it!"

He slammed on the brakes, and the seat belts did their thing. He'd stopped inches short of a beauty in a minikini who was Rollerblading across the PCH while playing a violin.

"I think we've arrived at the party," I told him.

Frush was nestled among an assortment of high-end boutiques, salons, and spas operating under the umbrella name of The Malibu Collective. Or as the local teens called it, "The 'Bu'tive."

Brueghel drove around the lineup of cars near the valet service and parked his Crown Vic himself near a night-padlocked shop called May's Flowers. As we approached the restaurant, where a small, nervous woman in a pantsuit checked off names on a clipboard and a huge bull-necked gentleman observed her and the guests with a bored expression, Brueghel said, "Am I having fun yet?"

I have to report, in all humility, that my arrival at the door caused something of a sensation. That happens when your picture has been popping up on news shows and websites all day in connection with . . . celebrity murders!

Men stopped and gawked. Women stared at me longingly. Or so it seemed. The name-checker waved us in. Even the bouncer seemed impressed.

There must have been some Malibu Collective insistence on a unified look to the exteriors of its shops, since Frush's façade, like the Pet Shampoo Parlor to its left and the Anime Art salon to its right, had a distinct washed-out tan adobe quality. Its interior, for purposes of this party, at least, resembled a Universal TV set designer's idea of a classy, top-of-the-line brothel, subtly lit, plush furnishings, small tables, and lots of loud, self-important men and beautiful but languid ladies.

"Nice crowd," Brueghel said. "I always wondered where Satan hung out during his frequent West Coast visits."

A buffet dinner awaited on two long tables lining the right side of the large room, manned by a group of men and women costumed in prison striped shirts and trousers and toques. The members of the serving staff, circulating through the crowd, also were garbed in prison chic, minus the hats. I grabbed two flutes of champagne from the nearest tray and handed one to Brueghel.

"You'll have to tell me if I'm on duty," he said.

"Don't seem to be."

I searched the crowd of faces. Some I knew from films or sports. Some I knew from their appearances on the morning show. Most I didn't know at all.

"Looking for somebody?" Brueghel asked. "Our host is over by the stage, pawing the broad in the bikini."

She was wearing the same tiny thonglike outfit as the Rollerblader we'd almost run over. There were three others, similarly attired. One was seated at a set of drums. "I think they're the band," I said.

"They travel light."

The lady with Roger slid from his grasp, joined the others, and said something that snapped them to attention. She signaled a plump young man, their roadie, apparently, who, thankfully, was not in a minikini, and he did his thing with the sound equipment. She turned to face the crowd, raised her right hand, and, when she brought it down, the music began.

It wasn't awful. Like Katy Perry, times five. Bouncy, with lyrics that were seminaughty but cute.

With guests dancing or hooking up trying out lounge lizard poses, the detective and I decided it was a good time to take a run at the nearly vacant buffet. Calamari and olives salad. Two types of pizza squares, barbecued chicken, and boiled tiger shrimp. Mini sirloin burgers. And a special treat: abalone on the half-shell, which a prison-chic chef shucked on demand.

We commandeered a small table not far from the

buffet, coerced a server into providing two more champagnes, and dug in. Brueghel was at the buffet table selecting a second course when I heard that unmistakable voice say, " 'Illy, the hero o' the 'ay."

It was the wheelchair-bound Victor Anisette and his hot freckled nurse. He was swaddled in a too-full black shirt and black trousers, with an ugly black toupee stuck to his scalp. The nurse's white uniform was made of skintight leather. "He says you're the hero of the day," she translated.

Victor jerked his head toward Brueghel, who was approaching with his second full plate.

" 'Eeckey, hi ih a ang lace hohun hinhi who."

"He says, 'Detective, this is a strange place to run into you.' "

Brueghel looked at the nurse and I'd swear he licked his lips. Then he blinked and turned toward Victor. "How's the good life, Mr. Anisette?"

Victor glared at him with his working eye.

Brugehel put his plate on the table and sat, pretending to ignore the old man.

"Hug."

"He called you a thug."

"Well, that's praise from Caesar, sure enough," the detective said. "I like your nurse outfit, by the way. It's got that Helen's House of Pain thing going for it."

Surprisingly, she gave him a wide smile. Which he returned.

Victor wrapped one of his claws around the girl's wrist and said, "Ak e to aiya."

"He wants you to take him to aiya," Brueghel told the nurse.

She giggled. "Not aiya. Roger," she said.

"Nah!" Victor shouted angrily, and the nurse hopped to it, wheeling him away.

Brueghel stopped shoveling in the pizza long enough to say, "I'm a sucker for freckles."

"So is Victor," I said.

He winced and put down the pizza slice. "That's it. You ruined my appetite."

"Just as well," I said, pushing back my chair. "It's magic time."

I started making a path through the dancers. Following behind, Brueghel said, "What's up, Blessing?"

I didn't answer. He'd find out soon enough, I hoped.

To the left of the band, Roger seemed to be laying down the law to Victor, who wiggled in his chair. The nurse hovered just out of earshot.

Victor saw me approaching. He raised a bony claw, and Roger turned my way. He grinned and rushed toward me. "Billy, Billy. Goddamn it! The master detective."

Dancers stopped and stared as he wrapped his arms around me and hugged. "My savior." He released me and said to the crowd, "This man is the reason I'm free today."

Darned if they didn't applaud.

Then Roger saw Brueghel, and the smile on his face vanished. "What the fuck are you doing here?"

"He came with me," I said.

Roger gave me a cold look. "What is this? Some kind of setup?"

"Do you have an office here?" I asked. "Someplace we can talk?"

"What do we have to talk about?"

"After twenty-two years," I said, "don't you think it's time we cleared the air?"

He looked from me to Brueghel, who seemed no less puzzled than he.

"C'mon," Roger said. "Follow me."

He led us toward an open archway. Victor yelled something to his nurse, who responded by wheeling him in our direction.

"Hus hanana?" he cried out to Roger.

"He wants to know what's happening," the nurse said.

"He should join us," I said. "He was part of it, too."

We paraded past the customer restrooms, the service restroom, an unmarked door, an entrance to the restaurant's kitchen, and finally into the business office, where a bespectacled woman in her thirties sat at a desk, doing something with a computer. She was wearing a man's sport shirt at least two sizes too big for her, denim trousers, and gym shoes. She had a round, unlined, cosmetic-free face that seemed much too sensible and down-to-earth to be working for Roger.

Her name was Gina, I discovered, when Roger asked her to give us a few minutes alone. As soon as she left, closing the door behind her, he leaned against the other desk in the room—his, no doubt—and said, "Okay, Billy, say what you've got to say."

"I assume you all know I spent most of yesterday and last night in the company of three men who conspired to kill Des O'Day," I told them. "At the time, it was more than a little unpleasant. But in retrospect, it was pretty educational. Mainly, it taught me that living with a murder on your conscience tends to take some of the joy out of life.

"These guys were not happy campers. All three of them were at one another like rabid dogs."

"This is all fascinating, Blessing," Roger said testily. "What's it got to do with me?"

"Well, last night, I asked Stew Gentry what he'd do when Detective Brueghel here found out about his daughter and made the connection between him and Des. He had a very interesting answer. He said he'd tell the detective he had an alibi for the night of Des's murder."

I seemed to have captured their interest.

"Since it was Doc Blaney who did the actual crime, Stew could have gone any number of places to provide himself with a real alibi. But he was going to tell Brueghel that he'd spent the evening with Blaney. The 'beauty part,' as he put it, was that this would not only remove *him* from the suspect list, it would do the same for the guy who really committed the crime. It kinda struck me as sounding familiar."

Roger glared at me with that angry bull frown. "You're implying that twenty-three years ago, Victor and I colluded in a plot to kill Tiffany?"

"I am not implying that," I said. "How do I put this? For the collusion plan to work, neither Stew nor Blancy could have a real alibi. If Stew, for example, had decided to spend the night at a bar or in a poker game—"

"I get it," Roger interrupted me. "Anybody seeing him in the bar could have busted the fake alibi. And Blaney would have been left swinging in the wind."

"What the hell are we talking about?" Brueghel asked.

"Essentially, that Victor killed Tiffany Arden."

The old man still had a mean stink eye. He made some guttural sound that caused the nurse to shrug.

"That's ridiculous," Roger said. "Why would he . . . ?"

"Well, let's see. You and Tiffany had a fight that night. Maybe Victor thought he could take advantage of the situation. She rejected him. He goes a little wacko, things get out of hand, and he hits her with the tenderizer. Drags her out to the alley, tosses her into the bin. He cleans out the cash register and goes home, hoping everything will work out.

"Think of his relief when you call, panicked, in desperate need of an alibi. 'Of course,' I can hear him saying, 'anything for a pal.' "

"Hul hint!"

"He said 'Bullshit!' "

Roger stared at the old man, curious now but still not a believer.

"Did you know that back then, he forced . . . another girlfriend of yours to sleep with him by threatening to expose your affair to her husband?"

"Ayyyye!" Victor yelled.

" 'Lies.' "

"Your call, Roger. Do you believe him or her?"

"Jesus, Victor," Roger said. "You did that, didn't you? You son of a bitch."

Brueghel moved closer, ready to try and stop Roger from snapping the old man in two. But Roger wasn't showing anger. He looked beaten and betrayed, which was more disturbing, somehow.

"Whenever I showed any interest in a woman, Billy, he always took a shot at her. I used to think it was funny. And pathetic. But this . . . Why the hell didn't she come to me?"

My guess was Gloria didn't know how much he cared about her. Maybe *he* hadn't realized it before. "You should ask her," I said.

"Who're we talking about?" Brueghel asked.

Roger looked at him. "I think Victor did kill Tiffany, detective. It coulda been like Billy said, him losing it after she rejected him. But there's something else."

Victor let out another of his indecipherable screams and began writhing on his chair. The nurse made no effort to assist him.

"Tiff welcomed diners to Chez Anisette. But she also kept the books. After her death, Victor told me there'd been a discrepancy of nearly one hundred and fifty grand that she'd stolen.

"I was such a dunce. Like if Tiff had been sitting on top of all that cash I wouldn't have known it. But this man was like my dad. And he was such a swell guy, he even brought in an 'accounting specialist' to disguise the discrepancy. Leave Tiff's name unsullied.

"I'm dealing with the handiwork of some 'specialist' now. Gina's been going through our accounts, covering just the past ten years, and there's over two million dollars unaccounted for.

"So I'm thinking now that Tiff didn't take that hundred and fifty grand, but she might have discovered it was missing that night."

"Christ," Brueghel said. "We never even considered the bookkeeper angle."

Both men converged on Victor. He twisted his lips into what may have been a sneer and said, "Yll nehe conhi a crihi."

"He says you'll never convict a cripple." The nurse's pretty face hardened, and she added, "But if it'll help, I know where he keeps all of his records, business and personal."

Victor's claw shot up and clutched her wrist.

She pulled back his index finger until it popped. He released her, screaming in pain.

"I like this lady," Brueghel said.

So I guess I had become *his* wingman.

# *Chapter*
# FORTY-NINE

My flight to JFK was delayed forty minutes for some reason. Drunken copilot. Monster on the wing. It didn't matter, really.

I had forty minutes to kill. I could watch CNN, have a cocktail, buy a souvenir cap with a palm tree on it, but even if I hid out in the Million Milers Club, there'd be somebody wanting to know all about the Des O'Day murder.

I have discovered that the only place in an airport where you won't be bothered, outside of a bathroom stall, is when you're talking on a public phone. You can lean in, embracing the phone, turning your back

on the rest of the world, and it would take a kami-
kaze celebrity stalker, operating on their own or
under the aegis of *TMZ*, to invade your space.

There were only two problems with that plan.

It's not that easy to find a public phone anymore.
I uncovered one hiding behind a Burger King. Then I
had to think of someone to call. Which is why I
wound up returning Harry Paynter's message from
the day before.

"Yo, Billy, what's the hap?"

"You tell me. I'm returning your call."

"Oh. Yeah. Well. I was just checkin' in."

"You getting anywhere on the book?"

Silence on the other end.

"Harry?"

"Yea', bro. You, ah, talk to Wally the Winger
lately?"

"Not today. Should I?"

"Big changes, bro. Sandy's refocused."

"What's that mean?"

"New project on the front burner."

"What about mine?"

"You better talk to Wally. He and Sandy worked
something out. I think you got points in the new project."

"What is it?"

"The hottest property in town. Get this title:
*Blowout: The Stew Gentry Story*. It's got it all: sex,
showbiz, violence, heart, and lots of CGI potential,
including, wait for it, 3-D."

"Stew's cooperating?"

"Hell, yeah, he's cooperating. Wouldn't you for

two million bucks? You can buy a lot of defense with that."

"I thought there was a law against profiting from a criminal act."

"Listen to yourself," Harry said. "This is L.A., Jack. Five minutes after that rule went into effect, any contract lawyer worth his Century City address had come up with a half-dozen loopholes."

"Well, they just called my flight," I lied. "I've got to run."

"And I better get back to the old word maker. Man, it's great working on a project I believe in. What do you think sounds better, *Blowout* or *Blowup*?"

"How about *Blow Me*," I said, and replaced the phone.

The plane was actually an hour and twenty minutes late. I never learned why. Stardust in the fuel tank, maybe. Lotus leaves on the runway.

My seat in first class was beside an eighteen-year-old girl with Day-Glo yellow hair and a ring in her left nostril who'd just won a fourteen-million-dollar California lottery and was hooking up with her Internet boyfriend in New York for a monthlong trip to, as she put it, "Paris and other countries." She had a box of tiny rubber bands that were supposed to be for her braces, but every so often she'd shoot one at me and pretend it was a mistake.

A filter problem necessitated a shutdown of the AC, and things got a bit hot and clammy in the cabin. An attendant spilled half a Coke down my pants leg and into my shoe. And the movie turned out to be *Ghost Rider Two* with Nicolas Cage.

But I didn't care. I was alive. I had my health. And every hot and sweaty, Coke-drenched, Cage-mumbling, rubber band–dodging minute I spent was taking me closer and closer to the one and only Capital of the World.

If you enjoyed

# *The Midnight Show Murders*

you won't want to miss the next thrilling,
hilarious Billy Blessing mystery.


Read on for an exciting early look at

# *The Talk Show Murders*

Coming from Delacorte Press in 2012

# Chapter
## ONE

At roughly six-thirty on a Thursday morning that dawned bright and clear, members of the Chicago Police Department's Homicide Division and Forensic Services were lured to the city's Oak Street Beach by a body that had been deposited on the sand by Lake Michigan's ebbing tide. A drowning in the lake, accidental or otherwise, was not exactly remarkable. But this one was clearly unique, though that fact was not presented immediately to the public.

The CPD had dropped a cone of silence over the discovery. Even the hapless early morning jogger who'd nearly stumbled over the corpse was being forced to pursue his cardio perfection in seclusion somewhere off the grid.

Surprisingly, in this era of instant information, where members of the media are as persistent as they are plentiful, the news blackout lasted for nearly thirty hours. It was broken by a gray-haired, ill-tempered former cop named Edward "Pat" Patton. Since his retirement, Patton had begun a second career with an online blog, Windy City Blowdown, devoted primarily to outspoken and often outrageous political critiques, right wing rants and, adding a much-needed patina of credibility to his efforts, an ex-lawman's insider take on the city's criminal activity.

Blowdown's popularity had led to Patton's frequent appearances on local talk shows and on a few network offerings such as *Midday with Gemma,* where the eponymous hostess Gemma Bright had just welcomed him to share a periwinkle blue couch with her previous guest, Carrie Sands, a young vibrantly blonde actress who was starring in a new motion picture filming in the city.

When the applause of the primarily female audience began to subside, Patton plopped down on the couch. He leaned in close to the actress and whispered something in her ear that caused her smile to lose much of its perk. Then he turned his attention toward the show's hostess, adjusting his face in what he believed resembled a Gene Hackman–Popeye Doyle half-grin, *The French Connection* being his all-time favorite movie. "Okay, Gemma, I'm here," he said in his familiar, gruff voice. "So what d'ya wanna talk about today?"

"Oh, I think you KNOW, Pat." Gemma Bright's Australian accent was elaborate, slightly nasal and made more distinctive by her odd habit of emphasizing words and syllables in a seemingly random fashion. This, combined with her forty-something, zaftig but stylish good looks, an extroverted personality, and an ability to convey what seemed like genuine interest, had positioned her as the second most popular television personality in the Second City. "We want some DISH on that mysTERious body that washed ashore yesterdye."

"Dish, huh? Well, lemme tell ya, babe, it ain't all that appetizing."

"Death rarely is," Gemma said.

"That's probably why all those health-conscious wimps kept jogging past the body without stopping," Patton said. "Or, could it be that they were just too caught up in their own petty little lives to wanna get involved?"

"That's not fair," Carrie Sands chirped, evidently feeling he was talking about her people. "When you jog, you get in the zone and you block out a lot of what's happening around you."

"That explains why most of you bubbleheads voted for our illustrious illegal alien president. You were in the zone." Patton winked at the audience, which, surprisingly, rewarded him with scattered applause and laughter.


"Holy shit, Billy," my assistant Kiki Owens said. "Who is this trog?"

"You know as much about him as I do," I said, which was the truth at the time.

"I can't believe this birther crap is still around. And being allowed on our network."

"It's that nasty First Amendment," I told her.

We were in the studio six green room of Worldwide Broadcasting's Chicago affiliate, WWBC, watching the midday show unfold while I awaited my turn on camera. We were sharing the space with a pale, undernourished-looking guy in his twenties. His black hair was bowl-cut in what may have been an homage to the late Moe Howard. His concave chest was wrapped in a black T-shirt emblazoned with the statement "Down is the New Up" in yellow letters. His faded black jeans had slipped low enough on his hips to show an inch or two of candy-striped boxers, which in its way complimented his oversized pink high-top canvas shoes.

"Patton's a local celebrity," he said. "A real asshole who treats his employees like dirt."

"You work for him?" I asked.

He frowned. "Me? I'm Larry Kelsto. Why would I work . . .? I'm a comic," he stated, adding defensively, "I've been on a bunch of network shows. *Last Comic Standing, Comedy Brew, Later with Carson Daly.* Anyway, if you want to know about Pat Patton . . ."

He then went on to provide a Wikipedia-lite explanation of Pat Patton's semi-fame, concluding with, "The guy never met anybody he didn't hate. He's the opposite of Roy Rogers."

"I think you mean Will Rogers," I said.

"Who the hell is Will Rogers?"

"Roy's father," I told him, dismayed that a comedian, even a young one, would have to ask that question.

Larry Kelsto was not really interested in any of the Rogers, including, I assumed, Kenny or the late Mister. Lowering his voice, he said to Kiki, "You're an actress or a model, right?"

Kiki stared at him. She's an attractive, diminutive black woman who seems as fragile as an orchid but, as I once witnessed, she can make a six-foot-four, two-hundred-ninety-pound Russian mafia enforcer break down and cry like a baby. Her best weapon is a British accent with which she can draw blood faster than a buck knife. Judging by the look she was giving

Larry, she didn't seem to be into younger guys. Or maybe it was the candy-striped boxers. Or the shoes.

"Stick to comedy," she told him and focused her attention on the monitor.

That didn't seem to improve her disposition. "I'm picking up a really toxic vibe from Mr. Patton. We should leave now, Billy."

"Are you kidding? What business are we in, again? Show business. And what's the cardinal rule? The show must go on."

"I can fill for you," the comedian said.

"Thanks, Larry, but I think I can handle it."

Kiki shook her head. "Big mistake, Billy."

"Relax," I said. "It's just a talk show. After sharing a couch with Carrot Top, talking about weight-lifting, and Sean Hannity, just being Sean Hannity, this will be a breeze."

"Really? Listen to the guy. He's rancid, Billy. He makes Hannity sound like Walter Cronkite."

"Bite your tongue," I said.

On the monitor, Patton's face had turned a sanguine shade as he replied to something the young blonde actress had said. "Okay, I give you that, missy. Out of a couple hundred self-absorbed, gotta-stay-in-shape me-firsters, one little wimp shows some sense of civic responsibility by pressing a button on his cute little iPhone to call the CPD. Give 'im the friggin' key to the city, why not?"

"We TRIED to get him for the show," Gemma told Patton, ignoring the man's vitriol and thereby undercutting it. "But the police are treating this as if Homeland SeCURity were being threatened. We couldn't even find out his name."

"All you had to do was ask me, Gemma," Patton said. "It's Shineman. Carl Shineman. They got him locked up tight in his million dollar high-rise apartment on Elm."

"Why all the SEEcrecy?"

"Ah. If I told you that, Gemma, you'd know as much as me."

"How is it, Pat, that you ALways seem to be in the KNOW on every CRIME story?"

"Honey, as I've told you before, I put in a lotta long, hard years with the CPD, and I was payin' attention every minute. I understand how things work and where to go to get the info that citizens have a right to know."

"Then maybe you should TELL us why the police are being so SEcretive."

Patton hesitated, then said, "It's . . . all about the corpse, Gemma."

"The CORPSE?" It was our hostess's turn to address the camera. "This BAD boy will never even give me a CLUE about what he's going to say once he's out here."

"Where would the fun be in that?" Patton asked with a guffaw. "I get a kick out of seeing your reactions." He faced the audience. "You like to be surprised, too, am I right?"

Applause and giggles.

"Point made, Pat. So what's the big SEcret about the CORPSE?"

"The police don't want to look like clowns, but the fact is, with all their state of the art computer toys, they're having the devil's own time making an ID."

"Had the body been in the lake that long?" Gemma inquired.

"The water and the fishies did some damage to be sure. But that's not the real problem."

I noticed a tiny crease appear above Gemma's right eyebrow. Love that High Def picture. She seemed to be getting a little peeved at the way Patton was drawing it out. "And the REAL problem IS . . . ?" she nearly demanded.

Grinning, the ex-cop ran a thick finger across his neck. "The corpse's head had been chopped off clean. And they can't find it anywhere."

# *Chapter* TWO

Gemma blinked.

I'd written off as nonsense her comment about not knowing what Patton was going to say. Even if Standards and Practices didn't have their own often too-rigid rules of do's and don't's, talk show hosts are usually control freaks, at least professionally. But from where I was sitting, it looked like genuine surprise on her elaborately pancaked face.

She waited for the gasps from the audience to subside. Then she asked, "You're SAYing someone de-CAPitated the victim?"

"He sure as heck didn't do it himself," Patton said. "His hands and feet were chopped off, too."

"OhMyGod!" Carrie Sands exclaimed. "Then it had to be murder."

The view switched from a two-shot of Patton and Gemma to an angle that included the actress.

"The missing hands do kinda rule out suicide, babe," Patton told her. "But, like the old joke says, they could always use what was left for third base."

"That's disgusting," Carrie said.

Patton shrugged. "All in the eye of the beholder. I know people who say pole dancing is disgusting. Personally, I'm a fan."

Carrie glared at the grinning man.

"If you can get your MIND off of POLE-dancing for a few more minutes, Pat," Gemma said, "is there anything else you can tell us about the mysTERious body?"

The camera moved in on Patton.

"Sure," he said. "The vic was Caucasian. Male. That much is still in evidence. In his forties, they think. No DNA match so far. The feeling at Homicide is that he's somebody whose identity would point the way to the killer or killers."

The camera closed in on Patton and Gemma, catching the glint in her green eyes. "And they have no iDEA who the poor soul might be?"

"They don't."

"But you do?"

"Let's just say I've got a hunch. If it pans out, you and your audience will be the first to hear, Gemma."

"Does your HUNCH have anything to do with

the work you were doing before your reTIREment, on the Organized Crime Task Force?"

He smiled. "Good try, Gemma. But no. Those Outfit guys usually didn't bother cutting off any body parts. If they put somebody in the drink, they stayed in the drink."

"W-whoever did this didn't try to keep the . . . d-dead man submerged?" Carrie Sands asked, catching the camera operator off-guard. By the time he'd found her, Patton was answering the question.

"They tried. The theory is the body had been anchored by a heavy weight, but broke loose when the fish came to dinner. Judging by the teeth marks, they say it mighta been a bull shark did most of the dining. I been living in Chi my whole life and I never knew there were bull sharks in Lake Michigan."

Gemma Bright must have realized the idea of a shark nibbling on the corpse was one nightmare image too many for her lunchtime audience. "Yes. Well. NaSty business, inDEED."

She turned to the camera and said, "A real-life murder MYStery and we'll be bringing you the events as they unFOLD. Now, coming up is a CHARMing man—you all know him from *Wake Up, America!*, seen every WEEKday morning from seven to nine on WWBC Chicago, and on his own cooking show on the Wine and Dine Cable Network, Chef BILLY BLESSING!

"But first . . ."

As the show cut to a commercial, I stood, fully aware of Kiki's gimlet eye. She was on the verge of saying something but Larry Kelsto interrupted her.

"Only fourteen minutes left," he whined. "I'm

getting that bumped feeling. I knew it as soon as Patton showed up, the asshole."

I took a few deep breaths and tried to relax. A young woman appeared at the door, wearing jeans, a white WWBC T-shirt, a barbed wire tattoo on her left wrist, and a headset. Whispering into the headset, she approached and swiftly and efficiently checked a tiny wireless microphone and hid it behind my tie.

"This way, Mr. Blessing," she said.

"Lose the goofy grin, Billy," Kiki advised. "It's inappropriate with all the talk about a headless dead body."

As I followed my guide along the darkened backstage area, I heard Gemma announcing, "Here he is, one of your FaVorites and my VERY good friend, superchef BILLY BLESSING."

A stagehand pulled black a flap in the dark curtain and I stepped into bright lights and a response that sounded, to my ears at least, a little more enthusiastic than the blinking "APPLAUSE" signs usually produced.

The other two guests shifted on the couch as I took our hostess's hand and kissed it. I can be debonair when I want. I gave the still applauding audience a friendly wave and took my place on the end of the couch.

Gemma smelled of magnolias. Patton smelled of a spicy aftershave and, unless I missed my guess, a midmorning gin.

"Billy, it's WONderful to have you here again," our hostess said. "It's been MUCH too long since your last visit."

"About three years," I said, "Definitely too long. This is a great city."

Gemma faced the camera. "This is the busiest man I know. In addition to his so VERY entertaining television work, Billy has a MARvelous restaurant in Manhattan. He writes cook books and—"

"He was mixed up in some murders on the West Coast," Patton said.

A shadow of annoyance fitted over Gemma's face. She wasn't used to being upstaged, especially by a guest who'd already moved to the less-active middle of the couch. "How right you are, Pat," she said.

She leaned closer to me. Using a softer, more intimate voice, she said, "You went through QUITE an ordeal in Southern CaliFORnia last year, Billy. And before that, you helped the police with a series of murders in New York CITY, as we know from the fasciNAtingly suspenseful BOOK you wrote. What was it called?"

"*Wake Up to Murder,*" I said. "It's available in trade paperback."

"You're becoming a regular SUPER sleuth, like . . . Monk."

I myself would have opted for John Shaft or Easy Rawlins. Or even Guy Hanks.

"The police did most of the work," I said.

"Well, I'm SURE you contri—"

"You were right in the middle of the West Coast murders." This time, it was Carrie Sands, speaking up from the never-to-be-heard-from far end of the couch. "I just read poor Stew Gentry's book and he says you did all the detective work."

"Ah, yes," Gemma said coolly. "THAT book. We

had the young man on the show who helped poor, SAD Stew write the book. Harry something . . ."

"Harry Paynter," I said. There'd been a time when Harry was supposed to have helped me with my book, but he'd declined, in favor of *Fade-out: The Stew Gentry Story*. Just as well. Harry was a little too much of a hack for my taste.

"His and Stew's book garnished unANimous critical raves," Gemma said. "And it's at the TOP of the bestseller lists."

"In second place, actually," Carrie corrected. "Gerard's latest, *The Thief Who Stole Big Ben,* is number one."

The French novelist Gerard Parnelle had begun a series of thrillers about a scruffy Marseilles orphan who, through several improbable encounters, had been transformed into a beautiful, remarkably resourceful master thief. Book one, *The Thief Who Stole the Eiffel Tower,* had been the basis for a motion picture so successful in Europe and Asia it had heralded a Newer Wave for the French film industry. The movie Carrie was making in Chicago was an American version, *The Thief Who Stole Trump Tower.*

The recently published sequel, *Big Ben,* had arrived at the tipping point of the series' international popularity.

"Gerard's book is *numero uno,* of course," Gemma said. "Carrie, I want you to remind that BAD boy that he owes me a visit." She turned to me and without batting an eye asked, "Do you agREE with what Stew had to say about you in HIS book, Billy?"

"I . . . I haven't read it."

That was a lie, but, from what I've observed lies don't count on TV talk shows any more than they do in politics.

"Sandy Selman's making a movie based on Stew's story," Carrie, apparently the source of all that was literary in Hollywood, announced.

"Really? Will you be in it, Billy?"

"Doubtful," I told her. Hoping to close down the topic and move on to the reason the network's public relations team had arranged for me to be on the show, I added, "That whole thing is pretty much old news."

"Still, it's exCIting to hear about it firstHAND. As I recall, it was only by the MEREST stroke of good fortune you weren't killed. I'm sure our audience would love to hear what *that* was LIKE."

Sighing, I dutifully obliged with a brief wrap-up of my brushes with death, careful not to say anything that was not part of the public record. Having returned to Los Angeles for the trial, I'd had my fill of courtroom command performances.

"Do you think the punishment fit the crime?" Gemma asked me.

"Happily that was not my call," I said.

"What the hell does it take for those touchy-feely idiots in LaLa land to put killers away?" Pat Patton exploded.

"They didn't go free," I said.

"No. But they could be out in eight. And then they might come looking for the guy who helped put 'em away. Something to think about, huh, Billy?"

He was actually grinning. "Anything to make you happy, Pat," I replied.

Then, assumng that even a lame segue is better than none at all, I said, "Speaking of 'looking' for something, Gemma, I hope your audience will be looking in on Monday when *Wake Up, America!* begins the first of two weeks telecasting right here from Chicago. We'll be reminding the rest of the country about what a great city this is."

Thankfully, Gemma hopped right on board; we went back and forth on the glories of the Second City for a while.

I'm usually pretty relaxed even in this kind of environment, but I was thrown off a little by the sight of Patton in my peripheral vision. He kept staring at me—not in fascination or awe or even professional courtesy, but with narrowed eyes, as if I were an irritant that was causing him some internal distress.

I tried shifting on the couch until he was out of my line of sight, but that left me at an awkward angle. Which was making Gemma nervous.

During the commercial break, I turned to Patton and said, "So how do you like me so far?"

He continued to glare, ignoring my question. Then, lowering his voice, he said, "We've met before, right?"

"Not that I recall. But I'm on TV every morning. Sometimes people—"

"I've seen you on TV. Not so much on your show. I listen to the radio in the morning. It was on the news coverage of those murders. But I've got a crappy little screen. Eyeballin' you up close and personal, I'm pretty sure we met way back, Billy, when you had a lot more hair and less pounds. Yeah. Only the name wasn't Blessing. Billy . . . something else."

"We've never met," I said, wondering if that was true. Hoping that it was.

"We're chatting with one of our FAVorites, Chef Billy Blessing." Gemma signaled to us that we were back on camera. "He and the rest of the *Wake Up, America!* team will be greeting you LIVE from Chicago for the next two weeks over WWBC. Will all the co-hosts be here, Billy?"

I'm sure I answered the question and that I continued to keep up my end of the conversation, but my thoughts were definitely elsewhere.

I heard Gemma announce tomorrow's guests and apologize to Larry Kelsto for bumping him once again. She then informed the studio audience that each and every one of them was getting a complete makeover, courtesy of several local entrepreneurs. With the squeals of their delight almost drowning out her good-byes, the *Midday Show* wound to a close.

While the credits rolled, Gemma, Carrie Sands, Patton and I all stood and pretended to be chatting among ourselves as if we were old pals. Actually, Carrie was saying she'd be seeing me on Tuesday's *Wake Up*. We were giving her movie a big push because we'd made a first look deal with its writer Gerard Parnelle for a TV series idea he was putting together.

Patton was not playing our game exactly. He remained silent, staring at me, sly smile in place.

Given the all clear, I headed for the green room and Kiki, but Patton blocked my way. "Billy Blanchard. That's your real name, right?"

The sight of his smile had taken the surprise out of it. I stared at him. "My real name is Billy Blessing," I said, walking around him.

"Now maybe," he said, keeping pace. "But back at the tail end of the eighties, pal, you and I both know it was Blanchard. And you claimed a body that turned up in Cal City. I'll have the stiff's name in a second."

"I don't know what you're talking about, Patton," I lied.

Frowning, Kiki marched toward us. "I'm sorry, Billy, but we have to go now."

I nodded to Patton and allowed my very efficient assistant to pull me away.

"Judging by the helpless expression on your face," she said, "I assumed you didn't want to continue your conversation with that creep."

"Absolutely not."

"What was he saying to you, anyway?"

"Nothing very pleasant."

"I told you," she said. "He's a monster."

I turned.

Patton had been joined by a very tall, very muscular, very black man, neatly dressed in tan slacks and a tight white T-shirt. The newcomer was in his twenties, but the slicked-down hair and thin moustache belonged to another generation. He shifted from one foot to the next, somewhat impatiently, while Patton continued to stare at me.

The ex-cop raised one hand and gave me a jolly finger wiggle, as if he was seeing me off on a pleasant journey.

"A monster," I agreed.